the Secret Journey

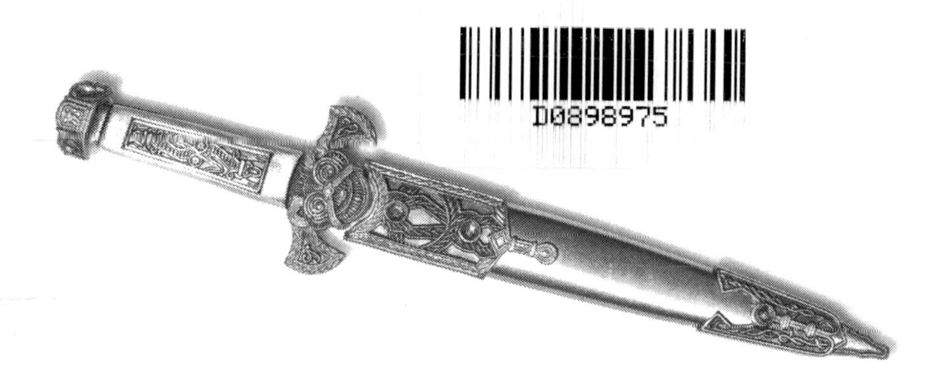

Brian Barnes
Judith Briles

Book 1: The Secret Journey
The Harmonie Books Series

Published by Mile High Press

Development Editor: Barb Wilson, EditPartner.com
Editor/Proofreader: Barb Wilson; Peggie Ireland
Cover and Interior Design: Rebecca Finkel, F + P Graphic Design, FPGD.com
Book Publishing Expert: Judith Briles, TheBookShepherd.com

Books may be purchased in quantity by contacting the publisher through the author's website: www.HarmonieBooks.com

Library of Congress Control Number: 2022920242
ISBN trade paper: 978-1-959737-99-5
ISBN trade paper Ingram Spark two: 979-8-218-06865-3
ISBN trade paper Ingram Spark three: 978-1-959737-96-4
ISBN eBook: 978-1-959737-97-1
ISBN audiobook: 978-1-959737-98-8

Historical Fiction | Women's Fiction | Medieval | Paranormal

First Edition
Printed in the USA

For Julie

my love and sunshine for 57 years

—Brian

For John

who introduced me to the nose of a fine red;

to limitless loyalty;

and companionship and love for 48 years

—Judith

Also by Dr. Judith Briles

When God Says NO: Revealing the YES

How to Create a Million Dollar Speech

How to Create Snappy Sassy Salty Success for Authors and Writers

How to Avoid Book Publishing Blunders

How to Create a Crowdfunding Campaign for Authors and Writers

AuthorYOU

Show Me About Book Publishing

Stabotage

Zapping Conflict in the Health Care Workplace

Stop Stabbing Yourself in the Back

The Confidence Factor—Cosmic Gooses Lay Golden Eggs

Woman to Woman 2000—Becoming Sabotage Savvy in the New Millennium

Woman to Woman: From Sabotage to Support

Smart Money Moves for Kids

The Briles Report on Women in Healthcare

10 Smart Money Moves for Women

The Dollars and Sense of Divorce

GenderTraps

The Confidence Factor—How Self Esteem Can Change Your Life

Money Sense

The Money $ense Guidebook

Raising Money-Wise Kids

Judith Briles' Money Book

The Workplace

When God Says NO

Woman to Woman—From Sabotage to Support

Faith & $avvy Too!

Money Phases

The Woman's Guide to Financial Savvy

Self-Confidence and Peak Performance

Contents

Enlightenment

Blowing out the candle,
my room is dark as a moonless night.
Falling asleep I summon a dream,
waiting for the Lady's light.

Her voice is soft and sincere,
a face of changing features and colors.
She brings knowledge and wisdom,
when she enters my dreams.

Who is this Lady I desire?
An enchantress?
A trusted guide?
One day we will talk, now I just listen.

prologue

Book 1

In the year 983, an infant was born in Marseilles, County of Provence, to a prosperous family. The girl was christened Lisa.

The infant's father was Alexander, the port commander of Marseilles, located in the southeast corner of France between the Alps and the Mediterranean, and under the influence of the church. Trusted by the people, he was the overseer of many of the ports along the coastline. He partnered with many of the merchants and made sure the orphaned children were cared for.

His wife Astrid did not want a girl child and took an immediate dislike to the infant, refusing to be part of her care and upbringing. She never wavered from her myopic and unconditional support of Fredric, her only son, who had matured to become a mean and ruthless failure in everything he did.

Knowing Fredric would inherit Alexander's estate and title as his birthright—and thus provide for and protect her if she were widowed—she openly resisted any discipline or correction by Alexander toward the now-psychopath Fredric.

Lisa's care and education were provided by Margaux, the housekeeper Alexander brought to the manor within the week after her birth.

The child flourished under her guidance, learning how to read and write. Her curiosity had no bounds. She studied her environment—the animals, the farming, the tradespeople in the port, and how her father worked. Young Lisa devoured anything that she could read and embraced her skills in writing and drawing.

And she had a secret companion … a voice that came to her infrequently, usually at night. She called the voice the *Lady*.

Now at thirteen years of age, her carefree childhood would soon be turned upside down. Contrary to the norms of the day and the teachings of the church, Alexander took her into his confidence, welcoming her advice as he shared the details of his business dealings with her.

Lisa was being groomed as the perfect protégé—and as the true heir Alexander desired.

the Early Years

one

The Solar

Hiding behind the tapestry was a way to spend time with her beloved papa without him knowing she was there.

Lisa ran through the great hall and down to Alexander's solar, the room where her papa held all his private meetings with important people.

Fredric, the older of Alexander's two children, was chasing her in hot pursuit, screaming all the while, "I will beat you when I find you!" Entering the solar, red-faced and breathing heavily, he scanned the room, searching for his sister.

The power and ambiance of the room was oblivious to him. The opposing wall displayed a striking array of weapons, swords, bows, knives, and daggers on the right side of a large hanging tapestry. Most of the weapons displayed had been acquired from the many conflicts Alexander had engaged in. In the center of the display was his most prized possession: a priceless dagger, its hilt studded with jewels.

Covered with magnificent tapestries, the remaining walls caused the room to glow softly with color. The only light in the room at this hour flowed in through a single large window in the southern wall. A most impressive tapestry hung next to it, covering a niche in the wall.

"Where did she go? I know she turned into this room," Fredric muttered.

Hidden behind the tapestry, Lisa was curled up inside the niche. She knew he was there. She waited silently, hoping to go undetected by the brother she never trusted; the brother she hated.

Lisa discovered the wall niche when she was young. For many reasons, it was her favorite place. Hiding behind the tapestry was a way to spend time with her beloved papa without him knowing she was there.

As time passed, the conversations he had with his visitors began to intrigue her. Instinctively, she knew to remain quiet and still when he talked with his important visitors. It was her secret place; no one knew she was there.

Her body tensed when she heard Fredric's foul language as he moved about the room. First, he looked beneath the stocky rectangular oak table centered in the room and then behind each of the handsomely carved chairs that surrounded it.

"I know … you are behind the door!" he shouted. He grabbed the handle and whipped it back, fully expecting to find her there, then slammed it against the wall. "Where are you?"

There was no sign of the sister he wanted to purge from the household.

Fredric's eyes searched the room, landing on the tapestries.

Smiling to himself, he stealthily moved toward the first tapestry closest to the door. With a solid blow, he kicked the bottom of it, expecting to hear a scream. Nothing happened.

Lisa heard the anger in his voice as the words spewed out of his mouth.

Feeling his nearness, Lisa knew the tapestry covering her hiding space was next in Fredric's attack. With eyes closed, heart and head pounding, she held her breath, biting her lip so she would not shout out. She knew what was coming.

Fredric passed the wall of weapons and delivered a hefty kick to the tapestry she hid behind. Shaking a little, it quivered itself back into place.

Not a sound nor movement came from her. Silence filled the air. Lisa was safe.

Unbeknown to either, Alexander had heard the commotion and followed his children to the solar. Hesitating at the doorway, he watched the scene unfold. Alexander was a man in black. From the leather boots that few men could afford to the belt that cinched his tunic. His stature was tall for men and the black tunic he wore accentuated it, as if to stand out in any crowd. The purse hanging from his belt filled with coin was made of leather from hide of a bull. His black beard was short and neatly cut as was his hair. His eyes were a rich hazel that danced when in the sunlight and when surrounded by candlelight. Only when angered did they deepen to a browner hue. No one questioned his authority. The only thing missing was a dagger that he usually wore when he was out in the port.

"What is going on in here, Fredric? Why are you kicking my tapestries and slamming my door? This is my solar. No one is allowed in here unless I invite him and that includes you."

Rebuked, Fredric whined, "Papa, Lisa tried to make me sick. She put a worm in my porridge."

Glaring at his son, he continued, "I will talk to her and put an end to this childish nonsense. Now get out. I have a guest arriving soon."

Fredric pleaded, "I am seventeen and a man, and I should attend these meetings you have. Mother thinks I should and it is my right." Not moving, he stood defiantly in the middle of the room.

Silence followed. Neither male moved.

Anger flowed through Alexander's body. *Who is this vile boy?*

Finally, he spoke. "You may attend when you prove your merit and not until then. Get out."

Shooting a hate-filled look at his papa, Fredric turned and mumbled to himself as he exited the solar, kicking a tapestry as he left. *I hate him.*

Fredric was nothing like his father in size or presence. Thin, brown eyes, he smelled of sour ale. Rarely did he bathe like others in the villa did. He was unkept in his physical appearance. Where the wealth of the household easily allowed for changes of clothes, he looked as if they had been on his back for several months.

Alexander walked to the open window, letting his eyes rest on the countryside surrounding his home. "I do not think that boy can be my son. He looks more like an orphaned petty street boy," he murmured then sighed and shook his head.

What could that mean? How could Fredric not be Papa's son? thought Lisa.

two

Alexander

I have you to thank for my success.

As he turned from the window, the housekeeper Margaux entered, announcing the arrival of David, a local merchant. She escorted him into the solar.

Leaving, she closed the door behind her. Moving down the hallway, a voice called to her. It was not the first time she would hear the voice, but when she did, Margaux called it the *Lady*.

Margaux wore an ankle length brown tunic with an apron. A wimple covered her hair and what was most compelling was her dark brown eyes and high cheek bones with a look that demanded respect. Alexander thought of her as the heart and commander of the villa, and she did whatever Alexander asked of her. She thought of Lisa as her daughter. And to Lisa, Margaux was her true mother. She gave Lisa her love in words, hugs, and protection that her mother would not give and that the girl so desperately needed.

It was a familiar voice she knew that Lisa heard as well.

Lisa is safe with her papa now flowed within her, creating a sense of calm as she went about her duties.

Lisa was trapped behind the tapestry, her heart pounding wildly from the close encounter with Fredric.

I must breathe slowly and quietly. Sitting with her knees pulled up to her chest, she leaned back and rested her head against the stone wall, eagerly listening. *Will this conversation be boring like the last time, or will this man bring exciting news?*

As a successful merchant himself, holding the position of port commander, Alexander oversaw all the activities at the port of Marseilles. Merchants and townspeople alike sought his advice in matters of importance and respected his prowess in resolving disputes relating to their business interests.

She heard her papa say, "Welcome, David. Please sit with me. You have prospered well and I appreciate the swift return of the coin I lent to you to build your fleet of ships."

"Yes, Alexander, and I have you to thank for my success," David said in a raspy voice, a sign of his age. "Your advice to expand trading to countries east of here has brought great returns. But now I have new challenges facing me, and you are the only person I know who can help resolve them. My profits have been cut in half and I am losing patrons because their goods are being stolen!"

Lisa heard her papa's chair creak as he shifted in his seat to look at his guest. "Tell me what happened. You know I will help where I can." She could tell from his voice that David's words had distressed him.

"There are pirates who wait for my ships to leave the docks and they intercept them in open waters. Others have had it happen, too, yet nothing has been done to stop it. My ships return to the ports empty and the pirates sell goods they stole right in front of me at the marketplace here in Marseilles and along the western seaports of Italy. My men are reluctant to identify the pirates because they and their families are threatened with physical harm if they talk."

Alexander replied, "You are not the only merchant who has suffered at the hands of the pirates. I have been gathering information from others. My sources at the docks have told me of a particularly offensive pirate named Trebilock. We cannot allow him to continue to exert his control in these waters and disrupt the trade that has made our town prosper.

"It is time to stop Trebilock. He and his band of thieves are usually at one of the taverns on the docks. I will go to there tonight and deal with this."

There was a knock on the door of the solar.

"Enter," Alexander replied.

Margaux appeared, carrying a tray laden with wine, bread, and cheese, placed it on the table, and left.

Pouring wine for the two of them, he then offered the selection of bread and cheese to David. Alexander then lifted his goblet in salute to David. "To restoring your prosperity."

David nodded in agreement.

"I hope this wine is not part of your stolen goods." From her papa's tone, Lisa could tell he was smiling as he spoke.

David let out a hearty laugh. "If this is indeed my stolen wine, at least I know I have good taste."

With both men laughing, the conversation took on a more casual tone, with talk of families, and hopes for favorable winds and fair weather.

After a few minutes, Lisa heard David groan as he rose from his chair. "Alexander, I thank you for your time and assistance. I am grateful for anything you can do to stop the pirates' attacks on my and the others' ships."

"I will deal with Trebilock. The routes will be safer and more profitable for everyone."

Ignoring the uncomfortable position she had adopted in the niche, Lisa found the conversation with David intriguing, and listened closely. In her mind, she was developing a vivid image of her papa's guest and the events he described. He breathed heavily and spoke with a raspy voice. Lisa envisioned an overweight older man.

As he got up to leave the solar, David walked next to the niche where Lisa hid, and spoke. "This jeweled dagger is beautiful. If you ever want to part with it, let me know."

With a heartly laugh, Alexander swiftly responded, "I appreciate your offer—but it stays with me!"

Bidding Alexander his thanks, he departed.

Without seeing him, Lisa could tell he had a distinctive limp in his walk and he had an odor about him that filled her space. The odor was from a spice she knew but could not place.

Lisa envisioned David as he moved out of the solar, thinking, *I do not have to see people to know things about them.*

After David's departure, Alexander left to summon Jonathan, Margaux's husband. Jonathan was also the steward of his estate.

A quiet man, he was Alexander's ears and eyes on the estate and carried messages for him.

At the same time, Lisa slipped out to the privy chamber and then quickly returned to her niche behind the tapestry. She knew there was more to unfold. Settling behind it, she heard Papa's voice as he entered the room and settled into his chair.

When Jonathan entered the solar, Alexander looked up from the contract he was reviewing. "I need you to get a message to Isaac at once."

This got Lisa's attention. She knew that her father relied upon Isaac to assist in keeping order at the docks.

Leaning her ear closer to the hanging tapestry, she heard her father as he continued speaking.

"Tell him to prepare ten of his best men. We are going to visit a pirate at the Anchor Inn after the sun goes down."

Dismissing Jonathan, Alexander left to join his family for the evening meal.

What are Papa's plans with Isaac's men? Lisa wondered as she scrambled from her hiding place to join the family.

three

The Rivalry

You cannot do what Papa does—you are a girl!

At the evening meal, few words were spoken as the family gathered around the table.Lisa looked across at her brother, who was fair-featured like his mother with light-colored hair. She could tell that Fredric was still upset about the stern scolding he had received earlier from her papa, smiling to herself at the thought.

Fredric saw her smile. He glared at her and clenched his fists, holding one up to her. She did not care.

What she had overheard in the solar filled her with excitement and anticipation. *I want to be there when Papa confronts the pirate.*

Alexander smiled and flashed her a teasing glance. "Lisa, what did you learn from Margaux today?"

Lisa composed herself. "I learned some new uses for the herbs Margaux puts in our stew, and I learned about the many uses for the lavender that we grow in our fields."

Gathering her courage, she swallowed and took a deep breath. "Papa, today I told Margaux that I no longer wish to have sewing lessons because we have people who sew for us. And I no longer need to learn how to cook or run the kitchen for the same reason."

The conversation she had overheard in the solar that day had awakened her to a whole new world. She flashed a smile and, with her chin pointed cheekily in his direction, then said, "I want to learn how to use a sword. I want to travel and meet people in other towns. And ... I want to learn what you do."

"You cannot do what Papa does—you are a girl!" shouted Fredric across the table.

"You will do exactly what you are told, and you will follow the instructions given to you, Lisa!" Astrid interjected with anger. "Who do you think you are to demand your own course of learning and to do what men do?"

Lisa jumped up from the table and started to leave the room. She looked at her mother haughtily. "Why does Fredric get to do whatever he wants to do, and I must do what I am told to do? I learn things faster and better than he does. I know much more than he does. He cannot even read or write; everyone knows it."

Fredric's jealousy and dislike for her exploded. He spit out a mouthful of food and snarled, "I hate you! I will hurt you—I swear it!"

Alexander pounded his fist on the table. "Enough, Fredric! No son of mine would purposefully harm his sister. Leave this room immediately!"

As Lisa walked away from the table, she smiled to herself, mirroring how her father smiled. She gently patted her papa's shoulder as she left. Her hair and eyes matched his color and she had his height. Slim, she took pride in how she dressed. Where

Fredric stank, she bathed regularly using the special soaps that Margaux created for her. Mimicking her father's mannerisms and straightforwardness, Margaux often thought that she should have been Alexander's son. Where Fredric would kick the poor and hurt them, Lisa would share her coin and offer kind words. Back in her room, her brave appearance started to come down upon her and a feeling of loneliness enveloped her.

With parchment, quill, and ink, she began to write …

Fredric, you frightened me today.

You are not my brother.

My true brother would never harm me.

Mother, who are you ... what have you become?

You do not know me or like me.

Papa, I know you. I am part of you.

Do you know me?

Tears will not leave my eyes.

four

The Tavern

The noise-filled room grew deadly silent.

Early that evening, Isaac came to Alexander. "I have assembled ten men and they await us at the docks, as you asked. We have found Trebilock and his thugs at the Anchor Inn."

Alexander readied himself with weapons from his wall collection: a jeweled dagger tucked in his belt and a sword in its scabbard at his side. He and Isaac exited the manor, quickly crossed the courtyard, and mounted their horses.

Upon arriving at the docks, Alexander and Isaac rode up to a man holding a torch and dismounted. Alexander took the torch and inspected the assembled group.

"Good, all of you brought your weapons. We must be prepared for a fight, Isaac has told you why we are here tonight. I hope Trebilock and his band of thieves will put down their weapons and leave Marseilles willingly.

"If not, there will be a clash where some of us could be hurt. Isaac and five of you will enter the back of the tavern, and the rest of you will go with me to the front. I can see fear in some of your faces. None of us are without fear. Stay alert; we are here for the people of Marseilles. We need to stop these pirates. Are you ready?"

A full moon lit up the wooden sign over the tavern door and drunken voices from within filled the air. With no more than a nod and a gesture from Alexander, the men split up.

Taking a deep breath, Alexander pulled his jeweled dagger from his belt. He threw open the door and strode into the tavern.

The vile stench of vomit and ale-soaked dirt floor violated his nostrils. Flies circled around the leftover food scraps on the tables. Under the stools, rats raced back and forth, stopping in their tracks to get their share of the refuse.

Alexander quickly scanned the dimly-lit room that contained only a few flickering candles, the better to conceal any secrets or wrongdoings that were occurring. He was looking for Trebilock.

Stepping over a passed-out drinker, he spied where the pirate and his men were seated.

"Trebilock!" Alexander thundered.

Patrons' eyes were drawn to the dagger in Alexander's hand. A moment later, the noise-filled room grew deadly silent. Many of the men knew who Alexander was and immediately realized he was there to dispense justice.

The crowd separated, creating an open path to Trebilock's location. In six long strides, Alexander and five of his men advanced and stopped directly in front of the pirate. Isaac and the other five men burst through the back entrance and moved quickly to stand behind Trebilock.

Trebilock showed neither fear nor concern as he watched Alexander approach. With Alexander standing in front of him, he looked up from his tankard of wine, surveyed the numbers of armed men surrounding him, and slurred, "What brings *you* here?" Heaving his bulk upward, he struggled to his feet from the sturdy bench beneath him.

Alexander noticed a smile spreading across Trebilock's grimy face. The pirate was a huge man, taller and stouter than Alexander, and solidly built.

Standing as close to him as he was, Alexander could smell the stench of his body and his foul breath. He looked—and smelled—like he had not bathed in a year. His hair and beard glistened with grease, and his clothes and his boots were caked with mud and filth.

Alexander had met men like him before. Because of his imposing size, Trebilock thought he could force his will on anyone he chose. With each tankard of wine, he became even more cruel and aggressive.

Standing his ground, Alexander looked Trebilock squarely in the face. "You have pirated your last ship. As port commander of Marseilles, I find you and your men guilty of piracy. You are no longer welcome here or in the other ports I oversee. Lay down your weapons and leave now. If you are found in the port after sunrise, your lives will be forfeited."

The pirate sneered, "I am not afraid of you or your men. I go where I want and when I want. Leave now, before we cut you down." His threat ended with a drunken belch, spewing his wretched breath in every direction.

Swaying unsteadily, Trebilock attempted to pull his dagger from his belt. Just as he put his hand on the hilt of his knife, Isaac moved next to him and plunged his dagger into Trebilock's side. Alexander thrust his dagger in Trebilock's chest and, with an upward motion, jammed it into his heart as the pirate started to fall forward. Death was immediate.

Alexander stepped to the side and let him hit the floor, face-first. The tavern erupted into chaos as the patrons fled for their lives.

Trebilock's pirates leaped to their feet, and started swinging and slashing with every weapon they had. They were as drunk as Trebilock, resulting in a short, brutal fight, which ended with their deaths.

Alexander and his companions surveyed the blood-spattered scene. He gestured at the trembling tavern owner, motioning him closer.

Pointing to the dead pirate captain on the floor, he said, "Let the story be told … anyone who attempts to steal from our ships like Trebilock did will meet with the same outcome. Justice is swift in Marseilles." Alexander tossed him a small purse of coins. "Bury these men somewhere outside of the city."

Turning back to Trebilock's body, Alexander nodded to two of Isaac's men. "Turn him over." He dropped his boot onto Trebilock's gut and yanked his dagger from the pirate's now-limp body.

The patrons who scrambled out of the way when the fight began now flooded back into the tavern, the place erupting with cheers. The tavern patrons were relieved that the pirates were dead, and would no longer harass the merchants and townspeople of Marseilles.

When the excitement in the tavern finally quieted, Isaac and his men surrounded Alexander as they gathered by their horses.

"We pledge ourselves and our swords to you. We are honored to ride by your side," Isaac said.

"Isaac, the honor is mine. You and your men have a place at my table and on my lands as long as I am alive." With that, Alexander mounted his horse and turned it in the direction of the villa.

As he did, he noticed a young person hiding in the shadows beside the tavern.

Was that Lisa? Surely, she did not follow me here. Or did she?

five

Astrid and Alexander

Why do you not include Fredric in your affairs?

Jonathan met Alexander in the courtyard when he returned with the horse. Neither man spoke. Jonathan eyed Alexander's clothing and nodded to him. He offered two buckets of water to wash off the dried blood, then handed Alexander the clean clothes he had kept aside for him.

Later that evening, Alexander entered his bedchamber. Astrid had many candles lit while she combed her long golden-brown hair. Turning from her polished metal mirror, with a look of disdain toward Alexander and a voice that was more like a hissing snake than a wife, she spoke.

"What kind of father are you … you do not include Fredric in your affairs? He is a man now, no longer a boy. Has he not told you how eager he is to be at your side?"

Alexander grimaced. The thrill from his encounter with Trebilock was still coursing through his body, but Astrid's nagging words had stolen the excitement from the night's accomplishment.

"A man? No, he is not. Fredric has never told me or shown me that he wants to be anywhere by my side. All he wants is my coin. He doesn't care about the people of the port and he looks like scum. Your son is not a leader."

"Younger men than Fredric are already wed with families. You are his father. Why have you not found a suitable match for him to ensure his future?"

Instead of replying, Alexander sat quietly, reflecting on the early years he and his wife had spent together. *What has happened to her? Cannot she see what her son has turned into?*

Astrid changed after Fredric was born. Slowly, her sweet nature had turned vile and her tongue lashed out at everyone. Over the years, she transformed into a bitter woman, without kindness or consideration for anyone except her son and herself.

Not wanting any further conversation on the topic of Fredric, Alexander asked, "Do you remember how your mother changed after your papa was killed? She withdrew and lost all interest in life. She ignored you and your siblings—except for when she was beating you—and forced you to take care of yourself. She was a very unhappy, hateful woman … just like you have now become."

Taken aback, Astrid slammed down her brush and glared at him. "We were speaking of Fredric and your responsibilities to our son—the person who will take over your affairs. Why do you speak of my mother now? And how dare you compare me to her. I am not like her! All I want you to do is show some interest in Fredric and his future," Astrid blurted out.

Speaking softly, mostly just to himself, "Our son ... I do not think so ...."

Alexander knew Fredric did not have the capacity to step into his role. He was not equipped in any way to carry on the leadership of the family and his dealings with others was dismal. His mother had spoiled him in too many ways.

And now he realized that his wife was trying to undermine his authority.

Pulling himself from his reverie, Alexander stood from his chair and moved to her side. With arms crossed, he leaned forward and stated firmly, "Just because Fredric is a male does not mean he is ready to lead this family ... or any family. He is ill-tempered and thinks only of himself. He does not have the skills to manage anything or anyone. Fredric is more experienced in taverns and brothels than he will ever be with other responsibilities.

"I have grave doubts about him. No son of mine would behave this way." And then he added, "Fredric does not look like me nor act like me. Perhaps he is not my son."

Fear flowed through Astrid's body.

Turning from her, Alexander added, "I will speak to Commander Ramos of the Count's guard and request that he begin Fredric's military training. If he does not make a man out of him, no one can. Do not speak of Fredric working with me again. Now, this conversation is over!"

"It is far from over!" Flashing Alexander a hate-filled look, Astrid tossed her head back, and shoved him out of the way as she fled the room.

Glad to be rid of her, Alexander layed down, breathing deeply. *This woman has become a total stranger to me. The shortness of her height is now reflect in the shortness of her temperament. The woman I once cared for has taken on the form of a hag.*

Hearing a woman's voice, he opened his eyes and sat up.

What? Who said that?

Looking around, he saw no one. The voice he heard was kind and gentle. It certainly was not Astrid.

Getting up, he moves to the door. Is there an intruder in my home? A woman? I do not recognize the voice I heard.

Returning to his bed, sleep began to return to him.

There it was again … the voice.

Lisa is special. Support her. Be on the alert for her.

He had heard the voice before. Opening his eyes, he stares at the ceiling.

Who are you?

six

Lisa

Shadow, I am going to become like you, invisible to all except Papa and Margaux.

That night as she lay in bed, the conversation she had overheard between her papa and David was still swirling through Lisa's head.

I wonder what happened inside the tavern? What did Papa do to that pirate? I did not see any pirates leave the tavern. How do I ask him what happened, without him knowing I overheard him talking to David? If I keep listening in the solar, I wonder what else I can learn?

I wish Papa would teach me everything he knows, but I do not want to keep hiding behind the tapestry to learn it.

She leaned over to extinguish her bedside candle and caught a glimpse of her black cat, Shadow, at the foot of her bed. Shadow was very attached to Lisa, and the cat appeared only when she wanted to be seen. She spent all of her time feasting on the mice and rats that ventured near the villa.

Reaching down to scratch her cat behind the ear, she whispered, "Shadow, I am going to become like you, invisible to all except Papa and Margaux. People will get used to my absence here in the manor and my presence in the solar will go unnoticed."

In the past, Margaux had teased Lisa about her likeness to Shadow … long dark-brown hair, deep-set amber eyes, and a finely sculpted face. Like her cat, she was curious, independent, and agile.

Margaux was Lisa's confidante. Lisa constantly questioned Margaux about her papa's visitors to learn when they were expected. As a result, she had the opportunity to scramble to her favorite hiding spot before the visitors arrived.

In the meetings, Lisa heard a lot of words she did not understand. She would later ask Margaux to explain their meaning to her.

Within her concealed tapestry place, the thing she loved the most about his meetings and her secured eavesdropping was her new skill. By hearing their voices and the way they moved into the solar, she could sense their sincerity and whether they were telling the truth.

Lisa knew—mostly from the titles her papa used when he addressed his visitors—that there were some especially important people who came to seek his counsel. He met with dukes, leaders of the church, moneylenders, merchants, and peasants. Lisa wanted to do what her papa did, but she was a girl ... and managing businesses were something girls did not do.

Lisa was learning to "see" with her ears and trust her perceptions. She memorized voices, intonations, laughs, sighs, and themes of the conversations. That knowledge she could then attach to the title and name of any visitor when she encountered him.

Lisa had a feeling that one day all the information she was gathering would prove valuable.

It had been an exciting day. As Lisa closed her eyes, settling in with Shadow by her side, she was suddenly aware that a low voice was murmuring inside her head. The voice was always a soft female voice, speaking with wisdom and gentle assurance.

It was her *Lady.*

You will change the way …

"Change what way?" she mumbled as she drifted to sleep.

seven

Commander Ramos

Mine will have a detailing of his true progress.

Weeks after Alexander and Astrid had their heated discussion about Fredric's future, Commander Ramos arrived at their home. He was charged with gathering Fredric and his belongings and escorting him to his training. Fredric would be away from the family for a year.

Alexander greeted the commander warmly and escorted him into the solar for a private conversation.

Astrid was unaware of the commander's arrival in the solar until she was informed by Fredric, who heard Alexander greet him in the entryway. Upon hearing of Commander Ramos' presence, she stormed into the solar with clenched fists and pursed lips. Before she could say a word, a stern look was directed her way from Alexander.

"Commander Ramos, I am Astrid, Fredric's mother. Alexander said you are to train Fredric."

Commander Ramos stood, bowed, and inhaled slowly before he answered her.

"You are even more beautiful than I have been told. But, of course, my lady, what Alexander desires for Fredric is what all persons of authority want for their sons. Fredric will receive appropriate military training and when he returns, you will be impressed by his accomplishments."

The boost to her vanity diminished her anger and she smiled demurely. She was all aflutter as she struggled to remember the demands she was going to place on the commander regarding her son's training.

"You … you will keep us informed of Fredric's progress on a monthly basis," she spluttered.

"Yes, my lady. Your son will be treated well and his military training will be of prime importance while he is with us."

"Very well." With a toss of her head, Astrid straightened her shoulders, nodded, and flounced out of the room without closing the door.

Alexander turned to Commander Ramos with a shake of his head and sighed as he gestured to the commander to resume his seat.

"Send Astrid a monthly letter telling her of Fredric's progress and send me one as well. Tell her he does well, regardless of his progress. My letter, however, will contain a detailing of his *true* progress. And Commander, do not show him undue favor because he is my son."

Commander Ramos nodded in agreement.

As they made their way to the stables, Alexander and the commander chatted about other matters. Once there, they found Fredric and his mother waiting beside a large chestnut horse, laden with Fredric's belongings.

After a few words of advice from Alexander and a display of tears from Astrid, Commander Ramos turned to Fredric and said, "Mount up. We have a full day's ride before we reach the training camp."

Fredric did as he was told. With a resolute nod to his mother and father, he grasped the reins in his hands, unnecessarily dug his heels into the sides of his horse, and galloped ahead.

As they disappeared down the path, Astrid gulped back tears.

Alexander watched her with disdain as she stalked back to the villa and straight to her private chamber. Again, he questioned himself whether Fredric would ever be a man of which he could be proud.

eight

A Time to Rejoice

I am my papa's daughter.

With Fredric gone and Astrid in seclusion most of the time, no longer did the servants feel dread upon entering the villa. Smiles returned and laughter could be heard.

Lisa would spring from her bed at the rooster's crow, and join Margaux and her son Gerhardt to prepare the morning meal. It was a busy time, whomever dropped in was fed, and talk of the day's activities kept the conversation lively. Lisa felt accepted for who she was and not the daughter of the villa's lord.

With Fredric gone, Astrid went into a self-imposed isolation in her bedchamber for days on end. Meals were served only to Lisa and Alexander if he was in Marseilles. When he was gone, Lisa would share meals with Margaux, Jonathan, and Gerhardt, their son and her trusted friend. Gerhardt—scruffy brown hair, round faced with an abundance of freckles—was Lisa's age. He was her closest friend and companion to her when released from his normal work around the villa.

Without Fredric and the restrictions her mother demanded, it was a new time for Lisa. She would conceal herself in the niche in the solar, and spend hours intrigued by Papa's visitors and the many issues that she overheard.

When Alexander had business at the docks, Lisa would slip into the solar to read the books he had picked up on his travels and study manuscripts and contracts. Margaux knew where Lisa spent her time, just as she knew no one was allowed into the solar without Alexander's permission. She also knew Lisa's stealthy visits to her father's solar might endanger Margaux's position within the household.

One day, Astrid emerged from her bedchamber while Alexander was gone. She began yelling incoherently at everyone in sight. Lisa heard the commotion and went to investigate.

As she passed the entryway to Astrid's bedchamber, the gleam from the polished metal mirror Astrid used to admire herself caught her attention, and she stopped. Other than a wavering pale reflection in buckets of water, Lisa had never seen her own face.

Intrigued, she decided to look at herself in the mirror.

Turning her face from side to side, first smiling and then frowning, she began to giggle. To her, it looked as though Papa was staring back at her.

I look just like Papa without his beard. My chin and my nose are the same as his. I do not look anything like my mother. Maybe she is not my real mother?

Moving away from the mirror, she immediately left the bedchamber. Locating Astrid easily by following her shrill voice, she stared at her shrieking mother.

"What is the matter? Why are you so angry?"

"You should know. You act like a child and show no respect."

"How could I show you no respect when you never talk to me?"

Astrid quickly moved in front of Lisa, and the child held her ground. Astrid slapped Lisa in the face, and Lisa glared back at her with a slight smile.

"I do not look like you, not even a little bit. I am my papa's daughter … and maybe I am not your daughter after all!"

Lisa's words rendered Astrid speechless. As the furious woman spun on her heel and stalked away, a big smile spread across Lisa's face.

I do not like her and I do not want to be like her.

Later, Margaux pulled Lisa aside. "We need to talk. Let us go for a walk where we cannot be overheard." Once they left the villa, and were strolling in the orchard, Margaux began to speak.

"I have loved you as a daughter ever since I came to the villa. There are things about your family that you do not know and in time, your papa will reveal them to you. Until he does, do not underestimate your mother or your brother. It is best if you do not make them angry. Do you understand? To do so might put you in danger."

"I understand," Lisa replied. Moments later, she asked, "What things do I not know? Where does Papa go when he does not come home for many days?"

Margaux laughed. "Dear child, you are your papa's child. Your family is … complicated. As I said, one day your papa will tell you what is important for you to know."

Changing the subject, Margaux continued, "Do you remember the story I told you about what happened when you were young? You drew on the floor and the walls of the hall with the blacksmith's chalk."

Lisa nodded.

"I left out part of the story. At first, you created crude drawings of trees and stick figures, like every child does. But then you drew a woman, one with a beautiful face glowing with inner light. I had never seen anything like it—not even the monks at the harvest fair made images so perfect.

"Astrid made me scrub the chalk from the floor and walls, but before I did, I showed the drawings to your papa. We were both mesmerized by the image of your glowing woman. How could a child so young draw with such clarity and ease? Create something so marvelous? Since that time, your papa and I believe there is something more to you than even you know." Margaux stopped and turned to Lisa, gently embracing her. "We must get back."

Quietly, Lisa absorbed what Margaux said.

A woman … could that be the Lady I hear sometimes? I know her. At night, she talks to me in my sleep.

Over the evening meal with her father a few days later, Lisa was surprised when Alexander brought up the topic of art.

"I often find scraps of parchment containing poems and drawings inserted in my manuscripts. These things appear to be from someone in the villa. Lisa, do you know who the author and artist might be?"

In the silence, Lisa took a large bite of bread. Without looking up, she asked, "Papa, what do you think of the poems and drawings?"

"They are quite good. Every day I look for a new one. One day I will find out who the author is and learn more … about her."

Smiling, Lisa pushed her chair from the table, stood and kissed his cheek. "Thank you, Papa. There will be more for you to enjoy, I am sure. Look in your manuscripts tomorrow."

In her room that night by candlelight, Lisa began to write …

The Tree

When I tire of sewing to please and know my place.

The orchard is where I go, with apple and book, to be discreet.

Where my thoughts are my only care.

There is another place, a tree I climb, out of others' eyes.

This tree is where the whole villa lies at its trunk

None can come or go without being aware.

When people say I am under foot, this tree of solitude is what I seek.

A gentle breeze, the scent of the sea, faraway lands beckon to me.

Seaside towns waiting to see, beg many adventures waiting to explore.

I will dress as a boy: girls are not allowed.

To dress and act like a boy will be easy.

I will not hide my brash behavior for everyone to see.

nine

The Niche

Are you aware that Lisa has been sneaking into the solar and eavesdropping on my meetings?

For the past year, Lisa had made it a point to place herself behind the long tapestry whenever her papa had a meeting in the solar. Now that she had grown taller, she had to curl up to fit inside the niche and she had made it more comfortable by installing blankets to shield her from the cold, cramped surface.

In addition, she had craftily removed several stitches in the tapestry covering the niche so she could observe the guests who met with her papa. Now that she could see faces from behind the tapestry, Lisa noticed that her papa showed little emotion when conducting business until he was ready to reveal his position.

Standing at the solar doorway one morning as her papa was at his table, she asked, “Papa, may I come in?”

Looking up, he smiled. “Come in. What brings you here today?”

“Yesterday I saw the priest Loupe in your solar. Why did he want to talk to you?”

Raising his eyebrows, he scanned his daughter's face. *What is she up to? She is not like her brother and I need to know more.*

"He wanted to discuss my annual contributions to the church. Why do you ask?"

"Because he left in a hurry. Why is he upset every time he leaves here?"

"The priest and I do not exactly agree on the tithes I contribute. He expected more than I gave him."

"Maybe the lower tithes were due to the smaller harvests and the drought that has been everywhere," Lisa murmured.

Alexander heard what she had said. "Next year it will be better," Alexander replied, watching Lisa's reaction.

"Then the priest can fill up his tithe barns." Lisa nodded in agreement.

Intrigued and curious with her comments, Alexander asked, "What do you think about the priest?"

"I have seen the way he looks at you. He is not a good man and he frightens me." Lisa walked over, gave her papa a hug, and left the room.

Alexander rubbed his forehead.

How could she know what I discussed with the priest? She must have been in this room … but where?

Looking around the room, his gaze settled on the tapestry covering the niche. He walked to the tapestry, pulled it back, and found the blankets piled there.

Alexander smiled as he turned back to the letters on his table. *My daughter!*

Several days later, after a meeting with local merchants, Alexander sat at his table, then stood and turned to the tapestry covering the niche.

Looking at it closely, he said to the tapestry, “What have you learned today?”

A few moments passed as silence filled the room.

Again, Alexander asked, “What have you learned today?” Then, he added, “Lisa ...?”

Finally, a small voice whispered from behind the tapestry, “I learned that people do not trust the lords or church to keep their promises and that they are struggling to protect their families and keep them fed.”

“Come out, Lisa. We need to talk.”

Lisa crept out from behind the tapestry and looked sheepishly at the floor; her lip curled in a pout. She was upset and embarrassed about being discovered.

Alexander put his hand under her chin and raised her face so he could see her eyes. “Lisa, why are you hiding in here?”

“I hide here to be with you and learn about what you do, to learn from you. Papa, I want to do what you do. And ... I feel safe in here.”

Alexander moved to the center of the room and pulled out two chairs. He repositioned them to face one another. Sitting in one, he motioned to Lisa. “Sit.”

Taking her hands in his, he said, “I knew from your previous statements about tithes paid to the church that you had explicit knowledge of my discussions with the priest. It was not difficult to figure out that you had heard our entire conversation. I only had to figure out how.”

Looking at her papa, she said, "Do you remember the day that Fredric chased me into the solar?" Pointing to her hiding place, she said, "I hid in the niche so he could not find me. Before I could leave, David arrived, and I was trapped. That day I heard you talking to David about the pirate. What did you do? Please tell me what happened that night at the tavern."

Alexander raised his eyebrows. *So, my daughter* was *outside the tavern that night.*

"As the port commander, I have to know everything that is going on. It is my responsibility to maintain order and keep merchants and people at the port from harm. I had to protect our merchants. Now Trebilock and his men will no longer menace our ports and attack our ships."

"I would like to be a merchant someday."

Alexander threw back his head and laughed out loud. "Lisa … you should be thinking about getting married and having a family."

Lisa looked at him. Did she dare tell him what she wanted to do?

Having a life like her mother was not her choice. She did not want to do what her mother did—get married and have children. Gathering her courage, she leaned forward in her chair.

"Papa … I want to be like you. I never want to be like Mother. You know that I know more than Fredric. He never learned to read or write, so how could he read or understand your contracts? And … and there are things that I can do with animals. Sometimes, I can hear them speak and I know they understand my commands. I want to learn everything that you do ... things that I know he will never know how to do."

Quickly, she added, "Hearing your conversation with David about the pirates was interesting, and ever since then, I have been here for all of your meetings."

"Every meeting? There have been conversations held here that a young woman should not have heard," Alexander said, his tone stern as he rebuked her.

"Papa, I am not a child. How can I make decisions about my own life if I do not know what goes on beyond these walls? I want to know about everything you do. Besides that, I am getting acquainted with the beliefs and behaviors of some of the most influential men in our land. Some of the men you meet with threaten you. They just do not come out and say it, but I can tell from their behavior what they are thinking," she declared.

"Ever since I have heard you talking to so many different people, I know I want to do this, too. Until I hid in the solar, I did not understand what it meant for you to be the port commander, a successful merchant, and a strong leader. People come to you for advice and for your help in solving grievances. I want to know everything you know. I want to be able to do what you do."

"Lisa, there are consequences for the knowledge I possess and many reasons behind all the decisions I make."

Silence filled the room.

After a long pause, he added, "I will teach you, but you must follow my rules. You must never disclose any of the conversations you have heard or hear from now on. You cannot tell your mother and *definitely* do not tell Fredric. I believe he would divulge any information he obtained for his own gain. Your mother is blind to all of this and unfortunately, that puts our family in great jeopardy. One day you will understand."

Alexander sat back in his chair and looked at Lisa with a tender gaze.

She has grown so mature right in front of my eyes. How did I not notice that she was growing up? She demonstrates the desire to learn more than her years suggest. I know from the questions she is been asking that she possesses the ability to learn and understand my business affairs, and she shows a unique skill for reading people.

"Lisa, you are a special young woman about to face the difficult times we are in. Girls and women do not lead and they are not merchants. How can I help you stand up to the adversity you will surely encounter? I want to help you in any way I can. That's why you must follow my rules."

I feel as though I am being prompted to prepare and protect her. I wonder if these thoughts have anything to do with the voice I sometimes hear? I need to tell her more about Margaux and Rose.

The air had changed in the solar. He realized there was no longer a girl sitting in front of him. Instead, there was an intelligent, ambitious young woman—one he was proud to call daughter.

Making a decision, Alexander turned to a heavy wooden box he kept next to his manuscripts and contracts. With the two keys he removed from his belt, he opened the box.

"Papa, I have heard you open that box before. Can I see what is in it?"

"Yes, as long as you do not tell anyone what you have seen."

"Are those bags filled with coin?"

He nodded and took out a small purse of coins. Handing it to Lisa, he said, "If anything should ever happen to me, leave the villa at once and take this with you. Go to the docks and find a healer named Rose. She is a wise old woman and will tell you whose help you should seek and give you counsel on what to do next. There are merchant caravans that leave from the docks and travel to all parts of France. Rose will help you select the proper one and you must travel with the caravan to Paris immediately. Do not hesitate.

"Once in Paris, you must find a merchant and moneylender named Ezra. He is a good friend, and I have developed a solid business alliance with him. I trust him with my life as well as yours. This is important for your well-being. Do you understand?"

"Yes, Papa, I understand. I have seen and heard Ezra here with you in the solar."

Alexander smiled and reached for his daughter's hand. "Lisa, what *have not* you seen or overheard in this room? Keep the purse hidden. You will need the coin to pay for your passage to Paris, as well as other expenses along the way."

Confused, yet excited, Lisa took the purse from Alexander and placed it in the folds of her tunic. Sensing that their conversation was finished, she stood and hugged her papa, leaving him sitting alone in the solar.

He could tell from her footsteps behind him that she was headed toward her bedchamber to securely conceal her pouch.

Alexander walked to the window for fresh air.

Behind him, Margaux entered the solar with a wine decanter, placing it on the table.

Turning, Alexander asked her to stay as he closed the door.

"Margaux, did you know that Lisa has been sneaking in here and eavesdropping on my meetings?"

"Yes, Alexander, I know she loves to be near you. Perhaps that's why she hides in here."

"Margaux, last night I was awakened by an unfamiliar woman's voice. I got up to see if someone was close by. I found no one. The voice talked about Lisa. It told me that I must protect her."

Margaux gasped in surprise. "Alexander, I, too, have been hearing a woman's voice! Sometimes I hear it during the day; sometimes it comes to me while I am between waking and sleep. That voice tells me that Lisa is special, and I should watch over her."

"I have never had anyone say something to me directly or have voices come to me that I have wanted to heed like the woman's voice did. It is too real to ignore."

"We are both hearing the same message. I call the voice the *Lady*. What do you think it means?"

Alexander looked at Margaux with concern. "Lisa revealed to me that she hears the voice as well. And she calls it the *Lady*. For us to heed the *Lady's* message, we need to be protective of Lisa, and we must teach her of the dangers around the port. It is important that you are aware of Lisa's activities when she is not in the solar with me. If she ventures off alone, there's no telling what could happen to her.

"There is a reason we are getting these messages; the *Lady* is giving us fair warning that Lisa needs protection. I do not trust Fredric and I am fearful that he could cause her harm. I do not want Lisa leaving the villa without you knowing where she is going.

"The *Lady* ... why are we all hearing her voice? Fredric is gone. Where could the danger be coming from?"

Margaux's words, "There is something more to you than even you know," kept repeating in Lisa's mind as she sat up in her bed.

What do I not know? What did Margaux mean?

That night with quill and ink in candlelight, Lisa began to write …

The Artist

One day when I was small, the story goes, that I began to draw.

To people's dismay, with chalk, I drew on walls, floors and down the hall.

Margaux gave me parchment, quill and ink, stopped me drawing on floors and walls.

Parchment and guidance are what I need.

I drew birds and landscapes were easy for me.

While in the niche one day, with only people on display.

I drew people to pass the time away.

Then, a strange feeling came my way.

I drew the essence of the people in the solar that day.

What has come over me, I am frightened—I see the true motives of those on display.

ten

Daydreams and Thoughts

Why did I not see this before?

Lisa thought about hiding the coin bag under the straw mattress on her bed and then changed her mind. Hidden in such an obvious place, Fredric could easily find it and take it for himself. She layed down and stared at the ceiling.

Where would the purse be safe? I know … I will ask Margaux.

Shadow jumped up beside her and began pawing at her for attention.

Lisa snuggled with her cat and rubbed her belly as she whispered in her ear, “What just happened, Shadow? Why is Papa giving me these coins now? Is he in danger? What is he is not telling me? I must become strong and independent like you, Shadow. It is time for me to explore outside the villa. I must learn how to survive on my own. I am going to find the healer Rose that Papa told me about and ask her about the caravans to Paris.”

For a long while, she stayed in her bedchamber, daydreaming about people in faraway places and new adventures that were waiting to be discovered—dreaming of sailing the Mediterranean in search of exciting experiences.

More than anything, she dreamed about never seeing Astrid and Fredric again.

It is obvious from the way my mother treats me that she does not even like me, only Fredric. He puts on a good face to her, and despises all animals and other people. No one wants to be around him.

I want people to know me as a wise, compassionate, brave woman. I am going to make all this happen before I need to escape so I do not meet the fate she thinks I should have—marrying an old man and getting me away from here. The coin is important and I will need it to get away.

I wish Margaux had been my mother. She has protected me from Fredric ever since I can remember. Her kindness and strength have always been there for me and I have learned much from her.

While Lisa daydreamed with Shadow at her side, Alexander continued to sit in the solar, deep in thought.

Why did not I see how clever my daughter is before today? She has been spending many hours hidden away here, listening in on my business affairs. She is hearing some rough language, but she is gaining knowledge she will need to protect herself. I do not know how I know that, but inside my heart, I know it is true—just as I know how important it is that she learns everything she can. Lisa is beginning her journey in the safety of my presence, but that may not always be so.

I must teach her about the value of information and how to use it. I cautioned her to speak only to me about what she has overheard. The voice that I have heard carries a sense of warning with it. Because of that, I fear we are both in danger—and my senses are rarely wrong.

Tomorrow, I will go to the apothecary and tell Rose that I have given her name to Lisa. She needs to know about herbs and remedies if she gets ill along the way. When the time comes, Rose needs to tell Lisa about Ezra and how to get to Paris if something happens to me.

eleven

Fredric Returns

Alexander held his silence,
glaring at the petulant boy in front of him.

The final letter Alexander had received from Ramos—recapping the extensive training Fredric had undergone—was disappointing but expected. According to Ramos, the boy had no leadership abilities, and extreme difficulty in controlling his temper. Any type of strategic planning was beyond his mentality and judgment level. In the private evaluations that Alexander received, the commander could only recommend him for minor duties in any military situation. Any involvement in leadership should be avoided.

When Fredric returned after completing his training with Commander Ramos, Alexander realized he had not missed his son. Instead, Fredric's absence of a year was not long enough. Within a few days, Alexander was aware of a renewed division in the family. Fredric's return seeded it.

Alexander wrote back to Commander Ramos, praising him for the time and effort he had devoted in his attempt to train Fredric and thanked him for his honest assessment of his son's abilities.

As he finished writing the letter, Fredric abruptly entered the solar. Instantly, Alexander was on alert. The unbidden thought that flowed through his mind was *this boy is bad.*

"Papa, I need to talk to you."

"Come in and sit down."

Fredric did as he was told. "I have been home for two weeks and you have not asked to see me."

"I have been busy with matters of the estate and visits to the port."

"Why have you ignored me?"

"Fredric, what could you possibly want to talk to me about? In all your years, you have never asked to speak with me." Alexander frowned at his son.

"I spent a year training with that commander. I am a man now, and I want to be included in all your business affairs."

"Fredric, you are not capable of understanding anything about my business or the family."

"That's not true. I have seen what Commander Ramos sent Mother. His letters to her said that I did everything right."

Alexander held his silence, glaring at the petulant boy in front of him. *What a fool he is.*

Ignoring his papa's silence, Fredric added, "I am ready to take an active role in what you do."

Alexander searched through a stack of parchments to his left. He extracted the letters he had received from Ramos and tossed them in front of Fredric. "Read the commander's letters to me. They tell quite a different story, one that you know is the truth—his real evaluation. You have no leadership ability, your judgment is poor, and you failed to grasp the essential elements of military strategy."

Fredric's stunned reaction told Alexander everything as the boy leaped to his feet.

"Sit down, I am not done with you!" Alexander shouted. Fredric, now pouting, sat back down.

"You do not know what my business even does. Your sister knows far more than you do. Due to your lack of initiative, you have humiliated and dishonored this family. If I had my choice, you would not inherit my estate, ever. And, if you do, I am thankful that I will not be here to witness your destruction of all that I have created and the damage you do to others."

Fredric pushed the letters back toward Alexander. He stood, shoved the chair back, and shouted, "I hate you!" as he stomped out.

As Fredric retreated, Alexander heard him exclaim, "Mother, what are you doing here? Did I not tell you what he would say?"

Alexander looked down at the table in disgust. Now he knew exactly why Fredric had come to talk to him.

Astrid is behind this. If he inherits my estate, he will destroy everything I have created.

twelve

New Horizons

Papa, I went to the docks today by myself.

Margaux often took her son Gerhardt and Lisa with her on frequent trips to the village market square by the docks. It was within walking distance of the villa, and the two young people loved being together to explore.

Lisa was enthralled with all she saw there. She loved watching the activity and hearing the noise of the merchants as they shouted out their wares along with the myriad displays of fruits, vegetables, meats, fish, breads, and cheeses.

She noticed the different types of clothing worn by the people in the marketplace. For their outer clothing, the men wore rough shirts or knee-length tunics over breeches, either brown or gray, usually made of linen or wool from the sheep they raised. Women's garb consisted of long-sleeved dresses or tunics over a chemise, reaching to their ankles. During cold weather, they kept warm with shawls or capes. Their heads were often covered with wraps of material.

Coverings for feet varied, from pieces of wood with straps to simple shoes made from animal hides, sometimes taller boots made from leather. In the summer, bare feet were common.

Margaux's quest was to gather the ingredients for meals for the next few days. She and Lisa walked through the market, both carrying baskets to be filled with items for the estate's kitchen.

"Margaux, do you know a woman named Rose and where she is located?"

"Yes, why do you ask?"

"Papa told me about a woman who has an apothecary shop. I would like to see it."

Pointing out her location down the street, Margaux added, "Next time we will visit her."

Margaux had showed Lisa how to make the head coverings that all adult women wore, and the simple clothing she saw women wearing would be easy to acquire.

Lisa took it all in. She realized if she wore similar garments, it would allow her to blend in with the peasant women in the market when she explored on her own. Or if she headed to Paris, like Papa said she might need to someday.

They stopped at several of the tables. At each one, Margaux explained how she would cook the ingredients she was acquiring. She also noticed how Lisa's eyes wandered, as if she was searching for someone or something.

A few days after her initial market visit, early one spring morning before the household was up, Lisa quietly emerged from the servants' door at the back of the villa, clad in the newly-sewn attire she copied from what she saw at the docks. Her goal was the docks and to finally meet Rose.

She tiptoed out into the rear courtyard and vanished into a light mist before anyone saw her. Following the dirt path that wound through the orchard and ultimately ended at the road leading to the markets by the docks, she headed toward a place she was forbidden to go alone. Her curiosity was not to be denied.

Who is this woman named Rose? Why am I supposed to see her? How could she help me? I must meet her.

As the mist lifted, she could see the sun shining on ships in the bay. Excited by all that she saw, she was now ready to explore the area and satisfy her curiosity on her own terms and find Rose.

Spotting a large stone wall, she leaned against it to observe the hectic activity of men loading and unloading ships in the harbor. Focusing on one group, she noticed how orderly the laborers stacked their merchandise on the dock surrounding their ship.

There were several sellers, some with tables by the doorway already laden with vegetables, fruits, and various wares. Birds hovered about, looking for morsels to drop to the ground as the vendors added to overflowing baskets on their tables. The fish-mongers fended off diving gulls, while the wharf rats—both real rodents and hungry children—were shooed away by the sellers.

The merchants were hawking their items and competing for sales in exchange for coin, even bartering amongst themselves. In every direction she looked, people of all ages were roaming about, each one in pursuit of the day's treasure.

Deciding to break her fast, Lisa approached one of the vendors. With her coin, she purchased a slice of bread and a bit of cheese from the vendor, tart ale from another, and took her purchases to a large rock.

As she sat and ate, she scanned the area, focusing on everyone's activities as each moved about. Except for a few conversations, nobody seemed to be noticing who was around. They were so intent on the task at hand that they barely spoke to anyone unless a person wanted something.

As her eyes scanned her surroundings, she noticed an old woman sitting at a well-worn wooden table outside the door of a small store. The woman had a few bowls on display. But her look … it was directed at Lisa, as if she were beckoning to her with her eyes. Intrigued, Lisa pushed off the rock and approached her.

"Hello, Lisa … what brings you to the docks today?" the old woman asked with a smile.

Taken aback, Lisa shrugged her shoulders, not knowing what to say. *How did she know my name?*

The woman patted the space next to her on the rough bench behind her table. "Come, sit next to me. I have been watching you as you wandered through the stores and tables in front of them. I missed meeting you the other day when you were here with Margaux."

Surprised by what the woman had just said, Lisa hesitated, quickly observing the old woman. She had a tiny frame, weathered skin, and appeared slightly hunched over. A wimple of dark blue covered her head and shoulders and tightly framed her face.

Intrigued, Lisa could not look away from her dancing hazel eyes. The woman's soft, melodious voice charmed Lisa. Immediately, she began to warm up to the old woman.

There is something about her I need to know. Could this be Rose?

She felt safe, moving even closer as they sat on the bench together.

"Why were you watching me?" Lisa asked.

"It is what I do. Just like you have been doing the same thing since you first arrived here today. It is what people like us do; we observe people and things." Turning her head, she scanned their surroundings. "Look over there at the group of people by those two tables with vegetables on them. Tell me what you see."

Lisa studied the multitude of people milling about and then responded, "They are busy as bees, without knowing that they are all part of the hive. They are blind to one another."

"Excellent observation," said the old woman with a satisfied nod. "Now, let me tell you who *you* are," the old woman began.

"How do you have any idea who I am? We have never met before. Can you tell who I am by my appearance? And how do you know my name?"

"Yes, I know exactly who you are. Your clothes are crafted well—by your own hands, I suppose—to blend in here with the local people. Yet your hands are too soft, and your skin is too light. It is obvious that you are sheltered during most of the day from the harsh sunlight. I know that you have had a protected upbringing and you are educated because the words you use are not common to the people working on the docks or shopping at the market. You are bored and seek adventure."

"Just by these observations, it is obvious to you who I am?" Lisa asked in disbelief.

"Yes. You are Lisa, the daughter of Alexander, the port commander. You are everything he has described to me and more," the old woman said gently, reaching for her hand.

"You knew who I was before I approached you?" Lisa asked.

"Yes, dear, it is my job to know who visits the docks. I have seen you here before with Margaux. This time I also noticed your coin purse, which you tried unsuccessfully to conceal. A gift from your papa, I suspect."

Lisa laughed out loud, and then stopped herself. "So, you know my papa."

"Alexander has many business interests on the dock, including my space here. I see him and speak with him frequently," the old woman said with a smile.

"You are Rose … and you pay my papa for this space."

"Yes, I pay him for this space, but not with coin. There are many methods of payment in business. Information about what happens on the docks is most important; it, too, can be exchanged as payment to the right person," she said with a sly grin. "I am often your papa's eyes and ears for what happens here."

At that moment, Lisa turned on the bench to peer into the store behind the table they sat at. Her gaze traveled to the back where she noticed shelves full of containers. "You are a healer."

Nodding her head, the old woman responded, "Yes, for those who work on the docks. I sell the herbs, potions, and elixirs that arrive here from distant lands."

Lisa's attention was drawn back to the woman in front of her. "Is Rose your real name?"

"Roselle Du Maurier," she said softly. "The children call me Rose. Just Rose." Standing, she began to move slowly away from the table.

Excited, Lisa stood as well. "Papa told me that if anything ever happened to him that I should seek your help in finding a caravan that would take me to Paris."

Rose nodded with a knowing look. “Yes, he and I have discussed this in the past.”

Sensing that their conversation was over, Lisa untied her coin purse, gently took Rose’s hand, and emptied the coins into it.

“Rose, this is for the children I saw hiding behind the shelves that held containers.”

Rose caressed Lisa’s hand. “You truly are your papa’s daughter. He, too, helps me care for these orphaned children. I have enjoyed your company today, Lisa. Come back soon. We have much to discuss.”

“I would like to stay and talk more, but I need to get back. I will be missed.”

On her way home, the morning’s experiences danced through her head. Rose’s statement, “We have much to discuss,” kept running through her mind.

What did Rose mean? I can hardly wait to talk to her again. I like and trust her.

As Lisa approached the villa, a sudden thought came to her. Missing the weight of the coin from her small bag, she realized that it would be wise to not have a coin purse exposed. After thinking about the problem for a bit, she realized she could sew a small opening in her tunic to conceal a pouch from sight.

Before she knew it, she was standing in front of the door where she had exited that morning.

That evening, Lisa found Papa sitting in the solar reviewing maps of the area surrounding the villa. She skipped over to his chair and began telling him about her day’s discoveries.

"Papa, I went to the docks today by myself."

Alexander looked up from his work. He was not surprised by what he had just heard, only that she was so open about it. "And what did you learn today when you were at the docks *all by yourself*?"

Lisa sat in the chair next to him and recounted all the exciting tales of the people, sights, and sounds she had observed.

"Did you meet anyone?" he asked.

"I met Rose, the kind old woman that you told me about, Papa. We had a wonderful talk."

Alexander tugged on the cords of Lisa's coin purse, which was visible. "I told you to hide this. Now it is displayed for anyone to see, and it is substantially lighter than when I first gave it to you. Am I correct in assuming that you gave all your coins to Rose?"

Lisa nodded in the affirmative, remembering all the faces of the children she had seen while with Rose.

"It appears that you and I are both quite generous. I am proud of you for sharing your good fortune with others, and for sharing it with Rose. She is especially important to me. She also provides shelter and protection for many children and I make frequent contributions to her for their upkeep. What you did will buy food and clothing for them.

"But that coin was meant for your journey to Paris if the need should ever arise, and it was far too much coin to be carrying around. Promise me that you will not take that much coin with you again when you go out. There are people who would rob you —or worse—if they knew who you are and what you carry with you.

"Please listen carefully, Lisa. You took a big risk going to the docks by yourself today. If you do it again, take Gerhardt with you.

Never go further than Rose's table and make certain that Margaux knows before you leave the villa. Promise me that you will do this."

Surprised with how serious he had become, and with her eyes wide open, she said, "I will, Papa."

"You are smart and must keep your wits about you at all times. There are dangerous places for a young girl near the docks. Young girls are often harmed when alone or disappear and end up slaves."

Lisa listened closely to what he said, grateful that he had given her permission to visit Rose again … if Gerhardt was with her. She nodded in agreement to herself when alone in the room.

Alexander pulled out a large purse full of coins. Handing it to Lisa, he said, "Here is coin to replenish what you gave to Rose, and a bit more besides. Keep this purse safely hidden and do not use it for any purpose other than expenses to get you to Paris."

Refocusing on her papa's words, Lisa nodded again.

Alexander then handed her a second, smaller purse.

"This coin purse is to use when you go back to the market, but only a small amount is in it. Take with you only what you need for the day's purchases. Revealing any more coin than that puts you in great danger. Do you understand?"

"Yes, Papa."

"Good." He leaned forward. "Keep this in a safe place. If Fredric thinks you have your own coin stored somewhere, he will do everything he can to find it as will your mother. He has been visiting the taverns and brothels, and your mother has been supporting his behavior. He recently asked me for coin, and I refused his request. Promise me, Lisa, now."

thirteen

Papa and Daughter Bonding Time

Wealth is not everything.

At fifteen, Lisa was a smaller version of Alexander, slender and tall for her age.

Several years had passed since she had begun hiding in the niche. By now, her hiding place was cramped, but it was still the best seat in the solar. The small hole that she had so artfully opened in the tapestry was now concealed with a flap she had sewn on the reverse side. It allowed her to watch as well as listen to the conversations that took place and provided cover if necessary.

She noticed how her papa was attentive to body, hand, and facial gestures when his guests talked. And he knew she was there, just as he now expected her to be, her presence known only by him and Margaux.

She saw, too, that Alexander had the seating arrangement in a particular way. Deliberately, he always sat with the light from the window at his back. Lisa realized that it put his guests in full exposure and made observing their reactions quite simple. She had carefully rearranged the table and chairs a bit, so she had a better view of all the participants. When Alexander first noticed the new seating arrangement, he turned to the tapestry and smiled.

After his meetings, Alexander and Lisa would walk outside the villa and talk about what Lisa had overheard. He was amazed by her ability to remember even the slightest detail and depended on her to furnish those details later if he asked.

She is both the son and daughter I wanted, he thought to himself.

During one walk, Lisa was excited to show him she had heeded his advice about her purse and what she had created. Moving ahead of him, she slowed and turned a full circle. “Do you see my coin purse now?”

Amused, he watched her, then shook his head. “You do not have it with you.”

Laughing, she blurted out, “Yes, I do.”

Her hand disappeared into the side of her tunic. At the same time, her other hand moved to the other side of the tunic, disappearing beneath the fabric. Once again, she slowly spun in a circle and then stopped. Grinning, she withdrew her hands, pulling the newly added fabric out in each hand. Then she tucked them back into the hidden slots in her tunic. “What do you think, Papa?”

“What have you done, Lisa? I have not seen anything like this.”

“I took your advice about not carrying a coin purse when I was out. I sewed a hidden space in all my tunics where I could place coins or any small things I wanted to carry. I also added two of these spaces to my cloak.”

“Does Margaux know about this? If she does, I am going to have her add these to some of my tunics and cloaks as well.”

“She does … I call it *my secret.*”

"I am happy you told me about your secret ... now it will be ours."

With their exchanged smiles, their conversation and walk took on a different tone. Lisa asked him about the conversation she had observed in the solar between Isaac and him the day before.

"Papa, I heard Isaac ask you why you refused the count of Provence's offer to make you a noble of a vast estate. Do you regret declining his offer?"

Alexander reflected for a moment. "No, I do not. I have everything a man could possibly want right here. As commander of the port, I have my villa and grounds close to the docks of Marseilles, where it is convenient to conduct my business. I have sufficient wealth to feed and care for my family, and I have enough to share my good fortune with others.

"Wealth is not everything, Lisa. More important is what you do with it once you have it. I could have ten sprawling estates and it would not make me any happier than I am today. In fact, it would demand much more work. I have worked hard to acquire what I have. It was not handed to me and I am happy with what I have achieved. I did not do it all by myself and that's why I compensate those people who helped me along the way."

He took his daughter's arm and tucked it into his as they continued their walk.

fourteen

Dangers Abound

Lisa started crying, screaming, and trying to break away from the thug with the horrible breath.

Lisa woke to another cloudless day. During the night, the *Lady* came to her again.

Why does this voice keep coming more often in my dreams? Last night, I heard her say Rose's name and it sounded like a warning. I wish I could understand what she means. I know it will come to me.

Lisa had a plan for what she wanted to do today. Heading to the kitchen, she was ready with her request.

"Margaux, after my lessons, can Gerhardt and I go to the market to visit Rose?"

"Gerhardt cannot go today. He has work to do in the barn."

Hmm. Maybe I will just run down to see Rose by myself. I can return before anyone notices that I am gone, Lisa thought.

Astrid had begun tracking Lisa's behavior and whereabouts. Alexander's constant attention and devotion to Lisa and not to Fredric had created a strong wave of jealousy.

Upon exiting her own chamber, she saw Lisa slip into her room, looking rushed and excited. Standing back from her door, Astrid waited to see what Lisa would do.

What is she up to now?

When Lisa emerged from her room, Astrid was shocked to see that she was wearing a coarse wool tunic, like those worn by peasants. She watched as Lisa ran down the hallway and left the villa.

Astrid immediately set out in a different direction. Entering Fredric's bedchamber, she tried to wake him. Not surprisingly, he was sleeping off another night of drinking and whoring and did not respond.

With a grimace, she shouted and shook him at the same time. "You reek of wine! Get up and put your clothes on! I need you to follow Lisa and see where she is going."

Fredric grumbled and turned away from his mother as he got up.

"She was dressed like all the poor people around here … I do not understand why …."

Fredric turned and looked at his mother. "I saw her the other day with Margaux visiting the marketplace. She probably went there."

Astrid shouted again, "Get dressed, now! Follow her and report to me what she is doing there. Do not take a horse. You need to walk off last night's drink. And stay out of the taverns for one day."

Anything to get away from his mother ….

Fredric picked up the clothes he dropped on the floor the night before and redressed. He left the villa and staggered down the path on his way to the docks. A drink was the first thing he wanted, one that would soothe his foul mood.

As he neared the docks, he spied Lisa sitting at a table, speaking with an old lady he recognized as Rose. Unsteady on his feet, he stumbled just as he reached their table.

Rose gasped with fright as Fredric grabbed Lisa by the hair and pulled her to her feet. "Come have a drink with me," he slurred.

Rose stood to help Lisa, only to be shoved to the ground by Fredric.

Lisa tried to fight him off, but his hold on her hair was too tight and too painful.

"If you quit fighting me, I will let go of you."

Hearing her brother's words, Lisa stopped squirming for a moment. Fredric released his hold on her hair. At the same time, he grabbed her arm and started to drag her away.

"What are you doing? Where are you taking me?"

"Someplace where you can buy me a drink," Fredric growled with a smirk.

"I will give you coin, and you can do that all by yourself," Lisa pleaded, resisting his hold on her and failing.

"I want you to meet some of my friends. You never do anything with me," he whined.

"What friends? I have never seen you with any friends! I hate you … let go of me!" she shouted in his face.

Not letting her go, Fredric dragged her, thrashing and screaming, to the Anchor Inn, a tavern past the docks. It was his favorite drinking spot and a place where he spent time with prostitutes.

Theo, one of the orphan boys Rose looked after was close by.

Rose called out to him as she watched Fredric pull Lisa away. Pointing to where Alexander had boarded a boat, she told Theo to run and deliver her urgent message to him: Lisa had been dragged away by Fredric, heading toward the Anchor Inn.

Theo sprinted to the boat and started up the cargo ramp, only to be blocked by a stout, leathery-skinned sailor.

"Where do you think you are going?" the sailor growled as he blocked access to the boat.

"I need to get Rose's urgent message to Alexander—right away."

"If you are lying to me, I will toss your bones into the harbor," barked the sailor.

Alexander was close by and heard the commotion. As he approached the pair, he could see that Theo was quite agitated and had a frightened look on his face.

"I heard you say you had a message for me from Rose. What is it?"

"Lisa was visiting Rose, and Fredric came. He is dragging Lisa away and forcing her to go to the tavern with him," said the lad, relieved to have delivered his message.

"How long ago did this happen?" Alexander shouted to him as he fled down the gangplank and back toward Rose's stall in hopes of gaining more information. He knew if Fredric was involved, Lisa was in grave danger. He hoped he could reach her in time.

"Just now," Theo yelled at Alexander's back as he followed him down the dock. He matched Alexander stride for stride as both now ran toward Rose's tiny market stall.

"Where did he take Lisa?"

Pointing in the direction of the tavern, Rose said, "He dragged her to the Anchor Inn."

"Theo, run to the stables and get a horse saddled. Tell them it is for me and that I need it at once. Once the horse is readied, bring it to the Anchor Inn and wait outside."

Alexander tossed a coin to Theo and fled to the tavern.

Fredric barely managed to drag Lisa to the front door of the tavern. She was punching and kicking at him, trying to free herself from his grasp.

In a final attempt at subduing her, Fredric grabbed her by the hair once again. He threw open the door and shoved her into the dark interior that reeked of spilled ale and vomit. Once inside, he shouted to the tavernkeeper, "Give me wine!"

Two men, one called Blaxton and the other called Jaggor, drank regularly with Fredric and approached him as he stood in the middle of the room, restraining Lisa by her hair. Both men leered at her.

Fredric released his grip on his sister and shoved her in Blaxton's direction. "She is yours."

Blaxton caught her and swiftly pinned her arms behind her back. "We will give this little wharf rat back to you after she takes care of us."

Lisa started crying, screaming, and trying to break away from Blaxton, the thug with the rancid breath and filthy clothes.

Blaxton bellowed to his partner, "Look, Jaggor, a frisky fighter! We have got us some fun today."

The two men dragged Lisa into the back of the tavern and down the hallway that led to the brothel rooms. Blaxton chose an empty room on the right and shoved her inside. Lisa was at full voice, shrieking at the top of her lungs.

Jaggor, who had brought a cup of wine with him, grabbed Lisa's head and was trying to force her to swallow the contents. She spit the drink in his face, and he grabbed her around the throat, choking her, and stopping her wailing. While Jaggor held her forcibly, Blaxton yanked her tunic off. As he stripped her, he found her hidden coin purse.

Holding up the purse, Blaxton whooped, "Oh ho, Jaggor, this wench is going to pay us for using her! We can give her back to Fredric with our thanks for such easy wages."

"What is a wharf rat doing with a coin purse? What if she stole it?" Jaggor asked.

Cerise, a prostitute from the tavern's brothel, was slipping out to the tavern's privy when she heard the uproar. Eavesdropping shamelessly, she entered the room when she heard the comment about the coin purse.

A wharf rat with a coin purse?

Ignoring the two men, she crossed to the cot where Lisa cowered, naked and trembling. Looking at her terrified face and at the clean, unmarked skin on the girl's body, Cerise took pity on her.

There is something familiar about her; where have I seen her?

"You men … be easy on her, this is likely her first time," the prostitute said. "Let me see that coin purse."

Grinning like a cat that had just caught a fat rat, Blaxton dangled the purse where the prostitute could not reach it.

Cerise looked at the purse clutched in Blaxton's hand.

No … rats do not have purses.

She took a closer look at Lisa, studying her face. The girl still looked familiar. It was then that she knew who it was.

"You fools!" she screamed at the two men, horrified. "This is not a wharf rat … this is Fredric's sister—the port commander's daughter!"

Shocked, the men gasped, backing away from Lisa.

Free of Jaggor's choking grasp, Lisa covered her face with her hands and curled onto her side of the grimy cot they threw her on, facing away from the two thugs.

The prostitute fled from the room and raced around the corner to the common room of the tavern where Fredric sat calmly gulping his ale.

"Fredric, take your sister and leave now. You are going to get us all killed!" she shrieked.

Turning back to his drink, Fredric ignored her.

In the next instant, Alexander threw open the door to the tavern. For a moment, he stood, his eyes scanning the room, until he saw Fredric.

Most of the patrons knew what Alexander had done to Trebilock in this very spot, and they were certain what was going to happen next. Fear engulfed the room, and everyone scrambled away from Fredric, giving him a wide space.

"Where is your sister?" Alexander shouted across the room.

Slumped over his drink, Fredric seemed oblivious to what was happening. He gave no response.

Alexander immediately moved to Fredric's table. This time he bellowed louder as he grabbed Fredric's collar, yanking him up.

"Where is your sister?"

Fredric pointed to the back room of the tavern before returning to his slumped position.

Alexander was desperate to find Lisa. He would deal with Fredric later.

Heading to the hall, he turned into the first room he came to. His daughter was in a crumpled heap, terrified and naked, crying and quivering on the filthy cot.

Blaxton and Jaggor were still in the room, their attentions split between the naked girl and the coin purse. They, too, were oblivious to the initial presence of Alexander.

Yanking the still-dangling coin purse out of Blaxton's hand, Alexander threw the two out of the small room, crashing their bodies into the tavern wall as they dropped to the floor. Turning to Lisa, he quickly pulled off his cloak and wrapped her in it.

Pulling Lisa to him, he picked her up, and spun from the room. In a voice that made Blaxton and Jaggor, and all those in hearing distance quake, he roared, "I will tend to my daughter first, but I promise you, the two of you will be dealt with when I come back!"

With Lisa in his arms, Alexander rushed to the door. Leaving the tavern, he shouted over his shoulder, "FREDRIC! Get to the villa … now!"

Just as he had requested, Theo was waiting outside the tavern with a horse saddled and ready for travel. Alexander lifted Lisa onto the horse. He swung up behind her and gathered her into his arms once again.

Gently, he murmured in her ear, "I promise you, Lisa, this will never happen again. And I will deal with Fredric."

He turned to Theo and handed him the coin purse he had snatched from Blaxton. “Theo, take this coin and pay for the use of the horse. Take two coins for yourself and give the rest to Rose.” Urging the horse into a trot, Alexander took off for the villa.

Lisa wept most of the way back. At one point, she looked up at her papa and asked, “Papa, what is wrong with him? Why is he so awful and mean? Why does he hate me so?”

Alexander did not answer. Finally, he said, “I do not know. There’s a secret between his mother and him that I do not understand. He has been this way since birth. I have tried to teach him to be a man, but I have failed. He is coddled and protected by his mother. I promise you this, Lisa … his malicious behavior toward you stops as of today.”

When they arrived, Alexander carried her inside and gently lowered her to a standing position. Margaux had heard Alexander come in and went to greet him. When she saw Lisa standing there wrapped in her papa’s cloak, fear gripped her heart and she ran to Lisa’s side.

Alexander looked at Margaux. “Lisa was attacked by two drunkards at the Anchor Inn. Fredric initiated this by giving her to them—his own sister. Check her and tell me if severe harm has come to her. Be thorough. And then give her a gentle bath.”

Margaux nodded, understanding what he meant, and led Lisa to her bedchamber.

Alexander paced the entrance, waiting for Fredric.

Hours passed and everyone in the villa was now aware of the harm inflicted on Lisa. They all remained quiet and out of sight.

Many of them were stationed at windows facing the courtyard and they watched as Alexander paced.

Astrid summoned the courage to approach him. She, too, was aware of the fury burning inside him. He glared at her.

"Go back to your chamber, Astrid. You have caused this. Stay out of my way. I will handle Fredric, something I should have done years ago, and this time you will not interfere. No son of mine would ever harm a sister the way he did. Who have you been with to bring this bastard into my home? What monster have you created?"

Astrid shrank away, shaking for herself … and her son.

He knows. What am I to do?

Hours later, Fredric staggered into the courtyard with a drunken grin plastered on his ruddy face.

Unable to contain his rage any longer, Alexander grabbed him. "You sold your own sister for a cup of ale? And then you calmly sat and drank while your drunken friends attempted to rape her? What is wrong with you? Have you no decency? You are no better than the scum you associate with."

"I wanted her to have a good time. I told them not to hurt her," Fredric said as he wiped spittle from his chin.

"Did you tell them who she was?"

"No, why should I?" replied Fredric.

Alexander could not believe what he heard. *Why should he tell them this was his sister? Fredric is a disgusting idiot.*

"Do you know their names?"

"No," Fredric lied.

Alexander struggled to contain his anger; he was so furious he could barely speak.

"You drink with them daily, and yet you do not know their names? Well, I do. Lisa told me the names of her attackers.

"I will give you a word of warning. You should look for a new place to spend your idle hours. I sent Isaac to deal with those men and he was given orders to kill anyone who tried to stop him. By now, anyone remaining in the tavern knows you are the cause of all the trouble."

Fredric smirked and turned to enter the villa.

Alexander roared, "I am not done with you! Get back here!"

Fredric turned and staggered back to stand in front of Alexander.

In one swift movement, Alexander struck Fredric across the face. The slap was so powerful that Fredric stumbled and fell to the ground. Blood spurted from his mouth and nose.

At the same time, Alexander pulled a whip from beneath his tunic and began to flog Fredric about the back and shoulders, which caused him to roll across the ground.

"If you ever attempt anything again like you did today, your punishment will be swift and final. You will meet the same fate as Blaxton and Jaggor!" he yelled. Alexander discharged his anger with each lash.

"You put Lisa in terrible danger today! You are a weakling and a coward," he seethed. "And you are no longer my son. When Blaxton and Jaggor are found, they will be hanged, and you will dig their graves and bury them."

Alexander finally stopped beating his son, realizing he would kill Fredric if he continued. He bent down, grabbed Fredric by one arm, dragged him into an upright position, and then shoved him in the direction of the villa.

Fredric stumbled and fell once again.

As he did, Alexander yelled, "I am sending you back to Commander Ramos. Maybe he will succeed in making a man out of you this time. If not, you will be dead. And this time, your mother will not get reports that are written just for her .... She will hear the truth about all your failings."

Alexander turned and glared at Astrid watching from the window.

Disgusted with both of them, he stalked away.

From her.

And from Fredric as he layed on the ground, whimpering for his mother.

From the window overlooking the front yard, Astrid watched as Alexander beat Fredric. She wrung her hands and paced, wincing with each blow that her son took and snarled in rage, "If our roles were reversed, I would use the whip on Alexander!"

When the beating stopped and he looked at her, she turned away.

She was seething with hatred for Alexander. *I will show him.*

"Astrid!" Alexander shouted, his rage still evident. "Come out of the villa now!"

Jonathan and Gerhardt both retreated into their cottage. Margaux heard the shouting from the courtyard and stayed with Lisa to protect her.

Slowly, Astrid emerged from the villa entrance. There was no one else in the yard but Alexander, Astrid, and the terrified Fredric sobbing for his mother. Astrid had never witnessed Alexander in such a fit of anger or heard him yell the way he was doing.

Lifting his arm, Alexander pointed the whip at Astrid.

"This is your fault! You have brought disgrace and dishonor to my home. You have ruined *your* son, not mine."

Stunned, Astrid maintained her silence, yet her guilty look betrayed her. Feeling unsteady, her mind swirled.

How could he know?

He must be stopped ....

fifteen

A Time to Act

I promise you ... I will protect you from him and from Astrid.

Moving directly toward the door, Alexander's anger was heightened toward Astrid and her son.

As he moved past Astrid, he grabbed her elbow. "I have been lenient with Fredric and from now on that all changes. I must know where he is at all times. I do not trust him."

Seething with anger, she pulled away and fled to her bedchamber. He will pay for this ....

The cloud of rage that had entered the villa was inescapable. All Alexander could think was I want him out of my sight ... and gone. Both he and his mother are dangerous.

Alexander went directly to Lisa's bedside and reached for her hand. Despite the things she had heard listening in his solar, she was innocent, and he knew he had to protect Lisa at all costs.

Margaux was still sitting next to Lisa as she lay curled beneath her blankets. Looking up at Alexander as he entered the room, she whispered, "The best I can tell, she was not violated, but as you can see from the red marks around her throat and on her arms, she was choked and beaten. They were brutal with her."

Kneeling by her and gently touching her head, Alexander said to his daughter, "Lisa, I promise you … I will protect you from Fredric and from Astrid. He will never be able to hurt you again as long as I live."

Rising and shaking his head, Alexander turned to Margaux. "Stay by her bedside until she recovers fully. Let me know when she does. Do not let anyone into her bedchamber. Keep Astrid away from her. I do not trust her and I fear she will bring her harm. I have been concerned about Lisa's safety for some time now."

Margaux bowed her head in agreement. "I will sleep by her side until she regains her strength. I will have Jonathan bring food to us when we need it."

With his trust in Margaux, he knew he could count on her loyalty. Concern and love for his daughter showed on Alexander's face as he looked at her.

"Margaux, from this day forward, I would like Gerhardt to accompany Lisa whenever she travels outside this villa. I do not want her to ever be alone when she leaves these grounds."

She nodded and said, "Of course, Alexander. I will see to it that Gerhardt is her constant companion."

Alexander left Lisa's bedside and went quietly to his solar and closed the door. He slumped down in his chair and put his head in his hands. Tears dropped on the table.

To the empty room, he said aloud, "I have ignored the conflict in this family long enough. It is evident that I must protect the one person in this family who truly matters to me. That person is my daughter. It has become dangerous for her in this house."

Suddenly, he felt a warmth around him. The room's light changed.

He had experienced this sensation before.

And then he heard it ... a voice ... a woman's voice.

Alexander, there have been many warnings. You need to protect Lisa. Your life and her future depend upon it.

Sitting up, Alexander nodded his head. "I promise, with my life."

Margaux stayed by Lisa's side, offering her sips of water as she tossed and turned during the night. Moaning and crying out at times for her papa, she suddenly became very still as morning approached. The room felt warmer, and a soft light settled over Lisa's body, spreading to include Margaux.

I have forewarned your papa. You need his protection and he will give it. He has a plan. There is danger in your household. Always be alert.

Still at his table in the solar, Alexander opened his box and pulled out his writing paper and pen. Writing swiftly and forcefully, his communication was a letter to Commander Ramos, pleading with him to take Fredric back immediately for additional training. When he completed his letter, Alexander sent it by rider.

A week later, he received the commander's reply. The response was not what he wanted, but it was expected.

The man did not hold anything back. Plainly, Commander Ramos wrote,

Alexander, we will always be friends and allies. I will follow you into battle at any point, but do not ask me to do the impossible. Fredric does not possess the physical ability or mental skills to learn and use what you are asking me to instill in him.

I must respectfully decline your request.

–Ramos

Although disappointed, Alexander was not surprised by the commander's refusal to take Fredric. He realized that he would have to find another solution to protect Lisa.

The day after the letter from Ramos arrived, Alexander asked Margaux and her husband Jonathan to meet with him in the solar.

He clasped his hands together and addressed them.

"After what happened to Lisa at the tavern, I have given a lot of thought to finding a way to keep Fredric away from her. A plan I have come up with also involves Gerhardt. I will send Lisa and Gerhardt to train with Sir Roland. He is renowned for his abilities to train men for battle. He will teach both how to defend themselves."

Margaux and Jonathan exchanged concerned glances.

Finally, Jonathan spoke. "Gerhardt would welcome the change and the opportunity to learn new and useful skills. The two of them are friends and will support each other. And Gerhardt will learn things he never would have otherwise."

Alexander smiled. "Thank you both for protecting my daughter and for your loyalty to me."

Lisa was tucked away in her niche in the solar. Curled up. Safe. She had not been in there since Fredric and his friends attacked her.

Sensing footsteps, she knew that they belonged to her papa.

Barely breathing, she waited as he entered and shut the door. Pulling his chair away from the table, he turned it toward Lisa's place. Gently, he said, "Your *Lady* came to me the other night. She wants to make sure that I protect you. I promise you, I always will, Lisa."

From her place behind the tapestry, Lisa responded, barely above a whisper. "I know, the *Lady* came to me, too, after she spoke to you. She says you have a plan."

"I do. Will you come out so we can talk?"

Slowly at first, Lisa pulled the tapestry back. Unfolding her legs, she rose, watching her papa's eyes. They were concerned, yet kind. Her face, neck, and arms were still badly bruised.

Alexander's anger swelled as he watched her stand, yet he knew that he must comfort his wounded child. Reaching his hands toward hers, he whispered, "Come to me, my daughter. When you are ready, I will reveal my plan .... I want you to be strong enough to undertake it."

"Fredric will never hurt me again. I am ready, Papa."

sixteen

The Training Begins

Be aware of what is happening around you, whether it be day or night.

The following day, Alexander made arrangements with Sir Roland to send Lisa and Gerhardt to meet him and make plans for their training.

His camp was not far from the villa. The two had passed it many times on their trips to the market-place, but they never realized that the secluded large stone cottage perched on the hill overlooking the docks belonged to Sir Roland. They knew nothing about what occurred behind its walls or what they would be doing there.

As they approached the cottage from a winding stone walkway that was sheltered with large trees and overgrown shrubbery, they saw that the land surrounding the cottage was sectioned off into individual training areas. There was a large structure on the west side that appeared to be bigger than the cottage itself.

Lisa whispered to Gerhardt, "Do you see how big the stables are? Sir Roland must have many horses in there."

"I hope so!"

They walked up the steps to the door of the cottage and knocked. A tall, broad-shouldered man with several scars on his face and piercing dark eyes opened the door. His short, dark brown tunic was leather, belted with a dagger in its sheath at his waist. His hands were huge and heavily calloused. Lisa notice that fresh blood was oozing from what appeared to be a wound on his forearm and dripping on his boot.

Lisa and Gerhardt exchanged glances, both thinking *what have we gotten into?*

Sir Roland sized them up, noting the bruising on Lisa's face, neck, and arms. His gruff voice then bellowed out, "You must be Lisa and Gerhardt." *Alexander was right to send her to me.*

Lisa gulped when she heard his loud voice. "We are. Are you Sir Roland?"

"I am." He left the two standing as he walked around them. Both felt his eyes on their backs. Gerhardt's knees began to quiver. Lisa touched his hand as an assurance.

He spoke again. "Get to the training area. You two have much work to be done."

Lisa pulled Gerhardt forward as they followed Roland to the back of the cottage.

"Your training begins starting now. You will do exactly as I say. I will teach you how to fight with your hands and your body as well as with weapons.

"The first thing you must learn is personal discipline ... listening is essential. Listening is not just what you hear. It is what you see with your eyes. It is what you sense in your belly. I will teach you how to recognize danger and how to respond in a variety of ways.

"From this day forward, you will run everywhere you go, not walk … RUN. You must build your endurance. Your legs might be the one weapon that will save you when danger strikes. Your work today is to run back to your home. If you are instructed to go anywhere by Alexander or Margaux, you will run. Only within your home or at the docks will you walk. Everywhere else, you both run for long distances and sprint for short distances. You will return tomorrow and every day forward at sunrise until I instruct Alexander that your training is complete.

"Do you understand and agree to my terms?"

Excited with their new venture, Lisa and Gerhardt did as they were told. They ran all the way home and collapsed when they arrived. It was a long run.

"Gerhardt, let us go find Margaux and ask her to wake us both when she comes to the villa in the morning."

Finding her in the kitchen, Margaux was preparing bread for the evening meal.

Lisa spoke up first. "Sir Roland wants us to be at his camp at sunrise every morning. Will you wake us before first light so we can get there on time? He told us we must run everywhere to build our endurance, and we must always run both ways."

"Running? You will be hungry all the time."

Everyone laughed when Margaux said that.

Then Lisa became quiet. Finally, she said, "Margaux, I cannot dress like a girl in a full-length tunic and run. I want to dress like Gerhardt and wear clothes like his when we train. I cannot do all what Sir Roland wants me to do dressed as I am. I think breeches and a shorter tunic would be more practical for me."

"What if I give you some of Gerhardt's clothes to wear to start with?" Margaux asked.

Lisa looked at Gerhardt. "That's a great idea! Gerhardt, what do you think … is that all right with you?"

"It makes sense to me. Mother, I will get her some of my clothes now."

The next day began just as they had planned.

Gerhardt was already in the kitchen. Margaux went to Lisa's bedchamber to waken her.

Not surprisingly, she was up and dressed in Gerhardt's old clothes—her new ones that consisted of breeches and a tunic that stopped just above her knees. She liked being free of the ankle-length tunic she was accustomed to wearing. With the pants and shorter tunic, she could see how defending herself would be easier

Tucking her long hair under a tight-fitting cap, she was ready for the day's run and training. *I am going to sew my secret holes in the sides of all my tunics and the breeches. I want to make sure that I can always have some coin with me when I am away from the villa.*

Leading Lisa back to the kitchen, Margaux helped pack the foods they wanted to take with them for the day. Gerhardt slung their packs over his shoulders.

Margaux's parting words as they left: "Never forget: Always be on alert."

Lisa looked at Gerhardt as if to say, *Are you ready?* They both nodded to each other and took off running with the lingering moon behind their backs as the promising sunrise beckoned them forward with its rays of bright light. They did not attempt to talk. Each was focused on the pace and the destination … and how fast they could get to Sir Roland's.

They arrived at the cottage and circled around to the back. The sky had become afire with clouds of red and yellow, and the sun was just ready to announce itself when Roland stepped out of the stables.

"You two look happy this morning. What is the cause of your merriment?"

"Sir Roland, we did just as you instructed us. We arrived at sunrise," Lisa said, beaming with satisfaction.

Not to be outdone, Gerhardt chimed in with, "And we ran the entire way!"

"Now tell me how you figured out what time to be here this morning."

"We were not exactly sure when sunrise would occur, so we left the villa before the moon dropped below the docks. We ran down the cart path in the direction of the marketplace since we have done that many times. The moon was still in the sky and we had plenty of light to see where we were running. We arrived here before the sun fully rose." Lisa sat back, took in a deep breath, and waited to hear what Roland had to say about her summation.

He took a moment. Looking from one to the other, he said, "I am pleased with your reasoning. You arrived on time—well done.

"One reason I wanted you here at sunrise was to teach you this … when you go into battle, always keep the sun at your back and stay positioned on high ground. You want your enemies to be blinded by the sun and you want them to have to climb up to reach you. The other reason for traveling here at this hour was to have you observe your surroundings in a different light. Be aware of what is happening around you, whether it be day or night.

"I am also pleased with your honesty. While some might see honesty as a weakness, it always serves you well. When faced with a difficult situation, it is more honorable to speak the truth than to lie. There are ways to communicate the truth so that it is suitable for all who hear it."

He continued, "The reason for having you run to and from each destination is to build your strength up. If you ever need to escape, your legs can take you far. It is unlikely that you will encounter others who are skilled at endurance running. Running is your first weapon. And it will train your mind to stay focused on the task before you. You have done well. Continue running as you travel everywhere."

"Today, you will focus on personal protection using hands, arms, legs, and feet to stop any attacker."

Roland demonstrated how to use the heel of the hand to drive a blow to the bridge of the nose; how to use fingers to stab the eyes; and how to jab a blow to the throat. After showing them, he had each of them stand before him and he went through the drills.

Both Lisa and Gerhardt took turns pretending to be the attacker. Groans, grunts, and ouches vibrated within the yard. They learned quickly. And although Lisa's bruises from her attackers had faded, new ones surfaced with the physical work Gerhardt and she were doing. They viewed them with earned pride.

For the next several months, the training progressed from physical contact to the use of knives, swords, bows, and arrows. Their days were filled training with Roland and continued as they practiced all he taught them when they returned home.

One day as they entered Sir Roland's courtyard, he was waiting. He had a stern look on his face as Lisa and Gerhardt approached. Of course, he always had a stern look.

As they got closer, his grimace turned to a broad smile. Pointing to the stables, he said, "Bridle the horse you each want to train on and bring it here."

Before he finished speaking, they turned and ran to the stables. This was the day they were waiting for. Gerhardt was first to return and Sir Roland nodded his approval.

There was commotion in the stables. Concerned, Sir Roland started walking to the stables when Lisa led a snorting, agitated stallion into the courtyard. Stopping in an attempt to settle him down, she began to speak directly and quietly to the horse.

Sir Roland watched with concern, then amusement. *She knows animals.*

Immediately, the stallion settled down. Reaching up and gently stroking his face, Lisa leaned in and hugged his neck. Then, she proudly turned and brought the stallion to Sir Roland.

With a glint in his eye, he said, "The one you chose has thrown the best men to the ground. Are you sure you want him?"

"He chose me, Sir Roland. He started to snort and kick until I went to him. I told him that if he wants out of his stall, he has to obey my commands."

"We will see how long you can stay on him. If you can ride him, he is yours; he has been nothing but trouble."

"What is his name?"

"I call him Trouble because that's what he is. What are you going to call him?"

Thinking for a moment, she replied, "I will call him Valiant because he is strong and if I had to, I would ride him into battle."

Lisa stretched on her toes and took a handful of his mane, pulling herself up. Once on his back, she leaned toward his ears that were turned in her direction and whispered to him. Valiant began walking slowly around the courtyard.

Sir Roland shook his head in disbelief, thrilled with what he saw unfolding, while Gerhardt just cheered her on. *This Lisa is special. Alexander is right in protecting and training her.*

Months went by and their riding skills improved daily. They were responsible for feeding and grooming the horses, and cleaning all the stalls. Sir Roland let them ride to the villa and beyond, but they were still expected to return the horses and run home.

On their last day, Sir Roland said, "You have learned well, and you have been excellent students. I am proud of you and all that you have accomplished. Alexander will be pleased."

Lisa was touched by his words. "At first, we did not think we could master all that you taught us. It was a lot … and it was hard. You encouraged us to achieve everything that we did. Thank you, Sir Roland."

"Lisa is right, Sir Roland. You gave us the strength and confidence to stand up for ourselves."

"Your papa has compensated me for your training and for your horse. Valiant is now yours. You and Gerhardt are always welcome here. Lisa, give this written message to Alexander when you return to the villa. It tells him that your training is complete."

With that, Lisa and Gerhardt both mounted Valiant, turned, and left Sir Roland's facility. The two friends rode down the hill, all the way to the villa.

seventeen

New Clothes

Always be on alert.

Lisa dressed differently now.

During the training sessions, she wore breeches and the shorter tunics that she and Margaux had fashioned after Gerhardt's clothing, along with Lisa's secret holes that she was now adding to Alexander's clothing, and to Jonathan and Gerhardt's as well. Margaux knew that it made no sense to be learning and practicing fighting moves in a long tunic like she usually wore around the villa. And Lisa clearly liked these clothes better.

After several months of running to and from training, everyone they passed on the road knew who Lisa was—Alexander's daughter. And they knew she and Gerhardt trained daily with Sir Roland. But for what, they had no idea.

At first, when the two set out each morning, some of the village women would come to their doors and shout at them, "What are you boys running from … what have you stolen?" A few recognized that one was not a boy—it was Alexander's daughter, Lisa.

Then, the rumors started ….

Does she think she is a boy?

What is wrong with her?

What will Alexander say when he finds out?

Why does Alexander not stop her?

It is not proper for a girl to dress and act like a boy!

Many found it odd—some even declared it sinful—that a young girl wore boys' clothing and took part in military training. They all knew what was going on at the cottage and why many young men were sent there … but a girl? What was Alexander thinking?

The younger girls who saw Lisa in her training clothes knew why. It was to protect herself from her brother, along with the thugs he was constantly around.

The younger girls knew Fredric was bad, very bad and someone to avoid.

They also thought her clothing was a more freeing way to dress. Feeding pigs, chickens, and milking cows in long tunics got them filthy. The village girls wanted to dress the way Lisa was now doing, too. Mothers complained to each other that their daughters wanted to wear the same clothes as their sons. What would others think?

Lisa was aware of what was being said … and she did not care. She was glad that the younger girls had taken notice. She knew that she needed this training and she needed to learn all that she could quickly, in case she was attacked again by Fredric and his friends.

Her life depended on it.

But there was something else that lingered in her mind. She was not sure what the nudging was. She only knew she needed to know how to defend herself.

The sooner, the better.

eighteen

The Warning

What kind of dreams are you having that tell you to be on alert?

Almost a year had passed since the tavern assault.

One day Alexander summoned Lisa into the solar. "Sit down, my daughter. Let us talk. You are happy of late. I can see it in your eyes."

Lisa smiled. "Papa, I have much to be grateful about. Gerhardt is my constant companion and we enjoy practicing what Sir Roland taught us. I rarely see Fredric anymore and Astrid keeps to herself. I am on my own ... and I learn about people and what you do all the time."

Then her smile faded. "Not knowing where Fredric is or where he might suddenly appear concerns me, but I do not feel threatened by him anymore. I can take care of myself. Sir Roland advised me to always be alert. Now that my legs are strong from all the running, Fredric would never catch me. With all the strength in my arms, he could not drag me the way he did before the attack by the others. I am grateful for the hard work that Sir Roland put me through."

"Lisa, you are right. I believe there is something wrong with Fredric. Be careful. Your *Lady* has advised me to that we all need to be on alert. My agreement with the duke was to protect the port with whatever force is necessary. With that charge, dealing with your brother and the thugs he drinks with fall under that authority.

"When Isaac found Blaxton and Jaggor, he summoned Fredric to be part of the punishment I decided was appropriate. Blaxton and Jaggor had to watch Fredric dig a large hole—one that would be their grave. Isaac was repulsed at how Fredric seemed to enjoy putting the rope around their necks and watching both kick as they slowly died."

Alexander looked down and nodded. "Your mother knows he is usually at a tavern and whoring with women. She knows where he goes. Rarely does she mention what he does. I have an uneasy feeling about both. I have dreams that tell me to stay on alert. And then there is the voice of the *Lady*."

Pausing, Alexander reached for his belt where he kept his many keys. Removing two, he said, "I want you to have this key to the solar. When you are here, always keep the door locked."

With a smile and a glance at the wooden chest, he added, "This other key unlocks everything here, including my chest. Keep these in your niche behind that tapestry. They will be safe there."

Turning to the wooden chest, he took his key and opened it. He then extracted a leather coin purse and handed it to Lisa.

With eyes widened, Lisa watched him. *Why is he doing this?*

"I want you to add this to the coin you have already hidden away. Also enclosed in the purse is a map, along with directions, to my friend Ezra's home in Paris. You remember Ezra from our meetings here?"

Reaching for the coin and sensing the seriousness of her papa's words and tone, she nodded her head. "Yes, Papa."

"Ezra knows about you and the training you have learned from Sir Roland as well. He is a loyal and trusted friend and we have made an agreement. It is part of my plan to protect you. He knows that if someday you arrive at his door, you are in grave danger. Your presence means something has happened to me and he will take you in and see to your protection."

"Papa, why are you telling me about Ezra again? Why are you giving me more coin? And the map? Are you in danger? Am I in more danger than what happened at the tavern? What has changed? And what kind of dreams are you having that tell you to be on alert? Are they from my *Lady*?"

"You are different, Lisa, from others—from women and from men. I am aware that people have talked about your altered dress. It amuses me. Being different threatens others; sometimes it can make them afraid. I think what you are doing is courageous and wise. Most do not value women. I do, especially smart ones. You are smart and so are Rose and Margaux. Along with Ezra, it is you four I trust the most. Three women and one man."

Leaning forward, Alexander lowered his voice and took her hand in his. "My dear daughter, I just have a feeling that something bad is going to happen. I cannot explain it, but I have a feeling that we must be prepared for the unexpected. Last night, I heard the *Lady's* voice and it warned me to be careful when I was here.

"Add this purse to the coin I gave you before and be ready to leave with little notice. Above all, be mindful of Fredric. He is a cunning, dangerous coward and has been quiet for far too long. Astrid will do anything to protect him ... not you."

Lisa jolted when she heard him say he had heard the *Lady's* voice.

I know this is the same voice I have been hearing in my dreams. The Lady is talking to both of us. She is watching over us.

Alexander continued, "It has been many months since you have attended any of my meetings because you have been busy with your training. Let us start again today. I think you will want to hear what Karl has to say when he arrives later today. He owes me for financing his ships and does not want to pay. I want you to tell me what you hear and feel."

Lisa smiled with anticipation and left to hide the coins, now wondering about their shared voice ....

nineteen

The Betrayal

It turns out I misjudged his trustworthiness.

Anxious to settle into her secret space in the solar, Lisa arrived there before her papa. She was not there long before she heard a familiar voice whispering. It was Astrid's. Peering through the hole she had made in the hanging tapestry, she saw a man produce a small vial from beneath his tunic and hand it to Astrid.

Suddenly, Alexander entered the solar. "There you are, Karl," he said as he greeted the man.

Flustered, Astrid dropped her hand with the vial to her side. She excused herself and quickly left, keeping her hand tucked between the folds of her tunic.

"Sit down, Karl. I asked you here to settle your debt over the money you owe me," Alexander said. Maintaining his silence, he then added, "You are robbing me."

Karl squirmed in his chair. Sweat started to bead on his brow. He said nothing in response.

Lisa breathed quietly, not wanting to move. Today, her papa's conversation grew loud and animated as he rose and glared down at Karl, reminding the man of his original promise of support and Karl's agreement to share in the profits with Alexander. She watched Karl as he squirmed, then noticed him clenching his fists as he sat with Alexander towering over him … almost as if Papa's words had exposed his dishonesty.

"Karl, I know that you have brought in several shiploads and unloaded barrels of spices, selling all your merchandise. You needed my coin and my contacts to establish the shipping route to the Far East, and I gave them to you. Now, you have failed to give me my share of the profits we had agreed upon as a condition of my coin to you."

Karl offered no excuses, insisting that his expenses exceeded what he had been paid for his cargo. Once his expenses were paid, there was no money to give Alexander.

Alexander glared at him as silent tension filled the room and then stated firmly, "I know that not to be true. You are lying." Alexander then added, "You have two days to pay your debt or forfeit all your ships to me as per our agreement. Now leave."

With that, Karl rose and stomped through the doorway. Alexander followed behind him to see that he left the villa. He glimpsed Astrid's tunic at the edge of the room, but when he turned around, she was gone.

When he returned, he closed the door. Lisa was standing by his table. "Will he pay you?"

She was aware that he financed other merchants to help them establish their own trade ventures. She knew that was how he met Karl.

"He has two days to honor his commitment. If he does not, I will own a fleet of ships."

A day had passed after the meeting. Lisa found Papa at work in the solar, reviewing various merchant contracts. She settled into a chair at his table.

Looking up from his work, Alexander asked, "Lisa, what brings you here today? I am not expecting any guests."

Smiling at his remark, she said, "I know that. I have some questions about the meeting with Karl yesterday. Can I ask them?"

Amused, he smiled back at her as he leaned toward the back of the chair. That was all the permission she needed.

"You do not show any emotions when you meet with people, but you looked and sounded angry with Karl. Why?"

"I thought Karl was a smart man and worthy of becoming a business partner. He was successfully trading with the Far East, and I loaned him enough coin to expand his fleet of ships. He has not attempted to repay any of the debt he owes me, although he has made several voyages.

"In fact, he has not spoken with me since I gave him the coin. Yet, I know he is highly successful with this new trade routes. Now, I just want him to pay his debt. I do not trust him and I do not want to work with him in the future," Alexander said, his tone filled with disappointment.

"What if he does not pay?"

"I can make his life miserable and force him out of business here by closing the port to unloading or picking up anything from Marseilles. I can also contact other port authorities and block him along the coastlines."

Satisfied that he would eventually succeed in collecting the coin owed him, Lisa then added, "Papa, you know that I was in here before your meeting with Karl. I thought it was strange that Astrid escorted him into the solar, not Margaux. That's not like her.

"Both stood in front of my tapestry whispering to each other. Then Karl handed her a vial of some sort, which she hurried to tuck into the sides of her tunic when you came in. She left the room when you entered. Did you notice her hiding her hand? That is what it looked like to me. It all seemed unusual. Do you have any idea what could have been in the vial and why she hid it?"

"I have no idea what he gave to your mother. I will ask her about it later."

At the evening meal, Alexander was quiet and distant. He looked as though he was mulling things over in his mind.

Both Lisa and Astrid had joined him. Looking at his wife, he asked, "Astrid, did Karl bring you a gift when he was last here? I thought I saw you with something in your hand as I entered the solar."

Astrid pretended to be shocked. "Whatever do you mean? Why would he bring me a gift? He is your business associate."

Now looking at his daughter, he noted her eyes widening as she heard Astrid's lie.

Alexander continued, "You have been reclusive since Fredric and his friends attacked Lisa. Yet, the morning Karl arrived, you were quick to greet him and bring him into my solar. That's something that Margaux does."

Astrid became indignant and stopped eating. "Alexander, I do not like what you are saying." She then leaped from her chair and quickly moved away from the table.

Alexander remembered the voice in his dreams. He knew Astrid was hiding and withholding information.

As he looked at his daughter, he wondered: *What is that woman plotting?*

Later that night Alexander went to the solar to think. At that hour, wine was normally brought to him by Margaux, but to his surprise, Astrid entered, carrying two goblets.

She never joins me at night. Maybe she is trying to make amends for her earlier behavior.

"I see you brought my wine," he said in a pleasant voice. "Thank you."

Astrid handed him a goblet. "I am here to talk about Fredric. I want you to pay as much attention to him as you do to Lisa."

There was nothing pleasant in the way Astrid spoke. The tenor of her voice was sharp, not friendly.

Alexander was put off by the direction the conversation was taking. Fredric was the last thing he wanted to talk about, but he indulged her by saying, "Lisa is interested in my work and she is learning a great deal by talking with me about things that happen in the world of trade. Fredric, on the other hand, is nowhere to be found and shows no interest in anything but taverns and brothels."

Alexander noticed an unusual hesitancy in Astrid.

Why is she restraining herself? Rage usually shows on her face and surges through her body when I speak of Fredric.

Drinking from the goblet, he tasted an unusual flavor and picked up a strange odor. At the same time, he was distracted by her attempt at hiding her rage toward him rather than the taste of the wine.

"He has grown up. You just do not want to see it … to see him and what he can do," she insisted.

"Maybe I should put him to work in the fields or have him load and unload ships like other young men his age."

Astrid's eyes narrowed. "He is your son, not a common laborer."

"His behavior is more of a drunken peasant. He has shown no strength or learning after I placed him in the training camp under the direction of Commander Ramos. He failed at everything he was asked to do. The letters you received from the Commander were untrue. I asked him to send them to you, withholding all the problems and failures Fredric created daily.

"No, Astrid, I do not think Fredric is my son …. In fact, I know he is not."

Glaring at her, he took a gulp of wine, wishing the conversation were over and she would leave.

Astrid hesitated. *How long has he known?*

She knew very well that she was irritating him, but she continued as she noticed the sweat on his face increasing.

It will not be long now.

In fact, she wanted to annoy him. "You acted the same way when you were his age."

"Yes, I did some of the things he has done, but I knew when to stop and go to work. Fredric must make his own decision to change. He has demonstrated no responsibility for others and no trustworthiness. Remove yourself from my room now."

Suddenly, Alexander dropped his goblet on the table and watched it roll off. He sat still, looking at Astrid with a knowing stare as he realized what his wife had done.

"You poisoned the wine …."

Slurring his words, his speech became more difficult to understand. “I expected this from … a bishop or a pirate … never you. You … poisoned … me. *Why?*”

Astrid smiled, thin and cruel.

Then her mannerisms and voice became menacing.

Alexander tried to stand, but could not. He was paralyzed, but for the moment, still alert. Based on how his body was reacting, he knew his life was ending.

Astrid moved and circled Alexander, then stopped by his side. Lowering her head to his ear, she hissed as she pinched his nose, pulled his head back, and began pouring the rest of his goblet down his throat while he heaved and choked. “Finish your wine, husband.”

Dropping the goblet on the table, she spat out, “This is for the beating you gave Fredric and for ignoring him. Your favored child, your precious Lisa, will now be punished severely for the beating her brother received. And I will see to it that she is destroyed. I never loved you, nor her ... she is part of you, a man I despise.” And then she laughed out loud, evilly. “Fredric is my son ... never yours ... and he will get everything you have worked your life for, starting tomorrow.”

As his life slipped away, all he could think about was Lisa. *Will she get to Ezra in time?*

Alexander slumped to the side of the chair, dead.

Satisfied, Astrid maliciously smiled at him, picked up both goblets, and walked out of the solar.

Fredric, my son ... my work is done.

twenty

The Discovery

There is grave danger for you in this house now.

A loud scream ricocheted throughout the stone walls of the villa the next morning.

Coming from the solar, Astrid had pretended to find Alexander's body. Her loud wails brought servants running to the solar to discover Alexander slumped in his chair and Astrid hugging his body.

Lisa heard her mother screaming and raced to the source. The scream she heard was not one of fright but rather laced with icy triumph.

When she arrived, she saw Astrid over her papa's lifeless body. She also noticed there was no emotion in her mother's eyes. They were darker than she could ever remember, as if evil was looking at her.

Rushing to his chair, she pushed her mother aside. Lisa encircled her father's upper body, taking him in her arms and sobbed with uncontrolled grief. In his ear, she whispered, *I will avenge her evil, Papa. I promise.*

As she held him, she noticed the absence of his large ring of keys. *They are missing.*

Turning to Astrid, she realized that her mother looked indifferent, defiant, and victorious. There was nothing grief-stricken about her. And hanging from the belt of Astrid's tunic was Alexander's ring of many keys.

I know that she murdered him ....

Rising, Lisa yelled at her, "You killed him! I know it!"

Turning her back on Lisa, Astrid left the solar in a huff, pushing Margaux aside and glaring at her with a look of satisfaction.

Lisa heard her papa's keys clanging as Astrid went through the door.

She does not know that I have the same set of keys. She will never see what is in the chest!

The servants were speechless. In front of them was the dead body of a master who had been kind and caring to them. They also heard what had transpired between mother and daughter, and the shouted accusation.

Turning her head back from the door, Margaux went to kneel next to Lisa, who had dropped to the floor, laying her head in her papa's lap. She wrapped her arms around her as Lisa held her papa. There was nothing she could say in that moment, nothing that would be able to comfort Lisa.

Margaux looked up to see who was still in the room. Leaning in close to Lisa, she said in a whisper, "There is grave danger for you in this house now. Come with me to my cottage right now."

Hearing her, and understanding that danger surrounded her, Lisa released Alexander's body, kissing his hand as she stood and left with her.

When the two were settled safely in Margaux's cottage, she took Lisa's hands and looked sadly into her eyes.

"Lisa, it is my fear that your own life could come to great harm. Several of us have seen and heard much in the last few days. I believe that Alexander was murdered, just as I heard you say to your mother. Quickly, gather your clothing and find the coin that I know you have. Your papa would often confide in me. When you started your training with Sir Roland, he told me his plans for your safety.

"You must now carry out the plans he put in place for you. Prepare your essentials for traveling to Paris and bring everything back here at once. If you do not, you will not be able to escape the danger that surely is churning around you in the villa—all of it from your mother and brother."

With eyes streaming with tears of sorrow and her heart breaking, all Lisa could do was nod in understanding. Gathering everything she could get her hands on, including all the coin, she took everything to Margaux's.

Lisa spent a sleepless night crying, tossing, turning, and vowing to exact revenge.

The light started to glow above Lisa.

Your Papa has prepared you for this journey you are about to take and I will be with you.

Lisa was fully awake. The *Lady* ... her *Lady* ... had come to her. "Do you promise you will be with me?" she said in a whisper to the light.

Yes, I promise. It will start in the morning. You must prepare quickly and do everything Margaux asks. The plan your papa made for your journey will begin immediately after his funeral. You are ready, Lisa.

"Am I? I am afraid of what Astrid could do to me."

Your mother will not stop you. You will discover many strengths and insights as you travel. You will change the lives of others. You are ready.

Smiling, Lisa put her head down and drifted back to sleep.

Now reassured, she was certain. *I will change the lives of others.*

twenty-one

The Revelation

The woman is beyond evil. I hate her.

Early the next morning, Lisa received a summons to the solar from Astrid. Her eyes were red and puffy, both from crying and little sleep, when she entered the room. Just past the door, she stopped abruptly.

Based on the timing and the way her papa died, she was certain her mother had killed him. And it had something to do with Astrid's odd behavior in the solar two days ago.

"You are sitting in Papa's chair," she said in disbelief as she looked at her mother.

Fredric sat beside her in a guest chair with his filthy feet up on the table. Astrid stood and motioned Fredric to take her place.

Rising to his feet, he slowly moved to Alexander's chair. Holding his shoulders high and his back straight and chest puffed out, he stood in front of the chair. Slowly, he turned and with head held high and chin pointing out, he slowly sat down with a mock appearance of authority. Then, he put his feet on the table, an insult directed to and felt by Lisa.

Astrid displayed her triumphant glare at her. "Yes, and now it is Fredric's chair," she snapped back.

Lisa's face turned red with fists clenched as she glared at Astrid, then raised one hand and pointed a finger at them. Her voice vibrated within the walls of the room.

"One day." Turning to leave, she stopped in mid-stride with Astrid's next declaration.

"You are not leaving. I have arranged for your marriage to Lord Neliphis. He has expressed his interest in you, although I cannot understand why."

Lisa turned around, walked slowly toward Astrid, and halted directly in front of her. She bent forward with clasped hands and said resolutely, "I will never marry that old man. I accept no part of your arrangement. I will choose my own partner when I am ready."

Astrid shrieked into Lisa's face with the look of a she-devil, her foul breath offensive. "You will marry Lord Neliphis or I will sell you to the next slave ship that enters the harbor!"

"You will not …." Fury in her eyes, Lisa glared at Astrid and uttered the words, "It was you," as she pointed her finger once again. "You killed my father. I saw you plotting with Karl before Papa demanded that he pay money he was owed."

Astrid 's look shifted from anger to fright.

Turning to Fredric, Lisa knew there was nothing keeping him from trying to hurt her. Her feeling was confirmed by his sly smile.

Turning back to her mother, she continued, "Your time will come, I promise you. I will get my revenge for what you have done to my father." Without another word, Lisa abruptly turned and walked out.

Astrid twisted her mouth into a scowl as she looked at Fredric in disbelief.

He smirked at her as he snapped the quill end off Alexander's pen and picked his teeth with it. "What did you expect? I told you that's how she would react."

Lisa's thoughts were frantic and jumbled as she walked down the long hallway from the solar. *I must get out of here right away. I need to talk to Rose.*

As she approached the door of the villa, she made her decision as she passed the kitchen. Darting into the room, she threw the door open and started running toward the docks.

As she ran, the same thoughts kept coursing through her brain.

What has happened? Astrid's attitude has changed overnight to joy. Why is she suddenly announcing my marriage to Lord Neliphis, a marriage Papa would never want or approve of? Why is she doing all this when Papa is not yet buried? I hate this woman; she is beyond evil.

When Lisa arrived at Rose's shop, she saw her handing a small vial to a woman at the door of her shop. Just then, she knew.

That was the same type of vial Karl gave to my mother.

When the woman left, Lisa approached Rose and asked, "Can we talk in private?"

"Of course, dear, let us go inside. I am so saddened to hear about Alexander's death. I was told early this morning."

The two had reached the back of the apothecary shop behind the shelves of bottles, where, thankfully, no children were present.

Turning to Lisa, Rose added, "It looks like there is something else …."

Through her tears, Lisa began to unfold the story of Karl supplying the vial that looked like the one in Rose's shop to her mother in the solar, of her papa's sudden death, of Astrid's abrupt shift to joyfulness, and finally, of her mother's threat to banish her on a slave ship if she did not marry Lord Neliphis.

As Lisa spoke, she saw how Rose paled and began to tremble.

"I have to sit down," Rose said shakily. Lisa found a stool and placed it so Rose could steady herself.

"What is wrong?" Lisa asked.

"That was poison in the vial your mother received from Karl. I sold it to him," the old woman gasped in utter remorse. "She poisoned your papa. When used in small quantities, it is effective to treat many illnesses. My God, what have I done? I killed the most kind, gentle, and caring man I have ever known," Rose choked as she began to sob.

Now Lisa knew what she suspected was true.

Astrid ... she did *kill my papa.*

"Oh, Rose, you did nothing wrong. If Karl had not found the poison here, he would have found it somewhere else. Astrid would have demanded it. Do not torture yourself with these thoughts," Lisa said, attempting to ease Rose's obvious pain and guilt.

Lisa reached out with both hands to capture Rose's cheeks. She bent down, kissed Rose on the forehead, and spoke with a gentle tone.

"I still love you. I will always love you. You have done nothing but care for others your whole life. My papa saw the best in you and you saw the best in him. Rose, this will be one of our last times together. Margaux has advised me to prepare to leave the villa as soon as Papa is buried. She is worried that if I do not leave at once, Astrid will try to fulfill her threats and bring great harm against me.

"Now is the time to begin the plan Papa told me to follow if anything should happen to him. He said you are part of it. What do I do?"

Rose wiped her tears and nodded her head in understanding. She and Alexander had discussed his plan to protect Lisa on many occasions.

Lisa appeared to gain strength as she spoke, understanding what needed to be done. In front of Rose's eyes, Lisa became a warrior, taking command.

"Gerhardt will inform you when Papa is to be buried. On that same day, I will leave the villa for the last time as his casket is being placed in the ground. Will you arrange for me to travel to Paris with a caravan on that day?"

"I will take care of it. You need to get back to Margaux right away, before you are missed and Astrid sends Fredric after you."

Both women sensed that events were unfolding at a rapid pace and their lives would change forever. Alexander had prepared them both for this day, but they were saddened tremendously that the day had occurred before any had anticipated.

Holding one another tightly, and with no attempt at restraining their tears, they whispered simultaneously, "I love you."

Stepping back, Rose reached up to Lisa's face, wiping her tears away, saying at the same time, "Truly, you are special. You are both the son and daughter your father desired. I know that we will meet again, long after you leave Marseilles."

twenty-two

The Final Goodbye

Lisa looked at both rings and revenge flooded her mind. I hate her.

When Lisa returned to the villa late that afternoon, she knew there were more things she had to do before she left for Paris. The first of which was saying her final private good-bye to Papa.

Alexander's body had been placed in the great room, cold and gray. He had been prepared for the final rituals that would take place before his burial. Jonathan had seen to it that he was outfitted in his finest battle garb, with his favorite sword at his side.

She approached the bier where he lay and placed one hand on his folded hands and another on his shoulder. Suddenly all the hate and fear she had felt since his death disappeared. A calm overwhelmed her; the presence of the man at her fingertips removed all her anger.

Lisa stood motionless and looked down upon his face.

Memories flowed through her mind of the man that was her father, protector, teacher, and confidant.

The conversations, walks, and the looks he bestowed on her as she hid behind the tapestry in her secret niche returned. Tears filled her eyes with the joy of those moments that she would cherish forever. A smile came to her as she bent over and gave him her last kiss on the cheek. "I will make you proud, Papa."

As she lifted her hand from the top of his, she saw the gold signet ring on his right hand.

The ring was a wide gold band that displayed the family crest in the center. It represented power and responsibility, a ring worn by one who had achieved great things. Alexander used it to impress his crest into wax, sealing all his business contracts and his written communications.

On his left hand, he wore another gold ring. It, too, was a wide gold band that held a finely faceted ruby in the center. He loved the ring and always wore it. He once told Lisa that the ring had been made for him when he was visiting Ezra in Paris.

Lisa looked at both rings. "Papa would want me to have these."

As heir apparent, Fredric was entitled to the signet ring, something that would give him power and authority because it held the family crest.

But was he the heir?

Alexander had said that no son of his would treat his sister the way Fredric had treated her. And, in Lisa's opinion, the ring had to be earned before it could be worn.

A thought came unbidden into her mind, and she vowed Fredric would never see the signet ring again, let alone wear it. She had the same thought about the ruby ring.

These are my rings. I know I am the true heir.

Lisa eased both rings from her papa's fingers, tucked them inside the hidden compartments she made in her breeches, and gently returned his hands to his sides. Determined and bold, she knew there were two more tasks for her to tend to before departing, with the solar her final destination.

Lisa procured two large pieces of cloth and lengths of rope, then went to the solar. She smiled as she unlocked the door, *Astrid thinks she is the only one with keys.* Entering, she lit more candles and immediately went to her papa's table to find parchment, ink, and a quill pen. Finally, she sat in his chair to write a letter to Astrid.

Astrid—

I saw you accept the vial of poison from Karl and now know you used it to poison my Papa. You are evil ... and are now cursed.

I know where his wealth lies.

And I know that Fredric is not his son.

You will get what you so rightly deserve.

I will see to it. I promise you.

—Lisa

Finished with the letter, she walked to the tapestry that had shielded her for so many years. Folding the letter, she placed it in her niche behind the tapestry. She knew Astrid would find it one day.

Next, Lisa turned her attention to the wooden boxes that held Papa's manuscripts, contracts, gold, silver, gems, and coins. Opening the boxes, she removed the poems she had written for him, a few contracts, and everything of value she could find.

All the while she smiled, saying softly to herself, "Astrid will rue this day." As she said this, she left one silver coin in the box.

Opening the shutters, twice she carefully lowered her heavy bundles of newfound bounty out the window tied in the large cloths, to be retrieved later that night.

As Lisa turned, candlelight reflected off the jeweled handle of Papa's favorite dagger hanging on the wall. The light flickering from the faceted gems called to her. Moving to the wall of weapons, she gently lifted it from its perch and tucked it inside her tunic.

Papa, I am ready.

He will soon be resting in his final burial place. I will leave something for him to protect.

Lisa then headed to her bedchamber to get some things she wanted Margaux to have for safekeeping; items she could not take with her to Paris

Opening the door, she called out to Shadow. At the same time, she was surprised to see many candles were lit around her bed. *Who did this?* She did not hear Shadow's typical guttural meow.

Instead, as she approached her bed, her horrified gaze brought bile to her mouth as her screams flowed. Her beloved cat had been dismembered and its body parts were strewn all over the bedcovers. It was a horrific sight and she felt her knees begin to give way.

Lisa collapsed to the floor in shock, agony, and fear. Her screaming and wailing brought people running to her room from every part of the villa—all except for Fredric and Astrid.

In her heart, Lisa knew there was only one person who was deranged enough to slay her beloved Shadow: *Fredric*. And because he had killed Shadow in such a personal place as her bedchamber, she felt certain that she would be Fredric's next target. She realized nothing would ever stop him from inflicting pain on everyone and everything in his path.

Margaux attempted to comfort Lisa as the other servants disposed of the cat's remains. The maids wrapped what was left of Shadow in the bloodied and soiled blankets from Lisa's bed and cleaned the room as best they could.

Holding Lisa as she wept, Margaux whispered to her, "It is not safe for you to be in the villa any longer. Dear Lisa, I am so saddened by what you experienced these last two days. First your papa's death, and now your sweet Shadow is gone. I saw Fredric chasing Shadow earlier today and I believe he killed her. I think you feel that he did as well. Now, Fredric will come for you. Stay watchful. Be careful who you trust. And remember your training. You must be ready to leave here as soon as the burial is over.

"Your papa's burial will take place tomorrow. After the burial rites, return immediately to my cottage. The bag you packed with your essentials is stored in the back of the pantry. I will prepare food and drink to last you several days and I will place it alongside your bag. Gerhardt will take everything to Rose.

"Jonathan will have Valiant ready and waiting behind our cottage. Together you and Gerhardt will ride to Rose's shop. Gerhardt will get a message to Rose tonight when he takes your clothes and to food and let her know that you will be at her shop after the burial. Rose has made arrangements for you. She will tell you how to find the caravan that will head you north toward Paris.

"Tonight must be our final farewell. I will be tending to Astrid all day tomorrow … and keeping her away from you. I have loved you since the first time I held you in my arms, as dearly as if you were my own daughter. Concentrate on your lessons that prepared you to be who you are and who you will become. I pray we will one day meet again. Until we do, know that I love you and will forever hold you in my heart."

Lisa could barely breathe. All she could do was cling to Margaux as she sobbed and rocked in her arms. She managed to sputter out a few words.

"I would not have survived this long if it were not for you. Thank you, Margaux, for all that you have taught me and for showing me the only love I have ever known outside of my papa's. Immediately after the services, I will start feeling ill, and say I need to lay down at your cottage. There, I will meet up with Gerhardt, and after that, I will leave the villa forever."

Lisa was grateful to be at Margaux's for another night. Her thoughts focused on all the memories, events, and people that meant so much to her—people she might never see again after tomorrow.

Her head spun with all that had happened in the past few days and how her life would change forever. Papa's sudden death—his poisoning, Shadow's massacre, the rushed goodbyes with Margaux, Gerhardt, Jonathan, and Rose, and now an impending departure from where she had grown up. All of these roiling emotions had brought her to the point of exploding with rage and grief.

She now understood why Papa had prepared her with the plan and the financial means to escape to Paris if anything ever happened to him.

Astrid might think she was now in charge of Alexander's estate, but she and Fredric have no understanding of Alexander's true holdings.

Lisa did.

In the dark of the night Lisa returned to the bundles she had dropped from the solar window, retrieved them, and hid what was now hers.

When she returned to Margaux's, Lisa tried to calm herself and stay focused on the plans for tomorrow.

As she fell asleep, she murmured to herself, *I see you, Papa, but I cannot hear you. Please, please, please do not go. I need you, Papa....*

The last thing she heard was a soft, lilting voice as the dream slipped away.

twenty-three

The Burial

Alexander was never afraid to step in with ferocity if a loved one's safety was in jeopardy.

Early the next morning, Gerhardt returned to the cottage after chores and found Lisa sitting at the kitchen table. From the morose look on his face, she knew he was thinking and feeling the same thing she was ... the final goodbye.

He looked at her sadly. "Lisa, I wish you *were* going to live here. I am sorry that your papa is gone, and now you will be gone, too. All our lives have changed in a few days. What will I do without you?"

Lisa hugged him. "You are right about everything, Gerhardt. I will miss you, too. This is what Papa prepared me for and this is why he sent us to train with Sir Roland. I will be all right, Gerhardt, you will see.

She did not want him to see the tears welling up in her eyes as she turned to leave.

The morning of Alexander's funeral was sunny and warm for January.

Because of his sudden death, only nearby villages and local townspeople had been notified in time to attend. The burial rites were not scheduled to begin until late morning, but shortly after sunrise, a steady stream of people began arriving at the estate. Gathered there were peasants, merchants, shopkeepers, sailors, knights, and nobles from neighboring estates.

The kindly old priest from the town was to give the funeral mass.

Astrid had washed her hands of anything to do with Alexander on the day she had "discovered" his body in the solar and had left all the final arrangements to anyone who cared to cope with them. She saw no reason to pretend she was a grieving widow. She had hated Alexander for years.

Jonathan, Margaux, and Gerhardt had taken it upon themselves to prepare Alexander's body and notify the priest. They also decided that the orchard was ideal for his final rites and resting place—and for the ease to allow Lisa to escape.

Gerhardt had notified Sir Roland about Alexander's death and together the two of them had planned a military ritual they felt would be appropriate for his final goodbye. Once everyone had gathered, and after a sign from Jonathan, the ceremony began.

A horse-drawn wagon driven by Gerhardt made its way from the stables to the front door of the villa. The wagon was followed by Sir Roland and twelve of his men, all on foot. When the procession halted at the villa, Jonathan held the door and the men filed in, two at a time. Once inside, they were led to the great room. They surrounded the bier, and at Sir Roland's direction, lifted it, carried it outside, and carefully positioned it on the waiting wagon.

This time, the men surrounded the wagon, with Sir Roland taking up position at the rear of the procession. Upon his command, Gerhardt and the wagon moved slowly in the direction of the orchard where the crowd of mourners were gathered.

When they reached the orchard, they once again lifted the bier and carried it to a wooden platform that Jonathan had built for the occasion. Placing it on the platform, each bowed in respect and then backed away three paces. They had placed Alexander so that he was facing the sea he so loved and from which he had earned much of his wealth as a merchant.

Margaux, Jonathan, and Gerhardt stood together on the left side of the bier; each of them solemn and trying to control their tears. Lisa stood on the right side of the bier, gazing at her papa's lifeless body, making no attempt at restraining her tears. Her heart was broken. Her rock was gone. She knew she was truly all alone now, and her life as she knew it was also gone.

Danger was nearby. She sensed that as well.

Glancing up to see where Astrid and her brother were, she saw them standing behind a group of neighboring nobles. Astrid locked eyes with Lisa for a moment and looked away. She was neither solemn nor weeping; to Lisa's eyes, Astrid looked bored.

Lisa raised her arm, pointing her finger directly at her mother. Defiantly, her lips mouthed the words, *you killed him.*

Fredric stood to the side and behind Astrid. He caught Lisa's gaze, held up his hands and tapped each ring finger. He realized the rings were gone, and he smiled a devilish grin. She knew by his actions he was aware she had them. Even at this hour, he appeared to be in the early stages of drunkenness; nonetheless, his expression gave her cause to be concerned.

Lisa knew danger was circling around her. *Someday, I will return here when Fredric and Astrid are destitute.*

She took a moment to survey the crowd. It was a surprise to see the huge crowd of people who had turned out to pay their final respects to her papa: peasants, merchants, knights, and nobility were all present.

Lisa's eyes then settled once again on Astrid; Priest Loupe had moved next to her. She learned from observing people in the solar that she could see the essence of people and their conversations. Astrid was telling him of her good fortune and Loupe was looking at her as a wolf looks at its prey.

She turned back to look upon her papa and closed her eyes. All sound disappeared, and now she and Papa were alone.

Reliving her last walk with him as he revealed his life story, she remembered that he wanted to be judged fairly. In her mind, she saw him as he turned to her, remembering his last hug, and the feeling of finality it conveyed.

One day I will write his story, our story.

The priest's prayer was over when Lisa opened her eyes. Her goodbyes to her papa had been said. It was time.

As she looked up, a huge hawk was circling and staring down at her. It dipped one of its wings toward her, exposing a red sheen across its tail feathers. Then, it flew to a nearby tree, landing on one of the branches as if to watch what would happened next.

At that moment, Sir Roland took a few steps forward and stopped at the foot of the platform facing Alexander. Swallowing hard, he took a few deep breaths and began speaking from the heart.

"Alexander's courage and abilities in battle inspired us all who rode with him. His fairness as a merchant helped those living in the Marseilles and surrounding areas. Many have experienced his generosity and compassion and know he never shirked his responsibilities. Alexander was respectful to and respected by people of all social classes. He was an excellent negotiator and facilitated settlements favorable to both sides of an issue.

"He was never afraid to step in with ferocity if a loved one's safety was in jeopardy and above all, we know of his strong devotion to his daughter, Lisa."

Hearing Sir Roland's comment, Astrid stifled a cough and rolled her eyes. As soon as she did, all eyes focused on her and she sensed the hateful mood of the mourners directed at her.

As soon as Alexander was found dead, rumors ran rampant that he had been poisoned, most probably by Astrid. Lisa had heard the rumors early on and did nothing to stop them. Instead, she encouraged them.

Roland was nearing the end of his speech, and as he did, he paused for a long moment and bowed his head in thought. He looked up at Alexander's face, placed his hand over his heart and said, "Sir Alexander, it is my honor to call you my friend. You will be sorely missed by me and by all whose lives you have touched so profoundly."

With that salutation, Roland nodded to his men. In unison, they approached the bier. Each placed a hand on Alexander's body, drew the sword from its scabbard, raised it to the sky and saluted him with the words: *"May you meet with fair winds and smooth sailing."*

As their salute ended, the huge red-tailed hawk rose from the branch and again circled over the gathering, dipping toward Lisa, then soaring steadily higher and headed toward the port.

Several in the gathering wondered … was it a sign?

twenty-four

The Escape and the Naming

Grabbing a handful of hair, she started hacking away at her long, dark locks.

As soon as Lisa saw the hawk soar overhead, she put her hand to her forehead. "I do not feel well. I am going to lie down." She said the words loud enough for those standing close by to hear.

Standing next to her, Gerhardt took hold of Lisa's arm to support her, and together they turned and walked back through the crowd of mourners to Margaux's cottage.

Once inside, she headed to Gerhardt's room at the back of the cottage. Lisa recognized the breeches and tunics to which she had added the secret pockets, boots, and a cap that Margaux had laid out on the bed for her. She quickly changed into the attire.

Holding her papa's dagger that she had found lying beneath the breeches, she bent over a bucket of water and looked at her reflection. Grabbing a handful of hair, she started hacking away at her long dark locks. She cut until she was satisfied with the short length of her hair all around her head, and then lifted the boy's cap from the bed and put it on her head.

Lisa took one last look at her reflection and was astonished at how young and boyish she appeared. Through the sewn opening in her tunic, she concealed the sheathed dagger and wrapped the remains of her hair in a kerchief that Margaux had left to dispose of later.

She rechecked her satchel to make certain it held the coins and map Papa had given her and the other essentials she had packed for her journey. Taking the coin purse and map, she tucked them tightly in the cloth-lined opening she had sewed beneath her tunic. The food Margaux had prepared for her was waiting at Rose's

Finally, she felt for her papa's rings, which she had looped on a cord she had tied around her neck. It, too, was tucked beneath her . Patting the rings, she said aloud, "Papa, my secret journey begins today."

Lisa stopped when she saw Jonathan, Margaux, and Gerhardt standing at the door. They had all slipped away from the group of mourners and come back to the cottage to tell her goodbye.

Her new look surprised them. No longer was the young woman they knew as Lisa in front of them. With her chopped hair and tight cap, she had taken on the appearance of a tall, lean peasant boy.

Margaux smiled. "You will fool many people. Perhaps you may even attract some girls."

With that, the first laugh flowed from Lisa's lips ... and a smile. Approaching Jonathan first and giving him a quick hug, she thanked him for all he had taught her and for seeing to the villa's estate. He gave her a smile and a nod, and promised her he would do as she asked.

Turning to Margaux, she hugged her tightly. At the same time, she gave her a purse bulging with coins.

"I do not know what Astrid will do, but I know Papa would want you to have this. Now, go back to the villa and do what you are expected to do. Pretend to be shocked when you hear of my disappearance. You know Astrid will lash out at all around her when she realizes I am gone for good. Continue as if nothing has changed. Thank you for preparing all my things for me. You have always shown me a mother's true love. I treasure you, Margaux. Goodbye … just for now."

Margaux whispered, her tone urgent, "Rose is waiting for you at her shop. Go at once. Travel safely, dear one, and stay alert." Lisa did not see the look of Margaux's heartbreak on her face as she turned away.

Lisa looked at Gerhardt. "Let us go." His farewell would wait until they reached Rose's.

He loaded the satchel onto her horse.

Both mounted the same horse and headed to the southern gate of the property where no one would see them leave.

He murmured, "Lisa, lean into Valiant's neck as we leave. If anyone sees us, it is me and the horse they see, not you." They rode off toward the forest that hemmed the far side of the estate—quickly blending in with the trees and shrubbery, riding slowly and calmly so as not to draw attention to themselves.

"Let us stop here, Gerhardt." She then turned to take one last look at her home. Tears welled in her eyes as she realized, not only would her life change profoundly from this day forward, but those she loved and left behind would also be affected: Rose, Margaux, Gerhardt, Jonathan, and the orphan children —all who benefitted from her papa's guidance and generosity.

Gerhardt spoke softly. "Come ... we must go quickly."

"Yes, I know. I must tuck these memories away and focus on joining the caravan. Papa gave me the knowledge of life outside this estate. Now I must use every skill I have to survive. One day, I will return to this land, and Astrid and Fredric will be dealt with."

They resumed their leisurely gait until they had cleared the forest and found the road leading to the docks, then they quickened their pace.

Both jumped off the horse as soon as they arrived at Rose's shop. Tying Valiant to a post, they ran inside to find her arranging bottles on a shelf.

Running to her side, Lisa caught Rose's hands and breathlessly exclaimed, "Rose, we are finally here. Gerhardt told me he came to see you last night, to tell you all that would take place today. Did you find a caravan I can join to make the journey north?"

Despite being startled by Lisa's changed appearance, Rose nodded in assent.

"I found someone I trust. His name is Jericus and he is a good man. I have known him for years. He is aware of your situation and knows that you are Alexander's daughter; he will see to your safety. Armed guards have been contracted to travel with the caravan, which left at first light today. There are many wagons, pack horses, merchants, and other travelers who will be making the trip as well. Other than Jericus, no one should know you. Stay to yourself. There are people who know you by sight and may not be fooled by the change in your appearance. The further you are away from here the safer you should be."

Lisa listened to Rose's concerns. "I will do as you say."

Rose looked at Lisa. "You have done well to change how others will see you. This might be a good time to become someone else as you make your way up north so that no one can easily tie you back to Alexander or Astrid."

"Yes!" Lisa thought a moment, leaned in close to Rose, and said, "From this day forward, I shall be known as Nichol, Nick to those I meet. I have always loved that name."

Rose smiled and put her arm around Nichol's waist. "It is a beautiful name for a beautiful young lady." From under her table, she pulled out a full-length woolen cloak. "You will need this to keep you warm, Nichol."

In her haste to leave the villa, Nichol had not included a cloak, and was thrilled with the gift. As she slipped on the cloak, she noticed a purse sewn into it. Opening it, she withdrew a bag, opened it for better viewing, and looked questioningly at Rose.

Rose smiled and said, "The leaves come from various herbs I use, and they are infused with rose hips from my garden. I call the mixture white rose. My children love its smell and I love its soothing effect. It is something to remember me by. And I have something else …."

Removing a leather string from her neck, Rose placed it around Nichol's neck. Examining it, Nichol saw a stone with a feather attached to it.

"This, too, is for you, child. It has protected me and now it will protect you. The hawk is important to you and will always now be with you."

Looking down, Nichol grasped the stone and immediately felt a sensation as her fingers touched the feather. A sense of energy and well-being flowed through her. *Papa.* Then, looking up, she saw him ... the red tail hawk circling above. *I knew he would be with me.*

Refocusing on Rose, she heard her friend continue to speak. "I have enjoyed our visits immensely, and I will miss you and your papa very much. Alexander raised a wonderful daughter."

Nichol wrapped Rose in her arms. "Thank you for the gifts. I will cherish them always. I will never forget you and all that you have done for me, taught me, and shared with me. I love you, Rose."

Finally, she handed a coin purse to Rose. "Papa would want you to have this."

"Now, gather your things and perhaps you can catch up with Jericus before nightfall. Godspeed, my sweet friend. Goodbye ... Nichol. Travel wisely."

Nichol turned to Gerhardt and embraced him. "I will miss you and I will keep our adventures in my thoughts. We will meet again; I promise. Now return to the villa and act as if you know nothing of my disappearance.

"Valiant is now yours. Take him to Sir Roland's and tell him of my wishes, but say no more and he will not ask. Papa has told him of his troubles and he is a true friend. I whispered to Valiant that you are his new master. You will be the only one that he will permit to ride him."

Hugging him one more time, she turned and left and started on a slow run.

After she left, Gerhardt stood still with his head bowed. His only true friend had walked away.

Rose went to him and grabbed his arm. "You must leave at once and return to the villa without being seen."

Astrid did not wait for people to leave the service for Alexander. She abruptly excused herself soon after the last words over Alexander were spoken. It was time to collect her prize.

With the key to Alexander's solar in her hard, she entered the villa and rushed to the room, unlocking the door. She went directly to the locked box. Fredric was not far behind. "Fredric, we finally have the wealth that we deserve."

Fumbling with her keys in nervous anticipation, Astrid opened the box and lifted the lid. With a blank look on her face, she just stared into an empty box with one silver coin in the bottom. Falling to her knees, hands covering her face, she started wailing with uncontrolled anger.

Pushing his mother aside, Fredric stood over the box. "It is empty; it probably has always been empty." Roaring in anger, he smashed his fist on the desk.

When she heard the wailing, Margaux moved quickly to the solar. When she got there, she stood quietly standing by the door and out of sight. She took pleasure in Astrid's misery.

Knowing that Alexander's box was always full of items, a smile crossed her face as she turned away.

Lisa has been here.

Astrid ceased her hysterical crying and removed her hands from her face. Once again, she stared into the empty box. The longer she stared, the angrier she became.

Turning to Fredric, she howled, her voice hoarse from sobbing, "Do not be a fool. This box was never empty! Lisa has taken its contents and robbed us of what we deserve. Find her and bring her back to me—dragging her by her hair if you have to! I know this is her doing."

In his usual state of drunkenness, Fredric did not fully comprehend what his mother said. He just stared at her.

"Do not just stand there, get her! Bring her to me at once. I will make her tell me where she hid my gold and silver!"

The Confrontation

I am not stupid, old woman.

Before Fredric began his search for Lisa, he needed to get to the Anchor Inn. A drink, maybe several ... then he would go back to the villa and search everywhere.

Just as Gerhardt walked out of Rose's shop to mount Valiant and return to the villa, he saw a rider fast approaching … Fredric. Stepping back, he hid out of sight.

Inside her shop, Rose also heard a rider's approach. The next thing she saw was Fredric riding up to the horse tied at the post.

Jerking the reins free from the post, Valiant reared on his hind legs and then firmly planted his hooves into the ground.

Fredric dismounted and tried to approach the horse. Valiant put his head down, then kicked at Fredric while trying to bite him. The horse backed away, snorting, as if daring Fredric to try and touch him.

Realizing the horse could not be mastered or bullied, Fredric turned into the shop.

Rose had watched Valiant's reaction to Fredric from inside the shop. Glaring at him as he entered, she snapped, "Get out of my shop!" *The horse knows he is bad. It is protecting Nichol and Gerhardt.*

Fredric grabbed her by the arm and growled hatefully, "That is my horse! Where is she? Which way did she go?"

Rose looked at him, her gaze puzzled. "That is not your horse. And who is *she* that you are asking about?"

"Do not be a fool, old woman … tell me where my sister is!"

Pointing to a ship that was barely away from the pier, she said, "Lisa is not here. If you are looking for her, she is gone. I saw her talking to the captain of that ship–the one that just left the harbor."

Shoving her down, Fredric snarled, "I am not dumb, old woman. I know she is still around here somewhere. I will find her when she comes back to get the horse."

Looking up from the ground, Rose said, "You are a drunken coward. The next time you enter my shop will be the last."

He was not accustomed to a woman talking back to him or threatening him.

With a blank stare, he was speechless at the old woman on the ground. Turning in a huff, he left the shop, mounted his horse, and headed in the direction of the Anchor Inn, leaving Valiant at Rose's.

Exhaling a deep breath, Rose whispered, "*Dumb* is not the first word that comes to mind with that fool."

Spying him on the wharf nearby, Rose beckoned young Theo into her shop. After giving him several coins, she instructed him to find the tavern owner of the Anchor Inn and give him the coins. "Give him all of this, and tell him a friend wanted to make certain that Fredric's wine cup is never empty tonight."

Emerging from his hiding place, Gerhardt peeked around the door of her shop. “Did he harm you?”

With a smile, Rose shook her head. “I have been treated worse. Take the horse back to Sir Roland’s right now and do so without being seen. Make sure you visit there often so you remain bonded with Valiant as Lisa wanted.

“And tell Margaux that Lisa is safe and making her way to the caravan. Do not worry about Fredric. He will spend the rest of the night at the Anchor Inn.”

twenty-six

Nichol's Journey Begins

What she was not prepared for was the danger following her from her past.

Nichol reached the caravan that evening just as the sun slipped over the horizon. Jericus and the caravan were off the road and stopped for the day.

Nichol went to the head of the caravan and found Jericus, recognizing him from Rose's description. She introduced herself as Lisa, but asked him to call her Nick.

"I have been expecting you," Jericus replied.

Motioning to her to follow him, they moved away from the caravan for a quiet conversation. Turning his back to the others, he spoke directly to Nichol.

"I knew your father well, transporting some of the goods from his ships in the port. Rose told me what has happened. If you are with me, I will protect you."

"Thank you, Jericus. I am most fearful of my brother Fredric. I know he will be looking for me. He does not know how I am dressed or that I have cut my hair …."

"I hired guards for protection of the caravan. They will be alerted."

The next morning, Nichol marveled at how quickly Jericus organized everyone as they got ready to set out for the day.

He reminded those who could not walk far to load into the wagons. Those who could walk were told to stay close to the wagons on either side.

Because of the size of the caravan—ten wagons, thirty pack animals and over forty people made up the caravan—he had hired armed guards who flanked it at various positions. At the rear, two heavily armed guards followed behind the last wagon.

Nichol lined up on the right side of the lead wagon along with some of the other travelers. Jericus motioned for the horses to pull forward as he headed them to the road leading north.

For Nichol, it was a new life. Seeded by a murder, what she felt was the guidance of the hawk, the voice of the *Lady*, and the gentle care of Rose and Margaux. She felt safe for the first time since his death.

Breathing deeply, she was on her way to Paris.

As she walked, Nichol was lost in thought. At this point she could not fathom how her new life would unfold or what would lie ahead, but she knew full well the danger that would greet her if she returned to the villa.

This is where I need to be now. This was part of Papa's plan.

Margaux's last words kept echoing in her mind:

Your papa always thought it would be a pirate or a bishop that would be his undoing. He never imagined his own family would betray him. Alexander had survived many conflicts in business and battles on the field, only to die by poison at the hands of his wife.

Nichol's thoughts returned to the present and with a resolute gait, she straightened her shoulders, let out a huge sigh, and affirmed out loud, "I cannot let Papa down. My journey has begun."

Life lessons she had learned from Alexander, Margaux, Rose, and Sir Roland would prove invaluable from this day forward. Because of all the time she had spent observing the docks in Marseilles, Nichol had witnessed the behavior and activities of many different cultures and had a good ear for learning their languages. Due to the time spent in the solar, she could converse easily with the educated elite. She adapted to situations easily and readily.

Her training with Sir Roland taught her skills that women did not know … but she did. Her curiosity to learn all kinds of things would prove helpful as she set out on the next phase of her life.

When she joined the caravan, Nichol noticed the group of travelers accompanying Jericus on this trek to Paris was very diverse. Because the caravan and the troupe associated with it was a large one, they traveled slower than she would have liked.

While they moved along, Nichol began to file information and descriptions of the other travelers. She noted a priest, two monks and their fellow worshipers in one group, several men and women who walked next to the wagons so their children could ride inside, and various individuals who did not belong to any party or group. Toward the rear and in front of the two guards, there were two merchants who had their wares packed on mules and donkeys.

At the end of the second day's travel, Jericus circled the caravan into an open field where everyone could camp together for the night to ensure their safety. At Jericus' direction, several people began unloading the supplies they would need to make a fire as well as food and beverages for the evening meal.

When the meal was finished, people pulled out whatever they had brought with them to sleep on. Some had nothing more than the clothes on their backs and searched for the cleanest patch of grass they could find to call a bed.

Everybody tended to reassemble into the same groups they had been traveling with to set up sleeping arrangements for the night. Anticipating this, Nichol had befriended two young mothers before the evening meal. Both had more than one young child to care for and she had offered to help with their children during the night. As a result, she could blend in with the group of young parents who gladly accepted her help with crying babies. Everyone was exhausted and immediately fell into a deep sleep.

It was the middle of January, and the air was crisp. The next morning, they rose at dawn, and ate a generous meal to fortify them for a full day's travel. Packing their supplies, the younger children got into the wagons and were on their way quickly. The caravan moved slowly but steadily the whole day and stopped again that night to camp in a meadow on the east side of the road.

The following day, Nichol chose to walk at the rear of the caravan among the merchants gathered there. She thought she might learn something valuable since they were frequent travelers on this route.

Keeping to herself, she overheard the merchants talking about an inn in the town of Arles that they thought they would reach by nightfall. It would be a welcome place to spend the night.

After a midday meal, a light rain began to fall as they set out on the final leg of the day's journey. The dampened dirt on the road provided relief from the choking dust they had encountered all morning, and then the sun broke through once again.

A young couple with two children had also opted to walk at the rear of the wagon and began to fall behind when the sun hit its peak. They were one of the young families Nichol had helped the previous night. Sensing that the mother needed a break, Nichol offered to carry one of her tiny daughters. At the same time, the father adjusted his hold on the baby he carried and they walked on.

"Where are you going?" Nichol asked the young father.

"We are going to any town where I can find work. I was a carpenter's apprentice in a small village outside of Marseilles until the work ran out. I need to find work and shelter soon. My wife and children cannot continue at this pace. We need to find a new home."

Quietly he continued, "I heard the merchants talking about an inn they say is not far from here. We do not have the coin to stay in the inn tonight, so we are going to camp somewhere off the road and rejoin the caravan in the morning."

Looking down at Nichol, who held his sleeping daughter nestled close to her heart, he said, "Thank you for carrying Rosalie. This trip has been hard on my wife."

Nichol's eyes began to water as she thought of Rose. She whispered, "Rosalie, what a beautiful name."

She was drawn to this young couple and their children when she first met them. *Someday, I hope to have a family like this.* "If this sweet person is Rosalie, what name do you and your wife go by? My name is Nick."

"I am Colin, my wife is Liliane, and this new baby girl is Viviane," he said proudly as he looked down at the tiny bundle he carried.

Smiling, Nichol said, "I am pleased to meet you, Colin. If it will be of any relief to you and Liliane, I am happy to camp with you again tonight and help with the children. And if it will make traveling easier for you both tomorrow, I am happy to carry Rosalie or Viviane."

Colin hesitated only briefly before he said, "Thank you. We would both appreciate that." They walked in thoughtful silence as they approached the caravan.

As the travelers reached the small village of Arles, Liliane set about pulling their bags out of the wagon and handed them to Colin. He took the bags and went in search of a secluded spot not too far from the main road where his family could sleep for the night. By staying close, he would see when the caravan was ready to start up in the morning.

He spied a small grove of trees and laid out their belongings amid the grove. They would be protected from weather and travelers there.

Many of the others in the caravan headed for the inn. They preferred some warmth and food for the night. Still others decided to sleep in or around the wagons.

Seeing where Colin had settled his family's things, Nichol removed her own bags from the wagon and followed them to the stand of trees. She gave them plenty of space for privacy and laid out her things several feet away. She unpacked the food she had in her satchel, and as she did, she saw the look of hunger on the faces of the young couple. She knew immediately they had little food.

Taking her pack to their spot, she said, "I want to share this with you. There is water in the waterskin. I will go to the inn to get ale for all of us to drink." She handed the food to them and started off.

On her way, she saw Jericus tending to his horses. She approached him and reached inside her tunic. Extracting some coins, she extended them to him. "I would like to buy food and drink for you and the family that is traveling behind the last wagon with me."

"Put your coins away. Rose told me of your situation. Your father was always good to me. It is time for me to repay some of that goodness. No one yet knows who you are, but I would advise you to stay out of sight until we are far away from Marseilles. I will return soon with food and drink for all of you."

Nichol motioned in the direction of the grove where Colin and Liliane were sheltered, and said, "I will be over there with them."

Jericus headed off to the inn and returned promptly to the grove with bread, cheese, roasted rabbit, and ale that was strong enough to soothe the aches and pains of the day's travels. He gave it to Nichol, who passed it on to Liliane.

Nichol said kindly, "Thank you, Jericus. Tomorrow I will buy your evening meal." Jericus simply nodded, turned to leave, and stopped abruptly.

Nichol followed his gaze to the road and saw a rider approaching the inn at a furious pace. Her senses told her to hide immediately.

twenty-seven

The Past Becomes Present

I cannot go on like this.
I will put an end to him tonight.

As the rider drew near, her eyes narrowed and recognition surfaced.

Fredric.

How did he find me and so soon?

Stopping in front of the inn, Fredric dismounted, and threw the reins around a nearby post. His horse was lathered from the run and was gasping for air.

Jericus watched Fredric rush into the inn. Turning to her, he said, "I know who that is and I have dealt with him before. Stay hidden in this grove until I come to tell you what is happening."

He left to go back to the inn, and Nichol turned and looked at Colin and Liliane with a worried look.

"Something has frightened you. What is it?" Liliane asked.

She shivered and then told them part of her story. "I am not the boy you think I am. I have had to disguise myself because of the threats by my mother. She demanded I marry an old man she had chosen. If I did not, she would sell me to a slave ship. I refused her demand and immediately escaped. Jericus understood my danger and took me in. It appears she has sent my evil and vindictive brother to find me and take me back. I must stay hidden.

"Now I need your help as well. Please call me Nick—that will help protect me. Will you promise?"

Nichol was hesitant to divulge any more information than that. She did not want to compromise the young couple if they should be questioned later, so she changed the subject. Then she added, "The children are fast asleep. Did you all have enough to eat and drink?" she asked.

"Yes, we ate more than we should have," replied Colin. "Thank you for sharing all that you did. Come sit with us and eat your meal, Nick. We will help you."

Nichol joined them and sat so she could see Jericus when he returned from the inn. She picked at her food and ate what little she could manage to swallow. Her appetite had vanished now that she knew Fredric was so close. Barely able to speak, she encouraged Colin and Liliane to talk about their lives.

"We left our home because I am a carpenter and I could not find enough work in our small town to sustain us. We want a better life for our children other than working the fields and living in a hovel furnished by a lord. It was not easy leaving our families, not knowing what lies ahead, but now I am desperate to find work and will do anything—even working in the fields—to provide food for them." He finished with, "Thank you for your generosity in feeding us tonight. We had no food left when we got here."

Looking at the young couple and their two babies, Nichol thought, *I have no worries compared to this family. They have no food or coin while my worries are a vindictive brother and a malicious mother. Until now, I have had all that I ever needed. Seeing the poor children on the docks in Marseilles and now watching this family struggle for survival, it is selfish to think just of myself.*

She shook herself from her thoughts when she heard footsteps in the brush approaching the grove. In the now-fading light, she recognized Jericus. She could hardly wait to hear what he had to report.

Standing from her spot on the ground next to Colin and Liliane, she looked up at Jericus to hear what he had learned. He did not look concerned.

"Jericus, what is Fredric saying and doing in the tavern?"

He looked at her calmly and shook his head as he began to relate what was occurring in the inn. "Your brother certainly has not made any friends inside. He was quick to down several cups of ale and, just as quickly, began bragging of his wealth and importance. I sat at a table at the back of the room and listened. He said he is on a quest to find his sister Lisa and asked if anyone had encountered her. His description of you made me wonder if he really knows what you look like.

"The more he drank, the more slurred his speech became. When I left, people were ignoring him. Soon he will be too drunk to walk. I think you are safe to sleep here in the grove tonight. I will check on him once more before I bed down this night. If anything has changed, I will let you know. For many reasons, I wish to be on our way tomorrow. Be ready at first light."

As he turned to leave, she felt some relief. "Thank you, Jericus. I think we will all sleep better tonight knowing that Fredric will be drunk in the tavern. Knowing his fondness for drink, I will wager he will not stir until midday tomorrow. We should be safe when we leave at dawn."

After Jericus left, she helped the young couple clear the remains of their meal and wrap their babies in blankets. After bidding them good night, she sauntered over to where she would sleep. And though Jericus' input was promising, she would sleep lightly all night.

In the middle of the night, she woke in a cold sweat from a frightening dream. Jumping to her feet, she quickly surveyed her surroundings. All seemed quiet. *I cannot go on like this. I will put an end to him tonight.*

Walking slowly to the tavern, Nichol quietly opened the door and stepped just inside the room and paused. She observed that only a few candles were lit in the empty tavern and at a table straight ahead, Fredric was facedown on the table. He appeared to be asleep—or more likely, unconscious from drink—with his head resting on his folded arms.

Glaring at Fredric she reached in her tunic and slowly but firmly grasped the hilt of her dagger. Taking a deep breath, she cautiously approached him. Her anger when she woke had started to subside; all she saw in front of her was a pathetic drunk.

Now standing over him, Nichol pulled out the jeweled dagger from the sheath beneath her tunic.

Wait, Lisa ... you are not a murderer like your mother.

She moved her hand away from the dagger's sheath and stepped back. Her thoughts rambled. *Maybe I should shake him awake, giving him a chance to defend himself. When he tries to attack me, I can justify plunging my dagger into him.*

Her mind cleared and Sir Roland's training took over. She knew that the best place to thrust her knife would be into his side, close to his heart. Lifting her arm, she raised the knife back as far as she could, and with a glare of uncontrolled hate, she clenched her teeth.

Death was what Fredric deserved.

Just as she was ready to strike, a coin purse looped around his belt caught her eye. Leaning forward, she carefully cut the strings and tucked it inside her tunic.

Whispering in his ear, she said, "Tonight I let you live. But the next time, I will not be so merciful."

Returning the dagger to the sheath, she slipped out of the tavern with a slight smile on her face and a purse full of coin.

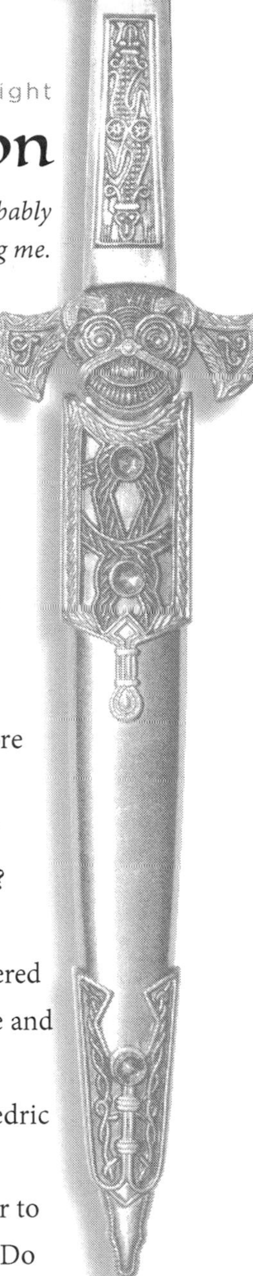

twenty-eight

Avignon

If I was flailing about, it was probably about my brother threatening me.

Before the sun rose, Nichol was up and helping Liliane and the children, anxious to get Arles behind her. After consuming a light morning meal that Lillian prepared, all bags were repacked. The wagons were their destination.

Jericus was preparing to hook up his horses to the wagon as Nichol approached him.

Smiling, he said, "Do not worry, Fredric had more than his fill of ale last night. If he rouses before the evening meal, I would be surprised."

"If true, then he will not need his horse today," she replied with a sly grin. "Do you know where it is? I do not see it tethered in front of the inn."

"I took pity on the horse. Last night, I fed it, watered it, and put it in the field behind the inn. The saddle and reins are on the ground close by."

Jericus smiled. He knew her intent. "When Fredric discovers his horse is gone, his anger will soar."

Tilting her head in thought, Nichol put a finger to her lips. "How far do you plan on traveling today? Do you know where you will stop for the night? The young family and I can travel faster than your wagons today if we take Fredric's horse. One of us can ride and carry the children, while the others walk alongside. We can meet up in the next town."

"The next town is Avignon, and it will take at least two days to get there. I have business there and I plan to stay over a few days. Avignon is a large village and there is an inn at the market center, just as you enter. I will seek you out once we have arrived."

"Jericus, Colin wants to find work to help his family. Maybe there is a chance something will be there."

Nichol clasped her hands cheerfully and left to talk over the idea of traveling on a horse with Colin and Liliane. She detailed the plan for them, and they agreed. When she said there might be work for Colin in Avignon, she could see his mood lighten at once.

"Take your family behind the inn. There is a dark chestnut horse with white markings on his face. The saddle and bridle are on the ground close by. Saddle and bridle him and have your things all packed. We will leave as soon as I get back."

Nichol went back to talk to Jericus and outlined their plan, telling him they would be leaving right away. Thanking him for protecting her, she ran off to find Colin and Liliane behind the inn, saying over her shoulder, "We will look for you in Avignon."

Colin found the horse and readied it with saddle and bridle. Loading their bags, his family waited for Nichol to join them.

Looking to Liliane, Nichol asked, "Do you know how to ride a horse."

"No—we did not have one. I do not know how to ride."

"It is not difficult. I will teach you how after we have left Arles. Until then, I will ride the horse. Rosalie can sit in front of me and

I will carry Viviane. You and Colin will walk. Avignon is our next stop."

Nichol mounted up and Colin lifted Rosalie onto the horse, seating her in front of Nichol. Rosalie looked up at her and smiled broadly. Viviane was then handed to Nichol, and she cradled her in one arm as she handed the reins to Colin to guide them as they set out.

"Colin, take the reins and lead the horse. That way, the children can see that you are both still with them. I think once they are used to the rhythm of the horse, both will soon be asleep. Let us be off from here."

Feeling confident for the first time, Colin and Liliane enthusiastically moved forward.

The roadway ahead was flat and winding, and they moved at a steady pace. Observing the young family, Nichol suggested frequent short stops to feed and nurse baby Viviane, as well as to feed and rest themselves. The main road paralleled the river as they headed north. Each time they stopped, the horse was watered and they filled wineskins.

At midday, Colin saw a rock outcropping close to the river that was sheltered by trees. He led them to the spot, and everyone settled on the ground for a needed rest. Colin and Liliane fed the girls and the adults ate the bread and cheese they had saved from the previous night's meal. While the parents entertained the babies, Nichol stretched out on a grassy patch and closed her eyes.

The next thing she knew, Colin was shaking her shoulder to waken her. Nichol jumped up with a start and panic grabbed at her heart.

Colin said softly, "Nick, all is well. We have been here for some time and I thought we should move on."

Once she had her wits about her and realized they were not in danger, she exhaled and nodded in agreement. Quickly, she readied them to set out again.

Estimating that they still had a half-day's travel before they could stop for the night, Nichol asked, "Liliane, would you like to learn to ride the horse?"

"No … I think we can all travel faster if I walk now."

Nichol then looked to Colin. "Colin, perhaps it is time that you ride and carry the girls and let me walk some." It did not take a lot of persuasion. He mounted up and reached out for his two daughters. When they were settled, Nichol took the reins and led the horse back to the road. She walked on the left side and Liliane took up position on the right.

After some distance, Liliane said, "Nichol, you were having dreams as you slept back there and you were talking and thrashing about. Is all well?"

"I do not remember dreaming, but if I was flailing about, it was probably my brother threatening me. He is brutal, Liliane. He is a drunkard, does mean things to everyone, and only cares about coin. I am sure he is pleased that Papa was murdered. Fredric wishes to do me harm.

"I am fearful he will persuade other men to help him track me down and return me to Marseilles against my will. If that happened, I would be faced with not only my brother's cruelty, but also my mother's. Both are evil. That's why I must keep going. I cannot permit myself to be taken back."

Liliane did not ask for more details. Nichol had been so kind and generous to them that she hesitated to ask more.

"Nick, do you think there is a good chance that Colin will find work as we travel from here?"

"Jericus claims that Avignon is a village of some size and he thought there could be carpentry work available. The caravan will be there a few days so Jericus can deal with some of his regular business; he told me he will find us. Perhaps Colin can meet with him and get acquainted with some of the villagers. They will know what is available."

The two women continued walking, talking about many things: motherhood, raising two little girls, gardens, herbs, even marriage. All the while, they kept walking steadily toward their destination.

At one point, Nichol glanced back and smiled at what she saw. Colin had leaned back in the saddle with his two dozing daughters. From where she walked, she could hear him humming to them.

What a sweet family they are. They are kind and considerate to one another and seem to want what is best for their girls. I have seen the sparkle in their eyes when Colin and Liliane look at each other. They love each other. Someday, I will know this feeling.

They continued walking for hours, simply nodding and smiling at other travelers as they passed them. Nichol traded places with Colin once again and continued until they found a quiet spot in a stand of trees and settled down for the night.

Midday on the following day, they came to a halt as they reached the summit of the small hill they had ascended. Suddenly, Colin said, "I think I see Avignon ahead!"

Stretched out below them was the largest settlement they had seen since leaving Marseilles. Within the central marketplace, there were numerous shops. One building looked like it could be the inn where Jericus said he would meet them. Small houses lined both sides of the marketplace.

As they gazed further out, farms and fields and barns were on the horizon. This was the most welcome sight they had seen in days.

Colin could barely contain his excitement. Surely, he would be able to find work in a town such as this. He turned to his wife and Nichol. "It looks like we are here. Shall we find a place to settle in for the night?" All of them were pleased, relieved, and excited to see what lay before them.

Nichol had a sudden inspiration. Looking at the two of them, she said, "Colin and Liliane, I have a good feeling about this town. We can eat a good meal and find a place for the night. Tomorrow, we can walk around the town until Jericus arrives."

"Nick, we are grateful for your kindness to us, but we can never repay you."

Nichol said, "Colin, I believe you will find work here in Avignon. Soon you will be busy building a home for your family, as well as homes for many other people once they see your craft. One day when you have earned all the coin you need to care for your family, you can feed another family in need."

Heading into the town, they quickly sighted a tavern. They took little time agreeing that having a warm meal would be good for all, instead of eating bread and dried cheese that they carried.

Soon they were supping on rabbit, carrots, cabbage, warm bread, and plenty of ale. Rosalie and Viviane began to yawn and fidget. It was clearly time for them to bed down for the night.

"Why do not we just bed down in the stables? I see others doing it as well," Colin suggested. "I will go see if there is room for Liliane and the children. If there is, I will return after they are settled to let you know where we will be."

Bidding Liliane and the girls' goodnight, Nichol sat down and ordered another cup of ale. As soon as she did, the front door of the tavern opened, and a stream of travelers trooped into the room with Jericus at the rear. She stood and beckoned him to join her.

He ambled over to the table, exhaled a tired sigh, and flopped down onto a stool next to Nichol. "We are here," were the only words he could muster at that moment. Nichol found a server and ordered stew, bread, and ale for him as he relayed the day's travel events.

A few moments later, Colin returned and joined them.

Digging into his meal, Jericus paused. "Colin, tomorrow I am meeting with some men who want to build onto the community here in Avignon: more homes, farmsteads, barns, granaries, even merchant stalls and stores. I will be bringing them supplies they will need from the ports of Marseilles. Your carpenter skills would help them. Come with me to meet them."

Colin's expression was one of surprise and excitement. "Thank you for including me, Jericus. I am most grateful for your kindness. Liliane will be excited when I tell her."

Jericus and Nichol both grinned and told him to be on his way.

As he continued to eat and drink, Nichol leaned in close, chin in hand.

"Jericus, I have been doing some thinking today. I have a good feeling that Colin will find plenty of work here in Avignon, but he will need funds to buy his own tools and supplies. I would like to give you the horse we have been riding. I cannot sell the animal; I look like a peasant, so someone will think I stole it. Because you are known here, it would be natural for you to sell it. Do so, along with the saddle, and give the coin to Colin and Liliane. Take some of the sale for yourself and give the rest to them."

Jericus stopped chewing long enough to look at Nichol. "You are indeed Alexander's daughter. I will see to it that Colin gets the money from the sale of the horse. As for me, you paid for my meal. That is payment enough.

"Do you plan on traveling further with my caravan? I will be in Avignon for two days and I know you want to stay well ahead of Fredric if he is tracking you."

"I feel safe with you and I do not want to travel alone. But for the reason you just stated, I am eager to be on my way at first light. What do you think?"

"As your father's friend, I wish you were traveling with someone, Nichol. Still, I understand your need to leave and stay ahead of Fredric."

Nichol stood. "Jericus, thank you for all the guidance you have given me. I am forever grateful."

She gave him a quick hug and headed out to the stables.

twenty-nine

On Her Own

Anger—rather than fear—was her first reaction.

The next morning, she was awake and ready to leave before the sun was up. There was one thing she wanted to do. The aroma of fresh bread led her back to the tavern kitchen where two women had already baked many loaves and were working on the day's pot of stew. She nodded good morning to them and walked to the table where the loaves cooled.

The older of the two bakers smiled at her. "Do you want bread?"

"Yes, I have coin for six loaves. And if you have cheese available, I would like some, too." The elder baker gathered the items Nichol requested, wrapped them in clean squares of cloth and handed them to her. Nichol handed the lady a silver coin and thanked her.

The baker looked down at the coin and up at Nichol. She said, "This is too much for what I just gave you."

"What else do you have?"

"We have some dried rabbit …."

"Then I will have some of that, too. Thank you."

With food in her satchel and a waterskin full of ale, Nichol left the tavern through the kitchen entrance and headed back to the stables. Seeing Colin, she beckoned to him to follow her outside. Handing him four loaves of bread, some of the cheese and rabbit, she told him of her plans.

"This is for your family for today. When Jericus sells the horse, he is to give you the coin. It will be enough for you to take care of your family while seeking a job. Thank you … I will miss all of you. Please tell Liliane goodbye for me." She then circled back to the main road to start the day.

She had an uneasy feeling that Fredric was still in pursuit, and probably not far behind.

My taking his horse will slow him down but will increase his need for vengeance.

Because of the time she and Gerhardt had spent training with Sir Roland, Nichol was accustomed to running from place to place. Her endurance had continued to grow. The slower pace of walking with two children had slowed her down.

I need to run …. I have not done so for days. I need to feel the wind in my face.

This morning, the air was brisk and a cold, drizzling rain fell. She tightened the cap on her head, put her mind in training mode and began running north on the main road. Running kept her warm. When she slowed, her walking was always at a brisk pace.

At one point, she came to a split in the road.

The road branching to the left looked well-traveled and the road to the right appeared to be a local road. It had tall grass growing between the deep wagon ruts. Choosing the well-traveled road, she slowed her pace and began to take in her surroundings. In the distance, she could see what looked like a good-sized forest on the right side of the road.

Once she reached it, she entered and stayed within line of sight of the road as she walked. She loved the forest's solitude where she was able to breathe calmly, reflect, and relax in nature's presence. Sensing that there was something more within the forest, she proceeded, as though she was protected.

She had but a few precious moments of serenity when something told her to look back. When she did, she saw a lone, motionless rider at the edge of the road, staring at her through the trees.

Fredric.

How could he be here? I took his horse and coin and left him in a drunken stupor. He must have stolen a horse to get this far. Will I ever be done with him?

Anger instead of fear was her first reaction; spite was her second. She was going to make him work for it if he wanted to try to catch her, and work was something he was not accustomed to doing.

"You there ... stop! I am looking for a young woman and will pay you for your help in finding her."

"Does she put worms in porridge?" she taunted him.

Fredric did not respond, narrowing his eyes as she spoke.

"Did she know that her brother was a drunk and spent all his coin on whores?" Nichol then reached inside the neck of her tunic, pulled out the cord that held both of her papa's rings and dangled them for him to see as she yelled, "I have both rings now … and Papa was right. You are a drunken fool!"

She could see the expected reaction on his face as soon as she spoke.

In answer, he spurred his horse and plunged into the forest, directly for her.

He would try to destroy her for taking what he thought was his.

Nichol turned and ran into a deep ravine, carved out by flowing water as Fredric pursued her. She scampered up a loose dirt bank, then disappeared into a dense thicket.

Fredric attempted to follow, kicking his horse hard to follow her path up the bank. The horse slipped, falling on its side and sliding down the bank. Fredric landed at the bottom on his back.

His horse righted itself and shook off the water from the splash it had taken. Drenched and covered in mud, Fredric got to his feet. He swore furiously as he scraped the mud from his face, not knowing where she had gone.

Hearing his outburst, Nichol could imagine what had happened and walked back to the top of the bank. At the sight of him covered in mud, she laughed and shouted at him, "How does it feel to be bested by a girl?"

He flashed a hate-filled glare at her.

"I know Astrid poisoned Papa and you probably knew about it. And I know you slaughtered my beautiful Shadow. Some day when you least expect it, I will do the same to you!"

Furious, Fredric screamed at her, "You poisoned Father and stole his gold!"

"Do not be stupid. I would never harm him. Nor would I steal from him. Only you would … or Astrid, to cover her secret.

Who would benefit more by his death ... me, or you and her? I gained nothing and I lost the only person who cared for me. We have the same mother … we do not have the same father.

"You can tell Astrid that one day she will turn around to find me standing behind her. Then I will avenge Papa's death."

"I am the first-born son and the true heir …."

"The only son you are is Astrid's bastard son. You are not the heir."

With that, she laughed, turned, and disappeared from his sight.

Fredric's anger exploded once again. *I will destroy her!*

Ignoring the horse, he attempted to climb the ravine's steep bank. After several attempts, he succeeded. He pulled his sword and, waving it about madly, yelled, "Come out and say that to my face, you whore!"

Buried deep in the thicket, she mocked in a sing-song voice, "Not today. I like making a fool out of you. I could use a good horse. Where are you staying? Maybe I will take yours. Or you could try to find me now. Can you see me? I can see you."

Scanning the thicket and trees in front of him, he could not see her at all. It was like she was invisible.

Giving up, he finally slid down the slope to retrieve his horse.

She will pay ….

thirty

The Gift of the Forest

Glancing around, she silently thanked the forest and its creatures for protecting her.

Nichol knew what Fredric would do next. She also knew that he was foolish enough to attempt to follow her. W*ith any luck, his horse would stumble on the undergrowth and throw him to the ground again.*

Turning away, she swiftly ran deep into the heart of the forest.

Distance was needed … as much as possible. Running, she was grateful once again for her training. Occasionally, she stopped to listen and she could hear Fredric thrashing about and cursing. Over time, the sounds became more distant and she could tell he was heading in the wrong direction.

Stopping for a moment, she determined that she had been heading north through the densest part of the forest for a long time. Finally, a clearing appeared that crossed the main road. Quickly, Nichol moved to the west side of the road and down a hill that led to the river and followed it.

After several minutes, she stopped to rest at the base of a huge pine tree. Sinking to the ground, she listened for any signs of Fredric.

Of danger.

Once again, bird calls and the chatter of forest creatures surfaced.

He is not nearby.

Relaxing for a moment, she felt the sense of calm surround her. Nichol took a few minutes to eat, drink, and think before moving on.

I have outsmarted him so far and I know he will not give up trying to capture me. He is a dangerous fool, and I must never underestimate him. One thing in my favor is he has no stamina, except for drinking and whoring. He will soon have to stop for the day. When he does, I will move on.

She smiled and shook her head at her next thought. *Today is the first time I have said the truth to him. Did he understand it? Did he even hear me?*

Refreshed, Nichol left some breadcrumbs on a log for her forest friends and rose. *I will continue through the forest on the river side. With the horse, Fredric will likely stay on the main road. The next tavern awaits him.*

She made her way through the dense groundcover beneath the trees until she could no longer safely see her path. Finally, it was time to stop for the night. Surveying her surroundings, she gathered fallen pine boughs and leaves and made a bed under a tall oak tree to sleep.

The cloak that Rose had given her comforted and warmed her as she layed back to look at the moon as its light shimmered through the branches.

Tomorrow morning, I will find the main road.

As she closed her eyes, a familiar voice entered her thoughts.

I am here. You are safe for now, but you must stay alert. That was her last thought before she fell into a deep sleep.

Nichol woke with a start and sat up.

"Another bad dream—this time Astrid was a serving wench in a tavern and she poured a vial of poison into my ale," she mumbled out loud.

Sitting quiet for a while, she listened to the sounds around her. *Nothing seems odd or out of place.* Reaching for her satchel, she found the bread, cheese, and dried meat that she had planned to eat before sleep overtook her.

As she nibbled, she began to reflect.

How did it all come to this? What would Papa do in this situation? I miss him; he knew so much and taught me so much. His favorite question to me was always, 'What did you learn today?'

There were so many lessons. There were lessons about dealing with fear and lessons about using good judgment and choosing the right course. I learned that I must defeat my own inner fear before I can defeat those who want to harm me—Fredric and Astrid. My hatred of both is consuming me.

I realize that neither of them can be underestimated, but I must focus my thoughts on my goal … reaching Paris and connecting with Ezra.

Now thinking forward, Nichol remembered Jericus saying that the next sizeable town on her route would be Montelimar. Pulling out the map Alexander had given her, she saw that Jericus was right. Glancing around, she silently thanked the forest and its creatures for protecting her and set out in search of the main road to Montelimar.

Instinctively she knew that if she followed the direction of the sunlight, she would soon be out of the forest. Not only was she now in full light of day, but she had finally found the main road she had been on yesterday. She was ready to go.

I hope Fredric is drunk and will not be on the road until later today.

As she ran, the sun grew stronger, and soon she was dripping wet with sweat. Knowing that the river paralleled the road on the west, she headed toward it.

Finding a spot where she could safely descend to river level and get a cooling drink, she slowly walked along the bank until she found a shallow pool formed by two huge rocks. Looking around to make sure she was alone, she dropped her satchel. Her first impulse was to jump into the river, but it was January and the water would be frigid.

Kneeling, she washed her face. Taking a deep breath, she stripped out of her garments and quickly moved into the water. Dipping into the river, she drenched her hair, washing her entire body in spite of the cold water.

Stunned by the chill, she was immediately alert. Moving out of the water, she grabbed her belongings to start warming up and climbed up the bank to the road, ready to head to Montelimar.

I need to run to warm my body once again.

As was her new habit, she alternated between a run and a walk. To keep her spirits up, she reflected on the people who were important in her life. With Gerhardt, she had grown up with him. They had played, laughed, learned, and trained together for years. She missed his companionship.

Rose had taught her the uses of spices, herbs, and elixirs. She remembered how kind and loving the older woman was to all the orphaned children she cared for.

Thoughts of Margaux drifted through her mind. Nichol missed her warm hugs and quiet musings. The servant had taught her how to cook and sew, read and write, and showered her with love and affection. She also protected Nichol from the wrath of Astrid when she could.

Her papa was the most important—the one she missed the most. She missed him and the talks they shared as they walked around the estate and the knowledge she learned from his dealings when she was behind the tapestry.

And she missed Shadow, always there.

Each will be part of my new life. All that they have taught me, I will use for myself and those who become my new family.

thirty-one

The Respite

Nichol kicked some straw into a pile at the back of the barn and collapsed.

Her thoughts halted when she heard voices. She dashed behind a huge tree that was off to her right and peeked around the tree to get a view of the source of the voices.

A group of travelers were heading south. Talking and laughing amongst themselves, she heard several different languages and dialects spoken by the travelers, similar to what she would hear on the docks and in Papa's solar in Marseilles.

There appeared to be no apparent danger as they passed her.

Craving conversation, her mind spoke up. *I would love to speak with them, but I am a stranger, as well as a female in disguise traveling alone. Most would be suspicious of a stranger. I cannot take that chance.*

She waited until they were long past her location before she got back on the road and resumed her northbound journey. As she ran, she was now in the open and passed an occasional farmhouse off in the distance.

There must be somewhere that I can find food.

At that moment, she felt a few drops of rain. Suddenly the clouds opened and a downpour ensued. There was not a nearby tree or a structure to use as shelter.

Quickly, the road became impassable; ruts filled with water. She spotted a cluster of pine trees in the distance and ran for their protection. Stopping under their canopies, Nichol caught her breath.

Soaked, her stomach gnawed at her. The hunger pangs increased … and at the same time, she felt sad and alone for the first time.

For a moment she started to feel sorry for herself and then forced her focus back on her goal ... Paris. She would not allow herself to think about anything else except getting to Paris and finding Ezra.

She drank from the last of the water from her waterskin and pulled out the remaining sliver of the hard crust of bread from her satchel. Holding it out for the rain to soften it, she said aloud, "I must find food and water soon."

With that, she moved from the protection of the trees and out onto the road, running briskly as the rain continued to fall.

Finally, the clouds separated and a blue sky appeared.

Nichol ran to rid herself of the chill the rain had brought. As she rounded a bend, a farmhouse could be seen in the distance.

Is it worth taking a chance to ask for food?

As she drew closer to the house, a woman was in the yard. Her stomach again gnawed at her; this time louder.

Reaching for a coin in her purse, she approached, the coin visible in her hand.

Startled at Nichol's presence, the woman demanded, "What do you want?"

"Only food, if you have some I could purchase."

"Stay where you are."

The woman turned toward the farmhouse. A few moments later, she returned with a bowl of broth and two thick slices of fresh bread.

Nichol, hungrier than ever, devoured some of the bread and broth without taking a breath. When she was finished, she smiled at the woman, handed her the empty bowl with one hand, and with the other, handed her the copper coin. Thanking her for her kindness, she turned to leave.

"You look as though you could use a good night's sleep. Gather up your things and come with me. The barn will keep you safe and warm for the night."

In that instant, Nichol decided that she would be safe with this woman and followed her to the barn. They had barely gotten inside when the woman's husband and two sons appeared.

"Who is this?" the husband challenged.

"Just a young peasant asking for food. For a coin, I gave him some bread and broth. He is weary. I told him he could sleep in the barn."

"You can stay the night. Most travelers just steal from us and disappear," he muttered. The farmer directed his wife and sons out of the barn and swung the doors closed.

In the quiet, Nichol took in the space. With her eyes half-closed, she took off the wet cloak and laid it out to dry. Then she burrowed into the straw, using it as the only dry blanket she had. Too tired to finish the bread she had saved, her day ended.

After she awoke the next morning, she lay quietly in the straw. Finally, she sat up and brushed the straw from her hair and clothes and reached into her satchel for the last piece of bread. Rising and refreshed, she walked slowly to the barn doors and opened them ever so slightly as she ate it. Gathering her things, Nichol saw the woman and approached her.

"Thank you for feeding me and letting me stay here."

Nodding, the woman handed Nichol a small package. In it was a slice of fresh bread and cheese. Accepting it with a smile, she bid the woman farewell and headed up the dirt road.

She stopped when she reached the main road and looked back for a final glimpse of her short respite. A soft thank-you slipped from her lips, meant for the family who showed her such kindness.

A smile rose on her face as she remembered her papa. He had been charitable when he was asked for help. Another lesson learned. People were responsive when they were compensated for their resources, as this family had been with shelter and food.

Life is good, she thought. She was grateful for the bounty the woman at the farmhouse had shared with her.

Now I have enough food to last the day's travel.

thirty-two

The Inn at the Top

I feel protected. Other travelers will not think to look up.

Throughout the day, she ran, walked, and rested when she needed food or water. By midmorning, she found a tavern along the road to refill her wine sack and buy food to fill her pack.

Montelimar should be close.

Leaving the tavern, she headed into the quiet of the forest to rest and eat. Studying her map, the town of Valence was at least a two-day journey. Seeking a spot on the river side of the road, she hid her belongings and dipped into the water to wash her hands and face.

Refreshed once again, she took a moment to settle in and absorb the beauty that surrounded her. It was a breathtaking winter landscape. Again, she set out for the road, heading north. Valence would be her next stop.

With daylight fading, a safe place to stop for the day was needed. Once again, the forest offered the safe haven she was looking for. She spent the night and listened to the choir of owls nestled in the trees as she settled under the boughs of a massive pine and fell into a deep sleep.

Heading to the river as soon as she awoke, she filled her waterskin. *Today would be a full day of running.*

Doubting she would see anyplace that would have ale, she filled her wineskin with water as well. Grimacing at the frigid water, she thought of the villa, remembering the warm baths she enjoyed. *Someday, I will once again sink my body into a warm body of water.*

Fredric can come out of anywhere was her thought as she climbed the riverbank to transition into her running gait. Being constantly aware of who or what was ahead or behind her as she ran, she reminded herself to keep a keen eye on the surroundings on either side of the road.

I must stay alert at all times.

As Nichol passed small groups of travelers on the road, she acknowledged them with a smile and a nod, never lingering or engaging in conversation. She did not want to give anyone the opportunity to fully describe her or pick up on her dialect in case they crossed paths with Fredric, especially now that he knew that her looks had changed.

It was well past midday and she reached Valence earlier than expected because she had not slowed her pace all day. The sun was low in the sky as she strolled slowly, taking in all the sights and sounds of the quaint little village.

She found an inn where she could rest and replenish her food supplies. Purchasing food and filling her wineskin, she set out to explore a bit more.

After exploring the marketplace, it was not long before she realized how tired she was. Running at a steady pace for the last two and a half days had worn her down. Treating herself to a quiet, peaceful, and protected night's rest at the inn sounded very welcoming.

The next morning, she rose before sunrise and gathered her things and left. Today would be a run-walk day. Her sacks were full of ale and water and she had a goodly supply of food.

Before she knew it, she was moving at a rapid pace. At day's end, she once again sought a safe place to spend the night and found a cluster of pine trees. Instead of piling under the branches, her eyes scanned upward.

This is perfect. I will climb up. Then I can see what passes below me.

Once she was settled onto a perch that had many branches together and was broad enough to hold her, Nichol stretched out and marveled at her view.

I feel protected. Other travelers will not think to look up. Fredric would not.

Feasting on her bread, cheese, and dried venison, she tied her satchel to an adjacent branch and turned herself around so she could use the satchel as a pillow. With her belt, she lashed herself to the branch she was on and bade good night to all of creation.

Nichol was exhausted and thankful that her day had been pleasantly uneventful. Wrapping her cloak around her as she closed her eyes, a light … the light … surrounded her.

She heard a familiar voice—the voice of her *Lady.*

When you are quiet, and the time is right, you will hear me.

Finally, she asked, "Who are you, really? And why are you speaking to me?"

I have been with you for some time now. I chose you. Think of me as your inner spirit ... a trusted guide that will share options to events as they unfold. Right now, you are on the right path. You are safe here. Sleep now.

The squawking of birds roused her from a deep sleep at sunrise. A smile settled on her lips.

The Lady ... my Lady ... was with me last night. I trusted her to come to me. To be with me.

Wanting to keep the peace with her animal friends, Nichol untied her belt and satchel, gathered her belongings, and clambered down the tree. When she reached ground level and looked back up to where she had been, she thanked the tree for protecting her as she slept.

Absorbing the sights and sounds around her, she noticed a pair of rabbits scampering toward the roadway. The slight frost on the limbs created a picturesque scene as she took in the area.

Stretching her arms and legs, she tied her satchel to her side and began to run. Still feeling her evening meal with her, she would eat later after her body was warmed and hunger announced itself.

As she did, her thoughts turned to her satchel. *I need to figure a better way to carry it so it does not bounce at my side.*

Her next stop would be Vienne. On the map Alexander had given her, he had noted that Vienne was a monastery where she could find food and possibly shelter. To denote this, he had added a small square to the map.

My Papa was amazing … everything on this map has been true. The map she had with her was fully accurate in its directions and detail.

The road Nichol had been traveling on since leaving Marseilles was created by the Roman army over six hundred years earlier and had withstood the test of time. Worn and rutted in parts, it was still the main road used by travelers. The map showed the Rhone River on the far west side and was bordered by forest land on both sides.

Yes, she was traveling on this secret journey all alone, but so far, it was a journey to save her life, a life that had changed drastically in the two weeks since her papa had died and everything had been turned upside down. She missed Gerhardt and his companionship and wished he were with her now.

Despite her memories and momentary pangs of loneliness, Nichol reminded herself of her primary goal … to get to Paris and Ezra.

thirty-three

The Voice Again

Hello Nichol … I am with you.

Nichol was amazed to see that the sun had almost peaked at the point of midday. Her growing belly pains reminded her that she needed to eat. As was her new practice, she turned into the forest on her right and settled in behind a large pine. Basking in the sunlight, she nibbled on bread and cheese and sipped on her waterskin until she felt ready to start once again.

Margaux and Rose's last words, "Always be on alert … stay to yourself," flowed through her mind and into her eyes and ears as she picked up her running pace.

There were not many travelers on the road from the time she climbed down from her sleeping place. As evening approached, she knew it was time to stop, eat a bit more bread and cheese, and sleep. The afternoon had brought darkening clouds and a chill that promised a cold night.

Entering the forest to her right, Nichol walked amongst the huge pines. One beckoned to her as if saying: *Come to me; I will protect you.*

Smiling, she moved to the tree and cautiously ascended until she knew that she had her spot. Huge sweeping branches promised support, comfort, and protection from the cold wind that was picking up. Unwelcome eyes would not be able to see her, even if they looked up.

What she thought was a light drizzle of rain was not.

Holding her hand out, tiny snowflakes appeared on her palm.

Thankful that she had had another peaceful day, she settled in and secured herself to a thick branch. *No wonder I am cold.*

Suddenly the wind began to swirl, forcing her to hold on tightly with her belt to the limb as the pine swayed and danced throughout the night, while snow started to layer on the branches. As a result, fitful sleep followed, filled with vivid dreams.

The dreams surrendered to a calming soft light. It was then the voice came to her in her stillness. She seemed to sense the presence of her *Lady.*

Looking down, she saw the ground covered with an unmarked white coat. Not wanting to descend yet, she chose to lie still and simply listen to her surroundings.

Would the Lady still be with me? Maybe it was just the wind and my head is playing a trick on me.

Now she heard the voice clearly.

Yes, I am with you.

"Usually, I hear you in my dreams. That was when I was in Marseilles, before Papa died."

You are right. And I know he was poisoned and Fredric destroyed Shadow. It is now your time.

Quietly, Nichol absorbed what she heard. What she felt. And then a smile spread across her face. She was not alone: it was her time. *But what does that mean?*

Nichol, it is time for you to set out again. The sky is clear, as is the road. The fallen snow will melt and quench your thirst.

Speaking aloud, she murmured, "Thank you … you are now my *Lady* of the Light."

Untying her belt from the big branch, she carefully climbed down, shaking the snow off the branches as she lowered herself. Breathing deeply, she pulled the frosty air into her lungs as her eyes embraced the dawn.

As she took bread from her bag to chew on, Nichol started a slow, reflective walk, noting that the snow was not deep as she moved forward. She emptied her waterskin and added melting snow to refill it, and then sealed the opening. The road beckoned to her as she gradually picked up her pace. Before long, she was in a full run.

Overwhelmed with what had unfolded on her pine limb and the sudden appearance of the snow, she found that she was skipping and dancing along the road between stretches of running. She was genuinely happy, something she had not felt for some time.

As the sun drew higher in the sky, she knew it was midday, but she did not want to stop. Her body and her mind felt nothing but joy. She was not alone! Her *Lady* was with her.

As she ran, she remembered that when she and Gerhardt were running to and from Sir Roland's camp, they would chant sayings that they adapted to their pace. It helped them stay focused.

Today as she ran, she started piecing together phrases that would become her new chant, one that would keep her mind on her goal of reaching Paris.

After working it through, she finally settled on a saying that she sang out loud:

I am on my way to Paris, in many towns in many days.
That is where my future lies, my papa planned it that way.

She smiled at her craftiness in finding a saying that was in keeping with her goal and her pace. Singing it over and over throughout the day, the words became her mantra for all the days of her journey forward.

Vienne and the Monastery

In her mind, she could see the encounter unfolding.

Toward late afternoon, she realized there must be a village up ahead, as she had passed many people on the road late in the day. *I must be approaching Vienne.*

Even though she was walking, her walk was faster than most. Within a short time, she found herself behind a group of men, women, and children who were also heading north. Nichol attached herself to the group as they approached the monastery, so as not to appear as a lone traveler. Mingling at the back of the group with two of the women, she learned that the town they were approaching was indeed called Vienne.

"It is where we stay at night when we travel through here to Lyon," one of the women revealed.

The other quickly added, "There's a fair we attend, where we sell some of our goods."

Nichol absorbed what they were saying.

Then the first woman said, "It has a monastery that provides food and shelter to travelers and those who could not afford to stay at an inn …."

"... but they will demand coin if they believe you could pay," the other added.

This is interesting, thought Nichol.

"If you do not mind, can I walk with you until we reach the monastery? I have never been inside one before. Having food and shelter would be welcome."

"Yes ... what is your name, boy?"

She hesitated. *No one has asked me my name since I left the caravan.* "I am called Nick."

When they reached the gates of the monastery grounds, they were escorted by two monks to a long, low building that was connected to the southern wall of the monastery.

Nichol's eyes widened as she entered an oversized dimly-lit great room. Down the middle of it stretched a series of long tables with benches on either side. Along the walls at floor level, straw had been laid out.

One of the monks turned to them. "Women, you and the boy should select a sleeping location while there are a few still available. Deposit your belongings in the same place."

Thanking him, the two women moved toward a wall with open space. Nichol held back. Turning to her, one of the women said, "Nick, bring your things over here."

She followed the two women. Before she could drop her things, two men quickly grabbed the spot. At the same time, one of the monks called out, "Food will be served as soon as we determine how many people need to be fed."

This was all new to Nichol. She had no idea that monks or monasteries took care of the less fortunate. She was impressed, but wary.

Still looking for a place to put her bags, she decided her preference would be close to the entry door for sleeping. Thanking the women, she turned back toward where they came in and spied a place that would suit her by an elderly couple who she thought posed little danger.

She dropped her travel bags in the straw and turned to the center of the room to the tables where food would be served. Acting like she was traveling with the elderly couple who sat close to the end of the table, she asked if she could sit next to them.

The woman looked at Nichol and asked innocently, "Where are you going? You are all alone. It is not wise for a young one such as yourself to travel alone."

This was the type of talk Nichol wanted to avoid. She did not want to lie to anyone, but she had to create a plausible story and stick to it. Smiling at the woman, she replied, "I got separated from my group heading to Lyon. If I walk fast enough, I think I will meet them soon."

This was not a total lie. Nichol knew she would eventually travel through Lyon on her way to Paris. Smoothly she changed the subject to the old woman. "I see that you two are traveling together. Where are you going?"

"Yes, Herve and I come to the fair here in Vienne every year. We have done it since the first year we were married. We live a day's travel from here. The fair starts tomorrow. Are you going? My name is Bertrada. What is yours?"

Nichol noticed that the monks were beginning to place bowls on the tables. Hastily, she said, "Yes, I will be going to the fair tomorrow. It will be my first time at the fair in Vienne. My name is Nick ... and I am starving," as a monk placed several bowls on the table.

She was thankful for the distraction the food brought. There were over forty people gathered around the tables and all of them were hungry. Large bowls of stew filled with rabbit, carrots, turnips, and onion were served with brown bread and ale. *This is my first warm food since leaving Marseilles.*

The hungry people around the table praised the monks for their skills in growing and harvesting their own crops. Listening to the conversation, Nichol learned the monks' reputation for farming was known everywhere. They sold their produce at the fair every year and at the local marketplace. The proceeds from those sales helped the monks maintain the monastery and also to feed the many travelers who stopped for shelter.

The contents of the bowls disappeared almost as quickly as they were served. People stood in groups, talking softly. One by one, they started drifting in the direction of their straw locations.

Nichol went to her own patch of straw, lifted her satchel, sat down and leaned back against the wall. Herve and Bertrada did the same next to her. "What is behind the walls of the large building attached to this room?" Nichol asked.

"It is the monastery where the monks live and pray. It is also where nobles and other clerics stay when they travel through these parts. This room is for the poor. It is called the longhouse. It is not as nice as the monastery where the nobles stay, but these monks are very hospitable to the poor, unlike most that we have come across in our travels. We are fortunate to have stopped here for the night."

Nichol sighed deeply, relaxed against the wall, closed her eyes, and listened to the conversations swirling around her.

From her time on the docks in Marseilles, and throughout her travels so far, she had overheard and could mimic the slang and languages of the people she met. She seemed to have a special talent for listening to and creating a mental profile of the speaker.

As she sat there, she closed her heavy eyes. Immediately, she felt that she was back in Papa's solar. She could sense him. She could hear his voice.

Even though she knew it was a dream, in her mind, she could see the encounter unfolding. She was recalling the first time the Bishop of Marseilles made an unannounced visit.

The meeting was not going well. After listening to several minutes of demands, Alexander chastised the bishop for taking grain and livestock from the peasants in the way of tithes. He reminded the bishop that the poor depended on their grain and livestock for their survival in the winter, and they could not give away their sustenance to support the bishop's comfortable lifestyle.

The bishop protested, saying that he promised the peasants eternal glory if they gave everything the church asked of them, and implied eternal damnation if they did not.

Alexander had heard enough. He did not believe the eternal damnation story and said that to the bishop.

"Would you, Bishop, experience eternal damnation for abusing your power and position in the church and for not following your sacred vows of poverty, chastity, and obedience? I have heard many stories that would show you in an unflattering light to all."

The bishop was seething with anger as he grabbed his miter from Alexander's table and positioned it on his head. His tone threatening, he snarled, "You have not seen the last of me," and stormed out of the villa.

Her papa's voice was clear. Every one of her senses could hear and feel it.

Lisa, the bishop is a powerful and dangerous man. You need to stay very alert—his wrath can come for you from many directions.

Mumbling in her dozed state, Nichol woke and looked around. Had anyone heard her? Seeing everyone around her still sleeping, she layed back down on the straw.

She whispered to herself, "Now, Papa is dead and I am sleeping on the stone floor of a monastery with strangers. Could the bishop and his church have succeeded after all?" Again, she fell into a deep and disturbing sleep.

Nichol was startled awake by a voice close to her. Sitting up, she drew the dagger from her belt and prepared to defend herself. To her relief, no one was near her except Bertrada, and she was sound asleep.

Still, she was certain she had heard someone whispering close to her.

Is this a warning?

She lay back against the wall of the monastery, her satchel with her dagger hidden in her right hand and drifted back to sleep, reminding herself *I must stay alert.*

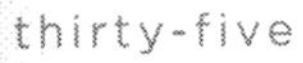

thirty-five

The Fair

I hope you will be satisfied with everything you have chosen.

Nichol woke to an overcrowded room of travelers. In the dim candlelight, she could see that many more people had arrived during the night. Bodies were everywhere, and the stench of body odor was overwhelming.

Collecting her satchel, she rose, and carefully stepped over slumbering bodies sleeping by the doorway and made her way out of the longhouse. The sun was beginning to rise as she got outside. Seeking the bench she remembered seeing at the front gate of the monastery, she sat down.

Based on what she had learned the night before, there would be plenty of food and ale sold at the fair. This fair was not the spring or summer fair; it was a winter fair to provide to those who had not enough to last the winter and also to provide people of the area with needed income by selling their wares. She decided she would see what they had to offer, make her purchases, and be on her way.

As the sun rose higher in the morning sky, people began to congregate outside the monastery, excited for the start of the fair. She recognized the two women she had met the day before and joined them as they headed to the entrance to the fair.

When they reached the fair, they were met by a magical sight. There were minstrels wandering, jugglers tossing brightly colored balls, corrals of baby goats for children to play with, and food vendors as far as the eye could see. The aromas that began to waft from the displays reminded her she had not eaten since the night before.

A large crowd surrounded the blue and white tent in the center of the fair. Under it were the monks where they displayed their array of vegetables and grains.

One of the key attractions was a selection of wines the monks had produced from the grapes in their vineyards. Nichol noticed several monks inside the tent who described every product grown at the monastery. Each explained how every item was sown, grown, harvested and how it could be used in cooking.

As she listened and watched, she realized that they were masters at selling their products. At the same time, they were teaching the buyers how to grow crops like they did in their own fields.

I wonder why the merchants in Marseilles did not explain their goods this way?

Nichol heard a name she knew. It was Brother Lemur, one of the monks who had served the evening meal the previous night. This morning, he was describing how and when to plant turnips, when to harvest, and how to use them in cooking.

Nichol was fascinated by all that she saw at the fairgrounds. She walked from stall to stall, sampling and evaluating the foods and beverages she would purchase when she set out once again. When she had seen and tasted enough, she went back to the tent where Brother Lemur was tending to patrons.

She selected dried fish, roasted mutton, various dried vegetables, fresh brown bread and a small pot of golden honey. She filled her waterskin with a delicious white wine that he recommended.

He wrapped her food selections in clean squares of cloth and tied each package with twine. He handed them to her with a gentle smile and said, "Thank you for your patronage. I hope you will be satisfied with everything you have chosen." He told Nichol the total cost of her purchases, folded his hands together, and stepped back.

Nichol was amazed at the paltry sum he had requested. She handed him double that amount, and nodded polite thanks. "You are to be admired for all that you do here in Vienne. You are masterful growers as well as winemakers. Your care for weary travelers is also noted and appreciated. Good day to you."

Surprised with what she said, and how much she had given him with the coin now in his hand, he watched her leave the fairgrounds and walk to the main road.

Hmm, I do not think that boy is a peasant, he thought to himself.

Nichol turned north and decided to walk the rest of the day. Her constant running day after day had exhausted her. She decided to make Lyon a two-day journey.

Moving forward at a slower pace would be a form of rest.

thirty-six

Maurice

God wants you to walk with us.

Having surveyed her map before leaving the fairgrounds, Nichol knew which way she would be traveling to reach Lyon.

Slowly walking, she chanted her new mantra as she progressed on the road:

> *I am on my way to Paris, in many villages in many days.*
>
> *That is where my future lies, my papa planned it that way.*

She approached a slow-moving group ahead covering the entire width of the road, and she decided to run past them. Nichol picked up her pace and started around them when a slow-moving old man in the last group chirped a good morning to her from the small wagon he walked behind.

Shortly after that, a mounted rider went by her, shouting at her to move off the road. She turned around just in time to see three more riders on the road behind her. One of them was a bishop, the other a priest.

As she waited at the side of the road for the riders to pass, the old man and his group pulled off the road and stopped next to her, leaving just enough room for the bishop and priest to get by.

As the riders passed the huddled group, Nichol caught a glimpse of one and recognized him immediately. *He was in my dream last night. He was the bishop that Papa was angry at in the solar!*

His beady eyes and big crooked nose that flared like the wings of a bat when he was upset had been imbedded in her memory when she observed the confrontation with her papa. The man was short and round and talked with a whiny, annoying voice.

A quick glance at the priest startled Nichol for a second time. He looked like the priest Loupe that also visited Papa.

At that moment, the old man standing next to her waved his arms at the bishop and yelled, "Your Excellency … God wants you to walk with us. Come join us in our journey."

Shocked, Nichol gulped and held her breath. *What was this old man thinking by addressing the bishop in this manner?*

She did not have to wait long to find out. The guard at the rear veered toward the old man, shoved his boot in his chest, and knocked him to the ground.

Nichol knelt next to him and gathered him in her arms, checking him for injuries, as his traveling companions encircled the two of them.

Blinking his eyes, the old man looked up at Nichol and asked, "Are you an angel? Am I dead? Was I struck by God or just the bishop's guard?"

She chuckled and said, "No, I am not an angel and you are not dead. And yes, you were knocked to the ground by the bishop's guard after you yelled out to him to walk with us rather than riding. Are you hurt?"

"I have been kicked harder. I am all right. I see that my request to the bishop had no effect on him."

Nichol helped him to his feet. He stood shorter than she, and was thin and frail in appearance. She was amazed that someone this old and small would show such defiance. Leading him to the shade of a tree, she offered him some of the wine she had purchased that morning.

He took a long drink and handed the skin back to her. "You are both brave and generous. You must be careful as you travel. If you fall or get hurt, people will pick you clean like buzzards on a dead rabbit."

"Are you able to continue on with your companions?" Nichol asked.

The old man thought for a moment. "No. I think I will rest here for a while. Would you tell the others that I will remain here? Let them know they should continue on."

Nichol was torn. She could not leave this old man alone to fend for himself. Yet, if she stayed to tend to him, she would delay her own journey. Walking back to the road where his group stood, she relayed the old man's request and waited while they discussed the matter.

A young man who appeared to be the leader of the group turned to her. "We cannot leave without him. We will travel north only as far as we can find a safe place to pull our wagon off the road. There, we will rest and wait for him to get his wits about him. Will you stay with him while we look for a clearing?"

In that instant, Nichol committed herself to stay with the old man. Something had tugged at her heart when she had first ministered to him. She felt a bond she could not explain. Nodding, she said, "Yes, I will stay with him. When he is strong enough to travel, we will come and find you."

Nichol returned to the old man and told him the decision his companions had made. He shook his head and smiled, as if he already knew what it was.

"I am hungry. Would you like to eat with me?"

He looked at her with regret. "I have no food to share with you."

"I have enough for both of us." Pulling packets out of her satchel, she divided the food into portions for the two of them.

This old man is different from the other people I have met on the road so far. I want to know more about him.

Encouraging him to talk about his recent travels, Nichol asked him where his group was heading. They had conducted a lighthearted conversation for several minutes when the old man stopped speaking and looked directly at Nichol.

"You are not who you appear to be. Your words are not those of a peasant or a servant … nor are your hands. You are a young woman, yet you are dressed in the garb of a boy and you are traveling by yourself. Why?"

Nichol felt trapped, afraid she had betrayed her new identity. She smiled at him. "Are you not doing the same thing, traveling by yourself? Perhaps you can explain who you are and what brings you to these parts."

To her surprise, the old man said, "My name is Maurice, and I knew your father. I saw you a few months ago when I was visiting Alexander. Even though you have changed your appearance, I recognize you now."

Nichol's heart thumped in her chest. Now she understood why she felt a bond with this man. "Yes, of course. I remember you. You gathered information for Papa about potential attacks the bishop was going to wage against him." She looked down and clasped her hands in her lap. "You know he is dead," she said quietly.

"Yes, I am aware. How did he die?"

"Astrid poisoned him. She wanted everything Papa had worked so hard his entire life for herself and for my horrible brother Fredric."

Strangely, she felt relieved. This was the most honest Nichol had been with anyone since she had left Marseilles.

"I am saddened that Alexander is gone and that he died at the hands of your mother. People like him are targets for men who think they are better than everyone else. He challenged their power, their authority, and their way of thinking. That's why the bishop started rumors and tried to attack him. He felt threatened by your father and had to show him who held the bigger sword.

"I am very tired now. Stay with me while I rest. When I wake, I will share information that may prove valuable for you." Maurice's head dropped to his chest and he was asleep. His breathing became shallow and labored and Nichol feared the worst.

There is so much about this man that is a mystery. I wonder what information he wants to share with me.

Hours passed and Maurice had not wakened. Nichol looked closely and realized he did not appear to be breathing. She lifted his chin, listened for sounds of life, and knew he was gone.

The kick to his chest had been a death blow. The guard had killed him.

Loneliness and grief overcame her. Nichol lowered his head and began to weep. For a few brief moments, he had been a connection back to her old life, a life with Papa. She would never hear the details he was going to share with her.

She wept for Maurice, for her papa, and she wept for herself.

It seemed an eternity before she was again aware of her surroundings. Through tear-filled eyes, she saw blue skies, felt the warmth of the sun, and heard birds chirping all around her. She knew what she had to do next.

Searching his clothing for valuables, she was amazed to find four copper coins loosely sewn inside the collar of his cloak. As she dislodged the coins from their hiding place, a tiny green gem dropped into her hand.

The gem that gleamed up at her was the type Alexander gave to all the people who brought information to him. It was his way of showing his appreciation. At that moment, Nichol felt Papa was with her and watching over her on her journey. She smiled in silent gratitude, put the gem in her purse, and stacked the coins on her satchel.

Nichol took Maurice's cloak from around his shoulders and covered him with it. Pulling together some fallen pine boughs, she piled them on top of him.

Gathering the coins, she packed the remains of the food into her satchel, hoisted it onto her back, and slowly walked to the road.

When she reached the entry point to the road, Nichol saw several multicolored stones lying in the grass. She laid them out in the shape of an arrow pointing toward Maurice's body and then started on her way to find his companions and tell them what had happened.

Recognizing Maurice's group with their wagon, she approached the campsite and found the young man she had spoken with earlier and motioned him away from the others.

"Maurice died from the kick by the bishop's guard. You will find his body covered in pine branches. I placed stones in the shape of an arrow near the edge of the road that will direct you to his body."

Nichol expressed her sympathies at Maurice's passing and turned to leave. Remembering the coins in her hand, she walked back and gave them to the group leader. "I found these coins when I removed Maurice's cloak to cover him. I am sure he would want you to have them."

The young man looked at her in disbelief. "I am grateful for your honesty. You could have kept the coins for yourself. No one else knew Maurice had them."

Knowing that she had the tiny green gem in the purse close to her heart, she added, "Maurice spoke highly of you when we were talking. It is only fair that you should have the coins."

The young man smiled. "Maurice died as he had lived … bold and unabashed. He always spoke his mind and was never afraid. Thank you for caring for him. We will go immediately and retrieve his body."

"I must be on my way."

Satisfied that Maurice's companions would see to him, Nichol walked slowly and deliberately on her way back to the road.

She was angry, sad, and she felt terribly alone. With her head hanging down, she talked to herself as she walked.

Why did I ever promise Papa that I would go to Paris? How did I ever think I could complete such a journey by myself? What will happen next? The only person I know is me, just me.

Immediately, Nichol took off running and did not stop until her sides were heaving.

thirty-seven

The Attack

I cannot keep running. I must defend myself.

Nichol ran for the better part of the afternoon, until her exhaustion crept in. She began searching for a secluded place to stop.

Just as she reached the crest of a hill, she came upon a group of travelers in front of her. She started to pass them on their left side when a man from the group shouted, "Come join us!"

She simply waved to them and continued.

Just as she was about to pass them, a man emerged from the group and grabbed her right arm. His wicked laugh and that of the man next to him as they both attempted to wedge her between them alarmed her.

Pulling her arm free, she turned her head to see who had grabbed her. What she saw sent chills down her spine. He leered at her with a nasty smile full of black teeth and his unwashed body emitted a repelling stench.

Pulling all her energy, she broke free and took off at a heart-pounding pace, gasping for air, fists clenched. The encounter with Black Teeth took her back to the day Fredric dragged her by her hair to the Anchor Inn.

Coming upon a small stream that trickled next to the road, Nichol bent to wash her face and hands to get the stranger's stench out of her nose. Stepping away from the stream, she gathered her things, and felt for the dagger at her side. She found a place to rest out of sight of the road and rested against an oak tree.

As she calmed herself by slowing her breathing, she fell asleep.

Startled awake when she heard voices nearby, Nichol stayed out of sight to see who was approaching. What she saw was the group she had passed earlier, led by the two men who grabbed her. The travelers stopped at the stream to rest and fill their wineskins. The two men stood with their backs to Nichol, unaware she was watching them.

Someone from the group noticed her and pointed in her direction. Turning toward her, Black Teeth and his companion broke away from the group and moved toward her.

Standing, Nichol backed against the tree so they could only come at her from one direction. One hand on her hidden dagger, she glared at Black Teeth as he approached.

Laughing his wicked laugh, he sneered, "I felt something young boys do not have when I grabbed you on the road. Let me see what you are hiding under that tunic!"

Her aggressive stare caught him off guard and she saw a look of intimidation cross his face. His cruel companion joined him and, side by side, they continued moving toward her.

Her breathing steady, Nichol continued to maintain her stare. Inside, her mind was shouting, *which one of you wants to die first?*

Shoving each other to get to her, Black Teeth arrived first, and stood face-to-face with her. His leering black grin surfaced again. "I will go first." He reached out with both hands to haul her in.

With feet planted solidly and knees bent to spring, Nichol lashed out with her left hand to grab the knife she saw beneath his belt. At the same time, she pulled her dagger from her belt and thrust it into his belly.

He looked down in disbelief at the dagger protruding from his midsection.

As Nichol yanked her dagger free, Black Teeth stumbled backward, reaching for the knife beneath his belt. But it was not there. Nichol held it up for him to see with a look of satisfied revenge.

Black Teeth caught his balance and lunged at her again. She sidestepped and as he fell past her, she reached out, slashing his neck. A pulsating stream of blood flowed from the wound as he fell to the ground. He tried to stand, but with the look on his face, Nichol knew his death was near at hand.

Without emotion, she watched as he collapsed to the ground, mortally wounded.

With heart pounding at fever pitch, in that moment, Nichol was ready to take on any man who was willing to test his manly strength against her female determination.

Turning, she growled at his companion, holding up both daggers for him to see. "Now, it is your turn."

Black Teeth's accomplice had watched the assault in total disbelief.

"I killed your companion faster than a hawk can snatch a snake. Are you next?" she snarled.

Shaking his head frantically, he yelled, "You must be a witch! I want no part of you!" Panicked, he disappeared, running into the forest.

Calling Nichol a witch caught the attention of the onlookers and they began chattering amongst themselves.

"Why would he call the boy a witch?"

"He cannot be a girl."

"We have never seen a boy act like him before."

"We have never seen a boy defeat a man."

"Where did he learn to fight like that?"

Nichol ignored their questions and comments as she walked to the stream to wash the blood from her hands, clothes, and weapons.

Reaction set in and she began to shake as she washed the blood away. *I never thought I would kill anyone. I never imagined Sir Roland's lessons would save my life from evil men. I feel justified.*

Hearing a hawk screech, she looked up to see one circling just above her, one with a red tail. *Thank you, Papa, for protecting me.*

Taking several deep breaths to calm her nerves, she left the stream and walked up to where the witnesses to Black Teeth's death stood in a huddle. All eyes were on the dagger in her hand. She approached a young woman standing at the front of the group.

Handing Black Teeth's knife to her, she stated calmly, "I am not a witch. I was trained to protect myself by my father. Take this knife. You never know when you might be caught alone and be threatened or attacked by bad men like the ones you are with. Keep it for your own protection."

Leaving the group standing there in disbelief, Nichol gathered her belongings and headed to the road.

Nichol was exhausted. Life as a single female traveler was filled with surprise and danger, and she had enough of both for one day.

Finally coming upon a dense section of the forest, she turned toward it, letting the massive trees welcome and envelope her. Immediately, she felt more at ease. Scanning her surroundings, she found a large pine tree to call home for the night. Her tired body desperately needed sleep.

Without a second thought, she jumped to one of the lowest branches and began climbing. She ascended until she found four limbs that were close together. Collectively, they fanned out to create a perch wide enough fto hold her body for her to sleep on. Securing herself to a branch with her belt, she searched through her satchel for something to eat.

Thinking back over the day's events, she murmured aloud, "Today could have been my last day if not for Papa and Sir Roland. Oh, my, death ruled this day." Shivering as she wrapped herself in her cloak, she put her head on her satchel. Closing her eyes, she took three long breaths and fell asleep.

Vivid dreams and the increasing cold penetrated her cloak and clothes. She woke shaking. Pulling the cloak tighter around her body, she thought, *I hope tomorrow will be better.*

Suddenly, a wave of warmth settled upon her, calming her quaking body. A voice followed … the *Lady* ... her *Lady.*

There will be other bad men on your journey. And there will be kind ones as well. Always be on alert, as you were today. You did well to protect yourself and the other women.

A smile crossed her face as she welcomed the sleep that settled in at last.

Can it be morning already? I am safe and dry here, and I did not fall out of the tree. I can see the frost on all the trees, yet I am warm. All is good.

Nichol reached for her bag, removing bread and a skin filled with water. She was in no hurry to leave.

Sitting in her nest high above the ground, she soaked in all of nature's beauty. She imagined the leaves on the bare trees and the bushes beneath them, all waiting for spring to show their beauty.

She watched a rabbit try to hide, staying motionless. The reason was soon clear. A red fox appeared and the rabbit started to run, but the fox was faster.

Nichol heard a shriek and knew the fox had captured its meal.

She knew it was nature's way, but she had seen and heard enough. It was time to leave. Before climbing down, she paused for a moment. Looking up and out, she said aloud, "Thank you for covering me with your warmth last night."

Climbing down from her secluded spot, she patted the pine tree that had held her in its safe embrace all night. Whispering the customary appreciation she gave to her surroundings, she set out on her journey.

Yet, as she looked about her environment, something felt different … nothing looked familiar. What happened last night? *This does not feel like the place I turned off the road.*

As she neared the road, she stood behind a large tree to survey who or what might be around her. Satisfied that she was alone, she left the tree and waded through the tall grass lining the road.

I do not remember this grass being this tall. Leaving the grass and stepping to the edge of the road, she looked up and down in bewilderment.

Where am I? She fell to her knees and covered her face. *What is happening to me? How did I get to a place I do not recognize?*

Pausing in thought, she pulled her hands from her face and turned them over.

These are my hands, but they look different. I feel different. Standing, she slowly turned around. A broad smile crept across her face as excitement overwhelmed her.

I see trees and their individual leaves and blades of grass in the field. I see clearly what will be there, the color that will come as spring comes forward.

The Lady … my dreams! her head shouted to her. Then a wave of calm flowed through her. The *Lady* has given me a gift ... a gift that will enable me to sense my surroundings in a way that I never could before.

Taking her first steps on the road forward, her legs quickly moved to a full run. Words started flowing from her mouth in a song ….

I am on my way to Paris, in many villages, in many days.
That is where my future lies, my papa planned it that way.

thirty-eight

The Lone Traveler

Trust your instincts. You have read the man's demeanor. What have you learned?

I*s that a traveler I see in the distance?*

It was … a lone traveler headed in the direction she wanted to travel. It appeared to be a tall man dressed in a long black robe and black hat. He was leading a donkey laden with sacks and several small barrels. The man and the animal moved slowly and methodically.

Quickly, Nichol weighed her options. Not wanting another confrontation, she could parallel his path and continue walking, using the trees as concealment. Or she could run as fast as possible past him.

The black robe and hat looked just like the monks she saw at the fair. Her curiosity stirred, she selected a route through short grass that allowed her to walk quietly, shielded by the trees as she watched his movements.

She continued in that fashion for quite a while. It slowed her down, but she felt safe doing it. Her plan worked well until she disturbed a flock of pheasants nesting in the grass and sent them flying in every direction.

Her heart jumped into her throat. She bent down behind a bush to watch the man's reaction to the sudden disruption.

Is he bad ... or is he kind?

He merely slowed the donkey, lifted his head, and turned to look in the direction of the flittering pheasants.

When she saw his face, her recognition was immediate. It was Brother Lemur, the young monk from the monastery in Vienne. What a welcome sight!

The day he had wrapped her purchases at the Vienne fair, she had a good feeling about him. Her first impression was that he was a kind and sincere person. He smiled with his eyes as well as his face, speaking in quiet tones, calmly, and with patience.

Standing up, she brushed herself off and made an immediate left turn through the trees that gave her access to the road where he currently stood. Humming to herself as she went, she knew he could hear her approach. She hopped from the embankment onto the road and with a questioning look, asked, "Brother Lemur, is that you?"

Though not frightened by her sudden appearance, he was certainly surprised.

"It is. And you are the young man from the fair who paid double for all your purchases. I am sorry to say that I do not know your name."

Smiling, she said, "My name is Nick."

"I am pleased to know you, Nick. This is my friend Moki who carries all my heavy bags." Moki was bigger than most donkeys. His coloring was light gray with a distinct patch of white between his ears that stretched down to his nostrils. A matching patch of white was at the top of his tail. At the villa there had been two donkeys. Looking Moki over, she knew that the animal could carry even more weight. Nichol reached out and scratched Moki behind one ear. "Moki and I have not stopped since sunrise and we are both in need of food and rest. We were looking for a flat spot in full sun off the road when you appeared. Would you like to join us?"

Nichol had another pressing decision to make.

Should I, or should I not? And if I travel with him, will he know I am not a young man … that I am really a young woman? She looked from him to Moki and back to him.

Nodding, she said, "Yes, I would. I, too, need a rest and something to eat. Do you think Moki can walk a bit longer until we find a spot close to the river?"

"I think he can manage that. Come on, Moki, let us go a bit longer."

They walked at a pace comfortable for the donkey, who was carrying double his weight. Brother Lemur walked on Moki's left side, carrying the reins and Nichol walked on the right. He was a tall man, as tall as her papa. His beard and hair were short and topped with a wide-brimmed black hat that kept the sun from beating on his neck. His hooded frock reached his ankles and tied around his waistline was a rope. What was on his feet caught Nichol's eyes. They were different from any that she had seen before.

It was not long before he exclaimed, "Ah ha! Look to our left. There's a clearing just ahead and I can hear water rushing. What do you think—should we see if Moki approves of our selection?"

They found a spot in the clearing with full sun to rest and eat. The monk secured Moki's reins to a low-hanging pine limb and moved to one of the sacks hanging from his right side. He removed a smaller bag that contained straw and a pot made of clay. As he scattered several generous helpings of straw on the ground in front of the donkey, the animal began eating it as it fell to the ground.

"I am going to get some water for Moki. Would you like to come along?"

Nichol looked at the donkey. "Do you feel comfortable leaving all your belongings here unattended?"

Brother Lemur looked thoughtful. "I suppose there's always a risk that someone could pass by while we are gone and steal my things. But knowing Moki, I am sure he would start braying to get my attention if someone was lurking about."

Patting Moki's neck, Nichol turned and went with Brother Lemur to find the source for water.

They walked along the riverbank until they found an area that was lined with small rocks. The rocks led out to a sandbar. Turning to Nichol, the monk said, "I think once we reach the sandbar, we will be in deeper and cleaner water," and off he went.

She did not care if she got her shoes or breeches wet, because she was used to it, but Brother Lemur wore a long heavy robe that would be even heavier if it got wet. Watching in amazement, she saw him draw his robe up from his ankles and tuck it into the rope that was already around his waist.

Mystery solved. She laughed as she watched.

Brother Lemur turned to her. "What has amused you?"

"I was just wondering how you were going to keep your robe dry and now I know. That's a creative solution."

Brother Lemur knelt on the sandbar and reached out far enough into the river to capture water into the clay bowl. Once he had accomplished that goal, he placed the bowl on the sandbar and sat down and faced the river. He removed his shoes, put them behind him, and dangled his feet and legs in the cold water. He sighed with relief and turned to look at Nichol, who was still standing on the far side of the sandbar watching him. It was his turn to chuckle.

He waved her over to where he was sitting. "I think you will find this most refreshing for your tired feet. Join me."

She finally did, but she left her shoes on just in case they had to make a quick exit. Brother Lemur did not say a word about the wet shoes or breeches as she sat.

Moki was the one that broke the silence before they began preparing to return to him.

Brother Lemur took in a deep breath. "Well, what do you know? That's my conscience calling. According to that noise, he is thirsty and lonely and I am late. I should go back. You can stay if you like. I will go see to my friend's needs." The monk dried his feet with the hem of his robe, put on his shoes, picked up Moki's water bowl, and left.

Nichol waited a few more minutes before she left the river. She hopped up, dusted the sand from her wet breeches and walked back to the clearing. When she arrived, Brother Lemur was talking to Moki as the donkey drank his fill of water.

The monk took a small pack from Moki's side and handed it to Nichol. "There is plenty in there for the two of us." Nichol took the bag and followed the monk to a fallen log, and they sat down.

"Before I left Vienne, I was given quite a store of food and wine since I will be on the road for some time. If you would like any of it, it is yours." He then closed his eyes, folded his hands in front of him, and silently prayed.

When he finished, Nichol looked over his shoulder and asked, "Brother Lemur, you said you will be traveling for some time. Where are you going? Are there other monks or other people who will be joining you as you travel?"

He shook his head. "No one will be joining me. Moki and I are traveling to various monasteries north of here. Lyon, Autun, Sens, Melun and finally to Evry. The monastery in Vienne is successful at growing fruits, vegetables, and grapes. I am taking seeds and cuttings to the monasteries I just mentioned. Once I reach each of those locations, I will teach them our new methods for planting, plant selection, pruning, and harvesting. Moki and I will be on the road for many days. Where are you going, Nick? You appear to be traveling all alone and you do not have a Moki to keep you company."

Nichol liked his calm manner and quiet banter, but she was not comfortable sharing her entire story with him. "I am on my way to Paris. I was with the group in Vienne where I first met you, but they were there just to visit the fair. I had to move on, so I struck out on my own."

Wanting to change the subject, she looked up at the sun. "The sun looks like it has passed midday. I should be on my way. Thank you for sharing your meal and allowing me to spend time with you and Moki. I hope you have a successful journey." She lifted her bag and stood up to leave.

Brother Lemur also stood, tilting his head and scratching his beard. "You just told me you are on your way to Paris. The monastery in Evry is my last stop and it is just outside Paris by two Moki days. Would you consider traveling with the two of us? I welcome your company and I can tell Moki has taken a shine to you. What do you think about that idea? I fear for your safety if you continue alone."

Nichol was immediately on guard. She welcomed his companionship and he offered an invisible shield of protection. People would risk a lifetime in hell if they harmed or stole from a monk. But could she trust him? Monk or no monk, he was still a male.

Papa, what should I do? If I go with him, it will take me longer to get to Paris.

The answer she heard was not Papa's. It was the *Lady's* voice.

Trust your instincts. You have read the man's demeanor. What have you learned?

Suddenly, she knew the answer to Brother Lemur's question.

Looking at him with a big grin, she nodded her head. "Yes, I would like to join you and Moki on your journey northward. Thank you for including me."

The monk was also pleased and said his own silent prayer of thanks. He lifted Moki's reins and said, "I am glad. Let us be on our way while the sun still shines on us."

They walked for a long stretch without saying a word. The energy around them seemed lighter and brighter; even Moki had picked up his pace.

Nichol felt relieved that she had someone by her side, someone between her and danger.

The thing she now had to consider was that she could no longer run at full speed as she moved along. Her journey would take longer. Moki certainly could not run with all the load he carried. Traveling with the two of them would add additional days—even weeks—to reach Paris and finding Ezra.

Still, it felt like a good trade. She had no specific deadline to meet, and Ezra was not even aware she was coming. Smiling to herself, she welcomed that she would live and learn as she traveled with her two new companions.

Before they left the clearing, the monk pulled a map from a satchel strapped around Moki's neck. He spread it across the donkey's flank and showed Nichol where they were currently and where his next stop would be. They were deep in a forest and it would take one full day of travel through it before they arrived at the town of Lyon.

She was amazed to see that his map and route to Evry matched the map and route her papa had charted for her journey to Paris.

This is too good to be true. It is almost as if I am being guided to travel with this man.

Brother Lemur suggested that they travel as far as they could on the road before the sun made its final descent. Then he proposed they look for a secluded area deeper within the forest where they could stop and set up for the night. He explained that he wanted to be a fair distance off the road and out of view of passing travelers.

She would have picked the same type of spot for the same reason if traveling alone. "I agree with you, Brother Lemur. This is what I have been doing when I stop at the end of each day."

All sorts of thoughts streamed through her head. Her new companion was a man. Granted, he was a religious man, but she had heard stories of other religious men and how they conducted themselves with women. There were no guarantees as to how he would behave toward her.

Will I have any privacy? Surely, he will need some as well. How do we handle this?

Now, she was not sure how any of these issues would be solved, but she did know one thing—she would deal with them once they found a place to stop for the night. She decided that it would be best to state her questions and concerns openly with him. And if she became unsure, she believed she could outrun him to escape if necessary.

The sun was on its lowest track of the day when they simultaneously declared that it was time to look for an overnight spot. For protection, they selected a place on the east side of the road, because it was uphill and more difficult to get to.

Brother Lemur guided Moki up and through deep underbrush until he found a spot that was flat and full of trees packed into a tight grouping. He looked at Nichol to get "his" input.

"What do you think, Nick? Does this look like a protected location to you?"

"Yes, it looks like everything we were looking for."

Brother Lemur began removing the packs, sacks, and barrels that Moki had been transporting. He started to lay them out in a circle in the middle of the group of trees. When finished, he pulled straw out of one of the bags and piled it on the ground in the center of the circle. Then he found the clay pot and filled it full of water from his waterskin and set it to one side of the mound of straw.

Nichol stood and watched. He seemed to have an established pattern to unburdening his donkey and staging the things he removed.

The monk looked at her as she studied his placements and grinned.

"Remember, I told you today that Moki gets a bit anxious if he is away from me for too long? We have established our sleeping arrangements so that he sleeps on his bed of straw next to me. I have created an enclosure around us, so we are somewhat protected from creatures wandering through the area at night.

"Donkeys tend to bond for life if they have another donkey partner. If they do not, they will bond with the next best thing. I am his next best thing. My advice would be to keep a safe distance from me during the night, so he does not show his possessive side. Once he gets to know you and trusts that you will not harm me, he will not be so controlling."

"I am glad you explained this to me. I think Moki and I are of the same mind. It is also my preference that you keep your distance from me during the night."

Brother Lemur looked at her. Quietly he said, "Nick, monks are required to take vows of poverty, chastity, and obedience. I have taken those vows and I intend to be true to them. You do not need to worry about me. I will honor you and I will honor God with my vows. You have my promise."

From the first time I met this man, I sensed that he was a good person.

They joined Moki and prepared their first meal as traveling companions.

As they ate, they chatted about things of little consequence when suddenly Nichol looked at him and asked, "You are now called Brother Lemur. Did you have a different name before you became a monk?"

Reflecting, he said, "My parents named me Timothée and that's what they called me when I was a baby. However, I have a brother two years older and all he could manage to say was Timo. After that, everyone in my family started calling me Timo."

"Timo. I like the sound of it."

There were so many questions she wanted to ask him. She was curious by nature, but she knew that with each of her questions to him, he would want to know the same of her.

"I am not familiar with the proper way to address a monk. Should I address you as Brother Lemur? Should I call you Brother? Can I call you Timo?"

The monk emitted a deep, hearty laugh. "Nick, you have a way of getting right to the heart of your question. I will try to answer your questions as directly as you asked them.

"In the monastery, we address one another in two ways. Out of respect, we almost always use the full title, which in my case is Brother Lemur. Other times we shorten the address to just the title of Brother. And to answer your third question, no one outside of my family knows about the name Timo except you. You can address me by any name you wish. I will answer to all of them."

She was beginning to like this free and open conversation with him.

He found her to be direct and humorous and she found him to be direct, humorous, and pleasant in his responses. He was not like some men she encountered since leaving Marseille who either ignored a woman totally or disparaged her if she asked a question.

She pressed on. "Were you born in Vienne? Did you come from a wealthy family?"

"No, I was born in Valence, which is not that far from Vienne. My father is a skilled tanner who makes saddles, bridles and harnesses, and shoes. Years ago, his craft was seen by the monks who live in the monastery at Vienne, and they convinced him he should sell his handiwork at the fair. He did, and his wares became much sought-after. Several lords commissioned him to create saddles and matching harnesses for their personal use. Additionally, various bishops hired him to make helmets and armor for their armed entourages.

"How is it that you chose to be a monk? Did you not want to follow him and be a tanner or some other tradesman?"

"I learned tanning and helped him with his creations, but my heart was not in it and I did not wish to do it for my whole life. Besides that, I have two older brothers who are the rightful heirs to his business and wealth, and who are more than capable to carry on his trade and legacy. It is a good fit for the two of them.

"Once, I went with him to sell his goods at the Vienne fair. While we were there, I had the opportunity to talk with several of the brothers from the monastery, and they took me on a tour. They showed me their farms, orchards, and vineyards, and explained to me their quiet way of living and praying. I have always been a hard worker and always worked with my hands, but after seeing how the monks produced edible life from seedlings, I knew my calling was to work with soil, seeds, and sunshine. It all seemed to agree with me.

"After we returned to Valence, I had time to think things through and talk with my family. Finally, they gave me their blessing and agreed that I should pursue the brotherhood. I made another trip to the monastery to talk with Abbot Cyprian. If he thought I was a good fit for the position, I would not return to Valence. That was five years ago. What about you? Where do you come from? What is your family background?"

Silence surrounded her. *Do I tell him everything? Can I fully trust him?*

"I was born in Marseilles. My papa was a successful merchant. As a young man, he was in the service of the count of Provence. Proving his loyalty, the count awarded him a Roman villa with surrounding farmland. He also made him port commander of Marseilles. My papa was well-respected." She finished and looked down at her hands.

Timo detected the sadness in her voice and asked, "You speak as though your papa is no longer living?"

She hesitated a bit, and then looked up at the monk with tears in her eyes. Trying to keep herself together, she whispered, "He died two weeks ago, and I miss him."

Quietly, the monk said, "I cannot imagine how badly you must be hurting. I am saddened to know about your loss. I would like to hear more about him whenever you are ready to do that."

Nichol shook her head slowly, and with a twist of her lower lip, said, "Thank you, but I think I have had enough for this day. I am going to join Moki for the night."

Picking up her satchel, she moved to the site Timo had assembled for their protection. She withdrew her cloak from her pack, wrapped it around her shoulders and stretched out on the ground to the right of Moki. Patting his head, she rubbed behind his ear and then settled her pack under her head.

She tried to count the stars as she lay there, but she could not see them for the tears spilling from her eyes. Turning on her side, she hugged her arms around her middle and allowed the tears to come.

Slowly, Timo settled down on the opposite side of Moki. He could hear her sobs as he prepared his own space. He whispered good night to Moki, who then sniffed Timo, rotated his ears, and closed his eyes.

Timo took a deep breath, folded his hands on his chest, and prayed himself to sleep.

There is much more to Nick … it is clear she is masquerading as a boy. I do not know why, but I will protect her … him.

She is so burdened.

thirty-nine

The Inn

I took my drunken brother's horse again!

Nichol woke with a start.

What was that noise?

Springing to a sitting position, she turned from side to side to see what the commotion was.

Moki was standing next to her, braying. Nichol soothed the donkey by scratching behind one ear as she talked gently and reassuringly into the other ear.

"Where did he go, Moki?"

Where was Timo?

Standing up to have a better look around their campsite, she saw Brother Lemur walking up the hill from the road carrying two waterskins.

When he reached them, he smiled. "Good morning, you two." Scratching behind the donkey's ears, he added," I see that Moki has gotten your attention."

"Yes, he did. You must have been gone for quite some time for Moki to start braying like he was."

"When I wakened, you were both sleeping peacefully, and I thought it would be a good time to go to the river to bring water back for all of us. I must have been gone longer than I thought. Now that I am back, are you hungry?"

Nichol nodded. Timo spread straw on the ground for Moki to eat and filled his bowl with water. Noticing the few scraps of food she had in her hand, the monk offered her cured bacon and berries from his pack. She accepted gratefully and munched away.

Finishing their quick meal, they loaded up the bags and barrels and headed down the embankment to the main road.

It was a marvelous morning. The birds were chirping and chattering, and squirrels darted across the road and up trees to avoid them. There were no clouds, the air was cool and blue skies promised a good day for travel.

The two walked and talked, enjoying their surroundings and each other's company.

Later that afternoon, they finally cleared the forest and were on a flat road heading north to Lyon. That was Timo's first stop to drop off the seeds he had brought from his monastery in Vienne. His plan was to meet with the monks in Lyon and teach them how and where to plant the seeds.

As they walked, he pointed out various plants, grasses, bushes, and trees. He explained their growing seasons, their growth habits, if full sun or partial sun was required, as well as the amount of rainfall they needed to thrive.

Nichol spied several herbs growing along the roadway. Pointing them out, she explained they were good for wound healing. He seemed surprised by her knowledge.

In turn, she was amazed at how much he knew, and she was taking in the information as quickly as she could. For every question she asked, he had an immediate and in-depth answer.

I wonder if he will let me join his training session with the monks? Ideas were popping through her head and she could hardly contain herself. She looked at him over Moki's bobbing head, and asked, "Brother Lemur, do the monks in Lyon shelter and feed travelers like those in Vienne?"

"Yes, they do. Every Benedictine monastery in France caters to travelers as well as to the poor who need food or short-term shelter. Why do you ask?"

"I am assuming you will be welcomed by the monks in Lyon and that you will have a place to eat and sleep inside the monastery. I am wondering if I can stay in the longhouse at the monastery for the same number of days you will be teaching there."

"Yes, you will be able to stay with the travelers in the longhouse. I will be staying inside the monastery with my brothers. That is the custom."

Doubt was creeping into her mind again. She was accustomed to planning her days based solely on her own needs. Now that she had a traveling companion, she was not sure how she should proceed.

Seeing her concerned look, the monk asked, "Nick, what is troubling you? You look uncertain about something."

"Timo, this is new to me, and I think that I may harm your good standing with the monks as well as hindering your progress moving forward. I am wondering if I should move on by myself."

"Monks do not travel often. When we do travel, it is safer to travel in groups with laypeople. When we are at the monastery, it is best to be discreet about our travel together. Gossip travels fast without understanding.

"As for you hindering my progress northward, please do not think that. If I have everything distributed to the other monasteries before the spring planting, everyone will be pleased. I have a feeling that you are the one who does not want to be delayed from getting to your destination. Could I be holding you back?"

He waited for her response as she shifted from foot to foot, debating her answer.

"Brother Lemur, we have been honest with each other thus far. Promise me this … if your being with me causes you discomfort in any way, you must tell me immediately. Until that time comes, I will assume we will travel on to Evry together."

One day, she must tell me why she is traveling disguised as a boy.

They entered Lyon through its southern border. The monastery was on the northwest border of town, and they had a while to travel before they would reach it. A few small structures lined both sides of the road as they approached the center of town.

Nichol had been traveling through forestland for two days since leaving Vienne, and almost all the food she had purchased there was gone except for some very dry bread and a little bit of honey.

They came upon an inn on the east side of the road and Nichol looked at Timo. "I know we will reach the monastery soon and we can get food there, but I am craving a meat pie, and inns are known for selling them. They are crispy and warm and full of vegetables, and one pie will feed both of us. Would you mind if I buy one at this inn? We can eat it as we go on."

"Go in and get your pie. Moki and I will wait here by these tethered horses."

As Nichol approached the door to the inn, she noticed one of the three tethered horses had been ridden hard and left untended.

The door was propped open, allowing light to flow into the otherwise candlelit room.

Quickly, she spotted a young woman behind a high table. Approaching her, Nichol asked, "Do you sell meat pies here?"

"Yes."

Nichol asked her bring one pie to take with her. The server nodded and left to get the pie.

While waiting, she observed the entire room was full of patrons. Then her eyes settled on the back of a lone man sitting close to the server's table. His head and neck looked familiar.

Immediately, she was on alert. She knew who he was when she overheard the crude remark he made to a man sitting at the next table.

Nichol's blood froze in anger and disgust. The word *Fredric* silently passed through her lips.

At that moment, the server placed the pie in front of Nichol and told her how much it cost.

Paying, Nichol quietly thanked the server, and turned to leave. She wanted the pie badly, but she wanted out of the inn even more.

It was too late.

"I know that voice!" Fredric shouted as he bolted out of his chair. Quickly, he moved behind her. Her body stiffened; she knew his smell.

He thrust his hand to the back of her head and grabbed her cap off her head. Nichol spun around.

"If it is not my little sister." They stood face to face, each glaring at one another. "Mother has had me scouring the country looking for you and here you are in Lyon. Imagine my good fortune. She told me not to return without you."

Fredric grabbed her arm, twisting it as he did and spraying spittle into her face with his vile words.

Nichol was fast. In one swift motion, she drew her right knee up and jammed it into his groin. He doubled over in pain, screaming out in agony.

The other patrons had been watching Fredric and were moving in to help Nichol.

Fredric saw feet approaching, released Nichol's arm, and pulled a knife from his belt. Struggling to his feet, he flashed his knife, yelling, "You will all stay out of this if you know what is good for you!"

Nichol drove her finger into his eye, causing him to shriek in pain, and charged to the open door. Glancing over her shoulder, she saw his hand covering his eye. At the same time, he staggered toward the door, attempting to stop her while screaming obscenities.

Timo was standing by the horses. He heard the commotion and Fredric's spiteful tirade when Nichol dashed out of the inn. As she ran by him, she thrust the pie into his hands.

Spying a saddled horse to her right, she hoisted herself up, *thinking this must be Fredric's horse, it is all lathered from running.*

Turning to Timo, she said, "I will meet you at the monastery."

Timo nodded.

Fredric limped out the door still holding a hand over one eye and lunged toward the horse as Nichol turned it to ride north. He screamed, "Lisa, get back here! You stole my rings and I want them back!"

Nichol turned her horse and hesitated long enough to stare at him with all the hate she possessed. With curled lips, she snarled, "I have nothing of yours. You are a bastard and not the son of my father!" Her words slapped him in his face, then his anger overflowed as he started toward her.

The horse's ears were pinned back and his nostrils flared as a misty cloud streamed from them. "Stay away! The horse remembers how you abused him."

Nichol leaned forward and whispered in her mount's ear, further agitating him as his hooves started churning the ground in anger. Grabbing a handful of his mane, she screamed as she released their combined fury.

Stunned by her quick action, Fredric did not move.

The horse responded to his new rider and leaped forward, trampling Fredric and leaving him lying on the ground.

Nichol brought the animal under control and commanded it to stop next to where Fredric writhed on the ground in severe pain. She swung her leg over the horse's neck and dropped to the ground, removed her dagger from within her tunic, and stood over him.

"I feel no ill will because of what you have done to me, but because of what you did to my Shadow, I bear anger for you that will never go away."

A reflection off her dagger drew immediate panic.

"Are you going to kill me?" Fredric gasped.

"Not today." Bending over, she laughed while she cut the strings holding his coin purse to his belt.

"No coin, no horse, and a long way from home. I wish I could see your mother's face when you crawl into the villa! Go now or I will fulfill Papa's promise to you—you will meet the hanging fate of Blaxton and Jaggor. Instruct Astrid that I will never give her what she wants … the details about Papa's business and the location where he hid his silver and gold. And if you ever seek me again, it will be your last breath."

Nichol leaped on the horse, turned, and was gone.

"Bitch!" Fredric spat, still sprawled on the ground.

Timo had observed Nick's violent encounter with Fredric. No words passed his lips as his mind processed what had unfolded. But he had heard plenty. A clear picture had just been painted for him.

Who is she?

Staggering to his feet, Fredric looked at the other two horses tethered to the post and started to limp in their direction. The monk guessed what he had in mind and stepped forward, stopping him.

Fredric attempted to shove past him to get to a horse, but Timo stood his ground and quietly said, "No … that would be unwise."

Heeding the monk's warning, Fredric limped slowly back inside the inn. Spotting the table he had occupied since early morning, he moved toward it, summoning the server. He resumed his seat, talking to himself and reminding anyone who came near him how powerful and wealthy he was.

Patrons drifted in and out for several hours, and all of them got an earful of Fredric's belligerence.

Finally, the owner of the inn had heard enough and asked two male patrons to throw him out, along with a warning to never come back.

forty

A Moment of Revenge

Who is this girl? I know she is not a man and I have never seen a girl move like she does.

Timo gathered Moki's reins and moved off in the direction of the monastery. Moki sensed his agitation but followed him willingly.

Once he arrived, he led Moki to the stables at the rear of the property, a benefit that the monastery provided to visiting clerics and royals to house their horses. After spreading straw for Moki to eat and filling a nearby bucket with water, Timo decided he would unload his packs later. Right then, he needed to find Nick.

Suddenly she appeared, riding in from the fallow field. He waited at the fence surrounding the stables until she noticed him and rode in his direction.

Dismounting, she led the horse through the gate and into the stall next to Moki. Saying nothing when she rode past him at the gate, she appeared upset as she started to remove the saddle and bridle from the horse.

Timo was almost to the stall when he heard laughter. Nichol was tending to the horse and she was laughing. Tears rolled down her cheeks.

Looking at her with concern, he said, "I went into the inn and retrieved your cap."

"Thank you. I would miss it on cold days."

Nichol put the cap on and continued, "This is the *second* time I have taken a horse and a purse of coins away from Fredric. There must be a God! I could not have planned this any better. When I spoke to the server, Fredric recognized my voice. Coming out of the inn, when I saw the condition of the horse, I knew it was his."

Wiping her tears, Nichol clapped her hands and shook with merriment. She was enjoying her moment of revenge.

Timo was mesmerized … and bewildered … and concerned. All he could do was stand there and watch her and absorb what she had just revealed.

I have never seen any man move like she does. With what I heard, I know she is not a man. Who is this girl?

Taking the saddle and bridle from her, he hung them on a hook at the back of the stable. Walking to the stall where Moki was still munching, he removed a basket from his side. Taking it to Nichol, he reached inside and pulled out the meat pie. Looking at her with raised eyebrows, he broke off a piece and handed it to her.

"I am not at all sure you still crave this pie, but I saved most of it for you. I think you might need it."

Accepting the pie, she said, "Why not? I chose to go into that inn on the same day my evil half-brother was there. Not only did I escape, but I also saved a horse from further abuse by taking it. Eating this pie will be the perfect ending to a perfect day. Timo, can I have one of your waterskins filled with that excellent white wine? I would like to take this pie, a skin of wine, sit out there in that field, and savor the ending to this day."

"Certainly, I will give you the wine, but it will be dark soon. Do you want to visit the longhouse first and claim your sleeping quarters for tonight?"

"No. I think tonight I will sleep right here between Moki and the horse and remember my papa. I cannot think of a better place to be."

The monk nodded and moved to Moki's stall to remove the cargo strapped to his stout body. He stacked the bags and barrels on the far side of the stall and rummaged through the last bag for the wineskin. He found it and took it to Nichol.

"I know you can take care of yourself, Nick. I have seen you do it. I think you will be safe here in the stables for the night. Now, I must go and let the brothers know I have arrived. I will look for you in the morning. Sleep well."

"Good night … and thank you."

Nichol took the remainder of the pie, the wineskin, and returned to the middle of the field to reflect on the day's events at the inn and her third encounter with Fredric.

I had hoped Fredric had given up pursuing me after his failed attempt in the forest outside of Avignon. I outsmarted him that day and today I escaped. But how long will I be successful at doing that? Fredric made it clear that Astrid is the reason behind his pursuit. She will stop at nothing to get me back in her control—her future depends on it. Who else will she send to find me?

By now, Astrid must have determined that she knows nothing about Papa's business affairs or his wealth, and she knows I am familiar with all of it. She must be furious because she cannot locate the piles of gold and silver that she thinks he has hidden. Maybe she thinks I am guarding it.

Fredric is a fool, thinking Papa's rings will give him power. I must stay alert, for he has no intention of taking me back to Marseilles alive if I am captured.

It is time for me to continue my journey to Paris and seek the protection of Ezra. But I have time before another hunter finds me. Without coin or horse, it will take weeks for Fredric to return home on foot. Who will Astrid engage to find me?

Standing, Nichol proclaimed aloud, "Paris is my future." Gathering her wineskin, she returned to spend the night in the stable with her four-legged friends.

Entering it, she did not notice the large red-tailed hawk perched on the rooftop.

The Lady is my guide.

I know deep in my heart my journey to find Ezra is what I must do. My life and future depend on it. I know little about Ezra or what Paris offers, but a life of unknowns is more agreeable than the life I left behind.

"I am doing what you taught and trained me to do, Papa."

forty-one

The Monastery in Lyon

We welcome you and all the knowledge you bring with you.

Timo entered the monastery and walked down the central hall to find Abbot Sebastos' room. Coming to a door that displayed a large cross, he knocked, then opened it.

Immediately, a loud welcoming greeting poured forth. Sitting behind a high table, with quill in hand, was a stout, cheerful man of middle age.

"I am Brother Timothée Lemur from Vienne. Are you Abbot Sebastos?"

Nodding, the older man stood, put down his quill, and came around to the front of the table.

Giving Brother Lemur a warm hug, he said, "Brother, we were so excited to hear you were coming to visit us. In the message I received from Abbot Cyprian, he spoke highly of you and your skills with growing things. A full description of all that you have achieved in Vienne was also included. All the brothers here are enthusiastic to learn from you. After you see our grounds, it will be clear that we need your help. We welcome you and all the knowledge you bring with you."

Timo was pleased. He was unsure how receptive an abbot would be to a new face, and this monk appeared to be genuinely agreeable.

"Thank you, Abbot Sebastos, for your warm welcome. I will do my best for you."

Placing a hand on his shoulder, Abbot Sebastos added, "It is nearly time to prepare food for our guests, but before we do, I want you to meet the other brothers."

The abbot led him down the hall and turned to enter the chapel. He rang the chapel bells three times, which was the call for all the monks to meet there.

One by one, they streamed into the chapel until all the monks were present. Abbot Sebastos introduced Brother Lemur to everyone. The monks welcomed him warmly and told him how glad they were to have someone teaching them about planting and reaping.

Brother Michael was chosen to show Brother Lemur to his cell where he could store his belongings. As he organized his things, Brother Michael left for the longhouse. The other monks went to the kitchen.

These monks were not only gifted farmers and winemakers, but they were also excellent hosts. Eggs, warm brown bread, cheese, and ale to wash it down had been prepared.

Brother Michael counted the number of travelers in the longhouse, and when he returned to the kitchen, he announced, "There are fewer travelers here than we usually have. We will not need quite as many servings tonight."

After feeding the travelers, the monks collected the empty bowls from the long table and returned to the kitchen to eat their own meals.

The chapel bells rang out once again, and the brothers moved to the chapel for evening prayers, then each went to his cell to sleep.

Timo took that opportunity to check on Nichol and bring her a few eggs, brown bread and cheese. He was also concerned that Moki would be unsettled because they would have been separated for so long.

Carrying a candle to light his way to the stables, his anxiety grew as he approached.

Moki was not braying, nor was he pacing about. When he got to the stall, he was astounded at what he found. Moki was curled up on a bed of straw and lying next to him with an arm around his neck was Nick.

Neither one stirred; they were sound asleep.

The monk stared at the blissful scene in front of him. *This young woman has a way of touching one's heart. Not only has she touched mine but Moki's as well.*

Leaving the food in the bowl he carried it in, he covered it with wood and a heavy stone and placed it by Moki's saddle, where it would be seen.

Timo exited the barn and returned to his cell in the monastery. He prepared for bed, settled onto his cot, said prayers of thanksgiving, and fell asleep with a smile on his face.

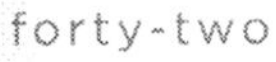

forty-two

Left Behind

Seeing that you and your horse were gone,
I had a moment of panic.

The next day the brothers were up before sunrise and in the chapel attending the first of seven daily prayer sessions. Immediately after that, Timo went to the stables. He was anxious to check on his two companions. He reached the barn, only to find the stalls empty.

Nick, Moki, and the horse were gone.

His heart dropped. *Did Nick's brother somehow find them during the night and force them to leave with him? Maybe, but he would have no need for a donkey. Where is Moki? Think. Think. Where can they be?*

He noticed then that the halter for Moki and the horse's bridle were missing and the horse's saddle was still hanging on the hook where he had placed it the previous day.

Now he had an idea where the three of them might be.

Exiting the stables, he saw large and small hoof-prints next to each other leading to the pasture gate and he followed them. The prints led to the south side of the monastery and turned west. *The river!*

Suddenly he heard the whinny of a horse off to his right and ran in that direction. He had gone only a short way when he saw Nick leading the animals up the hill toward the road.

"Wait!"

She spun around to see him running up the slope to meet them. "Good morning. What brings you here?"

"I went to the stables to check on you. Seeing that you and your horse were gone, I had a moment of concern. When I saw that Moki was also gone, I hoped you would all be at the river.

"Yesterday, when your brother tried to restrain you at the inn, I heard the remarks he made to you as well as your responses to him. When all three of you were missing this morning, I was afraid he had found you and forced you to leave with him. I am thankful to see that all three of you are alive and well. But then, watching you in action yesterday, I think it would have been difficult for anyone to force you …."

"We woke early, and I decided to take Moki and the horse to the river to drink. While they drank, I freshened myself and was thankful for the food that was under the stone. Now, we are ready to meet this new day."

A serious expression crossed her face. "Timo, I know you have a lot of questions. You are probably wondering who I am. When you and I have sufficient time alone, I will tell you the whole story. But for now, I suspect it is time for you to begin sowing your seeds of wisdom to the other monks."

Pausing, she then added, "I wish I could be present when you teach them."

"Everything I will teach them I have written down. I have made a set of illustrations that describes the types of seeds they will be planting, along with all the information on how and where to plant, tend, and harvest. I will leave it for them, and I am happy to give you a set of illustrations for you to keep. And if you want, I can teach you what I know."

This man is so knowledgeable about farming and plants. I can hardly wait to see what he has and what he does.

Returning to the stables, they put the animals in their stalls.

"If you stay with Moki, I will take your satchel to the kitchen and fill it with food."

"Everything I have eaten is good. Bring as much as you can. And thank you. I will wait right here."

Promptly returning, Timo handed the bag to her. "I think you will find some very good things in there."

Smiling and thanking him again, she peeked inside to see what he had brought.

"Yesterday, I had a brief tour of the monastery property. The monks here have done a fine job with their farmland, and they do not need as much training as they think they do. I expect I will be done by midday.

"When I am finished, I would like to leave immediately for the monastery in Autun. It will take about six Moki days to get there since we will again be traveling through dense forest. Is that agreeable with you?"

She nodded her head in agreement.

He continued, "Nick, what are you going to do with your horse? Do you plan on keeping him?"

"I have given that a lot of thought. A peasant boy riding a horse would attract unwanted attention to me. I cannot keep him, so I would like to leave him here at the monastery. He is too valuable to turn loose on the road and he is accustomed to being fed and cared for."

Pausing for a moment, she asked, "What do you think about this? When you are working with the brothers in the field, I will turn the horse loose and he will wander over to where he hears voices. If the monks wish to keep him, he is theirs."

Timo smiled. "I think your idea is a good one, and I know the brothers will take good care of him."

"There is something else to consider. How do we dispose of the saddle?"

Walking to where the items hung, Timo examined them closely. "Just leave it here in the stable. We will be gone when it is discovered. Along with the horse, the monks will credit God for their good fortune."

Nichol nodded her head. "Good fortune for the monastery, bad fortune for its previous owner. One more thing," she added as he turned to leave, "I have watched you load and unload Moki for days. Can I prepare him for travel while you are teaching? That way, as soon as you are finished, you can be on your way quickly and we will meet later on the road."

"Thank you. That will help us move on. At midday, the chapel bell will ring six times calling the brothers to prayer. When you hear the first bell, lead the horse out to the field of grain and release him. I will watch for him. Hopefully, he will be drawn to our location when he hears our voices."

"Agreed. Once I release him, I will leave the property and head north through the forest. I will watch for you and Moki when I stop for the day.

"Nick, I am amazed at how quickly and clearly your mind works." Turning, he left the barn and returned to the monastery.

forty-three

A Day with Brother Lemur

From one of the larger bags, he pulled out bareroot grapevines. As he did, he heard the monks' voices rise with enthusiasm.

The monks gathered in the great room around several tables that had been set up with parchment, quill pens, and ink for them to make notes relating to Brother Lemur's teachings.

Entering, Brother Lemur carried a large cloth bag and began arranging the contents on a table at the front of the room. Each variety of seed he had brought from Vienne was tied up in a smaller cloth bag.

The bags were sorted according to fruit trees, vegetables, and grain. From one of the larger bags, he pulled out bareroot grapevines. As he did, he heard the monks' voices rise with enthusiasm.

While Brother Lemur explained each variety of seed, the monks saw that his knowledge was illustrated and written down in a manuscript he had created, one that he would leave with them to refer to after he was gone. It was like nothing they had.

Throughout the morning, he described the fine points of planting in rows and furrows. He revealed the expected height and width at maturity for each plant and explained when and how to plant the seeds based on their growing seasons. The monks were amazed at his precision when he gave them an illustrated grid showing plant placement that took heights of the mature trees into consideration and the appropriate times to add animal manure to the base of each.

The last part of his teaching in the great room centered around the bareroot grapevines he showed them, explaining how to plant, stake, and prune them.

The brothers were full of questions relating to soil, sun, and water requirements for all the seeds, and when they should start the new seeds. They were intrigued with the bareroot ideas that Brother Lemur planted in their minds, along with the spacing of plants so that there was better growth.

Once all their questions were answered, he gathered the seeds and grapevine plantings and suggested they move to the areas behind the monastery so they could get a visual idea as to how the planting beds might be laid out when the time was right.

They were an experienced group of farmers, but they had not planted or worked with the variety of seeds or the bareroots he would leave with them. Moving quickly and efficiently, they made fast work of laying out the planting areas. They made and inserted the stakes required for the grapevines to come, and then they designed and systematically laid out the area needed to create the orchard when the ground began to warm, versus the random layouts that were routinely used.

The monks were used to manual labor and they worked well together, each one anticipating the next step and what supplies and tools would be needed. Brother Lemur was pleased with their efforts and the day's progress.

Anticipating that it was close to midday and time for the chapel bells to call them to prayer, he brought everyone together on the far side of the wheat field with their backs to the stable.

"What a fine job you have done today. You have learned well. Thank you for all your hard work and thank you for inviting me to work with you. I wish you bountiful harvests with greater production for years to come."

As he praised them, the first chime of the chapel bells announced the call to midday prayer. The monks began gathering their tools and supplies and prepared to head to the chapel.

Nichol had Moki packed and the bridle on the horse before she heard the first peal of the chapel bells.

When they sounded, she led him through the gate that led to the wheat field and took him to the south end of the field, out of sight of the monks.

Hoping the monks' voices would draw him to them, she turned the horse to head north and gave him a tap on his haunches that sent him sauntering through the middle of the field.

The bells continued to ring as the monks turned to make their way through the wheat field.

As Nichol had planned, one of the brothers spotted a horse with no rider. It was dragging its reins and wandering toward them through the field.

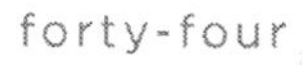

forty-four

The Hawk

The breeze washed through her hair and her heart sang as she sailed up the road.

Reaching the southern end of the property, Nichol scampered over to a grove of trees, waited to make sure no one had seen her and then picked her way through the trees until she was at road level. Continuing to walk amongst the trees as she moved northward, she made sure she was well past the monastery before she got back on the road.

Since joining Timo, moving at a slow pace as they traveled had been their routine. Deciding that it was time to revert to running, she took off. It felt invigorating. Removing her cap, a breeze washed through her hair and her heart sang as she sailed up the road.

As she ran, Nichol noticed that the forest on both sides of the road was becoming increasingly dense. Not wanting to get too far ahead of Timo, she looked for a tree she could observe from while listening for passersby. As was her habit, she looked for pine trees.

Finding one right next to the road, she hoisted herself up on a lower limb, adjusted her pack for easier climbing, and up she went. Stopping when she found a branch wide enough to hold her comfortably, she turned to face the road, and sat with her legs dangling over the limb.

There she would wait for Timo.

Knowing that it would be some time before he made it this far, she hung her satchel on an adjacent branch and began searching through it for something to eat and drink. There was the usual bread and cheese. She was delighted to discover a small pot of honey that she dipped everything in. Finished with her meal, she leaned back against the trunk of the tree, taking in her surroundings.

From her perch, she saw several mature oaks across the road. Just then, a red-tailed hawk floated down and settled on one of the top branches. When she saw it, she placed her open palm over the hawk feathers on the necklace Rose had given her and felt their calming presence.

At the same time, the hawk moved down to a branch close to her. Their eyes both met, as if they knew one another. Nichol leaned her head back.

The forest surrounding her was quiet, and the hawk began to move away, a movement having caught its attention and it flew off.

Nichol watched as it flew over treetops, dropped down over bushes, and soared upward again. Its wingspan was enormous. The hawk turned and dipped its wing toward her as it flew away. It then tipped a wing toward the river, circled twice over a collection of maple trees, and in one sudden movement, swooped to ground level.

She could not see what it had captured, but she heard a screech as the hawk made contact with some creature. After a short time, the hawk returned swiftly back to its perch in the oak tree.

The forest grew quiet once again. Nichol felt at peace. And safe.

forty-five

The Reunion

Timo, Timo, I am so glad to see you!

As the day wore on, the sun and the heat began to lull her to sleep.

Fighting the urge to close her eyes, she found her waterskin and sipped the sweet white wine that Timo had filled it with.

As she searched in her pack for more bread, she heard whistling down below. It was a high-pitched sound, the sound of someone whistling a beckoning signal. Leaning on the branch in front of her, she stretched out to get a better view of the source of the whistle.

Almost directly beneath the tree she was in stood Timo and Moki. Trying to mimic the sounds he had made, she whistled back. That caught Moki's attention, and his ears perked up. Timo stopped, looked all around, but could not locate the source of the responding whistle.

Nichol grabbed her satchel, turned around so she was facing the trunk of the tree, and carefully climbed down, stepping from limb to limb until she jumped to the ground from the lowest one.

Continuing her whistle, Nichol landed nose to nose with Moki. Hugging the donkey around the neck, she whispered greetings in his ear. At the same time, she looked up to see Timo smiling at her.

Being separated from him for almost an entire day made her realize how much she enjoyed his companionship. Giving it no further thought, she skirted around Moki, exclaiming, "Timo, Timo, I am so glad to see you!" as she threw her arms around him in a bear hug. Brother Lemur returned her hug with the same enthusiasm … the joy of being reunited with a good friend. Their embrace was swift and sweet ... and unexpected for Brother Lemur. He was taken aback by her use of his childhood nickname when she greeted him, and he was pleased. A sense of warmth filled him; he was happy to see her.

All Nichol could relate the feeling she had now was her friendship with Gerhardt. Granted, he was not a religious person, but he was her best friend and they always teased, played, waged pretend military battles, and hugged when they greeted one another.

Brother Lemur had taken Gerhardt's place. His presence and gentle way of being filled the void created due to the loss of her best friend Gerhardt.

Nichol stood next to him and smiled. "Shall we go now?"

Timo's return smile spread as he tightened the slack in Moki's reins and encouraged him to resume walking.

As Nichol walked beside him, many thoughts raced through the monk's head.

"Nick, when your brother came out of the inn, he called you Lisa. Tell me … who is Lisa? You dress as a boy but I suspected not long after we met that you were a girl." *I feel like she is the sister I never had.*

Silence fell between them. Finally, Nichol spoke.

"You are right. I am a girl. I changed my name to Nichol when I escaped from Marseilles, running for my life. I dressed in boy's clothes when Papa sent me to train as a fighter with a warrior to protect me from Fredric. I never wore my girl's clothes again. The boy's tunic and breeches were more comfortable and suited my activities. I felt that I would be safer traveling as a boy and the skills that I had learned would be acceptable and not raise alarm. I changed my name and cut my hair so that Astrid and Fredric would not be able to find me."

"Now that you have told me why you changed your name, now tell me … who is Lisa?"

Nichol hesitated. "I cannot … at least now. I am not ready. When we are with others, I think it is best you call me Nick still. To protect me … and to protect you."

Timo sensed her inner turmoil as she became quiet.

"We will be on the road for many weeks. When you want to talk more, I will listen. Who you are and what you say to me will be revealed to no one."

forty-six

Questions

Brother Lemur folded his hands, closed his eyes, and bowed his head.

Nichol had been asking questions from the time she could talk. When she was behind the tapestry in the solar, they remained in her head, usually with no answer. When Alexander discovered that she was his eyes and ears, her questions were encouraged and answered by her father.

Now, she was her own eyes and ears. Timo now became the recipient of her countless questions.

"Was your training successful with the brothers? Were they impressed with all the seeds you brought and your methods for planting and harvesting? What did they think about the illustrations you left with them? Did you save me a set of illustrations? And this I must know the answer to right away—did you find the horse in the wheat field—and what did the brothers say when they saw a horse with no rider?"

Laughing heartily, Timo shook his head. It was enough to silence her momentarily.

"I am not sure I will remember all the questions you just asked, but I will do my best to answer each one."

Taking a deep breath, she continued, "I have been living in the shadows by myself since my papa died. All I have done is run away from people, places, and bad events where I have had to protect myself. It is exhausting and lonely. Since I met you and we embarked on this journey together, I feel like I finally know someone I can trust and someone I can talk with honestly.

"You are here, I feel at peace, and I can finally be myself. And I have another set of eyes to see for me. I miss talking to people and having honest conversations. I missed your companionship when we were separated at the monastery.

"Timo, I am just so glad to see you! Forgive me for asking all those questions at once. Now that I have met someone who's kind and who has put no evil demands on me, I just want to talk like I did with Papa, Margaux, and Rose. Now, I will be quiet and let you talk."

Now Timo was silent. When Moki brayed, he spoke.

"Nick, you astound me. Words just seem to leap from your lips. We have at least another month, maybe longer, and we have time to talk for many days. I welcome your questions, your thoughts, your comments, your opinions, and your truth. But for now, let me see if I can remember all your questions and answer them to your satisfaction.

"Let us start with the brothers. They seemed pleased with their training and the information I shared with them. They also seemed pleased to receive the illustrations I left with them. And yes, when we stop for the day, I will give you a set to keep.

"Most importantly, the horse did just as we had hoped. After you released him into the field, he drifted toward us. There was much discussion about how he happened to be there. We searched for the rider of the horse but found none. The brothers planned to resume their search after prayers.

"I went to visit with Abbot Sebastos. I quickly described to him the plan to lay out the herb fields when the ground warms that included all the eating roots, the orchard, and the vineyard. I told him that he should be pleased with how well they worked together. After that, I explained that I would leave immediately to be on my way to the next monastery.

"The abbot thanked me for traveling to his monastery to share not only the seeds, but my knowledge and experience as well. He told me to fill my bags with as much food and wine as I could carry for my travels, and I did.

"When I got to the stables to load my seed bags on Moki, the horse was back in one of the stalls. Unless someone comes looking for him, the monks plan on keeping him to help in the fields. I am confident that they will treat him well."

"Did I answer all your questions?"

"Yes. Thank you. I am pleased that the horse will have a good home and be properly tended. Knowing that, I feel better. As we travel, I promise I will give you ample time to reply to any questions—but be quick about it," she said, followed by laughter.

They walked at a slow, steady pace for the rest of the day, quietly enjoying the scenery and each other. It was nearing dusk, and they agreed to find a place to stop for the night. Dense forest surrounded them on both sides of the road, and they chose to set up camp on the side near the river.

They twisted and turned through scrub oak until they found a relatively flat space amongst towering evergreen trees. Timo began his routine of freeing Moki from all his cargo, including his bundle of straw. He set the packs in a circle just as he had done the first night they stayed together.

"I am going to take Moki for a leisurely walk to get water. Would you spread straw for him to eat?"

"I would do anything for Moki," she replied. After spreading the straw, she sat and waited for her friends.

Returning, Moki was led to the straw and he began to munch.

"I am going to the river to wash my hands and face. I will not be gone long."

"I would like to do the same thing. It has been a long, dusty day.

Their camp was not far from the river and they reached it quickly. Nichol sat on the bank, removed her shoes, and dangled her feet in the cold water. Timo did the same thing.

Using the soap she had purchased at the fair in Vienne, Nichol scrubbed her face and hands. *I think I can make this soap better in many ways—smoother so it is not so rough on my arms and legs and with a scent. Why not add herbs and flowers when they are blooming again?*

They wasted no time. Both of them were tired and hungry.

Returning to camp, they sat on the ground next to one another and prepared to eat. Brother Lemur folded his hands, closed his eyes, and bowed his head.

Taking a drink of wine, she asked, "Timo, when you pray, what are you thankful for?"

Swallowing a bit of bread, he responded, "It depends. In general, I am thankful every day for many of the same things ... food, ale, and water to sustain my body, blue skies and sunshine, a day of safe travels, and for Moki, a sturdy helpmate to carry my cargo. Today I added one more—you. A companion to walk with and talk with."

Nichol was touched and pleased that Timo was thankful for her. It reminded her of long walks with Papa that she missed. "Timo, is it best to keep these things to oneself, or is it all right to say them aloud?"

"Either way is acceptable. Most do not voice their innermost feelings. They prefer to keep them between themselves and God. I believe that if you are giving thanks for the good things or good people in your life, it seems appropriate to share those thoughts aloud. To let them know that they are included."

Nichol folded her hands and bowed her head. "Today I am thankful that the horse that Fredric abused has a caring home. I am thankful that you, Moki, and I are reunited, I am thankful for all the food from the monastery, and I am thankful for a safe and quiet place to sleep tonight."

Having said all that, she stretched and yawned. "I am suddenly very tired. I think I will cover myself with my cloak and curl up next to a warm Moki. He has had a long day. Moki rarely sleeps standing up like most donkeys. Look at him. He has already found his spot for the night."

The monk agreed with her decision and stood to put his food away and prepare his own space on Moki's left side. With Moki between them, they settled down to sleep.

Just before drifting off, Nichol whispered, "I am thankful you are in my life. Good night, Timo."

He had not heard her words, but he was thinking the same thing about her as he fell asleep.

forty-seven

The Reveal

I feel a bond has been formed between us ...
one that I will never break or betray.

Nichol was the first to waken in the morning. Rubbing the sleep from her eyes, she stretched, checked on her sleeping companions, and rose in search of a private space.

When she returned to camp, Timo was up and feeding Moki. Turning toward her and smiling, he said, "Good morning." Moki twitched his ears in greeting.

Moving into their circle, she announced, "Good morning to you." Walking to Moki, she gave him a hug and a scratch behind his ear.

Seeing her display of affection, Timo experienced a moment of envy. *I wish she had done that to me.*

Suddenly, Nichol turned to him. "It is such a glorious morning. I am rested and eager to set out. What do you think about that?"

"I agree. Let us load our things and be on our way."

Talking little, they reserved their energy for the climb. Finally, the terrain flattened out and they picked up their pace.

Later that morning, Timo suggested that Moki needed a rest. A large smooth rock formation was ahead offering a sunny spot to sit on as Moki drank from the clay bowl Timo set on the ground.

"Nichol, you seem extremely happy today. What has caused your good mood?"

"This is the happiest I have been since I left Marseilles. There could be many reasons, but if I am honest with myself, I have to say that being with you and Moki is what makes me happy. I traveled by myself for weeks and only had myself to talk to. At all times, I had to remain vigilant. Now, I feel a sense of peace. I do not feel threatened by you, and I feel protected. I enjoy our conversations and you welcome my ideas and feelings in making decisions."

Timo was surprised and concerned by her response. "I had no idea you had been traveling alone for so long. You are different. Young women do not set out on their own. Not only did you do it for a day, but you also set out by yourself to travel all the way to Paris. I know very few men—and no other woman—who would attempt such a journey. I am in awe of you.

"Yes, you are different. You can defend yourself and you are quick thinking. You surprised me when you stated your wants and needs clearly when we first met. What touched me is your care and concern for animals like Moki and the abused horse."

Blushing, then pausing, she said, "Timo, only my father would have said things like that to me."

"In the work I do with the brothers, your traits would be deemed noble. Can I now ask what happened in Marseilles that caused you to leave your home and flee to Paris?"

Silence fell on Nichol as her eyes rested on Moki. Turning to Timo, she spoke.

"One thing you must know about me is that I trust no one until they have earned it. From the day I met you at the fair in Vienne, I felt you were a good person. I could see it in your eyes and in your actions. I trust you. It is time to tell you what happened and why I am headed to Paris."

After a long silence, she began to speak.

"The reason I left Marseilles is because of Astrid, my mother. She was jealous of the time, attention, love, and education my papa devoted to me. His name was Alexander and he was dedicated to teaching me about trade, people, and how to defend myself. He was also the port commander. When he discovered that I would often hide in a niche behind a tapestry in his solar, listening to his conversations, he realized that I was learning about his merchant trade and how powerful people think and behave. He learned that I have an excellent memory and could help him with what I heard and saw.

"Papa respected me. He trusted me. And he treated me differently than he did my brother. Astrid was angry that Fredric was not regarded the same way.

"There's more. You met Fredric. He is a liar, very mean, and a drunkard. Once, he sold me for two pints of wine to two other drunks. They beat me and attempted to rape me. Suddenly, Papa broke into the room where they held me prisoner and stopped the assault. Wrapping his cloak around me, I was rescued. Lifting me on his horse, he held me securely as we rode back to the manor. I never opened my eyes, knowing that I was safe in his arms. Calling for Margaux as he approached the gate, he carried me to my bedchamber and asked her to watch over me and not leave my side.

"The rest I learned from her and Gerhardt, her son. He flogged Fredric for his treachery and stupidity in the open courtyard of our villa for anyone to see and hear. Between the lashings, Papa roared that Fredric was not his son. Astrid witnessed the beating and was furious.

"Papa then sent him away for a year's military training and Fredric failed to meet any of the standards. During this time, Papa started to guide and teach me to be a merchant. Sometimes, he would tell me about contracts and how his trade worked. Sometimes he would talk about what he did and how he did it on long walks in our gardens. And sometimes, he would share things over meals at the villa. He would ask my opinion about people who came to meet with him and relied on my memory and ability to recall specific details of conversations I had heard. Astrid sequestered herself in her bedchamber, spending her time away from both of us and the rest of the household.

"While Fredric was away, Papa had me train with Sir Roland to increase my physical endurance and to learn how to defend myself. Gerhardt, my close friend, went with me. That's how I became such a strong runner.

"During this time, he gave me a map and bags of coin to secret away. He instructed me that if anything happened to him, to go to Margaux. She saw to our house and she was someone Papa confided in to watch over me when he was away. Rose—she was also a friend and confidant of my father—at the docks would help me hide and travel to Paris using the map.

"Papa also gave me keys to his box with all his papers, contracts, and another box where he kept his gold and silver. When Fredric returned from his failed military training, Papa started locking the door to the solar. He gave me a key to that as well.

“One day, Papa had a meeting planned. Before that meeting, he asked me to conceal myself behind the tapestry and be his eyes and ears. It was with a man that he had loaned substantial coin to for purchasing ships, but the man had refused to repay the loan.

“A few days later, Papa was dead. I had seen Astrid accept a vial that contained poison from the same man before the meeting in the solar. Later that evening, she told Margaux that she wanted to talk with Papa and would take his wine to him. She did so, and the next morning he was discovered dead. She poisoned him. I know it!

“The day after his death, she informed me that I was to marry an aging noble in a neighboring village. This man was an old man, much older than Papa. When I refused, she threatened to sell me to the next slave ship that entered the harbor.”

Timo made no attempt to interrupt her as she spoke. All he could do was listen quietly as she relayed her story. *It is hard to believe what I am hearing, but having been with Nick for a few days, I know she speaks the truth.*

“I do not think Papa was ever concerned that he would die at the hands of his wife. I am sure he thought it would be the bishop because he refused to bend to his demands for more than the normal tithes. I remember Papa telling him loudly that as a man of God, he should be ashamed of instilling the fear of damnation into his followers if they did not pay increased tithes to him and his church.

“After that meeting, the bishop made my papa’s life difficult. Papa sensed that his life might be in jeopardy and knowing my mother's and brother's total hatred for me, he prepared me with training to defend myself, a map, trusted helpers, and enough coin to make my way to his friend and business partner, Ezra, who lives in Paris."

As Nichol spoke those words, a cloud of mourning seemed to envelop her. She stopped talking for several moments. And then she spoke once more.

"The name Papa gave me was Lisa. I changed my name from Lisa to Nichol, cut my hair, and continued dressing as a boy to disguise myself and blend in with other travelers. That's how and why I left Marseilles, and why I traveled alone until I met you. I began my journey the day of Papa's funeral and have not stopped since. That is also why I have remained quiet and told no one my story. You are the first person I have trusted enough to tell other than Margaux, Gerhardt, and Rose."

Timo noticed that as Nichol relayed her story, she became animated as she talked through the events she had encountered.

"Timo, as you have told me, we will have many days to talk as we move northward. Now, how do you feel about getting Moki and us back on the road? We can talk as we continue."

"That's a good idea." He offered a hand to help her stand, and she took it. Enveloping her in his arms, he said softly, "I am sorry that this has happened to you Nichol."

Taking Moki's reins, they made their way to the road. This time as they walked, Nichol stood next to Timo. Previously, she had made sure the donkey stayed between them.

Timo noticed the change. *I feel a bond has been formed between us … one that I will never break or betray.*

forty-eight

The Comparison

I cannot imagine being raised in such a family.

"Were there good people in your life, Nichol?"

"Yes, there were many good people in my life … my papa, Margaux, Jonathan, Gerhardt, Rose, and Sir Roland. And now, Timo, I can add you to the group of good people in my life."

As they walked, Timo reflected on the differences in their upbringings. "You are a brave young woman who was born into a family that did not appreciate you … except for your papa. I cannot imagine being raised in such a family."

"Timo, tell me about yours."

"Mathias is my oldest brother, Francis is next, and I am the youngest. My papa, Wilum, is a successful tanner, and my mother, Claudia, has a gift for planting seeds and cultivating crops that kept my family fed all year. I am sure my interest in growing things came from her."

"Was your mother kind to you?"

With a twinkle in his eye, he said, "She showed love and kindness to each of her children as well as to her husband.

Nichol's mood lightened as she heard his story. "I see why you turned out the way you have. What you have described is something I never experienced, except when I had time alone with Papa. Margaux was more like my mother."

Walking for a long stretch in total silence, Nichol found herself comparing their two different childhoods.

I wonder what my life could have been if I had been raised in a family like Timo's. Sadly, I only know about the life I have lived. But I vow that if I ever have children of my own, I will never treat them as Astrid treated me.

They had talked with such ease and in such detail for so long they were surprised to notice the sun was on its downward descent and they needed to find a place to settle in for the night.

Finding one that was not slippery with the mud that they had encountered along the road, they settled by a grove of pines that had created a bed of dry needles under its massive limbs. As the sun dropped, a chill filled the air.

Nichol began to gather up needles from the other trees and dry grasses and piling them into a spot that was central to the grove. Moki had moved closer to her, as if he sensed that the fire would be comforting. Pulling a flint and piece of fire steel from a small bag, she placed the cotton wool on top of the flint. Striking the fire steel against the flint, the cotton wool began to glow. Placing the embers with the grass and pine needles, with rolled up parchment resembling a reed, she bent down with the end of the parchment close to the cotton wool and began to blow a slow but steady flow of air until a flame appeared.

"Where did you learn how to start the flame?" Timo asked.

"It is a way to keep my face from the smoke. I just started doing it; no one showed me. This is the first time that I have felt it was safe for me to start a fire. I could not draw any attention, traveling alone as I was. It was why I always climbed trees to sleep so that no one could see me. I feel safe now."

Without speaking, Timo moved about the area, now looking for burnable wood to enhance the promising fire for the night, and the warmth to come. Finding dead branches that were not soaked from previous rains, he gathered them, to add more wood when it died down.

Going to the packs that had been taken off Moki, he removed a strap and pulled out a small pot. Taking both the pot and Moki's water bowl, he headed to the river. When he returned, he said, "Let us create a stew from the herbs and roots we have."

Excited to have a warm meal, Nichol pulled out an onion, turnip, and dried beans. Cutting them with her dagger, all were added to the now-simmering pot. Reaching into her bag, she removed a few herbs she had brought with her, along with what she gathered along her journey. "This will be hearty, Timo."

Sitting by the fire, they settled in. They each had a spoon, using it to scoop up and serve the cooked ingredients. The bread they had was dipped into the pot, sopping up the rich liquid.

"There is a taste I do not recognize. It was quite distinct, suggesting hot … but it was not hot from the cooking liquids. What is that taste … is it something you added?"

Smiling, Nichol revealed, "You have just tasted pepper, Timo. It was one of the valuable spices Papa imported. I took a small bag of it with me when Papa told me that I might travel to Paris, far from the port of Marseilles and the ships that bring it in."

"You must tell me more about the other spices you have brought with you." Then, he added, "Oh, I almost forgot to give you something."

Intrigued, her eyes followed him as he got up and began to search his bag. "Here it is … the cloth package I wanted." Handing it to Nichol, he sat back and waited for her to open it.

As she removed the twine, the cloth fell away. Inside was the promise he had made to her—the copy of the same manuscript he had given to the brothers at the monastery they had left. And there was more: a quill, a small ink pot with a stopper, and several sheets of blank parchment.

This is better than the meal we just had and the warm fire I have longed for.

Silently, she moved to catch the firelight on the manuscript, looking through his writing quickly, thrilled with what she was reading.

"Oh, Timo, what a wonderful surprise! I can hardly wait to read every word. I am humbled that you have shared this with me and I am filled with joy to have your manuscript. There have been so many times that I have wanted to write down the events of the day and I have had nothing to do it with. Now I can. Tomorrow I shall begin to write *My Journey*. Thank you for everything!"

Conversation flowed as the moonlight night was their backdrop. It was time for sleep. This night was a special night for Nichol and she made sure Timo heard her prayer of thanksgiving.

"Timo, thank you for being the kind and caring man that you are and for being so good to me. I am thankful that you are in my life."

Smiling, he felt he needed to respond directly to her before he said his final prayer of the day.

"I, too, am thankful for you and your companionship."

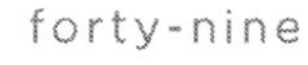

Divine Power

Do I dare speak up and tell him
what I really think and feel?

The next morning was overcast and suggested bad weather. The mist was heavy. Wanting to travel as far as they could before the promised wet weather set in, they ate bread and cheese, sipping from their waterskins as they immediately set out after Moki was loaded up.

The clouds continued to darken and thicken … the threat of snow surfaced. Suddenly, they were both covered in falling snow, with flakes the size of acorns. Moving a good distance off the road to a denser part of thc forest, they found an area where they could shelter under a tall pine and assess their options.

Timo started searching through his travel bags like a squirrel digging for food. Curious, Nichol asked, "What are you looking for?"

"I found it!"

He started unfolding a large tan cloth like the ones she had seen at the fair in Vienne. She jumped up to help him unfold it and together they found a space under the pines where they stretched it among several trees and secured it with the straps used to secure Moki's cargo when they traveled. Once it was constructed, Timo led Moki underneath.

"It looks as though we might need to stay here for some time." Timo searched for firewood while Nichol started a fire.

Nichol knew it was the smart thing to do. Their cloaks were wet, and the road was covered in snow and too slick to walk safely. She nodded her head and began to help Timo move Moki's cargo and spread it under their temporary shelter. Lighter items were placed on tree branches.

Timo began searching through his bags once again and came up with a long brown robe like the one he always wore. He offered it to Nichol, and she looked at him questioningly.

"What am I supposed to do with this?"

"It is my extra robe. I thought you would be more comfortable if you changed out of your wet clothes and into this."

More than willing to get out of her wet clothes, she was chilled and miserable, but if she did, it meant disrobing in front of him.

"Nick, it makes little sense to stay in those clothes and shiver. If you want to put this on, I will turn my back and you can tell me when you are changed."

Taking the robe from him, she stepped out of her wet clothing, slipped the robe over her head, and started laughing. Timo looked over his shoulder to see her doubled up with laughter.

"What is so funny?"

"I am a woman monk. Now Fredric would never recognize me!"

Taking a deep breath, she stood up and held both arms out to the side. "Timo, look at this. This is huge! Two of us could fit into this robe. I am laughing as I wonder what your fellow monks would think if they saw a female in a monk's robe. Could I get in trouble for wearing it?"

"You are welcome to wear that robe all by yourself and stay warm and dry. I am cold and wet. I have clothes in my bag that I have worn on occasion when I am working in the field, much like what you wear every day. It is my turn to change into dry clothes."

While Timo dropped his drenched robe and switched to breeches and a tunic resembling the normal wear of the area, Nichol started to gather the excess robe cloth that enveloped her around her middle. She then tied her regular belt about herself to hold it all in place.

Sitting and facing one another, they ate in silence.

"Nichol, what are you thinking?"

Hesitant to say anything at first, she finally said, with a chuckle, "Look at us. Now, I am dressed like a monk and you are dressed as a peasant."

Timo sensed there was more she wanted to say, and he remained quiet.

"I feel strange. Dressed as you usually are, I feel like I have powers that I did not have as a girl."

"What powers are you talking about?"

"The powers associated with the clothes worn by those in control."

"You think because I wear a robe, I have control over others?"

"Your church maintains control over all people. The fact that you wear a robe makes it obvious that you are part of the church's authority."

"I never looked at it in the way you described it. I have a feeling that it is not just the clothing that makes you think this."

"The clothing is just part of what I am talking about. It made me remember when the two men tried to rape me in the tavern. Men and boys seem to think that women are their servants and they can do and take anything they want from them, including their bodies. Why do men not care what women want? I am confused as to how all this came about."

Speaking slowly and quietly, Timo added, "My father treated my mother and other women with kindness. I would never treat a woman cruelly, monk or not. Tell me, did your father treat your mother poorly?"

"No. He was a master at including women in his life and in his business. He depended on them, especially Rose and Margaux, for information about happenings at the dock and in his own home. He sought their counsel and considered their input valuable. It is how he treated me."

"Why, then, do you make these accusations about men?"

"Because I have experienced all of it at the hands of my brother. And I overheard the conversations of men in Papa's solar. Since I left Marseilles, I have observed and been approached by vile men. Before I met you, I passed a group of peasants on the road. Two of the men in that group tried to assault me. I killed one of them and his accomplice fled for his life."

She has killed a man? I saw her take on Fredric, turning him into a whimpering coward. Nichol is someone with strengths that few have. She is not one to have as an enemy.

"Now I see why you would think men are not to be trusted. You have witnessed their worst actions, but I promise you, not all are bad."

Nichol was quiet, thinking hard. In her heart, she knew that some men could be trusted. *Do I dare speak up and tell him what I really think and feel?*

"Timo, I wished I had your family experience, but I did not. If it were up to Astrid, I would have been forced to marry an old man and subjected to his abuse.

"What I heard in the solar made me believe that a woman's value is less than a dying cat. It is an attitude that men display toward women that says they are superior. In all the meetings that I secretly observed and overheard, not once was there a woman merchant, trader, shipper, moneylender, noble, or religious sister in attendance. it was just me, listening behind the tapestry. Astrid rarely entered the solar, and never when Papa met with someone for business.

"Seldom did I hear anything said about women. The few times that the subject came up, it was only in a passing and scornful manner. If Papa had not told me with his words and trust that I was valuable, I would have believed what I heard and had seen.

"Look at the power of the duke. He is the ultimate authority over everyone in his realm. If there is a duchess, she is only good for breeding and bearing him sons. Her title brings her no power.

"And look at the church, your church, Timo. Who runs it? Just men … those who flaunt their power and wealth. The men of the church and the duke have declared themselves to be divine rulers. Those words I heard many times from my place behind the tapestry. They take their *divine* appointments so seriously that they severely punish their subjects for not heeding their every word. These men tell people what they can or cannot think."

Then Nichol went silent. Deep in thought, almost trancelike, her mind took her in a direction she had not been.

Soon I will go back and retrieve my inheritance—what is rightfully mine.

With Papa's gems, gold, and silver, I will start a revolution with women in trade and eventually gain the same power as men. I know that it will not be easy because no one is willing to relinquish power willingly. I will achieve it without those in power knowing it is happening. I know that the Lady will be my guide and we women will succeed.

Timo sensed that she was somewhere else.

Is her voice—the Lady—talking to her?

After several minutes, he added, "You are right to be angry. You have abilities far above most men I have encountered. Why should you not have the same privileges as men do? Peasant men have few rights—and women, they have even less.

"I do not have any answers for you, Nichol. Let us get some sleep and resume this conversation in the morning."

She gave Moki an ear scratch and then stretched out in readiness for sleep.

Timo leaned back, folded his hands, and gave thanks for this woman, this donkey, and this day.

Nichol has been abused at home, on the road, and has overheard some powerful people utter damning words in her father's solar. No wonder she has a deep anger at men and their hold on authority.

In his prayers, Timo softly said, "I am thankful that Nichol spoke up and trusted me with her thoughts. I understand her better."

Nichol's mind was not ready for sleep.

Tomorrow with ink and quill, I will write …

> I dream of wearing a tunic of my choice without fear.
>
> Of speaking my mind without retribution.
>
> Dreaming for now, that those in power might hear.
>
> Women of the world in bondage without choice.
>
> The Lady and I will be their voice.

Nichol moved in tight against Moki. Her thoughts disappeared as his warmth invaded her.

The voice … My Lady … I feel she is here.

I am here, Nichol … I am traveling by your side. You were right to share with Timo. Rest.

fifty

The Seeds of Change

Timo, you have inspired me to plant the seed.

The next morning was cold; the white blanket of snow was thick and beautiful. Moki was moving about and Timo had given him his straw.

Trying to gauge Nichol's mood, Timo said, "With what you said before we slept, it left me with much thought. Would you like to continue our conversation?"

Nichol nodded slowly. Hesitating at first, she opened up more.

"Timo, I do not understand why men are the only ones who can be powerful and have opinions. Only when coupling is involved are women desirable. Once the act is finished, women are ignored. If they attempt to question a man or his judgment, they are scorned or abused. How did this happen? Can these rules be changed, Timo?"

"I have no idea how all this came about. I confess, I have been working only with farming and seeds. I know how my own family treated women. As I have traveled, I am not involved with women and children, just my brothers. I will be more observant. Maybe then, I will understand more.

"You asked, 'How do we change this?' Maybe what I am about to say could help start a process that will impact many. You are aware that plants have normal growing seasons. How do you get an acorn to grow into a large and vibrant oak? You plant it in good soil, give it water, sun, and time, and eventually it sprouts into a sapling. You continue to nourish it and in time, the sapling becomes a tall and sturdy tree. After many years, that sturdy tree becomes a large oak.

"Nichol, I am wondering if that same approach could be used to create positive changes in how people treat others? There must be a purposeful planting of the seed, in this case, *change*. It must be planted in rich soil, nourished with words of wisdom and good intentions, and bathed in warmth to break open the hardened shell. With continued proper nourishment and light shining on it, in time, the seed will eventually bloom into the desired result."

Nichol looked at him with admiration. "I like that idea. Your comparison is both hopeful and believable. Timo, you have inspired me to plant the seed—for me and also for other women. If we start with the seed of change and give it the proper nourishment, we will one day witness the fruit of the seed we planted. Men will listen to women like Papa did to me. I hope we will live long enough to see how my sapling grows into a big oak tree."

Quickly standing up, she added, "Let us begin."

For the next four days, they made their way through the dense forest surrounding Chalon-sur-Saône and were now heading in a northwesterly direction that crossed the Loire River. Still many weeks from Paris, their friendship and trust of each other grew. The ideas that flowed through the days were stimulating.

For Timo, seeds of ideas began to sprout: *What else is there for me?* He now had someone he could talk to and confide in.

For Nichol, the internal excitement she felt for the potential strength and recognition for women, combined with feeling safe with Timo, eased her fears about traveling alone. She had someone she could talk to and confide in.

Their conversation took on a lighter tone as Timo shared his knowledge of plants and farming.

"Autun will be my next stop, and I estimate that we should arrive there tomorrow if we maintain our current pace. When you are walking with us, Moki moves faster, even with the heavy burden he carries."

Should I tell him?

"Timo … I can sense, hear, and feel the needs of animals. It is something I have known since a small child. My cat Shadow was my confidant for many years. Do you remember when I encountered Fredric? It was his abused horse I whispered to when I had to protect myself, telling him to trample Fredric. That is what it did.

"And when I whisper to Moki, we are talking with each other. When I ask him to move faster so we can find a safe place for the night, he nuzzles my arm to agree. When he needs to stop and rest, he twitches his left ear. When he is thirsty, it is the right. When he wants more straw, he swishes his tail."

"You two talk with each other? Why am I not surprised?" Turning to Moki and gently scratching behind his right ear, Timo said, "Moki, why have you been keeping secrets from me? I thought it was just you and me all along …."

Smiling to himself, Timo picked up Moki's rope as the trio set out.

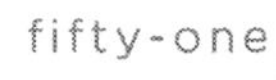

fifty-one

Autun

I hope my work here in Autun will finish quickly.

As expected, they reached the outskirts of Autun before dusk and settled in for the night. Timo's thoughts were filled with his tasks with the brothers that would start early the next day. As he closed his eyes, he envisioned his plans for the next two days.

Rising early, they set out for the monastery. Both were excited to see what the day would bring.

"Nick, do you plan on staying in the longhouse while I am working with my brothers? It might take two full days of training. You could meet some of the people who live here and get hot meals from the longhouse."

"I will stay in the longhouse and we will move on when you are ready. Food and a warm place to sleep with a roof is welcomed. I will fill my days exploring the village. But first, I have one question."

Laughing, Timo asked, "You have only one question? What is it?"

"If I need to talk to you in the next two days, how will I get word to you?"

Thinking for a moment, he found a small bag of seeds and handed it to Nichol.

"If the need arises, give this to one of the monks and tell him it is a bag of seeds that belongs to Brother Lemur. If I am given this bag, the first place I will look for you will be in the stables."

She nodded. "Yes, that plan will work. I will take the bag with me now. I will see you later."

As usual, Timo was taken aback by her openness and honesty of emotion. *I will miss Nick, too. I hope my work here in Autun will finish quickly.*

Nichol gave Moki a scratch behind the ear, leaned in and whispered to him, and waved goodbye to Timo as she headed for the road.

Timo tied Moki to a nearby post and approached the front doors of the monastery.

Entering, he saw how modestly the interior was furnished. There were the expected illustrations of saints, bible stories, and holy figures adorning the walls. The long hallway that led to the chapel felt soothing and peaceful. It felt sacred. He relaxed, absorbing the calmness that surrounded him.

Moving into the monastery halls, a brother approached him. Timo introduced himself and asked where he could find Abbot Filibert. Sighing, the monk pointed to Timo's left, bowed his head, and continued down the hallway.

Timo knocked on the door and was beckoned into the room. He was surprised to see a tall, thin young monk standing at the window of the room with rosary in hand.

"I am Brother Lemur. Are you Abbot Filibert?"

Making the sign of the cross as he turned to Timo, he said, "Yes, I am."

"Greetings, Abbot Filibert. I am Brother Lemur from Vienne. From what I have seen in the short time here, your fields display skill in planting. From what I saw in your fields as I approached the monastery, you are successful farmers.

"I had planned to be with you two days to assist the brothers, but I do not think they need it. I have put together a manuscript illustrating how to plant, maintain, and harvest the crops the various seeds that you do not have will produce. I could leave it with you along with the new seeds and be on my way."

Abbot Filibert smiled. "Brother Lemur, the other brothers and I will be pleased to hear your words. You are more than welcome to stay and rest for a few days."

Placing his hand on Filibert's shoulder, Timo spoke, "I do appreciate your offer. However, I must be on my way to the monastery in Auxerre."

"Before you depart, go to the kitchen and replenish your food and ale. Go with God, and may He keep you safe as you travel."

"Thank you for sharing your bounty with me. I hope we will meet again on my return to Auton."

Finding Moki tethered at the front of the monastery, Timo retrieved his food sack and waterskin and went to the kitchen to fill them. Returning, he loosened Moki's reins and headed toward the market to find Nick.

Autun was not a large settlement, but the village had outdoor shops that lined the roadway, including a stable and an inn.

Timo found Nichol leaning against a post with a clay pot in her hands. She had found a honey merchant and bought some of his wares.

Surprised to see him so soon, she put the pot in her travel bag. "Timo, what is wrong? Why are you here now?"

"There's nothing to worry about—I will explain it as we move on. I do not need to do the teaching over the two days I had planned for this monastery. I have left my manuscripts and new seeds for them to use."

Taking Moki's halter, Timo steered him in the direction he wanted to go.

At the same time, Nichol was eyeing Timo's feet. *His shoes are different from what others have. Did his father make them?*

"Timo, your footwear is unique. They are different from any I saw when I lived in Marseilles. Where did you get them?"

"I made them. My father taught his sons how to make leather boots and sandals. Why do you ask?"

"My feet are very sore from all the walking and running I have done, and Paris is still far away. I need something that protects my feet when I run, and if there is a way to support them better, my feet will feel better. The animal hides I am using do not work well. The leather is not supple enough and the soles are too thin for me to run in. I wonder if I could make my shoe soles thicker on the bottom to cushion my steps somehow? Would you teach me how to make shoes that would fit my needs?"

"Of course," he replied immediately, amused with her enthusiasm.

"When I found the honey merchant, I noticed that there was a tannery at the end of the road. I have an idea. Will you come with me? If we find hides that are suitable, I can purchase them."

"Nick, I will need to purchase several tools and waxed linen thread to make shoes."

"I have the coin for whatever you need."

Taking Moki's reins, they headed to the tannery where a variety of hides and leather were stretched out on two tables. The merchant had several types of skins hanging on straps stretched across the back wall.

They both examined the goods displayed. Timo spoke up. "This leather is good quality cowhide, very thick and strong."

Nichol had picked up a goatskin. "I also like the softness of the goat. This would be good, I think."

Timo nodded, agreeing with her choices. Both hides were quite large.

He asked the man in front of them the cost of the skins.

Subtly, Nichol moved away from Timo and feigned looking at other hides, pulling her purse out from her tunic at the same time and extracting the necessary money for the purchase. She slipped the coins into Timo's hand.

"I supply all the hides for the monastery. They have the tools to make shoes," the merchant said.

"I am Brother Lemur from the Vienne monastery. I have just left the monastery at Autun, supplying them with new seeds for their fields. I planned to be here two days to work with them with their crops and wine growing. Instead, I have left them with my seeds and instructions, and I am heading to my next monastery."

Turning his head to where Nichol was looking at the goat hides and then back to the tanner, he added, "This boy was hanging around the monastery and I noticed he needed shoes. I would like to make him a pair and a pair for myself as well.

The tanner looked closely at Timo. "Do you have the coin to pay for these goods?" he questioned.

"Yes, I am traveling to several monasteries in France and have been given extra coin for my needs if the monasteries where I am stopping cannot provide for me."

"We will need some linen and a few other tools; I have needles with me. I will need a punch, an awl, and a sharp knife. Do you have these here? Of course, any charity you wish to provide will be welcome."

"The monastery has been good to me. I have what you need and will give it to you for little coin."

"Bless you, sir, for your kindness."

Staying in the background, Nichol listened intently on how Timo handled the tanner. *Papa would want to do business with Timo.*

Timo thanked the merchant and they left with their new tools and hides.

"Let us see if there is a room at the inn and a place at the stable for Moki, since we will not be using the longhouse and the monastery's stable. I have the coin to pay for it and we can use the space to make our new footwear."

"Timo, will the innkeeper wonder why a monk and boy are traveling together when there is a monastery in the village? Will others know you are not connected with it?"

"That was taken care of with the conversation I had with the tanner. Everyone knows what everyone else does in villages. This one is no different. He will tell them about my connection and wanting to help a young boy because my father taught me how to make shoes."

"Would it be easier if you changed into the other clothes you carry? That way you would look like a peasant, too."

When those words tumbled out, Nichol noticed Timo was troubled with what she had said.

"Come, Nick, let us fetch Moki and leave. I have much to tell you. We can walk for a few hours and find a place to settle in that has some shelter from the weather."

Puzzled, she put the coin away that she had already pulled from her bag to use for the inn stay.

"Nick … I am getting used to you calling me that. I like it."

fifty-two

The Bonding

We both have something to hide.

Nichol followed Timo as they headed out of Autun toward Auxerre. "What did I say that upset you?"

"You have not upset me. I must explain my life as a monk and where I may have misled you. When we stop, we will start a fire if it is safe."

Silence followed. Nichol was lost in her thoughts. *What did he mean … he misled me?*

Turning to Timo, she said, "I am going to run ahead and see if there is anything suitable for us off the side of the road. If there is, I will hunt for wood for starting the fire later and come back to meet and walk forward with you and Moki."

Turning to Moki, she gave him his special scratch behind the right ear and then took off before Timo could say anything.

Starting to run, she turned her head and yelled back, "I will find the perfect spot where our fire and conversations will not be seen or overheard."

Running until her feet hurt, all she could think was *I need better shoes.* She saw a small stream crossing the road and turned onto the stream bank without slowing down. When she saw thickets on both sides, her pace slowed to a fast walk. She glanced back and realized she could not be seen from the road.

"The road has disappeared from sight," she said aloud, as if Timo was with her. Finding a clearing ahead, she climbed over the bank and stopped.

Speaking aloud once again, she said, "This is perfect. Trees for protection and wood for a fire — now I need to get busy."

The sun's placement told her that it was midafternoon by the time she finished gathering wood and setting up the rest of the site. Looking back as she approached the road, she could not see the area from the path.

I think Timo will like my choice.

Following her earlier steps at a slow run, Nick had no other thought than the making of her new shoes. *I need the ability to run farther, with more comfort for my feet. Other than Papa's dagger, running is my only protection.*

It was not long before she heard Moki's bray. Smiling, she began to slow down as she saw them and waved. Timo raised his arm … and at the same time, she noticed that Moki's ears seemed to perk up as well.

Finally slowing to a walk that matched Moki's, she reached over and gave him his scratch behind the ear. *I am back, little friend.*

At the same time, she said to Timo, "It is not much farther … I think we can get there before the sun sets. I have found plenty of wood for the fire and have it ready to start."

The threesome once again set out together. Nichol noticed that both Timo and Moki picked up their walking pace. An air of energy surrounded them.

"I told you that I had much to tell you. Now that we are settled here for a night or two, let us talk over food and the warmth of this fire," Timo said with a smile.

Passing bread, cheese, and dried meat to each other, he began to speak.

"The first years after I entered the monastery at Vienne were joyous. I felt a belonging, I enjoyed the structure of monastic life. I found my calling in sowing and reaping, and the gift of providing food to the monastery and the poor. What I could not adapt to was the petty behavior of certain monks. It wore on my spirit and I needed to find a way out of the monastery and still remain a monk.

"I approached the abbot with an idea to use our success with farming and see if it could benefit other monasteries. Monks stay with a monastery for their entire lives, so to see one like myself on the road is rare. Did you see the tanner, and how he looked at you and me?"

"Yes, I did see him looking at us strangely. From what you are saying, it would look worse if we entered an inn and asked for a room. Traveling with me could put you or me in trouble with the abbots of the monasteries we are visiting."

"Nick, we should not bend to the gossip of others, but we can continue as we have and stay separated except on the road. We both have something to hide. You are hiding who you are; I am hiding that I am traveling with a woman who I know is disguised as a boy. I am grateful to have you as a traveling companion."

"What I meant about the clothes is that clothes will not change who you are as a person. You will always be Timo the monk to me. I know who you are … I see you."

"What does that mean, 'I see you?'"

Her gaze unblinking, Nichol stared into the fire. "When I was hiding in Papa's solar, I observed people without them knowing I was watching. Occasionally a feeling would come over me and I could see people." Turning to Timo, she added, "It was something that Papa said about me—I could see people."

"I am curious; how do you see people?" Timo questioned.

"I could see them sitting there with my papa. The only way I know how to describe what I mean is that, despite what they said or told to my papa, I knew the true purpose of why they were there, what they wanted, and their motives without a single spoken word.

"If they lied when they spoke, I saw their body movements, the way they used their eyes and hands. I knew what their intention was before they said a word. I could see them further with the words they used and what sounds they made when they spoke. Sometimes, I could get a sense of the food they ate or what they drank by the odor of their bodies. And then there was their overall presence. My mind would tell me if they could be trusted … if they were decent or bad.

"When we met on the road, I saw you." Nichol turned to face him. "The monk I saw is true to his vows."

Silence fell once again.

Timo had never encountered anyone like her. *Who is this captivating young woman and what wonders will the future bring for her? And for me?*

"I must admit, I enjoy our journey and conversations on the road more than my time at the monastery. And now that we are here, I propose that we start work on your new shoes. What do you need? How are they different from what others have?"

"This is the extra pair of shoes I have worn through on this journey since I have left Marseilles. I run many steps each day, some days all day long. The sole is thin after so many steps; soon holes will be worn through the leather. If I step on sharp rocks and after I have run for long periods, this is where I feel pain.

"What I need is a thick sole of leather with a soft leather top tied at the ankle. If more thick leather can be added to just the toe and heel areas, I think it would feel better for my feet. And with the leather between the toe and heel being lighter in weight, it will allow the shoe to bend when I run. I will make a pad for inside the shoe from cloth to protect my feet and keep them warm."

Returning to the baskets Moki carried, Timo retrieved the leather and the tools he used to make his own shoes.

"Stand on this piece of leather so I can trace your foot. I can make the shoes you described."

"I have another idea. If we have enough leather left over from making the shoes, I want to make a new travel pack. One that I can carry on my back with straps over my shoulders."

"What is wrong with the one you have?"

"The side satchel I have now, has only one strap and it is not convenient to run with. The day I escaped from Fredric, I climbed a riverbank and ran into a thicket, and my bag caught on everything I passed. If I wear it on my back, I can move faster and more freely. And my hands will be free."

Timo absorbed what she said, then nodded his head, "Yes, we will have plenty for you to make a new satchel. You decide what size you want, and I will show you how to stitch it together."

Timo next made a pattern of one foot and then the other. Next, he began making what she had described.

Moki had given Nichol another idea that would benefit both her and Timo. Taking two pieces of leather and folding each, she stitched three sides closed with the awl and linen, leaving one side open. Gathering grasses and wild straw, she stuffed each one full.

That night, she revealed what she had made—a traveling headrest for sleeping.

"When I was resting my head against Moki and watching you pull out the hides we got, I realized having something that we could rest our heads on at night would be good. So, I made one for each of us that would not be ruined by the ground and could be restuffed as needed."

"I like this. Easy to carry and they will add no weight to Moki as we walk. I will use it tonight."

Encouraged with what Nichol created, Timo got busy.

Over the next four days, he worked on her shoes, having her close by so he could show her proper stitching methods that would endure rigorous wear. Throughout the process, he had her stand in them as he adjusted the new sole cushions, along with making sure her measurements were correct.

Finally, he was satisfied. Handing them to her, she immediately slipped them on and tied them at the ankle. Standing up, she sprinted to the closest tree, then turned and ran back to where he stood.

Returning to Timo, she smiled and said, "These are the exact shoes I described to you! They are sturdy and easy to move in. Thank you, Timo!"

"Seeing your smile made all the work worthwhile. Now, let me see the satchel you have been working on."

Holding it up for him to see, Nichol said, "I am almost finished. I just need to stitch on these straps to keep the flap closed."

Taking the satchel in his hands, his eyes took in her stitchery. He noticed that it was divided into sections and that she had added a flap to protect the opening. He had never seen straps that could be used as part of a garment.

"Nicely done. Your satchel is sturdy and well-crafted. Your idea to use two shoulder straps works. Now you can fill your bag and carry it on your back. Your hands will be free and you can run, all at the same time. Nick, I am impressed with your ability to solve a problem by creating something new."

"Look what we have done, Timo! A new type of shoe. A head-rest for sleeping. And a back satchel. Before I left the manor, I had everything a girl could want at home. Then you made a true pair of running shoes just for me, ones that I can run in all day long. You did not do this to make a profit, only to help me with your kindness. The kindness that I saw in you when we first met."

"And I see things in you that few others see. I know your papa did as well. And Margaux and Rose that you talk about saw it, too. You were privileged with how and where you lived. You had wealth that peasants and commoners will not experience. Yet, you are one of them—you understand them and their needs."

"It is true ... Papa made sure that I took care of the needy and orphans. I know that Rose was part of my understanding their needs."

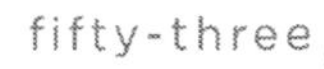

fifty-three

Auxerre

You were right. It seems I have a lot to learn about men and their evil ways.

Something had happened over the past few days.

A new sense of trust, of understanding had developed between them. The two of them had become united, yet they both knew they had separate paths to follow.

Moki was packed and Nichol's feet were encased in comfort. Each day she marveled over her improved shoes and how she was not as sore at day's end.

As they moved away from Autun, the dirt roads became rutted, narrower, and more difficult to travel. None of the surroundings delivered an adequate location to settle in for a few days. They had to continually watch for safe paths for Moki as well as themselves. As dusk came, they looked for their favored pines that they could sleep under.

They spent two exhausting days traversing the densely forested territory.

Early on the third morning, they heard loud talking and horses approaching.

Looking at Timo with concern, Nichol said, "We have not encountered people on horseback since Lyon where I took Fredric's horse. We should hide in the trees and see who is approaching."

Timo heeded her words and led Moki off the road and behind a nearby grove of trees.

Suddenly, three men on horseback came galloping up the hill from the direction of the river and stopped when they reached the road. They were dressed in tattered and dirty clothes. From their hidden location in the trees, Nichol and Timo could tell the men were heavily armed with swords and daggers.

The lead rider was waving a sword, and on its tip hung a long white tunic … a woman's tunic. His companions celebrated him with lewd shouts of praise concerning his male prowess.

As the riders bolted past their hideout, Nichol thought she knew the reason for their gaiety. She clenched her jaws and tried to quell the bile that was rising in her mouth. The riders headed north at a gallop, and Nichol and Timo stayed hidden. When the riders did not return, they nodded to each other and made their way back to the road.

Timo could tell from the set of her jaw that she was angry.

Her outburst was immediate. "Timo, did not you see what the leader had draped across his sword? It was a tunic, like peasant women wear. Based on that, and their excitement, I would guess the woman it belonged to did not fare well.

Timo tried to calm his friend. "Nick, are you assuming you know how the man came to possess it?" Immediately, he regretted what he said as the words flowed out of his mouth.

Nichol was infuriated by Timo's words. Through clenched teeth, she spat, "After hearing their words, why do you believe anything good or innocent about these men? They do not wear tunics and I doubt they robbed a washerwoman. Men are not all good, Timo —were not Fredric's actions enough to prove that to you?"

She left him standing there and backtracked on the path to investigate where the thugs had come from.

As she ran down the hill, her furor began to ebb.

Maybe Timo was right. She had imagined the worst when she saw the three horsemen, their bawdy words, and the trophy they displayed. If she was wrong, she decided she would apologize when they stopped to rest.

Rounding a bend in the path close to the river, her anger was quickly rekindled.

In front of her was a horrendous sight.

Off to her right, a naked young woman hung from a tree by her wrists. Blood had flowed from several stab wounds, darkening the ground beneath her. She had been beaten as well; bruises covered her body. It was obvious from her numerous injuries that she was dead.

Nichol ran to the bloodied site and cut the woman down. Was she still alive? Her eyes were fixed and stared out at nothing ... and everything. Checking for her breathing, there was none.

In a low voice, Nichol said to the young naked woman who lay at her feet, "I am sorry they destroyed you," and dropped to the ground in a fit of rage and sobbed at the cruel and senseless scene before her.

Flashes of the assault that had begun at the hands of Fredric's friends overtook her. She spat out every blasphemous term she knew to curse the men who had done this. If there truly was a God, she begged for the men to be dealt with in the same brutal manner they had used on their innocent victim.

Sitting up, she turned to the lifeless body, saying, "I will make them pay, I promise."

Turning, she saw Timo stop at the same spot where she had first seen the murder site. Horror and sorrow spread across his face. He slowly led Moki to the area and tethered him to a branch far from where the woman had hung.

Looking down at Nichol, he nodded solemnly. "You were right."

Nichol was not in the mood to talk. "Will you help me bury her?"

Scanning the area, Timo shook his head. "Unfortunately, this area is filled with rocks, and we cannot dig a grave. All we can do now is carry her body into the forest, cover her with branches and pray for the repose of her soul. I do not know what else to do."

They carried her body deep into the forest and layed her beneath a grove of trees. Fallen tree branches were collected to cover her.

When finished, they stood there in quiet sadness. Timo folded his hands, bowed his head and spoke words of praise for the woman. He concluded by asking God to lead her to the eternal light.

He could not go on. He had never witnessed anything this horrific, and he was having a hard time managing his emotions, let alone finding the right words to speak. *How could men be so cruel and purposefully destroy an innocent woman? How could a God allow this to happen?* He looked at Nick and knew she had endured enough.

Timo made the sign of the cross over the woman and turned to leave. Nichol followed. As they left, Nichol whispered, "Those were nice words you said, but words will not bring her back."

Timo could say nothing in response, he was so immersed in his thoughts and own anger at what he had witnessed. Both fell silent as they returned to Moki.

Timo felt the heaviness of grief, and withdrew inside himself to deal with it. They both walked for the rest of the day without saying a word.

Finally, Nichol broke the silence and asked if they could stop and set up camp. She led the way off the road and deep into the forest. They stopped when they found suitable space amongst the trees and silently unburdened Moki and spread his cargo out in the circular fashion they always did.

Timo scattered straw for Moki's dinner, poured a bowl of water for him, and left the campsite to be alone. When he returned, he saw that Nichol had helped herself to a few bites of food, and Timo sat near her to do the same.

He could tell she was holding a lot inside. "I can see that you need to talk. It might help both of us if we talk about what we experienced today."

Softly, she spoke. "I do not understand how these things happen. What did that woman do to deserve what they did to her. They raped her, beat her, and finally stabbed her to death. Where was your God when that woman was being brutalized? Why did not He intervene on her behalf? I do not understand. Why does not God stop cruel people?"

"I have no answers. I am asking myself the same questions."

"I want to find them and show them how it feels to be defenseless. I am tired of the strong and powerful maiming and killing the weak just because they feel like doing it—because they can. When I was in my papa's solar listening to the endless boasting of men's exploits and wars, I know what we saw today happens often, even though these things should not happen at all. I want to see justice administered, yet I know it will never happen."

She stopped to take a drink and that gave Timo time to talk.

Timo understood the rage she was expressing because what she had witnessed in the field very closely paralleled what she had suffered at the hands of her brother. She was finally expressing her inner feelings about the abuse she had experienced. Those suppressed emotions were causing her to lash out at all the bad people who did horrific things to innocent people.

"I have never seen the likes of what we came upon today. I hope I am never faced with it again. I do not know how or why bad things happen to innocent people, I do not know what drives some to such cruelty toward others. I am full sighted, yet I seem to have been blinded to what others have and are experiencing, as I just worked in the fields with my brothers. Was today my introduction to the true world that surrounds us? Are women unsafe if men find them alone? Are there many others like her who have died like she did?"

He shook his head before he continued. "I agree with you that the victims deserve justice. Up to now, I have never been exposed to the hatred and injustices that you have described, and I have never experienced the brutality we saw today. I have a feeling there will be more lessons on this journey.

"If I were confronted in a malicious manner, I am not certain I could defend myself. Monks are not warriors. People tend to leave us alone because we are religious figures. They are afraid

God will strike them dead if they attempt to harm us or steal from us. One thing I do know—if I had to physically defend myself, I would not fare well."

"You are a kind person, Timo. You see the best in people before they show you their worst. I am more distrustful. I have been trained to defend myself at Papa's insistence after I was attacked. I can teach you how to protect yourself. Would you like me to show you everything Sir Roland taught me and Gerhardt?"

Silence descended after she suggested that.

Finally, Timo said, "You are right. I think it would be wise for me to develop some defensive skills. But we have no swords or any other weapons to use for training."

"One of the things I learned in the beginning was that strength training was essential. Sir Roland made me run everywhere … not walk. Then, he continued our lessons using wood swords. I can do the same with you. Having Moki with us prevents you from running, but we can work on swordplay and hand-fighting. And, if I work with you, it will help me with my skills, too. Tomorrow, we will look for wood to make swords and begin your lessons."

"I am ready. And with what I have seen from you so far, you will be an excellent teacher."

Timo's Training

What a gift you are to me.

Whenever they stopped to rest, Nichol taught Timo the techniques of sparring, deflecting, dodging, kicking, and charging an opponent using wooden swords and daggers.

As she explained the strength training Sir Roland had demanded she and Gerhardt include in their daily routine, Timo said, "Let us try the run-walk as we travel."

Moki was the only drawback. They created a plan where Nichol ran ahead of Timo and Moki with her food pack on her back and found a spot where she could rest, eat, and wait for them. Then they reversed their roles and Timo ran ahead and waited for Nichol as she walked forward with Moki.

"It will take several days of practice before your legs and body get used to the pounding and the faster pace, but if you commit to practicing, both your strength and endurance will improve. You surprised me with how fast you are learning with the training. I did not expect you to be as agile as you are—you are catching on quickly."

"I had two older brothers I had to defend myself from, but I did not want to fight. It is why I always ended up on the ground, with them walking away laughing. I wish I had met you growing up I would have won a few of the battles we waged. In the end, Father settled whatever we were fighting over. Eventually, we brothers became good friends."

"Do you miss your family?"

"Yes, I do. One day I will return. Until then, I have fond memories.

"And what did I do to deserve a companion who is so smart and skilled? What a gift you are to me."

"Thank you." Laughing, she added, "You can be glad I am the one training you and not Sir Roland. And I am thankful to you for being my friend and for showing me a more thoughtful and gentle way of being."

Because they had added training and practice to their daily routines, time passed quickly and before they knew it, they had reached the town of Auxerre, where Timo would spend time at its monastery.

All of them, even Moki, knew what to do.

Timo headed to the stables with Moki to get him settled, then to the main structure of the monastery. Nick would head to the village, eventually settling in the longhouse.

"I will go to the village to see what is there later and join the other travelers in the longhouse. If I need you, I will send a message with the bag of seeds you already gave me." Scratching Moki's favored ear, she whispered in it and left.

What does she say to him? Timo wondered.

Taking Moki to the stables, Timo settled him in for the night. Entering the back entrance of the monastery, he stood for a moment trying to determine where he could find the abbot.

Passing a tall young monk who was crossing the hallway, he introduced himself and asked where he could locate Abbot Lothaire.

"You will find him in the last room on your left," the response came.

Reaching the end of the hall, Timo knocked on the door. The response was a gruff, "Enter."

Opening the door, he asked, "Are you Abbot Lothaire?"

As he said that, Timo's eyes took in the rich tapestries hanging on three of the walls, one with deep burgundies that featured a beautiful white steed charging forward. Another represented wine fields in full harvest. Whoever created these masterpieces had to be a weaver of renown. As Timo moved his eyes to the third, they were rudely interrupted.

The overweight monk sitting behind a table almost shouted at him, "Who did you expect to find here? Yes, I am Abbot Lothaire. Who are you and what do you want?"

Timo introduced himself and opened his mouth to explain why he had been sent to Auxerre. Cutting him off, waving dismissively, the abbot seemed uninterested in Timo's words.

Abbot Lothaire leaned back in his chair, bridged his fingers over his belly and glared at Timo. "You are not needed here ... or wanted." Immediately, he began praising himself. "Because of my knowledge and guidance, my monastery has been extremely successful."

Harshening his glare, leaning forward, the abbot squinted his dark eyes. "Brother Lemur, you can leave. The bishop has praised me for the farming methods I created and implemented. And the bishop has sent many groups to review our superb winemaking. They are all impressed with what I have accomplished. On his last visit, he gifted me with the tapestry of our orchards on the wall."

Timo stood listening to the boasting and embellishment. Since he had entered the abbot's office, he had not uttered a word after he introduced himself.

After several minutes of self-aggrandizement, Abbot Lothaire finally took a breath. He pushed his plump body away from the table, stood, and waddled to the door. Placing his hand on Timo's shoulder, he pushed him through it.

"So, you see, Brother Lemur, bishops and nobles alike have recognized and praised me for the success of our farms and vineyards. Surely you can see I do not need your training, seeds or ideas. You are free to go."

Abbot Lothaire turned back into his room and closed the door loudly.

Timo stood by himself in the hallway. He was so taken aback by what had just happened that all he could do was stand there.

He began to laugh.

At this point I am glad I will not have to stay here and endure his presence. This man's arrogance is enhanced with his gluttony and greed. I feel pity for the monks who live here and must tolerate the abbot's grand opinion of himself. He is one of the reasons why I am not living in a monastery.

Exiting the monastery, he went to retrieve Moki.

He found him dozing as he stood in his stall, and said out loud, "Moki, my faithful friend, it seems we are neither needed nor welcome here. We are free to be on our way. What do you say we go find Nick?"

Moki fanned his ears and waited for Timo to lead the way.

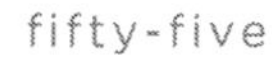

Justice

You must continue your journey
and stay away from them.

Nichol slowly walked down the road leading into Auxerre. Small shops lined the main street, with people entering and exiting. The day was a brisk and sunny one, a welcome relief from the constant overcast gray skies that permeate the winter landscape. Many lingered to speak with those they knew, as if they knew that the sun's warmth would not last long.

She stopped when a familiar smell caught her attention. Closing her eyes, she inhaled deeply to embrace a familiar scent, one that was attached to a fond memory —the burning of lavender that she so loved every time she visited Rose.

There must be a shop that sells herbs and spices nearby.

Opening her eyes, she scanned the surrounding shops to find the source of the delicate, sweet smell that blended flowers, herbs, and a hint of her evergreen bed each night. Nichol's intent was to let the smell guide her to the source.

As she set out, three horses that looked familiar distracted her. Tied to a post at a tavern, she was pulled to them. As she got closer, she saw a bloody tunic tied to one of the horses.

I know this tunic ... and I know these horses. They belong to the men who murdered the woman we found hanging from the tree. These vile men have no fear and do as they please.

I cannot let them go unpunished. I must go back and find the shop that has the familiar smell. I will purchase a remedy to combat their evil ways.

Returning to the spot of the scent that first got her attention, she let her eyes lead her to the source of lavender smoke and a narrow door, now ajar. Stepping just inside it, the sight and aroma of herbs and spices brought pleasant memories of Rose's shop.

Just then she heard the voice of an elderly woman. "Come in, you are blocking the sun. Do I know you?"

Nichol stepped aside. Through the haze she saw an old woman sitting on a stool, now basking in the warm sunlight of the winter day.

"No, I am just passing through."

"Are you in need of a remedy?"

"Not a remedy, but a poison for three rats."

Nichol went to where plants were hanging by string to dry. She rubbed leaves between her fingers and smelled the fragrance on her fingers that was released into the air.

"It was a memory that brought me to your door today."

"What memory would that be?"

"A fond memory of a wise woman, one that looked much like yourself. Someone I could trust and share my thoughts with. And one who gave me guidance."

"Come closer to me; my eyes are not what they use to be."

Nichol approached and kneeled in front of the small woman; her eyes were clouded with age. *She can barely see.*

"Your voice tells me that you are troubled. Is that why you want a poison?"

"Yes, I am troubled. Before I came in here, I saw three horses in front of the tavern. One had a bloody tunic draped across the saddle. The tunic belonged to a woman I found hanging from a tree. The men who rode the horses raped and murdered her."

The woman was silent a moment longer, then said, "If you knew a wise woman, then you must know why we inhale burning lavender, yes?"

"I do. Rose taught me it was to release fear and calm the mind."

She took Nichol's hands and spoke in a low, soft voice, "Now close your eyes and breathe deep."

At the same time, she crushed three lavender leaves between her fingers. Nichol took a deep breath. Her eyes began to close as her head slowly dropped, until her chin rested on her chest.

Neither spoke for a long time, until the wise woman observed Nichol raising her head and opening her eyes. The two pairs of eyes met.

"You must continue your journey and stay away from them. I knew from your first words that you are a young woman and if they captured you, they would show you no mercy. You would meet the fate of the young woman you found hanging.

"These men come and go as they please and are protected. They are henchmen for those who can pay. The church, dukes, and lords use them for protection and to collect tithes and rents and enforce against those who do not heed their word or meet their demands.

“The poor woman you found was probably a slave given to them for their service. No one will challenge them. Everyone is afraid because they are protected. They do as they wish with no consequences.

“You said that you are just passing through. Now, you must go and get away from here quickly. These men ride long distances, and there is no way to hide from them.”

Nichol stood and removed silver coins from her pouch. Taking the wise woman’s hand, she placed the coins in her palm, “Thank you for your explanation. Your words of warning show you care, but you know I cannot let the woman’s death go unpunished.”

The old woman’s head dropped again. In her soft whisper, she added, “When you touched my hand, I knew you would not heed my words ... go with her, she will guide you.”

Nichol looked closely at her, bent over, and kissed the woman on the forehead. “I hear you and will carry your words with me.” She turned and walked out.

She knows about her ... the Lady.

Reversing her direction, Nichol walked toward the tavern. As she entered, the stench inside the noisy, smoke-filled room was overwhelming. Her memory of her assault that Fredric had encouraged flooded her mind and she could feel rage entering her body.

The stench here is the same as the Anchor Inn. Clearing her mind and remembering the aroma of the crushed lavender, she glanced around the room, stopping at where the three men were seated. Her eyes moved to where the wine and ale barrels were stored.

Moving toward a man pouring wine and ale, she gave him enough coin to keep the wine flowing to the three men. Nichol ordered a cup of ale and sat on a stool in a corner of the tavern so she could watch them without being noticed.

Their voices thundered through the small tavern with each cup of wine and loud tales of their exploits brought glares from other patrons in the small tavern.

Impressed with their own stories, each one tried to outdo the other, not caring who heard them because they were untouchable. Other patrons began to leave, not wanting to endure their stories and company.

A plan was forming in her mind—a simple plan that did not involve poison or the dagger, one that would slow them down.

I must continue my journey with Timo to Paris and fulfill Papa's wishes.

Nichol stood and walked out. She mounted the horse with the tunic, took the reins of the other two and proceeded to ride to the monastery and Timo.

Halfway there, Timo and Moki met her. He quickly assessed that the horses were familiar—the same ones that belonged to the men who murdered the woman they had found.

Once he was standing in front of Nichol, his voice was very low. "How did you acquire these horses?"

Hesitating before she spoke, she knew that she must be completely honest.

"I saw them tied in front of a tavern and decided to take them to the monastery and tell the abbot that the men who own them savagely killed a young woman." Nichol paused, her expression changed, then asked, "Why are you not at the monastery ... are you leaving it now?"

"The abbot did not want me here. He even pushed me out of his cell and slammed the door behind me. He would not want to hear your story, nor would he want to see you. Nichol, this is not a safe place for any of us. We need to leave and be far from here before the men know their horses are gone."

Taking in what he said, she knew he was right. These men could even be messengers for the abbot or the bishop. *We could both be in danger here.*

"I can travel faster than you and Moki. Once I am far from here, I will separate the saddles and bridles, and hide them as I move away from here. Then I will turn the horses loose. It will take a day before you catch up with me. I will watch for you from a treetop. You will hear my whistle as you approach."

Before Timo could say anything else, Nichol turned the horses around and headed toward Montereau, their next destination. Moki and Timo followed her direction on foot and watched her ride out of sight.

Nichol rode hard the rest of the day. With enough light left, she found a safe place to stay for the night. Finishing what little food she had in her pack, she fell asleep with thoughts of meeting Timo and Moki the next morning.

She led one horse away from the road into a pasture and set it free. Taking the saddle and bridle from the horse and tying it onto a branch high in a pine tree, she laughed to herself. *They may find the horse but they will never look up to find the saddle or bridle.*

Continuing down the road, she did the same with the other horses, saddles, and bridles but on the opposite side of the road. As she carefully returned to the road, she remained hidden to observe any travelers passing by.

Pausing, she heard voices. A group of travelers were heading toward Auxerre, where she had just come from. Kneeling behind a cluster of bushes waiting for them to pass, she suddenly realized she had only one meal in two days and it consisted of a few bites to eat last night. Nichol walked to the road and started back toward Auxerre, keeping the other travelers in sight but far enough behind them to escape notice. *Timo would have food and we can continue together.*

At the end of the day with the sun low in the sky, Nichol stopped and climbed a tree to a point where she could see the road clearly in both directions. Wrapping herself in her cloak and covering her head with just a small hole to breathe through, she began to reflect. *I am halfway to Paris, sleeping in a tree and waiting for a monk with a donkey.*

Then, a smile spread across her face. *Everything must be all right. I miss Timo and Moki,* were her last thoughts before falling into a deep sleep.

The next morning Nichol woke with first light, climbed down from the tree and headed in Timo's direction. The air was cold and the sun was warm, and after a few hours of running, she heard a whistle. As she rounded a curve in the road, there were Timo and Moki. Running to Timo and into his arms, she then hugged Moki as his ears twitched back and forth with approval.

"Moki and I am glad to see you are safe I have much to tell you and I brought you ale and food. Let us find a safe place to eat and talk." Heading Moki off the road, they found a place to rest in the sun.

Nichol and Timo sat on a log Timo just handed her bread, cheese, and dried meat and watched as Nichol devoured the food.

"I think I will wait till you are done eating before telling you what happened after you left."

Nichol's eyes got big and she stopped chewing. Shaking her head, she mumbled with her mouth full. "Tell me."

"You created quite a stir after you left. As I was moving down the street, I saw people running into stores and homes. I could hear doors being bolted. The fear on the faces of the people told me that something terrible was happening. Then I saw the reason —the three men that you stole the horses from were drunk and assaulting anyone near them.

"They were brandishing their bloody weapons and several people were on the ground, bleeding from their injuries. Moki and I quickly went back to the monastery and this time I found a priest and told him what happened. We both quickly returned and the priest approached the men and was swiftly surrounded by them, knives out, and glaring eye to eye.

"Not retreating, the priest started to talk softly but in a stern way to get their attention. His abrupt and forceful hand motions could have told the story to anyone watching. They were unaware of me, as the priest's words were quiet enough to avoid being overheard. Their demeanor changed with each word as the priest spoke to them. Suddenly, the priest turned and walked away, back toward the monastery. As he passed, our eyes briefly met. I will never forget the look of anguish on his face. Defeated by the priest, their rampage was over and the men returned to the tavern."

Timo watched Nichol as his story unfolded. He could see her anxiety build and knew that questions were forthcoming. "Nichol, this is a good place to stay and finish the day. Tomorrow we can start out at first light."

Just then, she had only one question. “What did the priest say?”

“I overheard him say that they need to have a convincing story to tell the bishop of what just happened. I think they finally went too far. I suspect that the bishop and the duke will not be able to protect them once the people begin to complain. Then the men will have to be punished for their crimes—probably by hanging them in public. My fear is there are many more to take their place.”

Nichol stopped eating, staring into the distance in deep thought.

There is nothing to celebrate, no ending, just sadness.

Timo moved next to her and put his arm around her, and Nichol rested her head on his shoulder. Silence surrounded them. Forest noises were subdued; even Moki was quiet.

Recent events weighed heavily on their minds.

fifty-six

A New Companion

Shadow brought the much-needed spark of light they needed to brighten their lives.

Timo woke with a start when he felt something soft and wet against his face.

Turning his head, he saw a fuzzy gray and black creature hunched down next to him. The creature looked at him with bright shiny eyes, cocked its head, and backed up a couple paces, with tail wagging.

Timo whispered to Nichol to waken her.

Sitting up, she stretched and looked in his direction. What she saw made her heart melt. A tiny young gray and black dog was trying to get Timo's attention. From all appearances, it looked like a fluffy mixture of wolf and dog.

Nichol moved slowly, so as not to scare it away. Opening her food bag, she found some small scraps of dried meat, and offered them to the pup in an open hand as she called to it softly.

Inspecting her from afar with its nose, the dog turned its body slowly toward Nichol. Each paw step moved it closer. It stopped just short of her outstretched hand and sniffed some more.

With its tail tucked between its legs, the smell was too tempting. It could not resist putting its mouth on her palm to grab what lay there. It was a snatch-and-grab, and the creature quickly shuffled a few steps away to chew and swallow. With huge eyes, it looked at her as if asking for more. Nichol dug into her bag to get more scraps.

The creature's curiosity took over, and it scampered back to her open hand. This went on three more times before it settled down, resting its head on Nichol's leg and fell asleep.

Timo and Nichol had not spoken a word to each other since the first food had been consumed. They seemed to communicate with their eyes, intrigued by its actions.

Nichol looked at Timo and lifted her shoulders. "What do we do now?"

Almost in a whisper, Timo said, "The poor little thing was starving. It is not old—maybe ten to twelve weeks. My concern now is that the mother could be close by and may be looking for her. I am not sure what the mother is—whether she is a wolf or a dog of some sort. We need to stay vigilant."

Nichol agreed and they sat there for a long time, scanning the woods and watching for any movement. If the mother was around, she would have tracked its scent and made an appearance by now.

Still not knowing exactly what to do, they decided they would slowly get up. Moving the animal's head off her leg to his paws, the pup lifted its head and yawned. Nichol picked it up and cradled it on her shoulder. Instinctively, it snuggled against her contentedly.

On examination, Timo and Nichol determined it was a female. "I think we need to say she is a dog," Timo suggested. "If she has wolf in her, it will frighten others we meet along the way."

"I am going to call her Shadow," Nichol declared. Timo nodded in agreement, knowing that Shadow had been the name of her beloved cat that Fredric had killed.

Adding Shadow to their pack was a natural decision for Nichol as well as Timo. What had to be addressed was the introduction of Shadow to Moki.

Together they walked over to the donkey and Nichol let Moki smell the pup's scent on her hands. Moki fanned his ears back and forth a few times, trying to familiarize himself with the smell. Nichol turned and slowly held Shadow close to Moki's nose for him to examine as she talked softly to him and scratched behind his ear.

Shadow perked up. She was as curious about Moki as he was about her. They sniffed one another for a long while and Nichol finally put her on the ground by Moki's feet. Shadow was more interested in Nichol and stood looking up at her while Moki watched both.

Finally, deciding that this new addition was not a threat, Moki edged his way over to Timo and munched on the straw offered from his hand.

Introductions were made and friendships formed. It was obvious from the start that Shadow had no intention of wandering away. She had bonded with her new pack. From that moment on, Nichol had a little follower by her side. The two became inseparable.

All morning, they worked with the newest member of their clan. Timo fashioned a small harness and a lead with leather strips he had in his bags. Otherwise, it would have been impossible to keep Shadow from wandering off. Both took turns training her to walk alongside them.

Happy to be in their midst, Shadow adapted quickly to her training, bringing a much-needed spark of light to brighten their journey.

A short time after Timo experienced Shadow's lick, the puppy had brought laughter into their lives with her antics and the joy of discovering all the new things around her. Moki quickly became her companion, and the two teased and played with each other while Timo and Nichol sat and watched.

As afternoon approached, they decided to pack up and set out. Making their way to the road, Nichol took Shadow's lead and headed out.

Shadow was the diversion they both needed from the upheaval and disappointments they had encountered … the unspoken words were heavy in the air.

fifty-seven

The Voice

There is a better way … love, compassion, and truth.

Because of their late start, they decided to settle in before the sun set. Shadow was soon exhausted from all the walking; Nichol decided to carry her.

The following day, it was Shadow's first full day of walking with them. She tired easily and Nichol made room in her back satchel for Shadow. Sometimes, Timo walked with her curled around the back of his neck while Nichol led Moki. Occasionally, they would lay her across Moki's back, nestled between the bags and barrels he carried. No matter how she traveled, Shadow was at peace with her clan.

Walking quietly for some distance, Nichol broke the silence. "Why are you so quiet today?"

"Nichol, since we have been traveling together, I have noticed nights that you thrash about and mumble in your sleep. Last night you were talking plainly. Were you having dreams?"

Pausing before she answered, she said, "It was the *Lady* … she usually talks to me when I sleep. It started when I was a child. As years passed, the voice would come to me. It is always a woman's voice … gentle and soothing. That's why I called the voice the *Lady*. Often, I knew things that I had no experience in, or should not have a reason to know. I believe the *Lady* told them to me.

"The night before I met you on the road, she came to me as I slept in the tree. She comforted me, bathing me in a warm light that shielded the bitter cold. In the morning, everything I saw was different; I was not in the same land as the day before."

Nichol stopped and faced Timo. "At first, I was frightened, then I realized she told me that this was my first day, a new beginning. And you were the first person I saw."

She paused to see Timo's reaction. Standing calmly and not responding, he waited for her to continue.

"Last night, I fell asleep thinking about those men in Auxerre. She came to me as I slept and questioned my actions. I told her I did it for the woman."

"The woman?"

"Yes … the woman who was raped and hung by the men who we hid from in Auxerre."

Timo's eyes widened. "What was the *Lady*'s response?"

"She told me, 'Do not allow vengeance to cloud your judgment. There is a better way … love, compassion, and truth.' Timo, what I wanted to do to those men was kill them for what they did to her. Instead, I let my rage simmer until I thought of something that would make their short lives more miserable. The *Lady* told me to focus on getting to Paris."

"I like what she told you. Those are words we should all live by."

"I was beginning to wonder if I made the right decision to leave home. What if I make it to Paris and Ezra is not there? What do I do then?"

Sensing the melancholy in her voice, Timo said, "Nichol, it is natural to question the unknown. Who knows what Paris will hold for you? I am sure your future is in good hands … yours.

"Nichol, I too felt something different that morning and it was not long before we met. I cannot explain the feeling but I think our meeting was meant to be. This morning when I packed Moki, I saw you write on the parchment I gave you. Would you like to share your thoughts?"

Removing the poem she wrote from her satchel, Nichol read aloud …

My Journey

The sun is not up but it is getting light.

Warm light came over me on a cold winter's night.

Rubbing sleep from my eyes, something does not feel right.

Not hungry or cold, I climbed down from the tree.

Looking around, nothing looks familiar.

How can I tell what is true?

What I see is all new.

Yesterday seems so long ago.

My journey must continue, so down the road I go.

"I will finish when I add you and Moki."

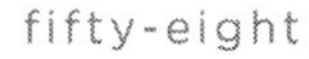

fifty-eight

Montereau

She will be your defender forever.

Timo and Nichol were in good spirits and chatted in a lighthearted way over the next three days as they made their way to the monastery at Montereau. They approached the outer limits of town early in the evening of the third day. Once again, they settled into the depths of the forest for the night.

Tired from their long walk, they quietly went about the task of unburdening Moki and preparing their simple meal. Shadow dropped down, exhausted from the constant movement, waiting for her share of the morsels.

"When I was in Vienne, the abbot there told me how magnificent the monastery in Montereau is. He told me I was fortunate to be going there. It houses about thirty monks—it is twice as big as anything we have seen. A vast property indeed, and I anticipate that my time teaching here might take more than two days. I will have a better idea after I see it tomorrow."

The next morning, they moved slowly through town, taking in all the sights and sounds as they headed north. Finally, they saw the spire of a church sitting high up on a hill on the east side of the road and realized it had to be their destination. The cross atop the church glistened in the morning sun and beckoned to them.

They turned onto a stone road that led to the church. Rounding a bend in the road, what stood before them took their breath away. Every structure was carefully constructed of matching stone. As Timo's eyes scanned the surrounding grounds, all he could think was *this is breathtaking.*

"It looks nothing like any religious community I have ever visited. Except for the presence of the church, this place looks like the estate of a noble or a wealthy merchant."

Nodding her head, Nichol whispered, "This is beautiful and reminds me of home and of Papa as he and I walked the gardens after his meetings. I miss his calm voice and guidance after I would share what I observed. I know you are excited to see what awaits you. Go now, Timo. I will take Moki to the stables and see you later in the longhouse."

Grinning, he replied, "You know me well."

Entering the monastery, Timo stood there in awe, admiring the courtyard and the placement of trees and shrubs that promised peaceful beauty when in full bloom. Hints of spring were already appearing in new leafing and on the grounds.

A tall, stately monk approached him. Taller than Timo, he had short-cropped blond hair and sparkling blue eyes. Smiling, he said, "This monastery has that effect on everyone who sees it for the first time. I am Abbot Jordanus. How can I help you?"

Coming to his senses, Timo said, "I am Brother Timothée Lemur from the monastery in Vienne. I have been sent here to share my knowledge and the seeds and plantings I have brought with me. As I approached, I saw how skillfully your grounds are kept. Perhaps I will be the student here and you will be the teacher."

"Ah, yes. We have been expecting you, Brother Lemur. We have heard such wonderful things about you and your abilities in working with seeds and soil."

"Thank you for your kind words, Abbot. I was told about the magnificence of this monastery before I left Vienne, but what I have seen exceeds what I was told. I would have expected to find a noble living here."

"My father was a successful merchant who died before his time, and this estate was left to me. I had no desire to continue my father's merchant affairs. Instead, I heard the calling to follow in the footsteps of Christ and to serve the poor. I studied at the monastery in Paris and took my vows there. While there, a thought occurred to me … why not turn my father's estate into a monastery? Only two buildings have been added since he built here. One is the church you see; the other is the longhouse."

"You answered your calling to serve God as well as the poor. And you have preserved your family's legacy."

For the rest of the morning, the two walked the fields. There were no clouds and Timo could see the promise of what the land would yield. The land was rich with robust smells of prior plantings. Pausing and taking in the breadth of what they had covered, Timo turned to his companion.

"Abbot Jordanus, you have excellent soil here and you have prepared your fields in a manner to reap the best harvest. I have only two suggestions. Plant the vegetable and grain seeds I will leave with you. Consider rotating them with your normal plantings and let crop land rest between seasons. They will add diversity and bounty to what you already grow. Integrate the hearty grapevines I have brought with your other vines, to ensure a fine selection of grapes and add to the variety you already have."

Going to the stables, Timo packed up Moki and returned to the monastery where Abbot Jordanus waited.

Handing him the seeds and grapevine cuttings, he said, "I have two more monasteries to visit before spring planting. I have enjoyed my time with you and look forward to seeing your fields in full bloom. When I come back this way on my return to Vienne, I will visit with you again. For now, I will be on my way."

"Thank you for your help and advice. I understand your need to continue on your journey, but before you leave, let us fill your bags with food."

With food bags brimming over, Timo returned to Moki, picked up his lead and said, "Let us go find Nichol and Shadow. I know where they will be."

While Timo toiled, Nichol and Shadow hiked along the river Yonne paralleling the town of Montereau. Loving the solitude of the forest that she had embraced as her new home base, she found a grassy spot and sat to share food and water with Shadow.

Devouring what Nichol had fed her, the pup wagged her tail in anticipation.

"Do you want to go to the river, Shadow?"

Removing Shadow's leash, the pup sprinted ahead. Finding a secluded spot, she first sat on the bank, enjoying watching Shadow explore the waters. *I need to do the same.*

Quickly disrobing, Nichol moved into the river and washed with a cloth and the soap she had and then dressed as soon as she left it. As she did, she noticed a large oak tree with acorns underneath. Wrapping the seeds in a square of cloth, she added them to her bag. Turning to Shadow, she said, "Timo will know how and when to plant these."

Nichol slipped the lead over Shadow's head and with a slight pull, the two made their way up to the road where she could see the town. *There must be a large market square here.*

Walking past the ale house in the middle of town, Nichol heard a commotion inside, and suddenly a drunk man was thrown through the door. Colliding with her, he grabbed her to steady himself.

Nichol stood her ground, but Shadow did not. In one leap, she launched upward, mouth open, and clamped the man's leg between her jaws. Stunned, all the man could do was hurl himself away from Nichol, swatting at the pup as she dangled from his leg. Shadow was latched on to him and she was not letting up.

Concerned for her pet's well-being, Nichol tightened the lead as she approached the man before he did something that would harm Shadow. Grasping her around the middle, she called out her name, and Shadow's jaws relaxed.

Cradling the dog against her chest, Nichol stepped further away. The man was not harmed. Rubbing his leg, he growled, "Let me have that dog. I will teach it a lesson!"

Shadow wiggled in Nichol's arms. Looking him straight in the eyes, Nichol laughed. "You are lucky she is young and did not maul you to death." Placing her on the ground, she turned away from him with Shadow prancing alongside her.

Walking but a few steps, Nichol looked up to see Timo and Moki approaching. Surprised, she asked, “What are you doing here? Why are not you at the monastery?”

“The brothers have done an excellent job in their fields. They did not need the amount of help that I thought they would. I gave them seeds that will thrive in their location and told the abbot I would be on my way. Now we can head on to Melun.”

Looking down at Shadow, Timo paused. “I saw what Shadow did to that man back there. I have never seen that side of her and now I know that she is a guardian to be reckoned with. You protected her the day she found us in the forest, and now it is her turn to protect you. She will be your defender forever.”

“I suspect she will defend you as well. You have been as kind and loving to her as you have been to Moki. Animals know who the good people are.”

As they walked, Nichol began asking questions about the inherited estate that was now the monastery.

After listening to what Timo learned, she said as he finished, “That explains why we thought the estate belonged to a noble and not the church.”

Smiling, Timo added, “And I saved the best for last. Abbot Jordanus’ father had established a lasting relationship with an importer and moneylender from Paris … a man by the name of Ezra. The abbot has maintained that relationship over the years. I do not know if it is the Ezra you are on your way to meet, but it could be the same man.”

For the moment Nichol was speechless. "Do you suppose ...?" she stammered. "Timo, I felt like I was back at my home in Marseilles when I first saw the grounds of the monastery. And now that you say there might be a chance that Ezra knew the abbot's father—it could also mean that maybe the abbot knew Papa."

Longingly, she looked off into the distance. *Could it be?*

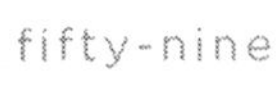

fifty-nine

Melun

If this is the entry road to the monastery, it certainly does not look very inviting.

They spent two full days making their way to the monastery in Melun. Nichol sensed that Paris had to be close. Both were becoming weary of traveling.

Turning to Nichol, Timo said, “I am glad Melun and Evry will be the last two monasteries to visit before I return to Vienne.”

Nodding her head, Nichol said, “I have been traveling for a long time to get to Paris and find Ezra. Hearing you say his name made me eager to get there without delay. I hope your time with this monastery is short like some of the others.”

As they typically did, they settled in the forest the evening before arriving at the next monastery. They satisfied themselves with the food and ale Abbot Jordanus had sent with Timo and enjoyed the silence of the night that followed.

Stretching out on opposite sides of their furry family, they readied for sleep. Shadow and Moki were snuggled nose to nose. Shadow’s legs twitched as if she was deep in a dream.

Tomorrow at the monastery promised another full day of training and planting.

Nichol heard Timo quietly murmuring his prayers of thanksgiving and she did the same. She thanked the *Lady* for another safe day of travel.

Before long, Timo and Nichol were asleep.

On the road early the next morning, Timo checked his map and thought the entrance to the monastery would be close by. Finally, they came upon a weather-beaten gate that had been haphazardly attached to two trees standing on opposite sides of a worn dirt path.

"If this is the entry road to the monastery, it certainly does not look very inviting," Timo said as they paused to take in their surroundings.

They made their way through the gate and started up a rutted and winding path that was strewn with debris and crowded with overgrowth on either side.

This may take longer than I planned ....

"They definitely need help in managing their grounds. I could be spending more than the two days that were planned. I hope you are not disappointed?" Timo said.

Rounding the last bend in the road, they stopped abruptly. What sat before them was a dilapidated old house that appeared abandoned. Next to it was a longhouse that was in the same condition.

What has happened here?

With an uneasy feeling, Timo looked at Nichol. "Something just does not seem right about this. You stay here with Moki and Shadow. Maybe my map is wrong, and this is not a monastery after all. If I am not back soon, you immediately head north through the forest."

With trepidation, she nodded her head, grasping Moki's lead tighter and calling Shadow to her side.

This is one of the most unappealing church properties I have ever seen. No wonder Timo is concerned.

As Timo approached the front of the house, his senses heightened. *Something is very wrong.*

Timo rapped on the wobbly door, and when no one came to open it, he turned the handle.

To his surprise, the door opened easily, and he walked through.

This was indeed an abandoned house. As he scanned the large room, he covered his nose with his sleeve. Debris and the remains of dead animals covered the floor, and the stench was overwhelming.

Taking it all in, he noticed another door on the far side of the room. Slowly, he opened it.

In front of him must be an illusion. What he saw caused him to stop and stare. Stretched before him stood a glorious stone monastery.

How could this be? What is going on here? Why would anyone deceive a visitor with a ramshackle façade to hide this glorious structure? This does not make sense.

Walking across the grounds, he approached what appeared to be a main door. Without knocking, he entered.

For, the third time, Timo was astounded at what he saw. He stood in the entryway in disbelief. Finding his voice, the words that loudly passed his lips were, "This place is sumptuous. It could be a palace … not a monastery!"

Timo's eyes feasted on the visual delight in front of him. Marble tiles covered the entire floor. The windows were covered in lush burgundy and gold tapestries. Timo stood in awe. Suddenly, a short, pudgy, middle-aged monk glided into the room and was surprised to see Timo standing there.

Eyeing him suspiciously, he bellowed, "What are you doing here?"

I am not off to such a good start, thought Timo, and he persisted with his introduction. "I am Brother Timothée Lemur. Brother Cyprian, the abbot at the monastery in Vienne, has directed me to help improve farming methods at several monasteries in the north of France. I have just arrived in Melun and wish to offer my services. Are you Abbot Florian?"

"Of course not. I am Brother Edotimus, his assistant. Abbot Florian is not in the habit of greeting strangers in the great room. He is a busy man. I will see if he has any time in his schedule to meet with you. Wait here."

While he waited, Timo noticed that the atmosphere here was not quite the solemn, peaceful atmosphere one experienced in a monastery. He could hear people yelling and laughing and he thought he heard someone crying. He could hear footsteps running across the floor above and wondered what it was all about.

Brother Edotimus reappeared. He stood back from Timo and interlaced his fat, stubby fingers across his portly stomach. He clicked his tongue against his teeth and said, "The abbot said he does not have time to talk to you. I have arranged for Brother Trystan to meet with you."

I hope that Nichol has headed away from here as I told her to do. I feel that there is danger here. This does not feel like a house of God.

Timo was conflicted. He had come all this way to share his knowledge. However, his reception here had been less than welcoming, and he was not looking forward to spending time in this environment. He made his decision and said calmly, "I understand completely. I am happy to meet with Brother Trystan."

Edotimus told Timo to wait again and left the room. He returned with a tall, lanky monk who appeared to be no more than sixteen years old. The older monk introduced him to Timo and the youngster looked scared and unsure of himself as his eyes flitted nervously from Timo to the floor.

Edotimus suggested they exit through the kitchen to get to the fields behind the monastery. Timo nodded and followed.

When they got to the fields, Timo was surprised at what he saw. The layout of the farmland was extensive and nicely designed. The thing that immediately caught his attention was that only peasants were working in the fields. The only monk in sight was overseeing the work, and he was shouting instructions at the workers—that was very odd and out of place.

My skills would not be needed here.

Turning to Brother Trystan, he said, "I have seen enough. Please tell Abbot Florian that his fields are well-prepared for planting and I can be of no assistance. Thank you for your time. I will let myself out the same way I came in." The shy monk nodded and returned to the monastery.

Timo walked slowly around the grounds of the monastery and ended up at the stables. What he saw surprised him. *There must be many wealthy visitors staying here, based on these fine-looking horses.*

Entering the monastery through the kitchen, Timo was greeted by Brother Edotimus, who stood chomping on a chicken leg as grease dripped down his beard. Before he acknowledged the monk, Timo saw a man dash toward the stairs at the back of the kitchen. Clutched in his grasp trailed a small boy who struggled to free himself. The man stopped to get a better grip and saw Timo watching him.

"Wait here. As soon as I deliver this one, I will be back to find one for you." He pulled the boy up the last few stairs and Timo heard the child crying in protest.

Shocked, his mouth agape, Timo looked at Edotimus questioningly.

The monk shrugged his shoulders and said, "There are many more where that one came from. Why do you go to the longhouse where we feed the peasants? You can take your pick of a boy, a girl—or both—and have a good time in one of the rooms upstairs. Their parents will not interfere. They know that if it were not for this monastery and the food and the shelter we provide, they would starve. It is a quick and easy trade."

Furious, Timo shook his head in disbelief. *This is a bad place. It is clear to me now that vile and depraved activities take place here.*

"I noticed some valuable horses in the stables. Do you provide horses for your visitors as well?" Timo thought he knew the answer, but he wanted to hear the monk's explanation.

"No, those beauties belong to our guests. Our location is close enough to Paris for the elite to come and stay and indulge in the finer things in life. Because we have a steady turnover of peasants, our wealthy patrons always have a fresh supply of young children to choose from. They pay us well to keep the pantry stocked, so to speak."

Timo's stunned silence enveloped him.

Who else knows about this place? Surely Abbot Cyprian does not know about this. That explains the beautiful surroundings I have seen. I do not think this is a monastery, and I am not sure these are real monks. I know one thing for sure … I have seen enough.

Turning to Edotimus, Timo swatted the chicken leg out of his fist. Glaring at him with a raised voice, he said, "You are a disgrace to God and to the Brotherhood."

Timo stomped out of the kitchen and through the great hall. He slammed the door of the monastery and did not look back. As he sprinted past the shoddy gate, he heard a familiar whistle. Turning, he saw Nichol beckon to him, and he ran to meet her.

Nichol had sensed that something was wrong at the monastery. After a short wait and when Timo did not come back, she did as he had instructed her. She led their animals up into the forest, but within sight of the ramshackle gate. Once there, she waited.

As Timo approached her, she could see that anger oozed out of him and his fists were clenched.

"Timo, what is it? What is happened? Why are you so upset?"

"We need to get away from here and deep into the forest immediately!"

Turning, the four of them disappeared into the densest part of the forest and did not stop moving until all of them were exhausted. Even Moki and Shadow sensed something was wrong and they had to move quickly.

Finally. Timo stopped. Turning to Nichol, he said, "I cannot believe what I saw and heard in that place. It is not like any monastery I have ever seen. It cannot be a monastery! It appears to be a secluded spot for the depraved activities of the elite. As I stood in the kitchen. a man was dragging a young boy up the stairs. The boy was crying and trying to break away. I was told the child's parents dare not protest this, or they will starve. That's when I left. Evil dwells behind the door and within the walls of that place."

Timo took a quick breath and continued in an even louder voice as he paced, his hands balled into fists. "The abbot's aide also made it clear that I could select a boy or girl from any family in the longhouse and spend time with the child in a room on the upper floor. He said they always kept the pantry well stocked.

"I have heard rumors that such things go on, but I have never witnessed firsthand what I did today. He told me that the rich and powerful go there to engage with young children and I am quite sure the monks—if monks actually live there—partake in the same indecencies."

"You do not think this is a monastery?"

"I am not sure. I do not know if they are real monks. It could all be a façade, just like the abandoned house that fronts the monastery to hide the truth from the unsuspecting eye. I am appalled that the rich and powerful prey on the innocent and less-fortunate people in this world. *Innocent little children ....*

"Nichol, I never understood the stories you told me you heard in your father's solar. And until today, I would not have believed that 'men of God' could lead such double lives—if they are men of God. I promised my life to God and I will never forsake that vow. I see now that rich and powerful members of the church may be entangled with rich and powerful members of the nobility. I have also learned bad people exist everywhere."

Nichol had never heard him talk like this. He railed against all the injustices and inequities he had recently experienced.

Walking to where he stood, she put a hand on his shoulder, "Let us sit and talk."

She waited for him to initiate the conversation, and when he did not, she did.

"Timo, I know you are disheartened. How could you not be? You have just seen the ugliest side of men. They preach right from wrong, tell us how to live our lives, and quote the words of God as if they had just talked with Him this morning. Yet for all the preaching they do, they practice the exact opposite.

"I understand how you feel. It is hard to make any sense out of it. I felt the same way when I heard powerful church people and others like them tell their sordid stories to Papa. Even though he never followed any religion, he studied many of them, and understood their basic doctrines. He lived his life by one rule … treat others the way he wanted to be treated.

"Papa talked about how difficult it was to stay true to just that one rule, let alone stay true to a book of rules written and interpreted by men who tell us that they know what God wants. Papa was generous with his time and his wealth and gave both to a lot of people, but when it came to sharing that with men of the church, he was very selective. He and a kindly priest, who ministered to our village, respected and helped each other. They had one common goal… helping the less fortunate. He did not have much use for the rest of the religious types."

"I wish I had met your papa.

"I realize now that I have led a very sheltered life. It was not until I set out on my journey that I have been exposed to the evil that some men can commit. Now, I am experiencing a crisis of faith that counters the vows I have taken."

Nichol looked at her disillusioned friend. Quietly she said, "My dear Timo, betrayal is brutal. I do know how you feel. I was sad and mad after all the things my mother and brother did to me after she poisoned Papa, and my brother set out to destroy me.

"The one thing that has kept me going was Papa's belief in me. He always told me how good and strong I was, and he made me believe in myself. He taught me to surround myself with good people. I know that's why I am with you right now.

"He taught me things that he never instructed my brother … he told me more than once that Fredric was not a leader. I became a confidant for him. He would ask my opinion after I had heard conversations within his meetings. He shared information about his businesses and his contacts. It was as if he was grooming me to be his successor, even though that was not the way for girls. And he made sure I knew how to defend myself.

"You have every reason to feel betrayed by those monks, but you must also admit that they are not all like the ones you encountered in Melun. If they were all that bad, you would have known about it much sooner. You represent the absolute best that any man can be. You have many of the traits of my papa.

"People need what you can provide. I believe in you and your goodness. You simply live your life from a place of truth and integrity. You treat others as you wish to be treated. You must believe that and believe in yourself. Because of who you are, you must continue the work you do."

Timo smiled at her with tears in his eyes. “You always say what is in your heart. I love that about you. Thank you for your kind words.”

sixty

Reflections

If she is as benevolent as you have described, perhaps she is guiding you and encouraging you to move on.

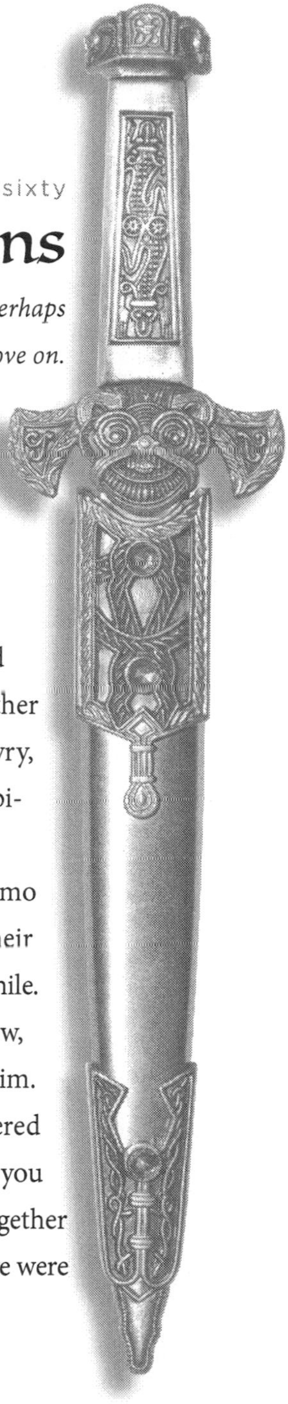

Timo wanted to distance them from Melun as soon as possible. Even Moki sensed it and walked a little faster. Shadow did not have to be encouraged to run ahead with Nichol.

Only today, Nichol did not run. Timo needed her presence. They traveled through the forest rather than taking the road as they made their way to Evry, not wanting to risk encountering any of the inhabitants or patrons of Melun monastery.

Nichol and Shadow walked quietly next to Timo and she only spoke if he spoke to her. Breaking their silence, he asked her if they could stop and rest a while. He put food and water down for Moki and Shadow, and sat on a log and beckoned to Nichol to join him.

Pulling more food from his travel bag, he offered it. As he broke off a piece of bread, he asked, "Do you remember when we first started on this journey together that we compared our maps and determined that we were both headed in the same general direction?"

"Yes, I do. We were amazed how two strangers could have the same route and almost the same destination in mind. Why do you ask now?"

"Because when we reach Evry, it will be time for us to part and go separate ways. I will miss you. You have become a dear friend."

Silence fell between the two friends. It was a comfortable silence ... and it was necessary. Then Nichol spoke first.

"I have been thinking about the same thing. I was leery of everyone when I first left Marseilles. But when I met you and Moki, I was surprised to see my defenses slowly breaking down. You have been my protector this whole time. You have taught me to trust again. And you are my friend as well.

"I am not looking forward to leaving you. For the last several days, I am being prompted to get to Paris soon."

"Do you think the prompting could be coming from the *Lady* that talks to you when you are asleep?"

"My sense is she needs me there. I am now hearing her voice when I walk and run."

"Nichol, you told me that you do things impulsively and you do not understand how or why. Maybe you are acting on the messages she is giving you and you do not realize it. If she is as benevolent as you have described, perhaps she is guiding you and encouraging you to move on … to become your own leader."

Looking at Timo, she nodded. "I have been wondering the same thing. I want to help other women. I think you could be right. If it is the *Lady* who's directing me, I feel I must follow her advice. Timo, you and I were protected as children. We never had to worry about having food to eat. Yet we have experienced hunger, cold, violence, and fear while we traveled. I know that I have grown from this and you have, too.

"I did not understand how desperate people can get when they have no food, shelter or means of supporting their families. And what they will do. I have come to realize that good and evil live side by side in this world. At first, I thought evil only existed in my family through my mother and brother. You have seen good and evil characters at the many monasteries you have visited. Nothing should surprise either of us again. Innocence is now part of our past. When I come across good and loving people like some we have met, it makes me happy. Life would be joyless without them."

"You have said everything I have been thinking, and I agree with you. Yet, I sense there's something more you want to tell me. What is it?"

"Timo, it is not only breaking my heart to leave you, but I feel I must also leave Shadow with you. I am just a few days from Paris. My intent is to run until my legs cannot carry me any farther. Shadow cannot run that long and I cannot carry enough food for the two of us. You will move more slowly for a while, and she will have you and Moki to look after her. She could become the shepherdess for your monastery when you arrive back."

Taking a deep breath, she willed the tears not to fall. Her whole traveling family was breaking up and she could hardly stand the thought of it.

"I had not thought about what we would do with Shadow. She is attached to you; it will not be easy for her without you. It is as if you are her light and she is your devotee. I am sure the monks would allow her to stay at the monastery. With more training, she will be a big help on the farm. Do you know who else will miss you? Moki. You tamed him just as you did me and Shadow. He will miss your gentle whispers as you scratch behind his ears."

Encouraged that Timo would take Shadow with him, Nichol pushed on.

"It seems that we are thinking alike. We have said what is circling around us. I am sad, Timo. Our journey is ending. It hurt me to think about it. Now I am saying it out loud. Promise me something? Tomorrow, can we part before we get to the monastery? I cannot bear waiting while you get Moki and Shadow settled in the stables. Agreed?"

Silently, Timo sat, thinking of her words. Standing, he reached for her hand. "Yes. Tomorrow it will be."

Calling Shadow to him, he encouraged her to settle by his side, stroking her ears and talking in a low voice. Eagerly, she wagged her tail and settled in, turning her head toward Nichol with one ear raised, as if she knew something was up.

"We will face this tomorrow, Nichol. For now, let us be happy and thankful for all the time we have had together. Today, we will make our way through the forest until it is time to settle in for the night."

Before their last supper, Nichol wanted to be alone. She took Shadow out for a long stretch, finally settling beneath a towering oak tree. Gathering her close to her chest, she held Shadow, burrowing her face in the back of her neck.

The two sat, loving one another for a long time before Nichol had the strength to rise and head back to the campsite. Shadow no longer shadowed her. Instead, she walked closely at her side, lifting her paw as if to match Nichol's every step forward.

Timo suspected why they had been gone so long. Just looking at his friend, he knew instantly she had spent the time saying her farewell to Shadow. He had spread out a selection of foods and sat waiting for Nichol to join him. He handed her a waterskin containing wine.

As she took it, he said. "This will be our last meal together. Not only is our innocence now part of our past, but the friendship we created also will become part of our past as well."

He exhaled deeply. "Starting tomorrow, we will not be together, but our friendship will remain a part of our hearts and minds."

Nichol nodded. "I felt the same way when Papa died. He prepared me, in so many ways, for this journey. You have been my strength to see it through. Now, I must continue alone. I am not looking forward to leaving you, but I feel driven to reach my destination."

They talked long into the night. Standing, they headed to where Moki and Shadow slept. Before settling in, Timo took her in his arms, holding her close. Neither spoke. Both knew what tomorrow would bring.

Breaking the embrace, Timo walked away to lie down.

Nichol watched over Moki and Shadow for a few moments, then moved several feet away, settling into sleep. As she closed her eyes, she sensed movement, then felt a wet nose nuzzling her head. Shadow gave her a gentle lick.

Nichol lay down and Shadow snuggled up against her, spending the night wrapped in her arms.

In the morning, Timo asked, "Did the *Lady* come to you again? You were talking more than usual as you slept last night."

"Yes. Her message was clear. She said she will guide me as I travel. She also said I will meet good people soon who will help me." Hesitating, she then added, "She talked about us. She said that we will be together again in the future.

"I am so inspired by her message. It will help to keep me strong and moving forward. And it means that you will not be in my past.

"There was one more thing. She kept referring to me as a leader … that one day, I will show women how to be independent and have their opinions be welcomed, even do more in the guilds and become merchants as men do."

Pausing, she continued, "It just occurred to me that you will now be able to get a good night's sleep since you will not be wakened by my muttering in the middle of the night."

"If I had my choice, I would gladly listen to you talk in your sleep every night."

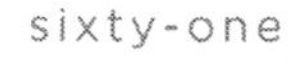

sixty-one

Choices

This feels good … it feels right.

Setting out for Evry early, they decided to stay on the road. There was little left to be said between them.

As they approached Evry, the usual farms lined the road. Soon, the monastery was in sight, and they both knew this was where they would part. Eager to reach Paris, Nichol knew she would commence running nonstop the moment they separated.

"If you decide to come north to Paris, you know you can look for me at Ezra's in Paris. Take good care of yourself and our animals."

Timo could only nod his head as she spoke.

Nichol then walked to Moki and whispered to him. Scratching behind both ears, she patted his head. Turning, she saw Shadow in the grass looking up at her. Leaning down, she picked her up, whispering words to her one last time. Fluffing her furry coat, she gently placed the dog across Moki's back, where she loved to ride.

Nichol turned and took her first steps on the final leg of her journey toward Paris and Ezra. Her walk turned to a trot, and finally she broke into a run. *This feels good … it feels right.*

Unbidden, her thoughts turned to the *Lady. You promised—I will see Timo again.*

Suddenly, Nichol was aware of a bark, followed by a whimper, and movement to her right.

Her thoughts left the *Lady's* words and her defenses were immediately up. Then her alarm dropped as a smile crossed her face. Shadow was matching her stride for stride, with her leash trailing behind her.

Slowing, Nichol stopped and dropped to her knees. Shadow almost knocked her over as she leaped into her arms. Snuggling Shadow close, she looked up and saw Timo smiling and waving as he turned up the road to the monastery.

The choice was made.

"Shadow, if you are going to Paris with me, you will need to learn to stay close and at my side at all times. You are not full-grown but you do look like a wolf." Picking up the end of the leash still around her neck, Nichol tied it to her belt. The two would walk and run in unison, alternating so the pup could keep up.

Over the next two days, with constant training prompts and whispers in her ear, Nichol and Shadow learned to keep their paces matched.

For those days, Nichol was lost in the joy of the antics of her companion.

On the third morning, while watching Shadow run about, she found a note in her bag. Timo had put it into her bag, wrapped around the acorns she had saved.

Remember to plant these.

They will grow into two mighty oaks.

Just like you and me.

Shadow stopped and came to Nichol and put her head on her lap. "I know you miss them, but I am sure we will see Moki and Timo again. Let us get on the road. We could reach the village Antony today."

As she set out again on the road, she remembered the mantra she sang to herself when she had first set out alone. She gritted her teeth, straightened her shoulders, and started singing with a few changes to it.

I am on my way to Paris,

Just a few more towns and a few more days.

Paris is where my future lies,

Papa planned it that way.

She took off at a full gallop, with Shadow by her side. Her feet felt comfortable in the shoes that had been created just for them.

Suddenly, her heart felt lighter. A smile spread across her face.

sixty-two

A New Chaperone

We would all feel better if the final leg of your journey ended with a new chaperone.

The afternoon sun was dimming when Nichol reached the southern border of the village of Antony.

Slowing her pace, she caught her breath and calmly walked to an area where she saw people moving about. It appeared to be a fair, set up in the meadow just outside of the town square. Tents and stalls surrounded the field, and she could hear noise and laughter. *This is where I need to be now.*

Checking her map, she knew she was only a few days away from Paris. Food was what she needed, and to her delight, a variety of vendors were just steps away. Slowly, she approached a young woman selling vegetables and dried fruits and next to that was one that had bread.

Removing her travel pack from her back, she filled it with enough food that it started to bulge. After that, she looked around and spotted a vendor with dried fish and chicken.

When she approached the meat vendor, people moved away from her. Some of them pointed at Shadow. As she paid for the chicken, the vendor asked, "Is it for the wolf?"

"She is not a wolf … wolves cannot be trained. As you can see, she is well-trained."

Both vendors commented on the straps she had on her travel bag. The older of the two quickly said, "Where did you get that? I could use it to carry my bread and have my arms free to carry more."

"I made it for myself. When I travel, I want to keep my hands and arms free."

"You could make them and sell them here."

Amused, Nichol thanked them and left. *Yes, I could make them and sell them. I could be a merchant, too.*

Yet she felt something different here. *What is it? I feel like I am being watched.*

Glancing around, her eyes met those of a young man staring at her. In an instant, Nichol looked away. Immediately, she moved to the next vendor's stand, out of the young man's sight.

Who is he? His stare was intense. Should I be afraid?

Nichol repositioned herself again, moving to the end of a vendor's tent where she could observe him and maybe not be seen. *I am curious—I have never seen eyes like his—piercing shades of green that were directed toward her. Mysterious, soft, and deep-set.*

He was tall, young, handsome, and thinly built with dark, curly hair. As he talked with people, he was very descriptive with his hands. At the moment, it appeared he was negotiating with another customer.

He began to scan the crowd, as if searching for someone or something. Suddenly, he turned in her direction and caught her watching him. Once again, their eyes locked. Raising his arm, a smile appeared on his face. He beckoned her to his stall with a friendly wave.

Nichol nodded. Slowly, she began her approach. His eyes maintained the connection while her eyes caught a movement to the side of his stall.

Watch out—a thief, her mind shouted. She knew the ways of thieves, after observing them for years at the docks in Marseilles.

It angered her … the customer that Green-Eyes had been speaking to was attempting to steal a bracelet!

Thinking he succeeded, that same man turned and was walking away from the stall.

Nichol picked up her pace and shouted, "Are not you forgetting something? You should pay this man for the bracelet you just took!"

Quickly, Green-Eyes looked at her quizzically and turned back to the man he had been talking to.

"He stole the bracelet you were showing him." Her outstretched arm pointed at the thief. "He is a thief!" Her voice was loud enough for everyone to hear.

People turned to see what was happening and watched the man withdraw the bracelet he had hidden and tossed it onto the table. Glaring at Nichol, he hurried away as people were shouting *thief*, and vanished into the crowded marketplace.

Thankful, Green-Eyes turned to her. "I am in your debt. I cannot afford to lose even one piece of jewelry. I noticed you were watching me. I am Robert. What is your name?"

"My name is Nick. And you were watching me first," she replied. *I need to stop calling him Green-Eyes in my head.*

"Yes, I was. I am in the habit of watching people to spot future sales," he quipped. "How did you know that the man was stealing?"

Ignoring his question, she replied, "You will not have anything to sell if you let people walk away with your jewelry."

An anxious silence followed while Nichol began to examine the jewelry. "You were distracted by looking my way. Is that how you attract buyers, by staring at them?"

Now embarrassed, Robert stuttered, trying to find the right words. "A boy with a young wolf is not what you normally see in town."

Nichol looked up with a broad smile. "This jewelry is beautiful. Is this your work, or are you selling for someone else?"

"This is just some of my work—and yes, I made everything you see. I sell most of my work in Paris. The patrons there have the means to buy my more expensive pieces. Can I show you anything in particular … for your mother or sister?"

I need to stop looking at his eyes. His craftsmanship is excellent; as good as any I have seen in Marseilles.

"Yes, I like that one." She pointed to a silver bracelet that was encircled with small gemstones. Robert picked it up. Reaching for her wrist, he placed it on Nichol, letting his hand hold her arm for a brief period.

Nichol held it up and admired the gleaming design of the bracelet from various angles. "This is lovely, but I need a sturdy necklace for something else."

Robert continued, "Do you like anything else you see here? Maybe something here for your mother?" *This boy is different. Is he a boy? Or is he hiding from someone?*

"You admire my jewelry like a woman, not a boy. Why are you dressed as a boy?"

With a shy smile, Nichol was startled as his words spilled out. *He knows; what can I tell him? I do not want to lose his attention.*

Suddenly, Nichol felt Shadow push against her legs. Looking down, she could see her tail wagging. There was no growling. *I think she is telling me he is safe to talk to.*

Nichol returned the bracelet and watched as Robert opened a silk pouch and withdrew a beautifully braided silver chain. The intricate detail was masterful, and it was just what she wanted.

He held it up for her to see. "I am going to show this in Paris where I can get top coin for it," he stated proudly.

Nichol reached her hand out and waited for him to place the chain in it. She examined it closely, judging its length and strength. She looked at Robert. "I will buy it if you tell me a fair price."

"You cannot afford it," he said, returning it to the pouch.

"I asked you how much?"

Robert paused and smiled, "Show me your coin and then we may agree on the price."

"If I show you my coin, you may know how much I have and ask for more than it is worth."

Nichol wanted the silver chain as much as Robert wanted to sell it. They continued to bargain, countering offer after offer, until Nichol had enough. "I will pay you ten silver coins less than your last price, which is my last offer."

"You drive a hard bargain. Your last offer is low but a fair one."

Reaching under her cloak, inside the opening in her tunic, Nichol opened the coin pouch without removing it and counted the right amount of coin by feel. Robert watched her count the coins she placed on the table.

"Would you like to have the silk pouch?"

"No, I am going to wear it." Nichol unclipped the brooch from her cloak and loosened her tunic. Reaching for the chain, she fastened it around her neck.

"I see you have a leather string around your neck. What hangs from it?"

"Rings."

"May I see them?"

"I have to go. Do you know of an inn where I can stay for the night?"

"Not for a young woman traveling alone."

Nichol was not sure whether to turn and leave, or stay. *I should be on my way but something about him tells me to stay.*

"The moment our eyes met; something attracted me to you. I watch people to give me a tell, whether they are interested in buying or not. The manner in which you talk, and the way you looked at the silver chain and admired my other jewelry told me you were a girl. When you loosened your cloak and put your arms up to fasten the new chain, I saw something boys do not have. Why are you dressed as a peasant boy?"

There were many questions he wanted to ask her … how could she be carrying the amount of coin needed to buy this silver necklace?

"I must go now." Nichol turned and began to walk away.

"Wait! As I said, there is no safe place for a lone woman to stay here. I can offer you a place to stay for the night."

Nichol turned. "And where would that be?"

"I live with my parents, my brother and my niece; you could stay for the night and leave in the morning. I promise you will be welcome and safe, and you will love the food my mother prepares. What do you say?"

Nichol paused and studied him for a moment, weighing her options, not wanting to be too eager. Finally, she said, “I accept your offer—but if I am not comfortable with the situation once I am there, Shadow and I will leave at once.”

Robert packed up his display and they walked a short distance to his home. As they walked, he asked, “Is Nick your real name?”

“No, my name is Nichol.”

Robert turned to face her. “Is Shadow your dog’s real name?”

“Yes.” Nichol slowed down and turned to him. As she studied his face and his smile, a shiver came over her. *I see him.*

Nichol was pleasantly surprised when they arrived at his family’s home. It was a small house solidly built from stone. There was a beautifully maintained garden on one side and a blacksmith shop on the other.

Robert entered the house first and stood by the door, waiting for Nichol to follow him. They were met at the door by Dinah, his mother. She hugged him warmly. “Did you have good sales today?”

Robert smiled. “Yes, it was a good day. A patron bought one of my best silver necklaces and in appreciation for her purchase, I offered her and her dog Shadow a meal and shelter for the evening.”

Finally, he moved aside, and Nichol stepped into the room. Shadow followed and sat by her side.

Seeing Nichol, Dinah asked him, “This is your patron?”

Laughing nervously, Robert continued. “Mother, this is Nichol. Nichol, this is my mother, Dinah.”

Dinah paused, then took Nichol’s hand, and said kindly, “Welcome to our home.” *This girl is filthy and dressed as a boy. What is she all about?*

As they closed the door, Robert's father walked into the room and stood silently watching. "Papa, this is Nichol. Nichol, this is my father, Achim."

"Who are you, and what brings you to our home?"

Robert interjected, "Papa, I met her at the fair today. She saw a man stealing a bracelet from my display. She stopped the thief, saving me a lot of coin. She also purchased one of my silver chains. When she asked me to recommend an inn to stay at, I invited her to spend the night here with us."

Just then two more heads popped into the room. A young man who looked like a younger version of Robert was introduced as his brother Gideon, followed by a tiny girl who ran up and hid behind Dinah's tunic. She peeked out at Nichol with one eye and giggled.

Robert reached down to pick her up. He squeezed her and said, "This little one is my niece, Raisa."

Raisa wiggled away from Robert and knelt in front of Shadow, putting her arms around her.

Nichol watched Raisa and without hesitation, turned to see concern on everyone's face. "She is a gentle dog and will not harm her." Then Nichol smiled as she looked from one family member to the next, committing their names and faces to memory.

It was Dinah who broke the silence. "We were waiting for Robert to arrive before we sat down to eat. Would you join us? Robert never brings anyone home with him; you are the first. Would you stay and let us hear everything about you? And your dog, of course."

Nichol entered and removed her travel bag, her cloak, and left them by the door. *I might need to leave in a hurry.*

Taking food out for Shadow, she asked Dinah for water for him.

"Raisa, would you like to feed Shadow?"

Raisa's head went up and down in reply.

Nichol removed Shadow's portions that she purchased from a vendor and gave them to Raisa. "Place this in front of her and step away to watch her eat—dogs do not like to be bothered while they eat."

Bowls were placed on the table and Achim served everyone from a large pot placed on the table. Dinah brought bread to the table.

Nichol was midway through her first bite of a cooked meal that had not been carried for days in her travel bag.

Without warning, Achim demanded in his gruff and grumpy tone. "Who are you? Why are you dressed like a peasant boy, yet you purchased expensive jewelry from my son? What brings you to our town?"

Nichol was prepared for the questions, but not in the manner that Achim asked them. She swallowed, washed her bite of food down with a splash of ale, and looked him directly in the eyes.

"My name is Nichol. I am the daughter of Alexander, the port commander of Marseilles. He sent me to Paris to find his friend Ezra, the merchant and moneylender. I am dressed this way so no one would recognize me or know who I was."

Achim listened closely. At the mention of Ezra's name, he stopped eating and leaned toward Nichol. The table went silent, each of them wondering what Achim would say next.

"The man you seek—Ezra the moneylender—is my brother. What business do you have with him? Why would your father send you on a trip across the country all by yourself just to meet with Ezra?"

Nichol's eyes met Achim's, then her gaze circled the table, stopping again at Achim's.

"I will tell you when we are alone, as she looked at Gideon and Raisa. The room turned solemn, all eyes focused on Nichol, then heads went down to finish their bowls of stew.

Achim could wait no longer. "Gideon, prepare Raisa for bed and then go to the blacksmith shop and make sure everything is secured for the night."

Gideon picked up Raisa and walked around for her to say goodnight to everyone. When he got to Nichol, Gideon hesitated, but Raisa did not. She held her arms out and demanded to be nestled by Nichol.

Nichol kissed her little cheeks, caressed her gently under the chin, and told her good night. Her sweet handling of Raisa was noticed by everyone. Of course, Shadow was hugged as well. Nichol whispered to Shadow to go lie with Raisa.

Seeing the concern on the faces, Nichol explained, "I do not know if she is dog, wolf or both but she is very defensive and if anyone but you or I enter that room she will protect Raisa. Tonight, she will sleep at your door. I am not sure how much to tell you; it might put you in danger just for providing me with shelter. I would like to leave coin for the meal and for one night lodging, you have been very kind."

Robert, Dinah, Achim, and Nichol then went to an adjacent small room.

Dinah tilted her head and gave a stern look to Achim, a look he understood. His demeanor and question to Nichol changed from gruff to a more sensitive one.

"Nichol, we would like to hear why you had to leave your home disguised as a boy and are traveling alone to seek out my brother?"

Nichol had expected the questions and remained silent while she debated how much she should tell them. *Achim and Ezra are brothers—the whole truth would be known to all soon.*

"My papa was murdered, and he prepared me with the means and the instructions to seek out Ezra if something happened to him. They had many business dealings together. He was one of the few that Papa trusted. Papa never intended for me to travel all this way alone. I started out with a caravan of travelers, but it turned out to be faster traveling alone."

Taking a deep breath, she folded her hands on the table, and looking from one to the other, she said, "I will start at the beginning."

She then reached behind her neck, removed the leather cord that held Alexander's rings and slid them off the cord. She then took the silver chain she had purchased from Robert and threaded it through the rings.

With the rings on display for all to see, she continued, "These rings were Papa's. I removed them from his hands after he died."

Nichol paused and closed her eyes and sighed. For a moment, she was with her papa.

She left the rings on the table as she told them the whole story. When she got to the part where her mother poisoned Alexander, Dinah gasped in horror.

When she explained that Astrid had sent her brother Fredric on a quest to drag her back to Marseilles, and then detailed the multiple acts of violence Fredric inflicted on her, Robert reacted and became visibly upset.

Turning to Achim, she said, "One of the things that Papa taught me was how to observe people. When he discovered that I often hid behind the tapestry in his solar to hear about business and shared what I heard, he began to teach me about his merchant trade. He explained to me about whom I should trust. And, if I got into trouble, who to go to if I needed help or needed to escape. Papa even sent me to Sir Roland's for training so I could learn how to defend and protect myself.

"One day, I was in my place behind the tapestry and heard my papa and Ezra talking. Ezra spoke fondly of you, revealing that you are a blacksmith, and that Dinah and Helene, Ezra's wife, are the best of friends."

She finished her story by filling in the details about how she met Robert at the fair in Antony. "I am who I say I am. I purchased the necklace from your son and asked him if he knew of an inn where I could spend the night. He offered food and shelter here in your home. I am happy to pay for that kindness.

Relieved that her story was out, she paused and waited for their comments.

Dinah was the first to speak. "My dear girl, what horrible injustices you have suffered. You are safe here with us for the night," she said, her tone kind.

Achim nodded. "My Dinah is right. You can stay here until you decide to leave for Paris. We can provide you with directions to Ezra's home. You do not have to pay; our home is yours."

Nichol could not believe what she had just heard. Tears of relief glistened in her eyes. She whispered, "Thank you for your kindness."

With that, they all rose from the table. Nichol collected her rings and necklace.

Dinah instructed Robert to show Nichol where she could wash up before retiring and where she could sleep for the night. She nudged Nichol toward Robert and they went to the back of the house.

When they were gone, Dinah looked at Achim.

Shaking her head, she said, "How could a woman do that to her husband and then take it out on her daughter? How clever and strong Nichol must be to have endured what she has and still be alive to talk about it. Achim, we must do all we can to help her."

Achim followed Dinah to the kitchen. "Yes, I agree. We will get her safely to Ezra."

sixty-three

The Farewell Meal

Is Robert leaving for Paris now because of me?

The next morning Nichol woke to the sounds of a rooster crowing and rustling in the straw surrounding her. Out of the corner of her eye, she watched Raisa and Shadow playing —she noticed that Shadow had learned how to fetch.

Making her own sounds so they would hear, Nichol stretched her arms and opened her eyes. As she turned her head, Raisa was sitting inches from her and staring at her. And Shadow was staring as well, with one ear cocked.

Nichol smiled and Raisa exclaimed, "I am a big girl now!"

"You certainly are. How old are you?" asked Nichol.

"I am three. Where are your mama and papa?"

Nichol thought it was an odd question, but answered with, "They are in a town far away from here. But they told me to find a young girl to be friends with. Will you be my friend?"

Raisa bounced her head up and down and cried, "Yes!"

Nichol rose from her bed and scooped Raisa into her arms to give her a hug. She could see Dinah in the kitchen and told Raisa, "Let us go help your aunt."

In the kitchen with Raisa smiling happily and clinging to her, Nichol turned to Shadow and signaled *stay* with her hand. Shadow positioned herself at the door and layed down. Nichol then lowered Raisa onto a stool near Dinah.

"Good morning. How can I help?" Nichol asked.

Taking in what she was watching, Dinah smiled. "Good morning. Yes—make sure this pot does not boil over. I need to get more bread."

While Dinah busied herself with the bread, Nichol asked, "Where is everybody at this early hour?"

Dinah wiped her brow. "Robert and Achim are at the forge preparing for the day's work and Gideon is drawing water from the well."

Just then, Gideon appeared with a bucket of water and placed it on the shelf. Thanking him, Dinah patted his arm. "Gideon, go tell your father and brother to come in."

"Dinah, I will go. Shadow needs to go outside. Raisa, come with us," Nichol said.

Dinah and Gideon readied the table with food and waited for them to return. The table was small and well-made of pieces of wood banded with an iron strap, and they sat shoulder to shoulder as they ate—all except Raisa, who sat on Dinah's lap. There was constant chatter about activities for the day and talk of neighbors and their lives.

Nichol could not add anything to the conversation, so she ate while everyone else talked. Tilting her almost-empty bowl, she sopped up the last of the porridge with a piece of bread, and began licking her wet fingers.

Everyone stopped talking and Nichol looked up to see what had silenced them. They were all staring at her.

Embarrassed, she said, "I am accustomed to eating food out of my travel pack and it is rarely fresh. This reminds me of the meals I used to eat at home. It is very good!"

Dinah smiled with pride that her cooking was equal to the meals served by the wealthy. Glancing at Robert, she told him to get Nichol another bowl of porridge. He did, and they resumed their conversations.

When the meal was finished, Achim asked Gideon to take Raisa and Shadow outside for a walk. They all noticed Nichol as she kneeled and whispered to Shadow, petting her animal gently when she was done. When they were gone, Achim slid his bowl to the center of the table, and everyone knew he was ready to talk.

Facing Nichol, he said, "The three of us have discussed how to help you. We have determined the safest way we can get you to Ezra's home. As Robert told you, he usually sells his jewelry in Paris. We all think he should accompany you there. He has agreed to help me finish some things at the forge today and he can be ready to leave with you first thing tomorrow. Because you have been through so much since leaving Marseilles, we would feel better if the final leg of your journey ended with someone who knows the area."

Nichol was touched. She looked at the three of them.

"I am so grateful to you for feeding me and taking me into your home, but I do not expect any of you to disrupt your lives to accompany me to Paris. It is only one day away on foot and I plan on running at full speed to get there."

Robert had been silent up to that point. He was glad that his father had made it sound like it was his idea to send him to Paris with Nichol. He was sitting close enough to cover her hand with his.

"Nichol, we want to see you end your journey safely at my uncle's home, and I know the way. You have made it clear that this is what your father intended for you, and we are honored to be included in the fulfillment of those plans. As it turns out, I have been accepted as an apprentice goldsmith in Paris and I can begin my training sooner than anticipated if I leave with you tomorrow."

Nichol looked at Robert. "I accept your offer."

Is it happening too fast? Outside of Timo, no one in the last two months had shown such care or concern for me.

She was silent, thinking about her options for a long while.

Nichol liked everything about him. Again, sharing with Robert her concerns about the danger that followed her, his only reply was, "I am willing to take that chance."

Nichol squeezed his hand. "All right. We leave for Paris tomorrow morning."

Now that plans were finalized, Robert and Achim left the house and went back to work on the tasks they needed to finish at the forge. Dinah sent Gideon and Raisa to the market.

Cleaning the remains of the meal away, Dinah asked Nichol to sit at the table. They talked throughout the morning.

Since Nichol had summarized details of her life to Robert's family the previous night, she listened quietly as Dinah recapped hers.

"Dinah, what is it like to have a little girl around the house?"

"She has been a joy for all of us. Raisa's mother was my sister. Both she and Raisa's father were killed when a wagon they were riding in overturned. Raisa survived the accident, and we took her in."

"Is Robert leaving for Paris now because of me?"

"Robert is an accomplished blacksmith, but he prefers making jewelry to hammering iron. He is twenty and has been accepted into an apprenticeship with a master goldsmith in Paris, and he is eager to begin."

"Would you tell me about Ezra and Helene?"

"Ezra is Achim's older brother. They each took a different path in life, but they are alike. They are gruff on the outside, but gentle on the inside. That's probably why your father chose Ezra to protect you. Helene is a dear woman and will capture your heart immediately.

"Helene and Ezra never had children of their own, and they were always happy to visit us when Robert and Gideon were growing up. Now that Raisa is with us, Helene creates excuses to come to Antony to be with her. Raisa loves the attention and kisses she gets from Auntie Helene."

Suddenly, Dinah stopped talking. She looked at Nichol with warm concern.

"It is plain to see Robert is taken with you. Achim and I know the real reason he wants to go to Paris with you. He does not want you to leave without him. For him to bring you to our home and insist that he act as your protector on the way to Ezra's told us all we need to know."

It was plain to see Dinah was struggling with the reality facing her. "Robert is my firstborn and, as his mother, I am concerned about his well-being."

"The love you show for your family touches me deeply. Papa was the only one in my family who showed me that kind of love. I cannot explain it, but when I met Robert at the fair, it felt like something magical drew us together. My life has been chaotic for over two months and Robert's protection as we travel to Paris is most welcome." Nichol apparently said just the right things to put Dinah's mind at ease.

To her surprise, Dinah jumped up from her chair and hugged her.

"Come, Nichol, let us clean you up. I made some new soap last week with lavender flowers I saved from the summer. I think you will like it. I suspect you prefer breeches and short tunics—Robert has offered a few of his for you to use. He told me that you had special slits in your tunic that you hid coin in. Show me and I will add them to the clothing he is planning to share."

"Thank you. There's one more thing. I have Papa's jeweled dagger I wore on a hidden belt for my protection. It would be best to keep it hidden by the tunic, but accessible if I need it."

That night, Dinah made a farewell meal for Robert and Nichol. She was amazed by Nichol's cleverness with her old garments and was planning to add hidden openings to Achim's and Gideon's tunics as well.

Gideon had already asked his father to make a back satchel like Nichol's.

Nichol felt like a different person—really clean for the first time since she had left Marseilles with Dinah's lavender soap and clad in clean clothes.

Nichol sat at the table with the others. After the table was cleared, Nichol, Gideon, and Raisa went to bed and Robert went to pack his things. When he was finished, he went to the kitchen to find his parents sitting at the table. He poured himself a cup of wine and joined them.

Achim withdrew a full purse from his belt and handed it to Robert. "We have saved this for a special occasion, and we want you to have it now. It is our gift to you for your expenses in Paris. Take it with our blessing."

Achim sat back and exhaled deeply. He was aware this was a turning point for all of them.

Robert was close to tears as he accepted the bag of coins. He had always been close to his parents. The tender-hearted words his father had just spoken touched him deeply.

"Thank you both for the coin, and the caring and the training you have always given me. I will work hard and make you proud."

The three stood and embraced. Dinah was openly crying as she held her son and whispered, "You could not make me prouder."

Achim nodded in agreement. "Let us get some sleep. Tomorrow will be here soon enough."

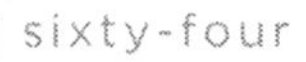

sixty-four

The Bond Is Formed

Nichol was dreading, yet anxiously anticipating, what would happen next.

Before dawn, Robert and Nichol left Antony as moonlight still lit the silent streets, slipping out the door as the others slept.

Robert was elated to be going on this journey. He grasped her hand in his as they wound their way through the back streets heading out of town. Shadow moved in synch with both of them.

The air was cool. Nichol slid her hand up his arm and snuggled into him as he drew her close to his side. She smiled up at him and quietly sang her chant:

I am on my way to Paris,
In many towns, in just a few days.
That is where my future lies,
And Papa planned it that way.

"What is that you are singing softly?" As he murmured the words, he looked at her, leaned down, and kissed her on the lips.

Her first kiss. How perfect it felt to her.

My life feels so perfect. How can I be feeling this way? I barely know him—yet I feel that I have known him always. The Lady directed me to him; I know because I see and feel him. Robert and I are together—reaching Paris is not such an urgent task now.

Oblivious to the world around them, they delighted in the intimacy of their own shared solitude. Their pace slowed.

On the road, they talked about their lives as they walked. Robert's mind was filled with questions for her.

"Nichol, you have experienced more in your few years than most people do in their entire life. I want to know everything about you—from what brought you to the street fair where I first saw you, to what it was like to live in a manor. Would you tell me about how your father trained you and taught you his business? And I would like to hear about the protection training that he had someone teach to you, too."

"I know that I had opportunities that you did not. But from what I saw and experienced since yesterday, you have had many things in your life that I would give all the coin Papa had to have. I would have preferred to have a family like yours."

The anxiety of what waited in Paris gave her pause. Slowing down, she moved to the side of the road and sat down. Shadow nestled close to her, cuddling under her arm.

Robert dropped down to sit on her other side. "Is something wrong? Why are we stopping?"

"For over two months I have been traveling with two goals on my mind: finding Ezra in Paris, and avoiding Fredric. And then, you came into my life. Being with you right now is all I want.

Now that my journey is almost over, and with some time to think, I am concerned about what awaits me in Paris."

I do not want to rush this moment with him, but why am I drawn to him; does he feel the same way I feel? Is Robert the one that the Lady told me about? Is this my life partner?

"Before I met you, all I could think about was to get to Paris —to find Ezra. Now, I do not think we need to rush to Paris. I want to know more about you as well, Robert. I want to know everything about you."

"Nichol, I like that. Let us walk until we find a place to stop, out of sight of travelers, for our protection. We can build a fire for warmth and set up for the night."

By early afternoon, Nichol followed Shadow behind a cluster of pines, far off the trail and near a small brook. With Shadow at her side, she called back to Robert. "Shadow found where we can stay the night."

Gathering wood, Robert started a fire. As she settled in, Nichol pulled out food that Dinah had given her. Smiling, she said, "Your mother included some for Shadow, too."

They sat together, eating their food, and talking of small things. Finally, Nichol added more wood to the fire, and began to tell Robert some of the things he was curious about.

"We are both connected to Ezra. He is your uncle. He was also my father's trusted partner. Before Papa knew that I was hiding behind a tapestry, I learned that he and Ezra were merchants together and they owned buildings to store goods. They also exported goods throughout France. Ezra even financed some of Papa's trade.

"I know that I can trust Ezra when I find him. Someday, I would like to be a merchant like my father was. What made you want to be a goldsmith, and not a blacksmith?"

"Over the years I worked hard to learn the blacksmith trade as my father's apprentice. One day, Ezra was on his way to Lyon. He stopped at the forge and showed us a gold necklace and broach. It was a gift for the wife of an important noble. I was so taken by the beauty of the intricate pieces, hammering hot iron on an anvil lost my interest. From that day on, I thought of nothing but being a goldsmith.

"When Ezra returned several months later, I begged him to help me become a goldsmith. Papa gave his approval, knowing that I would not be satisfied being only a blacksmith. I still help him on the forge when needed and I have labored hard and improved my craft. Now Ezra is financing my goldsmith business, and uses some of my work as gifts. Even though I am not yet a proper apprentice, he has received compliments on the quality of my pieces. Achim is proud of my accomplishments and Gideon has now taken my place at the forge."

"Outside of Ezra being your family, would he help sell your jewelry if you expand what you produce …not just in Paris, but in other places in France?"

Robert was surprised by what Nichol asked. "I know that my uncle does moneylending to merchants and nobles. I never thought of myself as a merchant, but I suppose if I am selling my work, I must be."

Laughing, she interrupted him. "You are the second person I chose to travel with on my way to Paris. The *Lady* told me that I needed to get to Paris. Recently she told me that I should not hesitate in my journey. I needed to get there. Yet, she directed me to you … you were her reason. Our meeting was not by chance."

"The *Lady* … who is the *Lady*?"

"The *Lady* is a voice I hear. She has become my friend and has talked to me since I was a little girl. Usually, it is in my sleep; she comes to me when I am dreaming. Sometimes I would hear things from her, and I would write with chalk on my bedchamber wall what I remembered. Our housekeeper Margaux was aware of her and Rose, the shopkeeper who was Papa's eyes in the port, said she was my special guide. Sometimes, she spoke to Papa while he slept, too—with warnings to protect me."

"You can read and write. That would be important for me to know. Would you teach me?" *Nichol is someone special. I cannot let her leave my side.*

Nichol had forgotten that most did not know how to read and write … something that Papa had insisted Margaux instruct his children to do when she was hired to run the villa. She used the books Papa brought back from his travels. When Nichol literally inhaled what Margaux taught, Fredriç did not bother with his lessons.

Turning to him, she continued, "Of course I will. I feel we have much to learn together. And first, we need to keep the fire going. The sky is clear and it will be a cold night."

With the fire built up, they leaned toward each other, nestling in for the night, the glow of the flames warming their faces … and their hearts.

In his excitement, Robert told her about the goldsmith guild he would be joining and shared his plans for learning his trade. Nichol listened eagerly and began to envision shapes for the jewelry he would make as he described how he worked and what types of gems he wanted to add.

Shadow crouched down and wiggled her way closer, separating them as she gave Nichol a lick on her cheek.

"Shadow is my protector; soon she will be yours."

Robert was amused as he looked at the two of them. "I would like to be your protector, too, Nichol." *Maybe tomorrow night I will sleep next to her without Shadow between us.*

sixty-five

The Union

Her body flowed with the joy she had longed to experience.

The next morning, they were up with the sun and continued their trek to Paris at the same leisurely pace they had set the day before.

As they walked, their life stories poured out.

"I would write stories for Papa and he would always thank me for them, usually at the evening meal. When he figured out I was hiding in his solar and listening to his business meetings, he was amused. Sometimes when he was alone, he would get up from his chair and turn to the wall and ask the tapestry questions … meaning me. He would wait for me to open the small flap I had cut in it so I could see. Then he would crouch down and say, 'What did you learn today?'

"One day, Papa told me that he did not believe that Fredric was his child after he had set me up to be assaulted by his friends. It was then that he began to interact with me as if I was his son—teaching me how his business worked and making me his confidant—and planning for my protection and escape if necessary."

"Do you really think your mother murdered him?"

"I saw the vial of poison given to her by a man who owed Papa money that was loaned to him. The next morning, Papa was found dead. Yes, I know she did it."

"Why would she do that?"

"She wanted Papa to allow Fredric to start taking over his businesses and learn to run the estate. Papa knew that Fredric was not capable of it and I had overheard him tell her that many times. Then I heard him tell her that he was not his son. He gave Fredric a brutal beating in the open courtyard for all to see after my attack, threatening he would be hanged if I was ever harmed again. From that day on, she started plotting her revenge."

Robert took in what she had said, squeezing her hand as she spoke.

"I have not experienced the hate and fear you have, Nichol. I do know that when you meet my aunt and uncle, you will be cared for, just as your papa planned. You will immediately take to Aunt Helene. She longed for her own daughter, something that never happened. When you walk through their door in Paris, she will love you.

"And remember how gruff my papa was when I first introduced you? Ezra is the same way. As soon as he realizes you are Alexander's daughter, he will make you his. You will have a new papa."

With tears in her eyes and joy in her heart, it was Nichol's turn to squeeze Robert's hand.

"Tell me more about Ezra. How did he offer to help you with the goldsmithing apprenticeship? Did he loan money to other jewelry merchants?"

Robert chuckled. "You were fortunate to understand your

father's business. I understood blacksmithing, but I knew nothing about moneylending. Uncle Ezra saw that I was interested in making jewelry at my guild trade and he was enthusiastic about supporting me. He ordered several pieces that he would use as gifts. He told me about the goldsmith apprenticeship in Paris and offered to underwrite the costs in trade for what I could make. I could not turn down such a generous offer. He was answering my dream to work with what I love."

The conversation was enlightening and gave each of them a glimpse into the other's family. Neither speaking of it, their hands naturally found each other, as if it was the most normal thing two people would do.

Their mutual discovery process was so blissful that their walking never returned to running—the hurried running that Nichol had assumed they would be doing to get to Paris and reach Robert's uncle.

Realizing they were moving more slowly, Robert laughed. "At the rate we are going, we might get to Paris in weeks rather than two days."

"I have been so happy with our conversations that I have not paid much attention to our progress. I cannot remember being this joyful since I took long walks with Papa in our gardens. It now seems like so long ago … yet it has only been a few months. If it takes us several extra days to get to Paris, I am content with that," Nichol said.

During their travels to Paris, they were becoming a couple.

Attracted to each other when their eyes first met at the fair, they were now teasing and touching throughout the day. They slowly walked, talked, and laughed their way into early afternoon before deciding to stop for the day.

That night, Robert drew Nichol close to him. She made no attempt to move, and Robert pulled her even closer and kissed her. It was a long, tender kiss that neither wanted to end, and it awakened the passion in both, stirring feelings that neither of them had had before.

Nichol was anxiously anticipating what would happen next. She felt a knot in her stomach every time she looked at Robert, and every time he touched her, her skin tingled with delight.

Shadow seemed to sense something different was happening. Perking her ears up, she crouched on the ground, ready to leap if her mistress needed her.

He layed her on the ground wrapped up under their cloaks as he whispered in her ear, "I have never done this … I do not know how or what I should do."

Nichol closed her eyes and folded her hands tightly across her stomach. *What if I do not know what to do …?*

Suddenly, she felt Shadow's nose on her hand. Laughing out loud, she turned her head toward her pet. "Shadow, it is all right … go lay down."

Amused, Robert decided to lead her into the topic. Lying next to her, he took her hand. "Nichol, are you nervous about coupling with me?"

"My heart is racing just thinking about what we might do. I … I confess to you that I am scared and excited at the thought of what will happen. I know how … coupling is accomplished, but I have no idea what I should do or when I should do it," Nichol admitted.

He held her face between his hands and kissed her gently on the lips. "I confess, I have never been with anyone before. What if we ... find our way together?"

Robert gently stroked her hair as he spoke, his voice soft, almost in a whisper. "I have never met anyone like you. You are beautiful, bold, courageous, and smart beyond words. May this be not only a journey together to Paris, but the beginning of our lifetime together."

Robert lifted his body, resting on one elbow and looked into her eyes. "I have a gift and a promise to you. Give me your hand."

Maintaining eye contact, filled with curiosity, she lifted her left hand that rested on top of her tunic.

Robert raised to a sitting position and gently wrapped one hand around her. With his other hand, he opened it and displayed a ring. "Will you accept this ring, and my pledge to protect and be faithful to you for as long as I live?"

Sitting up, Nichol was overwhelmed with what she heard. His voice was gentle, with a tenderness that she had never experienced with another. Her body flowed with the joy she longed to experience.

"Robert, I will accept your ring and your promise. I will be faithful to you and be your wife—and you will be my husband."

Tears streamed down her face. She cupped his face in her hands, kissed him, and held it for a long moment. When she withdrew from the kiss, she edged over by his side and snuggled into his embrace.

Robert laughed, kissed her, and said, "We have a lifetime together to figure this out. We will practice several times a day until we get it right."

Neither was aware of the soft glow of light that vibrated around them.

sixty-six

Who We Are

Neither of them wanted to be the one to break the spell.

The next morning, they woke to the warmth of the sun and the heat emanating from their entwined bodies. Nichol nudged her back against Robert's chest as he draped his arm across her and pulled her in even closer. She heard Shadow whimpering.

Lifting her head, she patted the ground. "Come here, girl."

Tail wagging, Shadow edged closer, her belly scooting on the ground. Robert raised his head and added, "Come, Shadow. Join us."

Now up on all four legs, Shadow leaped forward, nuzzling into Nichol's neck. Reaching up to scratch her favorite ear, Robert did the same. Settling down, Shadow put her head across Nichol's chest, tail wagging enthusiastically. Laughing and touching Shadow at the same time, Nichol reflected on their first night of lovemaking.

Robert had been gentle and patient with her as he explored her body and then she explored his … over and over. It had been painful at first, but once the pain subsided, they discovered a whole new world of pleasure.

Neither of them wanted to be the one to break the spell they were under, but after several minutes, Nichol sat up and turned to Robert. Shadow mimicked her mistress, her head moving back and forth between the two.

"Should we be on our way or just spend our day here?" Nichol asked.

"Let us get something first to eat. Shadow needs something as well, and I will take her for a run down to the river. My family never had a dog and I want her to care for me like she does you. Now we are a family."

Nichol pulled a comb from her bag and began gliding it through her clean hair. She did not want to move about, just be there, waiting for the two to return. When they did, Robert sat. This time Shadow sat by his side and Robert patted her head.

Nichol looked at the comb still in her hand and then gently put one hand on Robert's face and began combing his hair, filtering out the wooded environment and the sound of the river.

Robert put his hand on hers and pulled her to him. She was now a willing captive and he was hers.

All her fear and anxiety had disappeared. Feelings she had experienced the night before invaded her body again. They lay down and the world around them vanished once again.

Shadow did not whimper, giving them the space they desired as time slipped away.

It was midday before they packed up and started out.

They had walked far before Nichol asked, "Do you know what I would really like to do right now?"

Amused and open to anything, Robert looked hopeful and waited for her to tell him.

Reaching for his hand, she started to pull him toward the river.

They approached a shallow, slow-moving secluded section. Dropping to his knees, Robert put his hand in the water. "It is cold here. What are you thinking?"

Nichol smiled and pulled out a cloth and soap Dinah had given her from her pack. "Take your cloak and tunic and breeches off. We are not going to go in the water."

Intrigued with her proposition, Robert was quick to do her bidding, standing in front of her without clothes on.

Then it was Nichol's turn. Robert eagerly removed her clothes and spread her cloak on the ground. He forgot about the water as he pulled a willing Nichol down, wrapping his cloak over the top of them. "We can bathe later."

They embraced until Shadow stood and turned her head in the direction where they had just come from.

Nichol sat up and looked around, then rolled on top of Robert, "I think Shadow is warning us others are nearby. Let us wash quickly and prepare to leave." Whispering to Shadow to be on alert if someone approaches, she then turned her attention to Robert, placing her hands on his cheeks and kissing him.

Robert quickly rolled her over on her back. "I will only move from here if you let me wash you as well."

They washed and splashed at each other until the frigid temperature of the water stopped their pleasure.

As they dressed, they heard birds screeching in a nearby tree. Exchanging glances, they knew that they had to move on. Moving away from the river, they walked hand in hand back to the road.

They began walking as an elderly woman approached them, smiling as her eyes followed from where they came.

The three walked together, keeping Shadow at the edge of the road to avoid contact with other travelers. Paris was getting closer, Nichol's anticipation increased with each step.

Robert had become quiet. Finally, he asked, "Will you tell me about this Timo you mentioned to Achim? How long did you travel together?"

Nichol suspected where the questioning was leading, and she put his mind at ease immediately.

"Timo's true name was Timothée Lemur. I do not know when he joined a monastery or when he became Brother Lemur. The monastery is where he shared the skills he learned from his family about farming and grape-growing. I started to call him Timo soon after we met, it was what his older brother called him because he could not say his full name. After several days of traveling together, I asked him how I should address him, and he said I could call him by any name I chose. When I heard the name Timo, it seemed to fit his personality and that's how I addressed him in private.

"He became the brother to me that mine never was, just as I became the sister he never had. Contrary to opinions I once held about all church officials, Timo demonstrated to me that he truly is a man of God who believes and lives what he was taught. It was Timo who reminded me many times that he would stay true to his Benedictine vows of poverty, chastity, and obedience. And he did. I always felt safe with him."

"How did you two happen to meet and decide to travel together?"

She reached for his hand. "I met him at a fair in Vienne about ten days after I left Marseilles. The monks there hold a winter fair each year where they open their stores and sell to those who could afford to buy and give to those who could not pay. I filled my bags with things I purchased and Timo was the money handler for the monks. We had a short, pleasant conversation and I left to be on my way.

"I had been running through the forest for several days to stay hidden from my brother. One morning, I saw Timo and his donkey, Moki, on the road below the tree line. Recognizing him, I made my way toward him. He remembered me and all the things I purchased that day at the fair. We walked together for a time and it was during a rest stop that we discovered his travels took him on the same road and through the same towns I was heading for. When he stopped at different monasteries along the way, I ate and slept in the longhouse with other travelers. He made sure I had food."

"Why was he traveling alone? I thought monks stayed at one monastery?"

"He was at one monastery, but he was sent out by his abbot to help the other monasteries throughout the region to share his knowledge about plants, planting, and crops. He had created manuscripts on plants and how to care for them. A manuscript was left with each monastery after his visit. He also spent time working with the other brothers in the fields. When we parted, he gave me a manuscript showing his drawings and planting instructions. I will show it to you when we stop for the night.

"Early in our journey, we stopped at an inn so I could buy a meat pie. I heard a voice I recognized and it was Fredric, drinking the day away. He tried to capture me and take me back to Marseilles. I kicked him, gouged his eye, and ran out of the tavern, jumping on his horse.

"Riding the horse away from the inn, I decided his pursuit and treatment of me had to stop. Turning around, I halted in front of the inn. Fredric saw me and limped out, shouting, 'Give me the rings you stole. They are mine!'

"Glaring at him, I told him, 'I have nothing of yours. You are a bastard and not the son of my father.' Then I leaned down and whispered to the horse that he abused, 'Let us run him down.' Straightening up in the saddle, I gave the command to charge. The horse responded to me, and Fredric did not move. He stood there, angry and stupid with drink. The horse ran over him and he rolled under the horse as its hooves struck him.

"He was now screaming, curled up on the ground, and whimpering in pain. I leaped off the horse, cut off his coin purse, and warned him to return to Marseilles. I told him he was the bastard son of Astrid and his father was not my papa."

"Was that all you said?"

Nichol shook her head. "No. I told him if our paths ever crossed again, I will fulfill Papa's promise to treat him just like the two men he sent to assault me."

"What was your father's promise?"

"He told Fredric that if he ever harmed me again, he would kill him. That is how Papa treated the two men who attacked and beat me."

"Timo saw it all happen, including my brother's hateful and vicious behavior toward me. From that day on, he acted like the older brother that I never had, to support and protect me as we traveled together. Timo is kind, patient, generous, and a very loving person. He believes in his church and its teachings and is one of the few decent men I have met."

Nichol detected a bit of jealousy in Robert's look. She teasingly said, "You have been very indecent so far and I am learning to like it a lot."

They laughed and continued on their way.

As they walked, Nichol was deep in thought. Finally, she stopped and turned to face him. "I have a verse I would like to share with you. Would you like to hear it?"

"Is it about us?"

Nichol smiled and began …

> Purchasing food for my journey, ready to leave.
> I stopped and noticed a man watching me.
> What is he peddling, this man who stares?
> With his eyes like thunderbolts and clarity landing their hook.

The two faced each other, unseeing of travelers passing them on the road.

Robert hesitated for a few moments, thinking quickly. "I have a verse to share with you, too." He took her hands, kissed them, then looked into her eyes after a quick glance at Shadow.

> I see a young woman, a wolf by her side.
> Dressed as a boy, something to hide.

Laughing, Nichol added, "Oh, so my disguise did not fool you! Well, I have another verse."

Stepping back from him and pretending to be Robert, she moves her hands over an invisible bench as she begins her verse, beckoning as he did to urge her closer.

> A small bench, jewelry I see, must get closer.
> I can tell, this man is proud of what he sells.
> His pitch is mesmerizing, his hands tell the story.
> Every item he peddles is of exceptional quality.

Robert pulls her into his embrace, whispering in her ear,

> A glow surrounds her not a sound to hear,
> come closer, come closer, come closer, my dear.

Nichol smiled as she continued:

> I must approach this man who has me in his spell.
> Ignoring another man, who is there to steal.

Robert replied:

> She is in front of me ... what do I say,
> Take her hand, do not leave ... you must stay.

Nichol responded:

> This man turns to me with his appeal.
> I look away, I cannot resist.

Not to be outdone, Robert answered:

> I extend my hand; you hesitate at first.
> Our eyes meet, come to me, do not resist.

The words flowed from Nichol's mouth like magic:

> He pulls me closer with his every word.
> Luring me in to see his display

His eyes resting on my face.

Reaching for my hand, a touched embrace. I see him.

Can he see me?

Their final words to each other were almost uttered in unison:

What does she possess, that makes me so weak?

What does he possess, that makes me so weak?

sixty-seven

Ezra and Helene

I know she is telling the truth.

"Robert, look—there are more people on the road than I have seen in a long time. We must be getting close to Paris. Have you noticed how they stare and then move away from Shadow?"

"Shadow looks like a wolf and most people fear wolves. Let us move Shadow between us. I will keep her on a short leash."

The rest of the morning, they walked amongst groves of trees that were dormant with the season. It was obvious that the empty fields were fertile for the growing seasons after the winter chill subsided.

Finally, the empty fields yielded to a scattering of homes. Soon there were clusters of them. Nichol's heart picked up a beat. She knew they were nearing Paris.

A large river appeared next, with bridges spanning between its banks. On the other side, there were many buildings of all sizes. Travelers were moving in both directions and small ships were moving along the river. A wharf was located close to the entrance and exit of each bridge.

"Look … there are more buildings. And I can see another bridge and a gate in the wall. That must be what Papa told me about when he talked to me about Ezra! Of course, it is much bigger than Marseilles, but it reminds me of the parts where I would love to watch what was happening when the ships were unloaded."

"This is the Seine River," Robert said as they stopped to gaze across it. "We will cross here and then cross over another bridge. On the other side, there are many more people and homes. You will see the women dress differently from what you saw in the towns you have come through. And the merchants—you will hear them shouting out at passersby to visit their tables and stores. Many will be cooking on the streets and your belly will beckon to you to feast on the offerings. Merchandise will be moved up and down streets on carts. Sometimes the carts are pulled be a man; sometimes an animal. This is where Ezra lives. We are getting close."

Putting his arm around her, Robert said, "Yes, your papa was right in how he described it to you. That is the entrance to Paris. It is a large wall that surrounds a small island and was added to protect the people from the Norsemen."

At once, they picked up their pace. Once inside the wall surrounding the island, she slowed to take in all that she saw.

"Let us keep moving. We need to cross another bridge."

"Oh, Robert, this makes me happy. It reminds me of the markets at the docks in Marseilles. I miss that excitement and all the activity that I experienced when I went there to see the vendors and take in what was happening with the ships that were loading and unloading goods."

Knowing the area well from the visits to his uncle's house as a boy and then now to share jewelry pieces that Ezra had ordered,

Robert headed them to the second bridge. Ezra's home was not far away once they had crossed the bridge.

Within a short time, he slowed down as they approached an impressive two-story home built of multicolored stones. On either side of Ezra's home, there were houses of similar size but built with different material.

Knowing that her moment had arrived at last, Nichol said softly, "I was younger when he saw me outside Papa's solar. He may not even recognize me, but I will know him by his loud and distinctive voice."

All that she had experienced and endured on her journey was weighing heavily on her. The uncertainty of what might happen now that she was at Ezra's door only added to her anxiety. He owed her no allegiance, despite being a dear friend and a business partner to her papa.

Nichol took a deep breath and slipped behind Robert as he knocked on the door.

How will he receive me?

Will Ezra believe me?

Will he help me as Papa had suggested?

The chant she had sung to herself in all that time leaped from her lips with one final change. "I have finally arrived in Paris after two full months of travel. This is where my future lies; Papa planned this."

As Robert looked down at her, smiling at her song as her final words flowed through her lips, the door opened. Ezra stood before them.

Robert was a head taller than he was. Wearing a dark green cloak around his rotund body, his shoes were similar to the ones

Papa had worn when in the villa. What hair he had was shoulder length, with little on top of his head. A smile spread quickly across his face.

Without saying a word to her, his eyes settled on Robert. "Robert, what a surprise!" Turning, he shouted, "Helene, come quickly. Robert is here!"

Helene made haste to the door, wiping her hands on her apron. She was a head shorter than Ezra and now Robert towered a foot above her. A wimple covered her head with a few wisps of hair spilling out. Around her shoulders was a beautiful shawl of different colors, and on her two first fingers were gorgeous rings set with gems that sparkled when the sun lit on them. Ezra stepped back and Helene took his place. She hugged Robert tightly and kissed his cheeks. She was ecstatic to see him.

Nichol remained behind Robert as he greeted his aunt and uncle. She smiled as their familial display of affection was shared.

Turning to her, Robert took her hand and drew her to his side. Looking from Ezra to Helene, he said, "Uncle Ezra and Aunt Helene, I would like you to meet Nichol and our dog Shadow."

He looks just as I remember him … short and balding, with big round dark eyes. I do not think he knows who I am. I was very young when I met him, the rest of the time, I was hidden. Helene, with her silver hair and fine features, must have been a beauty in her day.

With a warm smile and cheerful greeting, Helene welcomed them inside, exchanging a glance with Ezra.

Robert and Nichol put their satchels on the floor and followed Ezra to the kitchen table as Helene gathered bread, cheese, and ale to serve.

"Is that a wolf?" Ezra huffed.

"No," Nichol displayed the palm of her hand and Shadow then layed down. "She only bites bad people," she said with a smile.

Robert looked nervous.

As Ezra bent down and rubbed Shadow's head, he laughed. "I guess I am not a bad person. I could use a wolf who bites bad people. Some days, I seem to be surrounded by them.

"Robert, we were expecting you a month from now when you were to start at the guild for your apprenticeship."

Smiling, Robert spread his arms in a broad gesture. "Uncle Ezra, I am here because of Nichol. And she, dear uncle, is here because of you."

Helene noticed the unusual ring on Nichol's finger. Her questioning gaze met Robert's, and when she saw his warm smile, Helene knew. *They are together; they are one.*

Ezra leaned in over the table, closer to Nichol, slightly tilted his head as he studied her features. "There is something very familiar about you," he muttered.

All eyes were on Nichol.

"You knew my papa, Ezra. We … I … used to live in Marseilles," she said quietly. "You met me one time when you visited Papa and I was very young."

She stood and removed the silver chain that held her papa's rings and placed the items gently in the center of the table. Next, she withdrew her papa's jeweled dagger from beneath her tunic and placed it next to the rings.

Ezra eyed the offerings on the table. Slowly, he reached for the signet ring and picked it up. As he rolled it in his hand, he clasped it tightly to his chest. Tears brimmed his eyes. A gentle smile touched at the corner of his mouth.

"This ring belongs to Alexander, and you bear his features. You must be Lisa."

"Yes, I am Alexander's daughter. You would have heard him refer to me as Lisa. Before I left Marseilles, I changed my name to Nichol to hide my identity and protect myself as I escaped. Papa told me that if he was to die suddenly, I should seek you out. He even gave me a map to find you, close to the time I had to leave the villa."

At first, Ezra was mystified by her words, and then concerned for her. His eyes first met Helene's, then quickly moved to Robert's before they rested back on her face. "Hide your identity? Why and from whom? And why would you leave Marseilles? Were you running from something?" Ezra asked.

"I was running … and it was to you … and it was for my life. Papa planned it. I have known of you, Ezra, for a long time. I hid in Papa's solar and crafted a hole in the hanging tapestry, which concealed me so I could see who met with Papa and listen to their business discussions. That's how I first saw you and how I learned about you.

"When Papa discovered what I was doing and where I was hiding, he had only two choices. He could let me stay in the niche to observe and listen—or ban me from the solar. He decided to let me stay and after his guests left, we would go on walks to discuss the meeting.

"Papa found out that my observations and memory for detail were sharp and that was valuable to him. He made sure that I knew about his meetings and who would be there. He also told me that I was more his son than Fredric could ever be."

Where everyone was intrigued with the story that was flowing from Nichol, her ease was apparent. The words continued to tumble out of her mouth. “Ezra … Astrid killed Papa. She murdered him by poisoning his wine.”

No one moved, as if the three of them held their breath. The room filled with silent tension.

This time, it was Nichol’s turn to hold her breath as each of them absorbed her words.

Ezra broke the silence. “How do you know it was Astrid who poisoned him?”

Finally, the lid was off her internal vial of secrets. She could no longer be silent with what had happened and was happening in Marseilles.

“I was in the solar, hiding behind the hanging tapestry as I usually did. Papa knew I would be there to observe how he handled a business problem with a shipping merchant he had loaned money to who had not paid him back. Before the meeting started, I was surprised to see Astrid enter with the merchant before Papa came in. She whispered with him as he handed her a small vial. Then, Papa entered the room, surprising them both. Astrid left the solar quickly, hiding the vial so Papa did not see it. That’s how I could see and hear the exchange between the merchant Karl and Astrid.

“At the time, I did not know the vial held poison, but when Papa was found dead the next morning in the solar by Astrid, I became suspicious. Our housekeeper Margaux told me that Astrid took him his wine the night before he was found—something she never did.

“At that time, Astrid had nothing to do with Papa and me, only with Fredric. She did not even speak to us. Papa told me that he thought she had gone mad. He also told me that he did not believe Fredric was his son.

"Before his funeral, I went to see Rose, the healer at the docks. Papa told me to go to her if anything happened to him. I told her about seeing the merchant Karl giving Astrid a vial like the ones she has in her stall.

"At first, Rose was quiet, then I could see anger cross her face. She told me that Karl had requested a remedy for helping him get rid of rats on his ship. Suddenly, Rose's hand flew to her mouth. Staggering to a stool, sobbing, her devastation shook her entire body. She told me, 'Lisa, he lied to me. He got the poison for your mother. I provided the means for Astrid to murder your father.'"

Nichol stopped talking. Once again, the room fell into silence, with all eyes on her.

Finally, Ezra spoke.

"Yes, I know of Karl. He is a despicable man. And I know of Rose—she was an important source of information for Alexander, and for me as well. I suspect that Astrid must have promised him something important for him to provide the poison. Does Karl know you saw him give the vial to her?"

"No. All that happened as I hid behind the tapestry."

"Before Papa's funeral, Margaux pulled me aside and told me I must prepare to leave at once—my life was in danger from both Astrid and Fredric. She moved my things to her cottage ... to send me on to Rose as soon as the funeral was over. Margaux said that Rose would guide me to someone who would help me get out of Marseilles and away from the threat of Astrid and Fredric.

"She said that there would be two horses waiting for me—the other was for Margaux's son, Gerhardt, who would ride along as

I left the manor. I dressed as a peasant boy, I hacked off my long hair, and then rode to Rose's shop."

Ezra had heard enough and felt it was time to reveal to all that he had heard of Alexander's death.

"I had received word of your papa's death, but the details you described are totally different from those I received in a written message from your mother. She knew Alexander and I did business together. The message said *you* murdered Alexander and that Astrid had sent people to find you to bring you back to Marseilles to face your punishment."

Nichol shook her head. "If I were not so sad and hurt about losing Papa, I could almost laugh at what you just told me. It makes sense Astrid would spread lies that blame me for his death. I believe she encouraged Fredric to pursue, capture, and return me to Marseilles. He tried to do this, unsuccessfully, several times after I fled. He is not smart enough to think of doing it himself.

"Astrid announced before I fled that I was to marry Lord Neliphis. And if I did not agree to marry him, she would sell me to the next slave ship entering Marseilles. Now she is saying I killed Papa so someone will capture me and return me to Marseilles."

Thoughtfully, Ezra asked, "Nichol, what would Astrid gain if you were captured and returned to Marseilles?"

"Papa's wealth." Nichol hesitated for a moment. "Papa had a locked box that he kept his coin, gold, silver, and gemstones in. Astrid took the keys from him the night she killed him. She did not know that Papa also gave me a set of keys to the solar and the locked box, telling me that I should take what I needed if he was dead.

"As his body was lying in the Great Room for others to come and pay respects, I went into the solar and took all that was in the box. I left one coin in the bottom. I then lowered everything out the window to the ground below and left, locking the door. I went to where the bags had been lowered and moved everything—his gold, silver, gems, and coin—to where she would not find it."

Pausing for a moment, a small smile spread across her face. "In a way, Papa is protecting it."

Ezra absorbed what she said, and then asked, "What drove Astrid to kill Alexander? From all I saw when visiting him, your mother led a privileged life."

"She was pushing Papa to include Fredric in his business and to begin learning to manage all his affairs. Papa had sent him to train with Commander Ramos for a year to gain the knowledge required to become a successful leader. Fredric failed the training. Papa told me his only interest was in wine and women.

"I visited the harbor dressed as a peasant boy so I would look like everyone else. One day, Fredric found me at Rose's table and grabbed me by my hair and dragged me into the tavern. He traded me for a cup of wine to his two friends. They stripped off my clothes, beat me, choked me, and attempted to rape me.

"Papa was on a ship in the harbor. As Fredric dragged me away by my hair, Rose immediately sent one of the orphan boys she tended with a message to alert Papa. Papa came at once.

"Rushing into the tavern, he told Fredric to get back to the manor. He then crashed into the room in the back of the tavern I had been forced into, and Papa stopped the attack on me. Wrapping me in his cloak, he took me back to the manor, shouting to the men who were trying to hurt me that they would be dealt with.

"When Fredric returned to the manor, Papa stopped him in the courtyard, beat him severely, and promised he would kill him if he ever got near me again. Astrid watched from a window and did not speak to Papa for a year. That is, until she brought him his wine one night.

"Papa had Margaux watch over me closely as I healed from the beating. Each day, he would come to my side and offer comforting words. At the same time, he made plans to have me taught how to protect and defend myself with weapons and fighting. That's when I started working with Sir Roland. What happened to me caused Papa to lose all hope in Fredric.

"I did not suspect the vial given to her was poison. I thought the beating was in the past and had been forgotten, but Astrid's hatred for Papa grew into rage that day. I should have …."

"It is not your fault," Ezra interrupted her. "The time spent does not matter—she is evil because she planned it. We will take care of Astrid—and Fredric, too—at the right time."

Silence again filled the room. Then Ezra asked, "Tell me how and why Alexander planned for you to find me."

"Papa sensed that he was in danger. Pirates threatened him frequently, and his relationship with the Bishop of Marseilles had deteriorated because of tithe demands. Papa accused the bishop of seeking personal power and wealth over the sanctity of the church. He wanted his coin to go directly to those in need and not to support the excesses of the bishop or the church.

"He had started to give me coin to hide. I would need it in case I needed to leave, if something happened to him. Then, just before he was murdered, he gave me a map and more coin for travel to Paris, plus the keys to his strongbox and instructions to take more if I needed it. You are the one person he trusted with my safety. He told me to seek you out."

Standing up, Nichol picked up her silver chain, put it around her neck and replaced the dagger in its sheath inside her tunic.

Ezra appeared to be lost in thought.

I know she is telling the truth. One day I will tell her the story behind the jeweled dagger she carries.

Noticing his uncle's expression, Robert said, "Uncle Ezra, is there something else you would like to talk about?"

"I am thinking that, with Alexander gone, all of my trade connections in Marseilles are in jeopardy. Alexander always functioned as my eyes and ears and negotiated on my behalf with my traders, and no one can replace him. I think it is time to end my business interests there. I can stay involved with traders closer to Paris. I should leave for Marseilles tomorrow to take care of this."

"Ezra, I have looked forward to the day when you stop traveling so far away, and spend more time at home," said Helene.

Laughing, Ezra replied, "Helene, if I am to spend more time with you here in Paris, I must leave soon and accomplish all I can as quickly as I can."

"Yes, I know, but I will miss you and will worry about you the entire time. With what Nichol has told us, if word gets out that she is here and you are protecting her, I believe you are in grave danger as well."

sixty-eight

New Beginnings

He did know ... he knew about the Lady.

The next morning, Ezra prepared to leave and sent a message to his guards to acquire horses for the trip. He wanted to depart as soon as they returned.

As they waited, the group gathered around the table to talk. Looking at Nichol, Ezra asked, "Would you like for me to tell anyone in Marseilles that you arrived here safely?"

"Oh, yes! Would you tell Rose, Margaux, and Gerhardt that I am safe? Only them, no one else. Tell each of them that I miss them terribly and love them dearly." She clasped her arms around her middle and tried to smile as she said this, but the faraway look on her face said much more.

Ezra put his hand on her shoulder. "I cannot imagine all the hurt and danger you have experienced since Alexander died. It saddens me that he met his death at the hands of your mother. And Lisa—I mean Nichol—I am sad for you as well." *And I also see great promise for you.*

"Thank you, Ezra. If it were not for Papa's foresight, I would not be here with you and Helene. And I would not have met Robert."

"Nichol, there was one conversation Alexander and I had the last time I visited him that I know you did not hear. We walked around the estate and he revealed much to me. He never talked about his personal life until that day. I knew things were bad … for him … and for you. I just did not realize how bad they could become.

"It was obvious he needed someone to talk with and I am honored that he trusted me enough to reveal his innermost thoughts. He told me he no longer trusted Astrid and that Fredric was a failure at everything he touched. You, dear Nichol, were the one person he trusted with his legacy.

"He revealed that you were the complement to everything he was. He told me about how clever you were. And he enjoyed it that you were interested in his business affairs, even offering ideas to help that had not occurred to him. As his daughter, you had all the traits and the knowledge that he had wanted a son to have. That conversation is why I know what you told us is the truth. And now I know the details leading up to his death.

"Astrid will fail—it is only a matter of time. She and Fredric have no knowledge of Alexander's business dealings. He told me that Fredric was pampered and protected by Astrid and now she is reaping the result of her actions. In fact, over wine one evening, Alexander told me that at times, he did not think Fredric was his son—that no son of his would act, think, or behave the way he did.

"I will speak to the people you have named and tell them you are safe and living with Helene in our home. Outside of those three, no one else will know that you are with us and are known only as Nichol now.

"There's one more thing. This is odd … Alexander said he heard a woman's voice—a voice with no physical body—that told him to protect you and that you were in danger. He did not know where the voice was coming from, but that he felt it was guiding you as well and that you heard it also."

Ezra paused, as if he were looking for the right words. "Then, Alexander stopped talking. There was a bewildered look that spread across his face. Then, he mumbled, 'It is too dangerous, hearing a woman's voice, heresy … forget what I said.' There's so much about your father that few know. When I return, I will tell you more. And Nichol, I believe there is much about you that you do not even know or understand."

Nichol's eyes grew bigger as Ezra revealed what Papa had said. Laying her face in her raised hands, a soft sob rose from her throat. *Papa did know … he knew about the Lady.*

Robert put his arm around her, smiled and whispered, "One day when you are ready, I would like to hear more about the Lady."

Everyone stood and moved from the table when they heard horses outside. Ezra opened the door and stepped out to greet his guards that were waiting. Helene handed them satchels of food and wineskins for the trip.

Turning to Helene, Ezra hugged her close and whispered, "I will be back soon. Watch over herr closely … she is in much danger."

Holding back tears, Helene responded, "I will keep her safe. Promise me that this is your last trip."

"I promise."

Mounting his horse, Ezra turned and waved goodbye to his family.

Standing in the center of the room with clasped hands, Helene surveyed the scene.

With a half-smile she said, "And so it begins. I have looked forward to this day for a long time. It is time for Ezra to slow down. When he gets back, we will see if he severed his ties with the southern ports. There are many things to keep him busy in Paris. And … I have a niece."

Ezra had been gone several days when Robert announced that he would leave for the goldsmith apprenticeship by the end of the month. Since he had been practicing the art of goldsmithing on his own for some time, his training would be only one year—less than the usual multi-year period.

As was the custom for all apprentices, he would accept residence there and would be allowed to leave only occasionally, even though the Guild Hall was not located far from his aunt and uncle's home.

Robert and Nichol took frequent walks to be alone as the day was soon to arrive when he would leave, with Shadow always at her side when they were out.

Robert knew Paris well. He showed her where to find the best food markets and the location of the closest apothecary. They would end their walks by sitting on the bank of the Seine, holding hands and enjoying the activity or just watching the river flow by.

With the joy of the moment, there was a sadness, the anticipation of their separation to come. The evenings were theirs alone.

One day, they passed the Guild Hall where Robert would be during his training. The street was empty and he stopped. As he gently placed a coin purse in Nichol's hands, he said, "I already own my own tools and have a good supply of raw materials. So, my expenses will be minimal once I pay the master for my training. I want you to keep the rest of the coin my father gave me and use it for your needs when I am away."

Looking at the bulging purse, Nichol pushed it away. "Robert, I still have coin Papa gave me. I do not need any."

"I thought you might say that. Do as you wish, but please know that my parents gave it to *us*; it is yours to use as well."

Accepting the purse, she moved closer to him. "I promise to keep your coin safely hidden."

One morning as they woke, Nichol rolled on her side facing Robert. "Have you noticed that there are stools that need to be fixed and doors are about to fall off their hinges in this house? If you make those repairs, I can undertake a thorough cleaning of the house."

"I have noticed. Ezra for all he is worth, has neglected his home but now he and Helene have us. Just the way they talk, I know that they think of us as their children and Helene looks at you as her daughter." Robert stood and offered Nichol his hand, pulling her up and to him. With his other hand he grabbed her rear and gently squeezed her backside.

"That will be yours when you finish your work; now go make the repairs."

As they entered the kitchen, Nichol greeted Helene with a bright smile.

"Helene, Robert is going to repair broken hinges on several doors. He will also repair some stools while I clean."

Helene motioned for Nichol and Robert to join her at the kitchen table. In a low voice, she said, "Ezra has always accepted things around here as they are, not as they should be. When I tell him of repairs that need to be made, he insists that he will make them in time.

"He does not want to admit he lacks the skills of his brother Achim. When Ezra returns and notices the doors and stools are fixed, he will thank you and say he was busy, but had it on his lists of things to do. Ezra is a blessing to me. He is a good provider and a good man."

Helene reached across the table and placed one hand on Robert's and one on Nichol's. "I think I will go visit friends and let you both work without my interruption I will announce my return loudly when I open the door."

With a smile and a wink of her eye, Helene rose. Nichol brought her cloak and placed it on her shoulders. Shadow jumped up and was by Helene's side.

"Would you like Shadow's protection?"

Helene reached down and rubbed her on her shoulders. "Yes, if she comes with me, I may also go to the market for our evening meal."

Nichol bends down and whispers in Shadow's ear and laughed gently as Shadow followed Helene out the door.

Robert was glad to see how comfortable Helene and Nichol were together. The two of them talked, laughed, and sang as they concentrated on their tasks.

He knew Nichol would be in good company after he left for his apprenticeship. And he liked the idea Shadow would always be close by for both Helene and Nichol.

The night before Robert was to leave for the guild apprenticeship, Helene excused herself shortly after supper. She wanted Nichol and Robert to have a quiet, private evening together.

The couple talked late into the night.

"Helene told me about their cottage in the country and said she would like to go and stay for a few weeks. She loves it there and wants to show me the countryside."

"I have been there before. Helene is right. It will be a good place for you to write, draw, and relax."

Their final night together was woven through with sadness, joy, and gentle, slow lovemaking.

The next morning, when Robert was ready to leave, he hugged his aunt and thanked her for all the food she had prepared for him.

Turning to Nichol, he gathered her in his arms and kissed her. "I will miss you and think of you everyday."

"I will miss you, too. We will be together soon."

sixty-nine

The Women

The kitchen table was the recipient of secrets.

The two women stood at the door and watched as Robert walked north. At the end of the street, he turned and waved.

Returning the gesture, each put an arm around the other's waist, and they walked back inside the house and closed the door. Silently they stood, looking at each other.

With a decisive nod, Helene said, "I know exactly how you feel. I have been through this scene many times in my years with Ezra and it gets harder each time. Our men are gone, doing what it is they do, and here we stand trying to figure out what we should do next. It is a very empty feeling.

"This time, the difference is that I have you here with me. I am so glad that you have come into our lives, Nichol. I know you have been through unspeakable grief and hardship of late. I admire your strength."

Nichol was taken aback as Helene's words fell on her ears. Tears brimming in her eyes, she hugged her. "I do not think of myself as strong. I had one goal to attain and that was to reach Paris to find Ezra and fulfill Papa's wishes. I did it. It was not easy and, at times, extremely dangerous. I feel like I have been guided along the way, and I was blessed to have had the protection of a very wonderful monk on my journey."

Helene smiled and said, "Let us sit here at the table and you can tell me about your entire journey. I want to hear about the monk. And I want to know more about how you met Robert."

Weeks passed by. The kitchen table was the recipient of secrets. And it became the hearer of all things … about hope, fears, anger, longing for lost ones, love, and much more.

Helene listened intently as Nichol revealed her journey path to Paris.

At times, she smiled at the naïveté of this girl who became a woman along her journey—one who showed no fear. At others, she was alarmed at the danger Nichol had encountered.

"Nichol, did your father really have you trained to fight like a knight would?"

Looking up from the beets she was cutting, tears brimmed Nichol's eyes. "If Papa had not had me trained, I would probably not be alive. I would have had no idea how to hide as I needed to at times. Or how to defend myself when I was attacked by both Fredric and bad men on the road before I met Timo."

"You were attacked by bad men?"

"Yes … two of them backed me into a tree. Then one came for me and I stabbed him with my dagger. The other man ran away.

"Before I cut my hair, it was as long as the top of my tunic. Now, I like it short. And wearing clothes like boys do make it easier for me to move about.

"There were also wonderful people I met on my way, Helene. Some offered me shelter for the night. Some welcomed me to walk with their family, so I would not be viewed as someone alone and vulnerable. When I met Timo, having a monk and his donkey to walk with offered me added protection as well."

Helene's eyes lit up as Nichol described how she would search for a large tree at the end of each day—a tree that she would climb up and nestle in for a safe sleep. She shook her head at the cleverness this young woman displayed who sat across from her.

Nichol told Helene how and where she met Timo, and how they became dear friends, along with his donkey Moki, the one that carried his seeds and cuttings to monasteries he visited.

Pausing briefly, she continued, "I know I alarmed Timo at first with my thoughts and opinions. He is a loving, trusting, and generous man and I know I challenged his beliefs about his church. By the time we parted ways at the monastery in Evry, he had witnessed firsthand all the things I had questioned about the deceitfulness of members of his clergy. Timo was feeling very disillusioned. It made him see things in a different light."

Once Nichol started talking, she could not stop. She revealed the ruthlessness of Fredric and how he attempted to accost her several times and return her to Marseilles and how she managed to escape each time. They laughed loudly together as Nichol described how she took Alexander's horse that Fredric was riding and abusing, and how she left it at a monastery where it would be treated well, while he was sleeping off a night of too much wine.

Helene was mesmerized while Nichol relayed the details of her journey. The entire trip would have been daunting and dangerous for any person—and Nichol had done it by herself until she met Timo.

"Why did you and Timo part ways in Evry? Why did he not accompany you all the way to Paris?"

Nichol looked sad and reflective. Quietly she said, "Except for the death of Papa and leaving my loved ones in Marseilles, saying goodbye to Timo was one of the saddest days of my life. We grew to understand, appreciate, and love one another. Due to some of the unseemly events we experienced on our journey, we both relied on one another's strengths to survive.

"His strengths included teaching, kindness, compassion, and listening. Mine included physical strength, awareness of my surroundings, and the ability to respond to them quickly. I learned to protect myself, which I had to do several times, including killing a man who was trying to rape me.

"Timo is a man committed to his faith and his calling as a monk. Originally, the monastery in Evry was the last stop on his journey and then he was going to return to the monastery in Vienne. But, after all he experienced in Melun, he decided he would stay in Evry. He told me he would pray for me and pray for guidance. He thought he could better serve God by helping people grow food and provide for themselves and families. I did not want to leave him, but I was determined to make it to Paris to find Ezra. After all, Papa planned it that way.

"The irony of all this is, I am now in Paris, but Ezra's gone, Robert's gone, and Timo's gone." Pausing, she then reached across for Helene's hand. "But I have you."

Helene took both Nichol's hands. "What courage it took for you to undertake this journey and come to us. You must take pride in your abilities to defend yourself and the fact that you never gave up. You achieved your goal. You are now safe here with me, and we must do our best to create a new life for you. I cannot speak for Timo, but Ezra and Robert are only gone temporarily. They will be back.

"We should get a message to Dinah and Achim and let them know you and Robert are here. They should know that Robert has begun his goldsmith apprenticeship and you are staying with me."

Days flowed into nights as the two women went about a daily routine of cooking together and touring the town to find their favorite foods and spices. At home, Nichol also used that time to sketch Helene as she cooked, along with drawing pictures of Robert and Ezra from memory.

Helene introduced her to some of the most prominent women in the community. They were all cordial enough at the outset, but they looked askance at how she dressed.

Helene overheard one of the women describing what an oddly dressed houseguest Helene had. When she heard the remark, she made no future attempt to associate with the woman.

I love Nichol just as she is. Her idea of wearing men's breeches makes sense to me. None of those pampered women could ever compare to her and all that she has achieved in her short lifetime.

seventy

Unexpected Visitors

The door to the cottage flew open.

Three weeks had passed since Robert left for training. Nichol kept busy, but the *Lady* had spoken to her in her dreams. Last night, the familiar light surrounded her.

Do not let your guard down, Nichol. Your awareness is one of your keen strengths. There is more than just you to protect.

Over porridge the next morning, Helene suggested, “I was hoping to visit our cottage in the country for a few weeks. Would you like that?”

“Oh, yes! It would be a pleasant change and I am sure Shadow would like to be in the country where she can run.”

“I will have Franco, a neighbor boy down the road, deliver a message to Robert, telling him where we will be and how long we expect to be gone. The cottage is only a half-day’s journey north of Paris. Robert spent time there as a child, and he can join us there if he is granted free time.”

The following day, they packed food and clothing to take with them. Helene arranged for two of Ezra's men to bring a cart and escort them to the cottage.

Arriving in the early afternoon, the men helped unload the cart. Helene paid the men and sent them on their way. Helene and Nichol went inside and opened the shutters to let in the fresh air and light.

Once organized, Helene invited Nichol to meet Jacob, the caretaker of the property. Finding him in the field, Helene introduced Nichol as her niece, and let him know they would be staying at the cottage for several days or more.

"It is nice to see you again, Helene. I will check on you while you are here and if I can be of help, let me know." Eyeing Shadow with a concerned look, he asked, "Is that a wolf?"

"No, do not worry about her," Nichol replied. "She is well trained and well fed and only bites bad people."

"Would she feast only on rabbits, then? Around here, the rabbits eat more from our gardens than we do."

Laughing, Nichol reached down to pet Shadow. Then she said, "I will bring her over tomorrow and we can see if she solves your rabbit problem."

Bidding goodbye to Jacob, Helene and Nichol left to prepare the food they had brought with them—lamb, vegetables, bread and butter.

Nichol chuckled, "Helene, this is enough food to last several weeks."

Helene turned to her. "We have a lot to talk about and it is always enjoyable to talk over a satisfying meal. We may want to stay for a while."

"I look forward to that. At home, our meals were rarely pleasant, unless it was Papa and me alone at the table."

"I anticipate cooking and having a wonderful conversation with my new companion. You are like the daughter I always longed for now coming to me as the wife of my nephew."

Nichol started a fire to roast the lamb, as Helene cut vegetables and placed them in a large pot suspended over the fire.

Helene poured both of them a cup of wine and with every sip, Nichol spoke more openly about her family and childhood. Helene was a good listener, and she could tell Nichol was still trying to make sense of the way her mother and brother treated her, so she let her talk.

I asked Robert, "What attracted you to Nichol?"

This is what he told me. "She was dressed as a boy but I was not attracted to her features, which I found out later were more than ample. He possessed a quality that captivated me and frightened me at the same time. When our eyes connected, I was in a spell and could not move my eyes from him. The closer he came, the more intense the attraction; I could not look away. I felt fear that comes when you are under someone's control. Then, when she stood in front of me, I knew immediately he was a girl. When she talked, her words drew me in. I wanted her more than anything I have ever wanted."

They both laughed as she said that. And then Nichol added, "It was the same for me. Our eyes met and we were pulled to each other. I kept moving so I could watch him and then saw that he was looking for me as I kept changing my position. Seeing what he was selling, I decided to approach him. At the same time, I saw a man was moving in to steal from his table. And you know the rest of the story."

It is a wonder that Nichol survived her upbringing at all.

By early evening, the lamb was ready to eat. Bowls were filled with lamb stew and fresh bread was sliced to sop up the delicious juices. They sat down at the quaint table by the fireplace, anticipating a sumptuous meal and enjoyable conversation.

Shadow was next to Nichol, eating from her bowl. Suddenly, she moved to a crouched, stalking position.

"Something is wrong, Helene. Shadow would not be acting like this if it was not." Nichol quickly uncovered her dagger as Shadow slowly moved to the door. She then stood and unsheathed it.

As soon as she did, the door to the cottage flew open.

A huge, faceless figure stood in the doorway with the sun at his back. Immediately, a deep guttural growl poured from Shadow's body. At once, the animal leaped, moving too fast for Nichol's eyes to follow, and locked her jaws down on the man's right hand—a hand that held a knife.

Shadow's jaw was like a vise as the intruder attempted to throw the dog off. With his attention on Shadow, Nichol rushed forward and plunged her dagger into his belly. The intruder swung his left hand and hit her in the face, causing her to fall to his side.

Nichol never let go of the dagger ripping his belly open. With his left arm, restraining his guts from falling out, the man fell to his knees. Shadow's weight dragged him lower, to the cottage dirt floor. Bellowing in pain from his wounds, and with Shadow not releasing her grip, his attack was over.

Instantly, another man appeared in the doorway.

Without hesitation, Nichol was up. Placing one foot on the fallen attacker, she flew forward with her dagger moving from behind to a forward thrust, plunging it into the second man's throat. He stumbled to the ground, holding his neck as blood gushed between his fingers.

Standing over him, Nichol recognized the mortal wound she had inflicted. His bulging, disbelieving eyes glared at her.

With no emotion showing on her face, she watched as his eyes glazed over, becoming a death stare. Reaching down, Nichol pulled the dagger from his throat, wiping the blade on his tunic.

Stepping back, her eyes took in the scene. Shadow watched her as she then pulled the second attacker farther out to clear the cottage door. With blood on her face, clothes, and hands, she raised her eyes and met Helene's gaze, who was still sitting at the table, her mouth hanging open in shock.

Immediately, Shadow came to her side, leaning on her leg. Nichol crouched down and pulled Shadow close to her as she scanned the cottage exterior to see if more danger existed. Her eyes stopped at the two horses tied to a low tree branch down the road. *They must be theirs.*

Stepping around both bodies, she reentered the cottage.

Helene had sensed her needs, and a wash pan with water awaited to cleanse the blood off her face and hands. Nichol turned and wrapped her arms around Helene.

"I am sorry I brought this to your home. They came for me. After all this time, I had thought Astrid would give up. These men must be buried at once and what happened should never be mentioned to anyone."

"Who are they … and why did they want to harm you?"

"I do not know. I can only guess that Astrid is behind it in some way. Sending Fredric after me did not work." Nichol paused in thought: *Is there someone else pursuing me?*

Silence filled the room as the two women looked at the door and the ghastly scene in front of them. Surprisingly, Helene was the first to speak.

"Do you think it is safe for us to be digging large holes?"

"We have no choice. Then we should return to Paris using the two horses tied up down the road. I do not think they belong to these men. The horses are of better quality than they could afford. I think the horses will lead us to who ordered them to attack me."

Helene released Nichol, gently stroking her hair. "The garden just outside is a good place to dig their graves and the soil is loose. We have two shovels here. Working together, we will be done before morning comes."

Nichol was astonished and thankful that Helene willingly offered to dig holes with her. What had just happened in front of her would have made other women frantic. *Helene has an inner strength that I did not notice.*

"With Shadow here to warn us of danger and the two of us, we will be all right. I am going to get the horses and bring them down to the cottage. Shadow will watch over them while we work. She will alert us if anyone else approaches."

The moon gave them enough light that they could see what they were doing. Once the hole was deep enough to contain both bodies, they dragged them and the weapons they carried into their grave and covered them.

Helene paused and stood up to stretch her back from the shoveling. "Should not we keep their weapons in case we need them when we start back to Paris?"

She must be afraid; I can sense it. "No … we do not want anything with us that would connect us to the men. It will only be a short time before we are back in Paris."

Adding the last shovelful of dirt and packing it down, Nichol then took Helene's shovel and returned both to where they were stored.

Looking at her bloodied tunic, Nichol added, "We need to restart the fire so I can burn my tunic. At the same time, we can heat your stew and eat. Both of us need some rest and nourishment before we finish cleaning up the entryway and return to Paris. When we do, I will learn who sent these men.

"Helene, we have to make things look normal as soon as dawn breaks. I will then take Shadow to Jacob's and rid him of his rabbit problem as I promised."

Relieved to be inside with Shadow crouched at the door, as if the animal knew it was her duty now to protect them. Helene started the fire in the kitchen and added the soiled tunic to it as soon as flames were ignited. It was consumed quickly.

She then filled two large pots with water that she heated over the fire that warmed the room, soaking two cloths in them, then wringing them. Handing one to Nichol, she kept the other.

The two women used the damp cloths to wipe the sweat from their bodies and faces.

As Helene layed down, thoughts of Ezra filled her mind.

She missed her husband and prayed that his trip would be successful, and he would return soon.

Lying there, she went back over the previous day's events and could only marvel at how quickly Nichol had reacted to the danger. Killing the man with skill and cunning, she showed no fear.

I have never seen anyone respond the way Nichol did. Her world has been torn apart by the people who should have loved and protected her. Why did God bring her to us? She is a story unfolding, and we are the witnesses to it. Her destiny has become ours.

Who, really, is this Nichol that we have come to love?

seventy-one

Return to Paris

Ezra uses Joshua, a messenger he calls the keeper of secrets.

Nichol woke with Shadow staring at her. She put her hand on her neck and started rubbing. Shadow's tail wagged and Nichol relaxed.

Getting up, she moved quietly so as not to awaken Helene. Covering her to stay warm from the morning chill, she turned to leave for Jacob's with Shadow.

"It is time to have some fun, Shadow."

Listening to her surroundings for any unusual noise, Nichol slowly went to the door and peered out. As she did, Shadow rushed past her and then abruptly stopped, turned around and sat outside the door, as if to ask *why are you waiting*? The horses stirred and nickered softly when Shadow ran by.

Helene's voice softly penetrated the morning chill in the room. Raising her head, she said, "You are not leaving without me, are you?"

Nichol turned and smiled. "Of course not, but I need to keep my promise to Jacob. Shadow and I are going up the road to solve his rabbit problem."

"Nichol, I woke before dawn and noticed that you were serene and had a smile on your face. I also noticed a dim light, almost like a glow, all around you. Then I went back to sleep again."

"The *Lady* came to me during the night. I could feel her warmth and her words that I would … *we* would … be protected. She told me to think of my past and the future will come together."

They both absorbed her words. Nichol could feel strength entering her body and then smiled at her friend, her aunt, and now, a mother to her.

Slowly, Helene rose from her bed, wincing at the pain she felt throbbing through her body from the unaccustomed activity of shoveling.

"Nichol, I will be ready to leave and have something ready to eat when you get back from Jacob's. It may be a while before we have another chance."

With a wave to Helene, Nichol set out. Arriving at Jacob's garden, Shadow did not need encouragement with her task.

Nichol kneeled down and whispered in her ear as Shadow wagged her tail, and then stopped. Quickly, the animal transitioned to a hunting crouch, slowly moving toward the gardens. Suddenly, she was in a dead run, scooping up a rabbit in her mouth. Turning, she brought it back to Nichol and dropped it at her feet.

"Good, Shadow." Nichol then pointed and Shadow repeated her hunt until there were no rabbits in sight, except for the ones at Nichol's feet. By then, Jacob had joined her.

"Hello, Jacob. As I promised, Shadow took care of the rabbits. These will make a delicious stew for your table. I will keep one for her to enjoy as well.

"I must also tell you something has come up. Helene and I must return to Paris. We just received a message in the middle of the night letting us know that Ezra is ill. It is not serious, but she is worried. We will return as soon as Ezra is well enough to enjoy the countryside with us. And if you have more rabbits, Shadow will be happy to get rid of them for you."

Eyeing the pile of rabbits in front of him, Jacob was elated to have food for his table and fresh vegetables still growing. Turning to Nichol, "I hope Ezra recovers quickly, Nichol. It looks like your Shadow will be welcome on my land any time."

Reaching down to scratch Shadow's head, he added, "You come back, too, Shadow."

Turning toward Helene's cottage, Nichol waved to Jacob and gave Shadow the rabbit to carry back.

This will be another training for her to learn to carry things I give her.

Another thought followed: *I need to make her a backpack so she can carry items for me.*

Helene was at the cottage door, sweeping dirt over the blood that had seeped into the ground. Looking up, she was relieved to see the two of them approaching.

Shadow was wagging her tail with the rabbit in her mouth as she approached Helene, proud of her catch. "I see that Shadow took care of Jacob's problem."

"She did. And Jacob did not mention that anything unusual happened last night. He did not say anything about the two horses or seeing any strangers. It looks like we are safe to slip away. I told him that you had got a message that Ezra was ill and wanted to return to be with him."

Much relieved, Helene said, "I have given the horses some water and I have packed our satchels for when we leave here. I have got everything ready to return to Paris. I did not want to start a fire, so the stew and bread from last night will not be warm.

While eating the stew, they watched Shadow devour the rabbit, her treat for the protection to both of them. Then Helene spoke.

"This morning I woke with a thought of how to find out who sent these men. Ezra uses Joshua, a messenger he calls *the keeper of secrets*."

"Papa used messengers, but I never heard him call them a keeper of secrets before. I like that."

"Ezra said that some messages are not written but memorized and kept secret for the recipient only. If the messenger is captured, he is not carrying a written message. We can take the horses to Joshua and let the horses lead him to where they came from."

"Do you trust him?"

"Yes, he is Ezra's cousin and they grew up together."

Gathering their things, Nichol helped Helene up on one horse and mounted the other.

As they headed out, Shadow's ears perked up. Nichol laughed out loud as she asked, "Do you think you are hunting rabbits again?"

For the first hour, not a word was spoken. Both were deep in thought.

Helene broke the silence. "When you stood outside the cottage covered in blood, I saw a look on your face—a bewildered look. Do you remember what you were thinking?"

Nichol shook her head. "I remember we were at the table and I looked at Shadow. Then I was outside looking at two men on the ground covered with blood, and I thought, who killed them? I looked down at the blood on the dagger and my hands. I must have killed them, but I could not remember."

"You never hesitated a moment. I have never seen someone move as fast as you did."

Pausing, Nichol gathered her thoughts. "Helene, I do not want to live like this, always waiting for another attack. If Joshua gives the horses freedom, they will find their way to their home. That way, he will know who set these men upon us, and we can learn who is behind the attack.

"Astrid and Fredric are far away. Could there be someone in Paris who planned this attack … someone who is powerful? It is not just Papa's coin they want. That is hidden in Marseilles and it would be immediately obvious that I do not have it with me."

"You talk about the days you spent hidden when your father had his meetings. Could you have overheard a conversation you were not meant to hear?"

"I do not recall anything right now. But perhaps I did. I will think about it."

"Nichol, we are going to find out who is responsible and I will be with you when we find out. Let us return to our home in Paris and stay there. We should be safe until Ezra returns."

seventy-two

The Secret Messenger

It is clear to me that they intend to harm you.

By early afternoon, Helene directed a slight change in the direction of their travels. "Joshua lives down this road. I hope he is here."

Dismounting, Helene knocked on the door. There was no answer. Then she knocked again, this time loudly. Again, silence.

Turning to leave, a voice from inside called out, "Who is it?"

"It is Helene. Open the door, Joshua."

A man with a trimmed beard and dark, piercing eyes peered out from a narrowly opened door. The man smiled. "Did you finally leave Ezra for me?"

"Open the door and let us in, you fool." Helene looked down at the knife in his hand. "What husband is after you now?"

Ignoring her remark, he looked past Helene to Nichol. "Who is your friend?"

"It is Nichol, and she is married to my nephew Robert."

Opening the door, Joshua gave a hearty laugh while embracing Helene. "You know me well."

Then, more quietly, he said, "I sense something wrong. That's why you are here. I know Ezra is not in Paris. Before he left, he came by and told me that you both would be at the cottage for about a month. I know him well and could see he was unsettled and had much on his mind. The sound of his voice told me he was concerned for you. I then told him I would visit the cottage in a few days to make sure you were settled. He seemed relieved and said no more."

"We need your help." Turning to Nichol, Helene added, "Would you tie up the horses and then come in so we can tell him what has happened?"

Shortly, Nichol entered with Shadow next to her. Joshua looked at Shadow and smiled. "What is the name of this mongrel?"

Nichol's eyes dropped to Shadow and took in how she had grown. Now, a powerful and poised animal, her body fur and tail were mostly black with gray highlights. Her ears crowned her head with gray ear tuffs. *I think she is a gift from the Lady.*

Looking up at Joshua, she replied, "She answers to Shadow."

Joshua knelt down and called her to him. Helene and Nichol looked at each other, afraid of what might happen next.

He petted her, stroking her fur. "See, all the ladies like me." A sigh of relief was heard from Helene and Nichol.

"Helene, what is wrong? Has something happened to Ezra? Do you need my help?"

Joshua was riveted and alarmed by the story that unfolded. He was horrified when he heard about the attack at the cottage. When Helene revealed that Nichol and Shadow had taken both men down and they had buried both bodies, Joshua's mouth dropped open with his stunned eyes directed at Nichol.

Helene spoke up before Joshua could say anything. "I watered the horses before we left the cottage this morning, but they have not been fed. If you give them a free rein, I think they will take you back to where they belong. Could you then find out who is behind the attack?"

"Most messages I deliver are not of importance. Some, like the messages that I must memorize, are the ones that interest me the most. What you have asked me to do more than interests me. I have a feeling that whoever is behind this attack is someone who is very powerful in Paris. Return to your home, Helene. I will find the owner of the horses and then come to you to tell what I learn. Unload what you cannot easily carry as you walk. I will get it to you later."

The women left and made their way back to Helene's and Ezra's house in Paris.

Just at dusk, a knock sounded on Helene's door.

"It must be Joshua." Nichol lifted a heavy wooden brace from its brackets and opened the door.

Joshua stood there, staring at Nichol.

Helene broke into his unspoken thoughts. "Come in, Joshua—what news do you have?"

"My thirst is great and I need something to eat."

Helene and Nichol just glared at him. Nichol quickly poured a cup of wine and brought bread to the table.

Joshua was acting out the messenger of secrets role—and that was trying Helene's patience. Helene was not inclined to be polite. "Out with it," she demanded.

After taking a long drink, followed by a large bite of bread, he finally spoke.

"I climbed on one horse and let the reins go loose on both. They did just as you said they would and led me to where they came from. It was a stable next to a bishop's house. A man came out of the stable. He looked at the horses and then at me. 'Where are the men who took these horses out?'

"I never saw any men. I found the horses on a road north of Paris with no one around but if no one tells me who owns them, they are mine to keep," I told him.

"Then he said, 'I will get the owner.'

"What happened next surprised me. He returned with a pretty boy priest. I asked him if he is the owner, and he told me that the bishop owns both horses. I then saw worry on his face and the stable man began to back away. It was obvious they were hiding something."

Facing Nichol directly, Joshua continued, "Nichol, you have powerful people who are interested in you. It is not clear to me if they were there to kill you or take you captive. Many who live here don't trust the clergy … they fear it, yet they succumb to its power. Ezra has held them off with his money, protecting him and Helene. Bishops have many secrets that only a few around them know."

Taking another drink, Joshua added, "I gave them the horses and left."

"Can you describe the two men? I know a place where men like these congregate. I think I should see if there is any talk about them," Joshua asked.

Nichol sat quietly, listening to what Joshua said. She knew that she was at risk … and that she had brought danger to Helene. Still, she needed to know more.

"Before we buried them, I carefully observed their clothes and features. They were fighting men, by the scars on their hands and faces. They had no coin on them when we buried them. To collect the coin they were owed, they probably had to bring us back to Paris. One thing is certain—we do not want people looking for bodies, Joshua."

Absorbing what Nichol and Joshua were saying, Helene wished aloud that Ezra would walk through their door. Refocusing on what Joshua suggested, she said, "I will make a place for you to stay with us."

Nichol whispered to Helene, "Can we keep this from Robert? I do not want him to worry."

"Yes, until Ezra returns. Then we must decide what to do."

Joshua stayed with the women for the next two nights, then he was gone for the next two days.

When he returned, he told them how his inquiry had proceeded.

"I went to a tavern that was common for men like your attackers to visit. I gave out their description, telling of meeting them two days ago. I said that I wanted to hire them, and I was sure they would consider my offer. I had a feeling that the men were well-known but nobody wanted to say. I took out my coin purse and held it up, and I told the men in the tavern that I would pay anyone who had information about these men. Then a man came to my table and sat down.

"Without a word, I dropped my purse on the table. He reached for it and I grabbed his wrist. I asked him to describe these men. He described the height difference, their clothes, and scars, exactly as you said. I asked him where I could find them. He told me that they only work for the bishop and they do all his bidding.

"When I added that they had large purses and maybe they did not need to work, the man leaned forward and said, 'Large coin purses … both of them?' I released my hold on him and his last words came at me with a warning: 'I would stay away from them or you might find yourself in the river.'

"Nodding to him, I left and placed myself where I was not easily seen. Almost immediately, the tavern door opened. He was walking fast … directly to the bishop's home. Everything that happened at the cottage had a bishop's knowledge and blessing. What would a bishop in Paris want with you? There is something you are not telling us."

"In Marseilles, there was a bishop that Papa had bitter disagreements with. But for a bishop in Paris to come after me?" Nichol paused and looked at Helene. "Could they have been after you now that Ezra has left town? Has he had problems with the church?"

"Not that he has told me. I think we will be safe here with Joshua around and when Ezra returns, maybe he will know."

seventy-three

The Surprise

I have seen that look before.

Helene and Nichol began to feel safe in Paris as they settled into a routine. Joshua would stay with them at night, then leave on another excursion to gather information.

At night, the conversations between Nichol and Joshua were revealing. Neither said too much or gave details, but after a time, each of them could almost finish the other's sentences and thoughts.

After one of their exchanges, Joshua simply looked at Nichol and asked, "Who are you?"

Nichol just smiled. "I'm your equal. I've been gathering information for years as I observed dealings with my father. I became his confidant as he asked my advice after I witnessed dealings and meetings with others when I was hidden in the solar. And he had me trained to defend myself."

I see you.

Pausing, Joshua sat back and observed Nichol. *Maybe she is more*, he thought.

During the day, Helene was fond of their quiet and easy conversations and Nichol's companionship. She was not altogether comfortable with Nichol's daily walks, but after the cottage incident, she knew Nichol and Shadow were able to defend themselves. And Nichol still dressed as a boy with a cap on all the time.

When she was out, most adults would give her a wide path because of Shadow. If there were children, Shadow became a magnet. Nichol welcomed them and Shadow enjoyed the attention she got.

The days turned to weeks and both felt safe. Joshua remained at the house, claiming he stayed for the food Helene prepared.

One morning after returning with Shadow, Nichol took her usual place at the kitchen table across from Helene.

Helene noticed immediately that something was special about her.

I think it has happened. Does Nichol know?

"Nichol, there's something different about you. I know a lot has happened since you met Robert in Antony. When you walked in this morning, you had a … shine. Do you feel different?"

"I am feeling relieved. With Joshua coming by, and knowing that Robert is not far away, plus having you and Shadow around, I do not have the constant feeling that I must be on guard at all times. I guess that would allow anyone to shine."

Smiling to herself, Helene started to hum softly. Then she said, "You have that glow and I know why. I have seen that look before, many times. My dear, you are with child! Dinah had the same glow about her when she was pregnant with Robert."

Nichol was stunned. When she heard Helene's words, she attempted a smile, but it looked somewhat uneven. Instead, a look of panic crossed her face. Her initial reaction to Helene's proclamation was one of shock. It never occurred to her that she could be pregnant.

A baby? How could I be pregnant?

Her thoughts were backing up in her throat like bile. Fear was kicking at the door of her heart because she did not want to expose a baby to the dangers that continued to follow her.

Nichol's look of panic brought words of comfort from Helene. "Ezra and I could never have children and I wanted them so badly. I am sure the child you carry will bring immense joy to you and our family," she said softly.

Tears were forming in Nichol's eyes. She felt lost. "Oh, Helene … defending myself was one thing, but now I will have to protect and defend an innocent life. How will I find the strength to do that?"

"Dear one, every mother carries the innate characteristics of a mother bear. With your courage, skills, and determination, no harm will come to your child."

Nichol liked the image of the mother bear and laughed. And then her laughter turned to sobs. Catching her breath, she said, "How will I know how to be a good mother? Mine was full of hate and revenge. She did not like me."

"You had other mothers around you. Think of Margaux and her presence—when did she leave you alone? Did not she fix your meals when you were little? Have your ever thought that she was your protector, along with Alexander's support? Is not that what she did?"

Slowly, Nichol nodded her head. "You are right. Margaux was always there for me … she raised me and made sure I was safe when Papa was away."

"Your body is changing … and it will change much more as it adjusts to the baby in your womb. And your heart and mind will change, too. Give it time. Soon all you will feel is joy … you will see."

Helene was right. Once Nichol admitted to herself that all the obvious signs were present confirming she was expecting a baby, joy and anticipation took over. She hummed as she went about her chores with a constant smile on her face.

As she lay in bed that night and closed her eyes, her hand rested on her lower belly. *Little one, I will be there always for you.*

And then a light came into the room. A familiar voice spoke to her.

All is well, Nichol. Your daughter will be special. She will bring you a joy that few experience. For women around you and her, she will bring a new voice for living. Love her and guide her.

The *Lady's* voice faded away as sleep overtook her.

Nichol's last thoughts were *I have missed you … please stay close to me.*

On awakening, she thought of the *Lady's voice* and what she revealed. *A daughter … a baby girl.* As a smile surfaced, she decided she wanted to keep the news to herself. Only she and the *Lady* would know for now.

Finally getting out of bed, she joined Helene at the table. Reaching for the fruit, cheese, and bread that had been laid out, she asked her, "How do you think I should tell Robert that he is going to be a papa?"

"Well, I think it would be nice if you could tell him in person. How do you feel about sending him a message and asking him to come visit us for a few days?

"You write the message and I will have it delivered and ask the messenger to wait for a response from Robert."

The messenger was duly sent off to the goldsmith Guild Hall.

It seemed an eternity before Nichol and Helene heard a knock on the door. The message was delivered by voice, not written. The messenger said, "Immediately, Robert asked me if you two were safe. I told him 'Yes.' He left me to talk with his master and came back with this answer … that he will be home at the end of this week."

Thanking him, Nichol gave him coin and closed the door.

Turning to Helene, she embraced her. "I can hardly wait to see him and tell him we are going to have a baby!"

Stepping back, a serious look crossed Nichol's face. "We cannot tell Robert … about what really happened at the cottage. At least, not yet. If we did, he would quit the guild to be with me. He needs to finish. After all, our future depends on him being one of the best goldsmiths.

"We can ask Joshua to return to his own residence until Robert returns to the guild. If he knew what really happened, he would never leave our sides."

seventy-four

A New Look

It took some time for the greeting to sink in.

At the end of the week, Robert arrived, just as he had promised.

Knocking on the door braced from the inside, Helene looked through the small hole that Nichol had made in the door at eye level that had a covering over it—one that was a rabbit hide saved when she hunted with Shadow.

Robert was surprised to see an eye looking directly at his.

Helene opened the door.

"I am glad you have the door barred," Robert said, kissing his aunt on the cheek. Turning to the door as he closed it, he eyed the rabbit hide hanging from a nail on the door inside. "What is this, Aunt?"

"It was Nichol's idea. She thought it was better for us to know who was at our door before removing the brace. Ezra keeps coin here for his business and we are alone right now."

"I like this idea. I am going to suggest it to the master at the guild. We have valuables there, too."

The whole time he was talking to Helene, he was looking for Nichol, but he did not see her. Helene knew why he was distracted and called for Nichol to come to the great room.

"Nichol? There's someone here for you …."

"I will be right there," she replied from the back room.

Gliding into the room, she was wearing one of the new tunics she had made. It was a cheerful purple color and she had attached fabric around the neck opening. She also wore darker breeches. Nichol held the hem of the tunic in each hand and pirouetted in front of Robert when she reached him.

"Nichol, I have never seen you dress so colorfully or act so playfully. Is this a new you? You look beautiful!"

Nichol could contain herself no longer. Twirling again, she asked, "Robert, do you notice anything different?"

"Well, yes. You have made a lovely new tunic and breeches, your hair is getting longer, and you are smiling from ear to ear. What have you been up to?"

Nichol looked at Helene, back to Robert, and said, "Welcome home, Papa. I am so glad you are here." Finally, she leaned in and gave him a kiss.

It took some time for the greeting to sink in. Looking between the two women, he refocused his gaze on Nichol. With a surprised look, he said, "Could this be true? Are you going to have a baby?"

Nichol and Helene laughed at his reaction and his questions.

Still laughing, Nichol said, "Your reaction is much better than mine was. Helene is the one who told me I am pregnant, and at first, I was shocked. Now that I have adjusted to the idea, I am thrilled that we are having a baby. We have just surprised you with the news and I know you need time to take it in."

"How do you feel? Oh, I can hardly wait to have a son that I can teach about goldsmithing …."

"Robert … what if it is a girl … would not you like to teach your daughter to be a goldsmith?"

"If we have a little girl, I will happily teach her to be a goldsmith … or anything she wants to be."

Sitting at the table, Robert held Nichol's hand as they talked. The more he heard, the more excited he got.

When Nichol noticed a change in his facial expression, Nichol asked, "Robert, what is it? Is something wrong?"

"Oh, how could you think that? Nothing is wrong. I am thrilled, excited, and more than just a little scared. I do not know the first thing about caring for a baby."

"I am feeling the same. I suppose we will learn together. Helene has helped calm my fears about being pregnant, and now that I have had time to get used to the reality of it, I am thrilled. I think you will feel more comfortable after a few days, too."

Helene talked about how happy and healthy Robert's mother had been when she carried him and how honored Helene was to be present at his birth.

Sighing, Nichol said, "I have no idea what Astrid thought or felt about her pregnancy with me. I would say, based on what she thinks of me now, she was not thrilled that I was even born."

She placed a protective hand across her belly. "I will never treat this child the way I was treated. I will give this baby all the love, affection, and nurturing that every child should have."

Helene put her hand on Nichol's. "We would expect nothing less. The child you carry is truly fortunate to have a strong, courageous, and loving mother like you, and I am certain Robert will be a loving, patient papa."

Robert nodded in agreement. "You are right, Aunt Helene. I will be the best papa I can be. And I would be happy to instruct any daughter of mine about goldsmithing."

Parenthood was all they talked about for the next two days. The one question they wrestled with was when the baby was expected to arrive.

Giggling, Nichol asked, "Robert, do you remember the first cold night that you kept me warm in the meadow?"

Grinning, Robert answered, "Yes, I certainly do."

Thinking back, Nichol offered, "If that night was the beginning, the baby should be born around the Winter Solstice celebration in December. It will be wonderful to welcome our baby during this time."

"I am going to leave the school. With a baby coming and the extra needs here, I should be here and …"

Nichole stopped him in mid-sentence. "No … you are not going to quit. We are a family and we will need the skills you are now learning to take care of us. Please, finish your training. It is for all of us."

Reluctantly, he agreed. "I am further along than most of the other students. My years of creating jewelry on my own has made a difference. The master often uses what I do as examples for the other trainees to copy. I have learned new and different techniques from him that had added some refinement to my designs.

"And I have news, too. The master gave my name to some of the lords and ladies who are patrons of the Guild. I am now completing custom pieces for three of them. I will share in the payment when the pieces are delivered."

"Robert, you are a talented, artistic jewelry designer. You are a natural salesperson. Remember, you sold me a silver necklace and won my heart the day I met you at the fair in Antony."

With the news of the coming baby, Robert never thought to ask about their visit to the cottage.

With Robert back at the guild, Helene and Nichol settled into a routine.

They gathered soft fabrics and the two of them sewed for hours every day to create swaddling wrappings for the baby that was coming.

Nichol stitched animal images on corners of each. Several looked like Moki and the birds that she saw in the trees on her journey to Paris. Layered blankets were created to keep the baby warm—winters in Paris were always cold.

Helene had never seen wrappings like the ones Nichol was making before. *How did she think to do this? I think other mothers would like these for their babies, too.*

The older woman was excited. A new little life would soon be living with her. She wanted this baby to have all the comforts and happiness it could have.

Nichol is the daughter I longed for.

One day during a sewing fest, Helene said, "You know, soon we will be making new clothes for you, because you will be growing out of everything you now wear."

Nichol laughed. "I know that will happen, but I am not sure how I am going to feel about being big and round. Do you think Robert will still love me when I get that way?"

Helene chuckled. "Big and round is nature's way of feeding and protecting you and your baby as it grows. Your body will change, but the woman Robert fell in love with remains. I think it is safe to say that you do not need to worry."

"Nichol, you seem sad this morning."

"I am. I have been thinking about all those I left behind … especially Papa, Margaux, and Rose. I miss them. I wish they could be a part of my baby's life and my life."

"I understand, but I am glad you are safe here with me. Nichol, you have become the daughter I never had."

Embracing her, Nichol whispered, "And you are the mother I wished I had and now have for real."

With a concerned look, Helene asked, "Nichol, are you aware that you talk often in your sleep? At night I wake at the slightest sounds. Lately, I wake hearing a soft a voice; it is your voice. When I go into your room, you seem to be having a conversation with someone."

"I am sorry … I do not want to disturb you."

"You are not, I am just concerned. When you awaken, do you remember any of the conversation?"

Nichol hesitated. *What should I say? How much should I say?*

Taking a deep breath, she began.

"There is a voice I hear. I call it the *Lady*. She has been talking to me since I was a child. I did not always understand her message, but now it is clear that she is guiding me. To what end, I do not know. Her voice is soft and soothing, the voice of someone who loves me."

"I would like to hear more about this voice … your *Lady*."

Helene added, "When I was younger, I used to have vivid dreams if I was trying to work through an awkward situation and could not arrive at an answer. What I found helpful was writing down what I could remember and later reviewing what had captured my thoughts during the night. It was very revealing and often helped me to arrive at an answer to the problem I was dealing with. Maybe it would help you understand what you are dreaming about and what is being said to you if you write down your thoughts upon waking."

"Margaux taught me how to read and write when I was young. I have not written down my conversations with the *Lady* because they are private and meant only for me. I have realized, because of what I learned from my father, that people are told what to think by the church. If the clergy knew of the *Lady* and her visits to me, they would consider her a direct threat to their power. That would be dangerous for me. And they would accuse me of being a witch. The church's power is absolute in these concerns."

"When you are ready to share with me, I will listen."

"So much has happened since Papa discovered I was listening to his meetings in the solar, and soon, I would like for you to hear it all."

Life with Helene was happy, quiet, and peaceful.

Nichol concentrated on remembering what she heard in her dreams. When the *Lady* came to her, she always told her to remain vigilant, and Nichol shared that message with Helene.

What she did not share was the big secret … that a daughter would be born.

The warning of being vigilant concerned her.

What could it mean?

seventy-five

Ezra Returns

It appears I have missed quite much in the last four months.

It was mid-October and Nichol was amazed at the frequent flutter and kick of her daughter as she grew inside her. She hummed a loving melody to the baby as she rubbed her belly.

She is an active one! I wonder how our lives will change once she is here? I vow that I will be a mother like the one that I never had.

Robert had been home to visit a few times as her pregnancy progressed. As he wrapped his arms around her on his last visit, he said, "I am always surprised to see how beautiful you look each time I walk in the door."

The roundness of her made him smile and her increasing size was now hindering her ability to move quickly. Shadow stayed near to her almost all the time, as if she knew her mistress needed her.

Late one afternoon, Helene and Nichol heard a wagon on the road. It stopped outside the house. They did not think much about it until they heard male voices and footsteps.

Shadow was up and crouched at the door. Her tail was thumping on the floor in excitement. The pounding on the door brought Joshua to it, with Helene directly behind him. He did not unbar it until he lifted the rabbit hide to peer out.

Instantly, the two sets of eyes connected, Joshua laughed out loud. He turned to Helene as he unbarred the door. “Ezra is home!”

Pulling it open, Ezra stood there, with his guards John and Roger behind him. Helene threw her arms around his neck and stood back to look at him. He had been gone for over four months and she scanned his body from head to toe to make sure it was really him, and that he was all right.

It finally dawned on her that she should move aside and allow him to enter the house.

Turning to his guards, Ezra asked them to bring his belongings inside. When they were finished, Ezra paid them, thanked them for their service, and released them.

Looking at the door, he raised his eyebrow as he looked at her. Laughing, Helene said, “It was Nichol’s idea—she thought it was unwise to open the door unless we knew who was on the other side.”

“I like this idea … where is she?”

“Resting. There have been a few changes since you left.”

Nichol, asleep in her upstairs bedroom, woke to voices on the floor below. Descending the stairs, one voice sounded familiar. Once in the great room she saw Ezra, and a wave of excitement and anticipation overcame her.

Ezra will have news from Marseilles.

Ezra and Helene exchanged whispered greetings and then he turned back to the great room. That was when he saw Nichol.

Ezra took one look at her and opened his arms wide to welcome her. Each held the other for a long moment, and then he stepped back to take in her rosy cheeks and protruding belly.

Smiling, he said, "Congratulations! It appears as though I have missed quite a lot since I left. Joshua, it is good to see you, I do not see you often and here you are when I return home to my women. Is everything all right?"

Helene laughed. "Ezra, you look travel-weary. Wash the road grime from your face and hands and come sit at the table. Nichol and I will make something for you to eat."

The women warmed the stew and bread they had eaten earlier in the day, and then they all circled around the table to eat and talk.

Helene finally felt at peace. Ezra was home.

As he took another mouthful, she said, "Ezra, it is a wonderful surprise to have you home at last! I have missed you. You look tired but well. How do you feel? Did you make it to Marseilles? What did you learn? Was there any talk about Nichol? Was there …."

"Stop … stop, Helene! Let me enjoy this feast you put in front of me. Then I will answer all your questions and a few more of which you had not thought of."

With Helene and Nichol quietly staring at him, Ezra swallowed the last bite and smiled. "It seems that I must talk and eat at the same time.

"Yes, I am tired. Tired of traveling and tired of the bumpy roads and rough seas. I am glad to be home." Ezra reached over and placed his hand on Helene's hand. "I missed you, too."

"Before we get too far into all that's happened since I have been gone, let us talk about the important news." Looking at Nichol, he added, "When is this baby coming?"

"We think around late December … in time for the Solstice celebration."

Delight spread across his face as he softly squeezed Helene's hand. Turning to Nichol, he continued, "This is good news for you and Robert. I assume he has been home to visit since I have been gone and he is excited that he is going to be a papa."

"Yes, several times, and he is thrilled and promises to teach goldsmithing to his son or daughter."

Quiet descended around the table. A seriousness spread across Ezra's face. Turning to Helene and Joshua, who was sitting next to his wife, he spoke, "I see a bed made up for a guest. I presume it is for you, Joshua. Is that why you opened the door for me?"

Helene hesitated, exchanging glances with Nichol and Joshua before answering. Finally, she spoke.

"Shortly after you left for Marseilles, Nichol and I went to the cottage in the country. We had planned to stay for up to a month."

Nichol knew what Helene would say next, and grimaced.

Ezra noticed the look and asked, "What is it? You look as though you are debating what to tell me. Out with it."

And out it came … all of it.

Helene continued with a thorough and lively description of the attack at the cottage, finishing with details of Nichol killing the abductors. "If it were not for Shadow, Nichol, and her quick thinking and actions, we would not be here today."

Taking a breath, Joshua finally spoke up. He revealed the plan the three came up with to return the horses to the bishop's house and of the men who only worked for the bishop.

Ezra was visibly upset. "I am sorry I left you alone. I should have hired men to protect you while I was gone. There's something we do not understand yet. There's an underlying reason someone sent ruffians to the cottage to harm Nichol."

Silence filled the room. Nichol could not contain herself any longer. "Ezra, I cannot wait to hear of what happened in Marseilles! Tell me about my loved ones. How are Rose, Margaux, and Gerhardt?"

Eyeing her, he reached across the table and touched her hand. "They are in good health, they miss you, and send their love. I had long conversations with Margaux and Rose before I left to return here. I will get to what we spoke about in good time but let me start at the beginning.

"Upon arriving, I spent three weeks visiting with associates to determine what had changed since my last visit. I inquired about Astrid and was not surprised to learn that the people of Marseilles doubt her version of Alexander's death.

"I went with John to the manor to meet with her. When Margaux opened the door, she immediately embraced me and welcomed me inside. I whispered to her that you are safe in Paris and that I wanted to talk with her and Rose at the docks the next day. Nodding agreement, she led me to the solar, took my guard to the kitchen, then summoned Astrid to see me.

"As I stood at the entrance to the solar, I saw the room that held so many fond memories in disarray. It was no longer the place where plans were made for businesses and the port was made safe. Now, it appeared ravaged. The walls were stripped bare of Alexander's battle weapons and tapestries. There were a few contracts and manuscripts on the floor that appeared walked over and pushed aside. It appeared as if the room had been hit by one of our sea storms and no one bothered to do the cleanup.

"Walking to the table, I saw a contract on the floor that held importance for both Alexander and me. Quickly, I folded it, tucking it into my satchel just as Astrid entered the room.

"Bowing to her, I pulled out a chair for her to sit. I told her I was in Marseilles on business and heard about Alexander's death and stopped by to pay my respects."

"How did she act when she saw you?"

"She was stately and confident until I asked how Alexander died. Fredric chose that moment to stumble into the solar, carrying a goblet of wine. He sat in Alexander's chair and put his feet up on the desk, pushing the few documents on it to the floor.

"His total disrespect for Alexander's possessions raised the hair on my neck. Leaning across the table, I demanded of him, 'What are *you* doing here?' Fredric grinned a wicked smile and belched. Not a word came out of his mouth. Astrid did not react to his behavior.

"Turning back to her, I asked again, 'How did Alexander die?'

"She shouted at me, 'Lisa killed him! Servants saw her in the solar late one night and the next morning Alexander was found dead. His empty goblet lay next to his lifeless body, and everyone knew she had poisoned his wine!"

"I stood and walked to where your secret niche was and leaned against the window ledge. Then, I asked, 'Who is everyone? And how do you know poison was the cause of his death? Could it not have been from a weak heart or a disease you were not aware he had?'"

"Astrid leapt to her feet and lashed out, 'What are you saying? Are you accusing me of lying? I told you … Lisa poisoned him!'

"Taking in the scene that was in front of me, I glared at [illegible] and then at Fredric. 'Astrid, what you are saying does not feel rig[illegible] *Only* the person who poisoned him would know how he died.'

"Fuming, she was on her feet. 'I have heard enough! Get out!'

"Walking to the door and peering into my satchel so they could see me, I said, 'I got all I came here for … the contract I had with Alexander. I also learned the truth about his murder. Lisa did not poison her father. My question is … which one of you did?'

"When I said that, Fredric stumbled to his feet and pulled a knife from his belt and pointed it at me. I turned away and walked out.

"Astrid then yelled to Fredric, 'Stop him! I want that contract!'

"I laughed as I walked down the hall. I heard a thump as Fredric turned the corner and stumbled into my guard. As I left the villa, I heard Astrid scream."

Exhaling, Ezra then added, "That is the essence of my conversation with Astrid."

Speaking directly to Nichol, he went on. "You were right about Astrid. She does blame you for Alexander's death and is repeating that story everywhere and trying to convince people of your guilt. She and Fredric are evil, Nichol, and I believe they are behind all the attacks you have experienced. As long as the danger exists, you must be ever watchful.

"You were wise to immediately escape when you did, and to change your name and looks. Your mother and brother are dangerous … and your father knew that they were."

Nichol sat with her face buried in her hands, sobbing.

Helene said, "Nichol, I know this is hard to hear, but you are safe with us."

"Should I continue?" Ezra asked.

ooking up, Nichol nodded.

"I met your mother several times over the years, but we had ew conversations. After what I witnessed in Marseilles, I know your mother is malicious, and your brother has been trained in her ways. She will stop at nothing to get what she wants. In her own way, she is still trying to manipulate all of your father's business associates. When I met with these merchants, I told all of them that Astrid killed Alexander, not you. Each should be wary of any current dealings with her and Fredric, and I advised them not to have any future dealings. The last thing I told them was to keep their distance.

"Before his death, Alexander had confided to me that the mood was not good in the manor and he thought you were in danger. Nothing seemed right. He thought it was coming from Fredric. And he was alarmed that Astrid did not see the weakness and cruelty in her son. Nor did she seem inclined to protect you. What I had learned in the short time I was there is that even Astrid should fear Fredric. Alexander told me there is something wicked that lurks behind his lifeless eyes. He told me when the two men were hanged who attacked you in the tavern, Fredric felt obvious pleasure as he placed the ropes around their necks and hoisted them into the trees to their deaths.

"When I was in Alexander's solar, I was troubled at the disarray I saw, with documents strewn across the floor. It told me a great deal—that no one was overseeing activities at the port and that neither Astrid nor Fredric had ever cared or respected Alexander.

"The next day, I met Margaux and Rose at her apothecary shop. Rose told me that Karl—the man who gave your mother the poison—was found dead in a ditch the day after the funeral. Both figured Astrid tried to solidify her version of Alexander's death by having him killed—probably by Fredric.

"There is great concern around the villa that Fredric has no one to hold him back. Everyone already knew him as a worthless drunk. Now he is considered a monster. Some even say that the day Alexander beat him in the courtyard is the day Fredric became a willing killer and would seek revenge against anyone he perceived had done ill will toward him.

"Margaux told me that Astrid was so upset when you disappeared, she went into Alexander's solar and ripped down the tapestries and removed his battle collection of swords and daggers, intending to sell them.

"Margaux went on to say she watched as Astrid picked up a piece of parchment from the niche where you always hid. Reading it, Astrid flew into a rage, screaming and howling. Then she saw her pick up the tapestry your father prized and you hid behind, and discarded it on the trash pile in the courtyard.

"She rescued it and took it back to her cottage in the villa. Both Rose and Margaux want you to know how much they miss you and how much they love you. They believe in your strength and goodness and wish you the absolute best that life has to offer. They hope one day you will return to Marseilles and take over where your papa left off."

Nichol sat lost in thought. Looking at Ezra with sad eyes, she revealed the secret of the note. "While everyone was out of the manor and at the funeral, I went to Papa's solar for a final time before I fled to meet up with Rose and then to come here. The last thing I did was write a note for Astrid to find. I left it for her to find in my niche.

"In it, I wrote:

> I saw you accept the vial of poison from Karl and now know you used it to poison my papa. You are evil ... and are now cursed.
>
> I know where his wealth lies.
>
> And I know that Fredric is not his son.
>
> You will get what you so rightly deserve.
>
> I will see to it. I promise you.

Nichol pulled on the silver neckless until all four of the items that hung beneath her tunic were in her grasp. She ran her fingers over Alexander's rings and the feather and stone that Rose had given her as she left Marseilles.

"Thank you for relaying all the messages to my loved ones and their messages to me. It seems like a lifetime ago that I left Marseilles. I am glad the people dear to my heart still think kindly of me. I am also glad they know the truth."

Ezra nodded. "Yes, they do. Seeing you touch your papa's rings reminds me of another conversation. I did not know about Rose's stone. Margaux told me that the ring with the family crest on it is the one thing Astrid so desperately wants returned. As you know Alexander pressed the ring in molten wax to seal contracts. For that reason, it is a symbol of power and wealth to her."

"My mother is desperate for many reasons. She will never see his rings again. They were of no importance to her before his death. They are a symbol of love … his for me and mine for him. Outside of the memories I have of him, these rings and his dagger are the only things I possess that were his.

"The stone is different. It has a special meaning and connection to Rose. As I traveled on my own, I always found safety in the trees. I would climb the trees at night to sleep and be protected from others who could do me harm. As I shut my eyes, I would often touch the stone for comfort. At times, it seemed like a soft light would appear … and sometimes I would hear the familiar voice of the *Lady.*"

"A light … what are you saying, Nichol?"

"Ezra … our Nichol is special. Alexander recognized and started training her to defend herself—far beyond what any young girl would know and do. He used her memory to help in his meetings. He confided with her about his business and what to do if something happened to him. That is why she is here now. The voice she hears …."

"Enough for now, Helene. I will hear more of this later."

Ezra turned to the large parcel he had placed beside his chair and invited Nichol to come see what was inside. "Margaux saved this for you. She knows how much it meant to you."

Nichol knelt next to the cumbersome package and began to unfold its contents. Inside was her papa's favorite battle tapestry, the one she had hidden behind for years as she witnessed the conversations and exploits of the visitors who came to see him.

Once she realized what it was, she stopped the unfolding, sat in her chair and drew the exposed corner of the tapestry to her heart as silent tears streamed down her face. "One day, this tapestry will have its proper place in my home."

Ezra and Helene sat quietly watching as memories flooded over her. After several minutes, Ezra put his hand on hers and said, "Nichol, do not let your mother's lies and deceit dampen your spirits. Her decisions will eventually be her demise."

"I want to be there when she and Fredric are destitute, on their knees, begging for help. And as I said in the note left for her, I will see to it. I promised her … and I promise you." Nichol's expression was stern and solemn.

"Have patience. Their fall will not be immediate, but Astrid is making enemies and before too long she will experience her last days of wealth," declared Ezra.

"Continue to stay alert. You are safe with all of us around you, but no one knows how long Astrid will continue her search, or who she will engage in the pursuit. Take the return of the tapestry as a sign of good fortune. Your papa will be with you always."

Nichol nodded. "This will add warmth around me as the winter unfolds."

That night in bed, Ezra whispered in Helene's ear, "Alexander was a wealthy man and never displayed it. He never forgot where he came from or who helped him along the way. He kept his gold and silver in a locked box in the solar. The gems he kept in that box were also worth much more gold. When I saw the box that day during my visit, the lid was up and the contents gone.

"Do you remember Nichol saying that she knows where his wealth lies? By the way they are living, Astrid and Fredric have not found it. They even desecrated his grave looking for it. This is why someone is pursuing Nichol, someone more dangerous than Astrid and Fredric. One day I will tell her the story behind the dagger she carries."

"After telling me this, you expect me to go to sleep? Ezra, tell me about the dagger," Helene insisted.

Ezra's soft snore was the only thing she heard.

seventy-six

Late December 1000

The Baby Arrives

You had to be in the room to understand.

By the first of December, Robert had completed the jewelry that he was obligated to make for the master's wealthy patrons. He was compensated for his designs and made the decision to end his apprenticeship to be with Nichol.

Ezra, Helene, and Nichol had decided not to tell Robert what had happened at the cottage until he completed his time as an apprentice. Now with the baby's birth getting closer, they decided to wait again.

By late December, Nichol was having a difficult time getting around. She was uncomfortable, but she felt the need to keep moving. Shadow, now fully grown, stayed close by.

The day was sunny, with a brisk wind outside. She and Robert had spent the day walking up and down the street in front of Ezra's home.

"Shadow seems to be more protective of you. Do you think she knows that a baby is coming and she will have someone else to watch over, too?" Robert asked on one of their walks.

Nichol tensed up, then relaxed. *He does not know yet just how important Shadow will be in protecting our daughter.* "I am sure she is aware of how my body has changed and that I am not running with her right now. That will all change soon."

Returning to the house, the extra weight she carried and the way the baby was lying in her body tired her. As slim as she was, it jutted almost straight out, putting her off balance. As she climbed the short stairway to their bedchamber, she told Helene, "I will rest before supper."

A light meal was eaten later and Nichol began helping Helene with the supper cleanup. As she moved the porridge bowls from the table to the kitchen, a horrible pain shot through her back and stomach, one that she had never felt before.

The midwife had prepared her for this, but experiencing it was a completely different thing. Nichol knew the baby's arrival was close at hand.

Shadow would not leave her side. Ears perked and alert every time her mistress moaned from the discomfort her body generated.

Helene was now alert and led Nichol to her bed, settling her in the dimly-lit room.

"I will have Robert get Sacha," she murmured and went to find Robert and Ezra in the lower great room. Helene's demeanor told Robert why she was there. As if she could read his thoughts, she said, "Yes, Robert, your baby is on the way. Go to Sacha's home and tell her we need her now."

Helene had hired Sacha, a midwife who lived nearby. She had visited Helene's home and explained to Nichol the birthing process and what to expect during the latter part of her pregnancy and during the birth.

Helene gave Robert directions to where Sacha lived and sent him on his way to retrieve her.

After he left, Helene started assigning tasks to Ezra. She remembered that Sacha said it would help the birth if Nichol drank hot water when she was laboring.

"Ezra, we will need plenty of hot water. Fill the containers so they can be heated. We will need wood to keep the fires going. And more soft linens for both Nichol and the baby." Her needs list grew for all the things she wanted him to gather.

Ezra could feel the excitement building under his roof. He collected everything that was needed and distributed to where it would be used.

As he gave Helene the linens, his hand lingered on hers. "We will have a baby in our home at last." Leaving, he handed her a piece of leather and added, "Give this to Nichol and tell her to bite down on it when the pain is great." Touching Helen's cheek gently, he smiled and headed down to the great room.

Robert burst through the great room door with the midwife, leading her up to Nichol's bedchamber. Helene sensed that Nichol's time was close.

Putting a hand on the shoulder of each man, she shooed them out of the room. It was not long before she heard Robert and Ezra laughing and telling stories … and consuming ale.

Sacha knelt by Nichol's side and conducted her first examination. "Your baby is close to birth." As dawn approached, the one narrow window in the bedchamber began to deliver the first of the morning's rays, bathing the room with a gentle light.

Once again, Sacha crouched by Nichol to check her progress. "Your baby is ready to come."

This has to be it. My daughter will be here soon.

Biting the piece of leather that Ezra gave Helene, Nichol let out a long and protracted moan. At that moment, a baby girl entered the world with a soft cry that brought joy to those in the room. While Sacha tended to Nichol, Helene took charge of cleaning the baby with the warm water and wrapping her in the soft linens Ezra had delivered earlier.

The men slumbered in the lower room, waking when they no longer heard Nichol's moaning. Then they heard the soft noises of the women murmuring above. They knew it had happened. Leaping up, they headed for the stairs.

As soon as they approached the door, Helene met them, cracking it just a few inches holding the infant in her hidden arm.

"Go away … we are not quite ready." She turned back into the room, closing the door.

Disappointed with her response, Robert and Ezra returned to the great room in low spirits.

Moving toward the bed, Helene placed the baby girl in Nichol's waiting arms. Taking her daughter, she bent her knees to create a backrest to lean her against as she observed her. A loving expression spread across her face.

Nichol touched her daughter's face with gentle strokes and marveled at the tiny hands and fingers that reached out to her. Sinking into the blankets that had been built up behind so she could sit, a huge smile spread across Nichol's face as she embraced her motherhood.

She cooed gently to her daughter and looked up at Helene. "It is time for Robert to come and meet his daughter. Please get him."

Turning to get the men, Helene felt a strange energy and motion behind her. She turned back to see a bright light dancing about the room, finally settling over Nichol. At the same time, she raised her daughter up as if she were offering her to the light.

Silence filled the room. All three women watched as the baby responded to the light … as if something was physically present in the room that only the mother and newborn could see.

Nichol smiled at her daughter's reaction, pulling her closer to her chest, snuggling the top of her head. Helene stood in awe. She knew … she had a feeling that the *Lady* who visited Nichol in her dreams was present. *The Lady is real.*

Helene glanced at the midwife to gauge her reaction.

The frozen stare on Sacha's face alarmed her.

Suddenly, Sacha looked at Helene, then back to the baby and Nichol, now surrounded by light. She backed away until she could go no further.

Her face contorted with fear and a howl came from her quivering lips. "The child and mother are cursed!" As she said this, her right hand made the sign of the cross.

Nichol caressed her daughter, oblivious to the midwife.

Shivers spread down Helene's back.

The light danced around the room one last time and disappeared.

Appendix Contents

Discussion Questions for

The Secret Journey

Book Club Leaders ... contact Brian and/or Judith to participate in a special meeting to discuss the book; the concepts; and the evolution of the series. We always encourage readers to post individual reviews on *Amazon.com*. And thank you.

In-person gatherings are possible if you are in the Colorado and either is available. Otherwise, Zoom is always an option.

Did the ending pull you in? Did you want more?

- Were you satisfied or disappointed with how it ended?
- How do you picture the characters' lives after the end of the story?
- If you were to identify the most important theme within *The Secret Journey,* what would it be?

What do you think of Lisa's transition to Nick, than Nichol?

- Do you know anyone like her?
- Do you think that there are women like her today?
- Do you think it's important for a women to be able to physically defend herself?

Was it right for Lisa to listen to Alexander's meetings without his knowledge?

- Why do you think she didn't tell him what she was doing?
- If he had known earlier, would he have forbidden her to be in his solar?

- Once Alexander invited Lisa to listen and watch, did he place too much responsibility on her?

Do you think Nichol should have had a man step in on her behalf versus dealing with Fredric herself?

- Should Lisa have asked for help?
- Were her actions appropriate when she took his horse and coin?
- What else could she have done to stop him from pursuing her?

What risks did Nichol undertake as she followed Alexander's map to Paris and his partner Ezra?

- Should she have left the manor and her villa as suddenly as she did?
- Should she have disguised herself as a boy? If she hadn't, what do you think would have happened?
- Was she right to accuse her mother Astrid of murdering her papa?

Would you approach a stranger in an inn, tavern, or bar for help? Have you ever had to ask a stranger for help?

- What fears would/could asking for help generate?
- What is the likelihood that adequate help would appear?
- What would you do if you felt threatened by someone you know as Nicole was by Fredric?

Was it appropriate for Nichol to travel forward with Timo and Moki? Or should she have continued on her own, running to Paris?

- Why did Nicole have a mistrust of men and the church?
- What steps did Timo take to make her feel safe around him?
- Did you think that Timo and Nichol would become a couple?

When Nicole slayed the two men at the cottage, was it her ... or was it the Lady guiding her actions?

- Did her actions and skills surprise you?
- Should she have taken Shadow to Jacob's or left right away?
- Should she have risked taking the horses?

If Nichol didn't have the voice of the Lady as a support, comfort, and guide ... would she have succeeded in her quest?

- Was the Lady real or part of Nichol's imagination?
- What would she have done if the Lady wasn't real?
- Did the Lady always have good intentions for Nichol, or could she turn against her?

When Nichol first sees Robert, it was his eyes that pulled her in. Should she have been more cautious?

- When did Robert figure out that Nick wasn't a boy? Should he have picked up that quickly?
- Should he have taken to his home as soon as he did?
- Did the Lady make it possible for the two of them to meet?

What themes surfaced in the story?

- Have you ever been in a situation where you needed someone to save you?
- Have you ever been in a situation where you did not want someone to save you?
- Have you ever had to step in and help someone out of a dire situation?
- Have you ever had to overlook or accept something so that you could have a relationship with someone?
- Have you ever had to trust someone you barely knew?
- Have you ever allowed yourself to cut off others you knew well because you felt they had become bad?
- Have you ever had inner voices and feelings that guide you?

Enjoy an excerpt from

The Harmonie Book Series, Book 2

available 2023

one

Meet Your Daughter

She shall be called Lucette ... Little Light.

Helene felt calmness return to her as she watched the loving, gentle touches between Nichol and the baby. *She will be a good mother.*

The midwife's panic was apparent to Helene.

Sacha pushed her aside with a sudden force as she dashed by her, rushing through the door, and almost colliding with Robert and Ezra as she fled from the house. Shivers slid down Helene's back once again.

Helene stood to one side and invited the men into the room. Grinning, she said to Robert, "You have a beautiful baby girl. Come in and see your daughter and her mama."

Robert was excited and nervous all at once. Forgetting to ask why Sacha fled, he was smiling from ear to ear. Nichol was lying back, cradling her daughter with joy apparent to all. Taking Nichol's hand, Robert bent to kiss her.

Nichol looked from him to their baby. "Robert, look at this beautiful little girl we made." She handed the baby to him and all he could do was look at her in wonder.

So tiny ....

A baby, his daughter, a beautiful infant with rosy cheeks and little features. As his smile widened and he looked at her face, her eyes locked in on his. He could not even speak.

Nichol looked at Robert and whispered, "You are a natural. You look like you have done this before." She was happy to see how at ease he was. He had always been gentle and loving with her, and he was acting the same way with their daughter.

"The only thing close to this experience was holding Raisa when she was a baby. This is much different. This little girl is ours."

"Robert, do you remember the most recent dream I told you about?"

He nodded.

"This is what the *Lady* told me in it. She said, 'She shall be called Lucette … Little Light.' When you and I discussed the dream, we weren't sure who the *Lady* was referring to. Now that we know we have a baby girl, how would you feel about naming her Lucette?"

Looking at the baby snuggled in his arms, he said, "It is a beautiful name. Lucette. Yes." The baby stirred when he said her name. Robert chuckled. "She is already responding to it. Lucette it is."

Helene and Ezra were standing close to the door. Ezra whispered to Helene, "Why did Sacha leave so fast? She had a look of fright on her face."

"I will tell you later."

Nichol invited them to come closer. Helene took Ezra's hand as they both moved to where Nichol was. Robert knew Helene could hardly wait to hold the baby again. Turning, he offered his tiny bundle to her. She took Lucette and cradled her in the crook of her arm.

Her face said it all ... Helene was in love.

She offered the baby to Ezra. He backed away, held his hands up and said, "Not yet. She is too little. Maybe when she is bigger, I will hold her."

Everyone laughed at his reaction—this tiny girl had already unsettled him.

"Ezra, I predict that before long she will have you wrapped around her finger," teased Robert. Ezra shivered just thinking about it.

Helene could see that Nichol's energy was fading and announced, "I think this new mother could use some rest. She has worked hard for the last several hours. Come to think of it, she has worked hard for many months just to arrive at this moment."

The men left—patting each on the back ... as if they had done all the work.

Still cradling Lucette, Helene carried her to Nichol. Nichol held the baby to her breast as Sacha had shown her. Lucette latched on and began to suckle. Nichol's milk had not yet come in, but with Lucette's help, it wouldn't take long.

Mother and baby quickly adopted the proper technique and bonded peacefully. Before long, both were asleep, and Helene tiptoed from the room.

Finding Robert and Ezra in the kitchen, Ezra began to speak.

Helene held up a hand to quiet him and said, "We must discuss what I just witnessed in the birthing room. It confirms what Nichol has told me. Not only is the *Lady's* voice real, but I am also sure she was present during Lucette's birth. A bright light came into the room and settled above Nichol and Lucette, and they responded silently to her."

"How could a newborn communicate with anyone, let alone a mysterious unseen voice?" asked Ezra with doubt.

"You had to be in the room to understand," said Helene. "Nichol has come into our lives not by chance, but for a good reason. I believe it. It is our duty to protect and nurture this special mother and daughter. Their welfare depends on us doing that.

"The midwife also saw what I saw. She saw Nichol offer up the baby to the light that hovered over the bed, and she saw how Lucette cooed with joy when embraced by the light. Not only did Sacha witness all that I did, but she began to turn pale with fear, making the sign of the cross and saying the child and mother are cursed."

Robert's and Ezra's eyes locked across the table. Robert was the first to burst out, "No person could look at what we saw when Nichol was holding Lucette and say that they are cursed."

Turning to Ezra, Robert pleaded, "What should we do?"

Before he could respond, Helene quietly said, "Robert, I do not have a good feeling about this. I am afraid she will bring trouble down on us." She turned to Ezra. "You must go to her tomorrow and buy her silence."

Looking at his wife and now sensing her fear, he nodded, saying, "I have never seen you so distraught, Helene. Of course, I will do as you suggest."

two

A New Role

I know that Nichol and Lucette must be protected.

Early the next day, Ezra walked to the midwife's home and knocked on the door. No one answered. Ezra was persistent and knocked again. He heard children talking and laughing, and he shouted, "Please, someone open the door! It is me, Ezra."

Finally, the door opened just enough for Ezra to see a man's face. "Is your wife at home?" The man paused and said, "Yes," and abruptly closed the door.

Moments later, the door opened, and Sacha appeared. "What do you want?" she snapped.

"I want to pay you for your services. Yesterday you left before I could do so." Ezra handed her a hefty purse of coins and said, "Thank you for your help with the delivery. Nichol and her baby are doing well."

"The devil is in that woman and in her child!" Sacha turned away and slammed the door in Ezra's face.

Stunned and surprised, he stared at the door.

Alarmed with what she said and her behavior, Ezra knew he must return to his family.

This woman is dangerous ... for Nichol ... and for us.

As Ezra entered the house, Helene almost pounced upon him. "Robert is with Nichol and the baby. Tell me what she said. Did she take your coin?"

In a lowered voice, he began to speak. "She would not answer the door at first. Then the door finally opened, but her husband closed it. Then Sacha came to the door. I thanked her for her services and told her that Nichol and the baby were doing well. She greedily took my coin and then spit out, 'The devil is in that woman and in her child!' Then she slammed the door in my face."

Helene took in his words and then reached across the table and put her hand on top of his. "Ezra, Lucette is special. A devil doesn't bring light. Nichol and Lucette have a great purpose; I am certain of that. We need to be part of their lives."

"Until now I have been careful not to judge Nichol because of what she has been through. After talking to Margaux and Rose, and then hearing you describe the birth, I know that you are right. There is something special about Nichol, and now Lucette.

"On the way home, I thought of Alexander telling me about a woman's voice warning him to protect Lisa and that she was in danger. He must have been referring to the *Lady* she and you talk about. I know that Nichol and Lucette must be protected. I promise to you that I will. I will be their defender."

About the Authors

Brian Barnes

Barnes spent decades in construction. While he built and could fix anything that required a hammer, screwdriver, saw, or drill, his mind filled with stories that only retirement gave him the time to write.

As avid reader of history, historical fiction and a follower of politics and world events, he is appalled when injustice and stupidity are prevalent in the behaviors of those who are in leadership roles. Much of the underlying theme within *The Secret Journey* was ignited by such events and the ignorance of what women are capable of accomplishing and achieving.

The Secret Journey is Brian's debut novel in the Harmonie Books series. He's now working on *The Secret Hamlet,* the sequel that will be followed by *The Secret Rise.*

Calling Colorado home, he's known as the "fixit guy" to family and friends. Summers pull him and wife Julie into gardening and maintenance within their community of townhomes.

About the Authors

Judith Briles

Briles is the author of 43 books and known as The Book Shepherd to thousands of authors she's worked with. Her construction tools are her words and imagination.

She is a book publishing expert and coach. Often, she must roll up her writing sleeves and become a Book Doctor, juicing up storylines and author words. Judith empowers authors and works directly with those who want to be seriously successful. Her recent books include *Snappy Sassy Salty, How to Create a Million Dollar Speech,* and *Author YOU: Creating and Building Your Author and Book Platforms.* Her personal memoir *When God Says NO: Revealing the YES When Adversity and Loss Are Present.* Her books have all been #1 bestsellers on Amazon. Collectively, her books have earned over 45 book awards. Judith speaks yearly at publishing and writing conferences.

Throughout the year, she holds *Judith Briles Book Unplugged* in-person and online experiences: Publishing, Speaking, Marketing, and Social Media. All are intensives limited small groups who want to be seriously successful.

Join Judith for the "AuthorU: Your Guide to Book Publishing" podcast she hosts on the Toginet Radio Network. Follow her at *@MyBookShepherd* on Twitter and join the Facebook group *Book Publishing with The Book Shepherd.*

Calling Colorado home, when she is not writing, she is most likely in the garden; or in the kitchen; or planning author events.

How to Work with

Brian and Judith

Book Clubs

Both Brian and Judith are available to book clubs to talk about *The Secret Journey* and forthcoming books in the series in-person in in Colorado or on Zoom.

Judith has also written several other books. Her memoir, *When Gods Says NO: Revealing the YES When Adversity and Loss Are Present* is about survival, thrival, and resiliency. Her many books on writing and publishing are ideal to create a discussion for club members who aspire to write and publish.

Bookstore Signings

Veterans at multiple book signings throughout the year, either or both would be delighted to come to your store, creating an event that customers will enjoy. They also will create a press release to support their appearance and push out social media as well.

Speaking

Both Brian and Judith would be delighted to speak about the process of writing; creating a series; and creating voices, attitudes, and behaviors for characters in fiction.

Judith has extensive expertise in publishing: how to get publishing; how to market books; how to use social media; how to create a speech on expertise and book; how to create a successful crowd-funding program; how to avoid publishing mistakes; and how to find the author's voice. Her personal website is *TheBookShepherd.com*

How to Contact

For Harmonie Books Series,
HarmonieBookSeries@gmail.com

For Brian

Brian@AuthorBrianBarnes.com

 @HarmonieBooks

 HarmonieBooksSeries

 Harmonie Books

 @HarmonieBooks

For Judith

Judith@Briles.com

303-885-2207

8122 S. Quatar Circle | Aurora, Colorado 80016

 @MyBookShepherd

 JudithBriles/

 JudithBriles

 BookPublishingHelp/

 Judith.TheBookShepherd

 http://bit.ly/BookPublishingPodcast

 https://bit.ly/Author-PublishingTips

Book One

The Secret Journey

At 16, Lisa's world unravels. Forced to run to Paris for her survival when her papa is murdered. Will she get there? Will Alexander's partner welcome and help her? Will she discover who killed her papa? Will the Voice that invades her sleep continue to guide her? Will she ever feel safe and loved again? The year is 1000 AD.

Book Two

The Secret Hamlet

With a priest coming for Nichol and her growing family, the *Lady* forewarns her that she must leave Paris at once and seek a new and distant land ... one that will bring peace and prosperity. Nichol's skills and movements are called upon repeatedly to protect them from thieves and the priest as they move toward their destination, the new hamlet of Harmonie. Available 2023.

Book Three

The Secret Rise

Harmonie has prospered under Nichol's leadership and vision. With Ezra's partnership, their commercial ventures have grown greater than her papa's were. The power of the Duke and Church threatens to destroy them and the business success they have created. Once again, Nichol must outsmart and out maneuver those in power and her evil brother. Lucette and Athena display skills that their mother doesn't possess. Available 2024.

Book Four

The Secret Awakening

The light that the *Lady* has surrounded Nichol with has extended to her daughters. The New Land, a land where women are not subservient to the church or to men, is the final destination with a port expanding trade to surrounding countries for the goods they produce. Available 2025.

Made in the USA
Middletown, DE
02 December 2022

16109531R00283